THE MIND MASTERS

Dr. Giles Todd was a brilliant brain surgeon. He knew as much as any doctor could know about the physical properties of that mysterious human organ.

Dr. Prentiss Fellkirk was a renowned psychic researcher, a pioneer in probing beyond all previous frontiers of science in his exploration of the secret depths of the mind.

Now they were rivals—in the most eerie, nightmarish contest that two men ever fought over a beautiful woman.

God help the man who won Fayre. God help the man who lost her. . . .

SINS OF OMISSION

Big Bestsellers from SIGNET

SINS OF OMISSION

A NOVEL OF OCCULT SUSPENSE

CHELSEA QUINN YARBRO

A SIGNET BOOK

NEW AMERICAN LIBRARY

TIMES MIRROR

for my agents:
Kirby McCauley (words)
and
Sarah Chambers (music)
with affection and appreciation

SIGNET TRADEMARK REG. U.S. PAT. OFF. AND FOREIGN COUNTRIES
REGISTERED TRADEMARK—MARCA REGISTRADA
HECHO EN CHICAGO, U.S.A.

SIGNET, SIGNET CLASSICS, MENTOR, PLUME, MERIDIAN AND NAL BOOKS
are published by The New American Library, Inc.,
1633 Broadway, New York, New York 10019

FIRST PRINTING, APRIL, 1980

1 2 3 4 5 6 7 8 9

PRINTED IN THE UNITED STATES OF AMERICA

□ ACKNOWLEDGMENTS □

The author would like to thank the following people for their kind and generous sharing of their expertise:

Dr. Michael Greenwald
Jacques Gautier
Grant Canfield
Joyce Donnell
Dr. R. P. Lloyd
Dr. Kate Davis
and my editor, Joan Hitzig

white-covered table the young woman
l the sounds were thin, as if coming

r?" the professor with the English ac-
side him.
er watching the young woman.
?" the professor said as he looked at

more or less. Longer than last time.
" The woman's tone was profession-
bulance should be here in ten more

, and leaned toward the screaming
er restraints. "Do you hear me? Can
k! I command you to speak!" He
doubt clouding his attractive face.
asked the woman beside him.
it a moment or two and try it again.
ambulance. You're fortunate this
b. You'd better be cautious." She
woman. "Drugs might make a dif-
or this sort of thing, remember."
ouder and more persistent. Mrs.
er eyes, but she stared at nothing.
eep her in the program? After this?"
n her jacket.
the doctors." He moved a little
himself heard through her screams.
ou speak?"
Fellkirk," Lupe said from the door.

"Yes. Fine. I appreciate your staying, Lupe." He waved
toward the closing door, then drew a chair nearer the white-
covered table. "Mrs. Schoenfeld?" he said after he heard the
front door shut. "Mrs. Schoenfeld?"

The staring eyes turned toward him, glazed with fright.
Then the screams faltered.

"This is Dr. Fellkirk, Mrs. Schoenfeld. Do you know me?" He kept his voice very level and watched her carefully.

Mrs. Schoenfeld's screams trailed off and she nodded slowly.

"You've had a seizure again, Mrs. Schoenfeld. There's an ambulance on the way. You've been out for about forty minutes." He watched her with guarded intensity.

"Where am I?" Mrs. Schoenfeld said in a whisper.

"You're at my home, Mrs. Schoenfeld. You came here at my invitation this evening. It's now somewhat after midnight. Some of the others from the lab were here. Do you remember?" He spoke each sentence with care and at last reached out awkwardly to pat her hand. "I'm sorry about the restraints. There was no other way." He waited while her face revealed her feelings.

First there were tears in her eyes, then the corners of her mouth drew down and she turned her head away. Her damp matted hair hung in tangles around her face. "Again." There was such anguish in that one word.

Professor Fellkirk did not answer her at once. "We'll see if something can't be done for you, Mrs. Schoenfeld. Certainly I have a degree of responsibility in this." He rose to deal with the restraints.

"No," she said in a muffled voice. "You shouldn't. It's me. It's me."

He had released her legs. "But you said that this had not happened until you came into my program. If there's a connection, then I feel I must . . ."

"No. No. *No!*" She started to cry, this time in deep, terrible sobs.

"Mrs. Schoenfeld . . ." Dr. Fellkirk put one large hand on her shoulder. "Come, Mrs. Schoenfeld. It may be harmful for you to cry so."

There was no response but tears. When her wrists were freed, she hid her face in her hands as she drew her knees up toward her chest. Dr. Fellkirk recognized the classic fetal position and found some sympathy for the poor woman.

A distant wail announced the arrival of the ambulance and Professor Fellkirk felt great relief. The ordeal was almost over. "It's the ambulance, Mrs. Schoenfeld. You'll be at the hospital in just a few minutes."

Her sobs lessened, and finally she choked out a few words. "What happened? What did I do?"

"Don't you know?" He asked the question sharply and waited for her reply.

"I don't remember anything. I don't remember coming here. I don't remember." She spoke in quiet horror as she stared at the far wall.

"Nothing?" The sound of the ambulance turning into his driveway took Professor Fellkirk away from the room. As he walked toward the door he very nearly smiled, glad to have a great burden lifted from his mind.

□ 1 □

At first Giles Todd wanted nothing to do with the case. He considered sending a polite recommendation that another neurosurgeon be consulted, but found that he could not: the request had come from Prentiss Fellkirk, who had been his friend for almost thirty years.

"Has it really been that long?" Giles asked the walls of his office, and, saying it, he knew that it had. He and Prentiss had met at school, not long after the war. Looking at the formal note on St. Matis stationery one last time, Giles picked up his phone and punched an outside line. The number Prentiss had given him was not particularly melodic on the phone buttons, and Giles wished again for his old-fashioned dial phone.

Then there was a voice on the other end, and Giles said, "Professor Fellkirk, please, if he's available. Tell him that Dr. Todd is calling."

He had to give his request to two more anonymous voices before he heard the familiar clipped greeting, "Fellkirk here."

"Giles Todd, Prentiss," he said. "I have your letter. What may I do for you?"

"Giles," Prentiss repeated. "How wonderful. I was afraid you'd refuse. I remember the last time I asked your advice—you admitted then that you hated this sort of consultation."

Inwardly Giles cringed. It was true, and his own frustration had led him to make certain scathing remarks he had later regretted. "Well, yes. But this matter sounds intriguing. You mentioned that the woman in question has had no history of seizures and that your preliminary tests appear to rule out some sort of tumor." He had seized on this at the spur of the moment.

Years of lecturing had given Prentiss a certain measured habit of speech, a sound that often made Giles think that there would be a quiz at the end of the conversation. "Apparently that's the case, but that's why I want *you* to see her. We've had her under observation here for very nearly three

1

weeks, and although the most alarming symptoms have ceased . . ."

"Alarming?" Giles knew that what he considered alarming was often quite different from what disturbed others.

"She hasn't had any serious episodes of amnesia, she has not assumed that trancelike state I described in the letter, and most of her actions have been fairly coordinated. But she is also very lethargic and has occasional symptoms of extreme anxiety." There was an awkward pause. "Look, Giles, I feel I *owe* the poor woman something. I got her into this, after all. If she hadn't been part of my parapsychological study group, this might never have happened."

"And it might have happened no matter what she did, or what you did," Giles reminded him with some asperity. "Very well. When do you want me to see her?" A knock on his door caught his attention and he called out, "Come in!"

"What?" Prentiss asked, confused.

"Sorry, Prentiss. I was talking to someone else." He waved Hugh Audley to one of the straight-backed chairs and went on, "I suppose you've checked for epilepsy?" It was so elementary that it seemed foolish to ask, but he had seen cases where this had been overlooked.

"First off. She's not epileptic, or if she is, this is a new version of it." On the other end of the line Prentiss hesitated, then said, "I'm going to be in San Francisco tomorrow. Perhaps we could talk then?"

It would mean breaking a dinner engagement, but Giles said without hesitation, "I'd be glad to. What time?"

"I'm supposed to be free at four. Suppose I come straight to the hospital?"

"All right. I might be as late as six, but I don't think you'll be bored. It's been too long, Prentiss." He gave a complicated shrug to Hugh Audley indicating that although he wanted to talk with Hugh, he still had to finish his phone conversation.

"As one relocated limey to another, Giles," Prentiss said with a tone of voice Giles knew went with a wry smile, "we shouldn't let so much time go by. It's been almost a year."

Giles felt a certain guilt. "Yes. And though work is the excuse, I'm afraid it isn't a very good one."

"It's my excuse, too," Prentiss admitted. "Well, perhaps tomorrow will be the first step in remedying the situation. As well as helping Mrs. Schoenfeld."

"That's the patient?" Giles asked.

"Fayre Claughsen Schoenfeld. Aged twenty-eight years,

five months, a widow, one child, a son, aged seven years," Prentiss recited. "Husband killed six years ago in Vietnam."

"You say in your letter that she's a master's candidate?" He gave the letter a quick glance to be sure he was remembering correctly.

"That's right. I've had her in one of my experimental groups, you know, ESP testing and that kind of thing. She was doing very well until the seizure hit." Prentiss stopped abruptly. "I hold myself to blame for it."

"You had no way of knowing," Giles said quickly. "You must not feel that way, Prentiss." He'd said this so many times before, to parents, husbands, wives, friends, that now the words came to his lips without bidding. "If this is a brain dysfunction, or a tumor, or some other problem, there was no way you could have known about it."

"That's wonderfully pat," Prentiss said. "But I'm the psychologist, remember. You can't beat me at my own game." He paused a moment. "Tomorrow, then. It'll be good to see you again. It *has* been too long."

"Yes. Tomorrow. Come to my office." Giles was relieved now that the conversation was ending. "Bring your information on Mrs. Schoenfeld, if you like."

"Thanks. I will. Good to hear from you, Giles." Prentiss made a sound that was very nearly derisive, saying, "I'm getting tired."

"Aren't we all?" Giles agreed. "Tomorrow, then."

"I'll be there. And thanks." Prentiss hung up.

Hugh Audley, who had been watching this with a faintly curious lift to his upturned brows, gave Giles a moment to gather his thoughts. "Another patient?"

"Not exactly. Not yet." Giles was still puzzled. "Prentiss is a very old friend. He wants a favor." Giles leaned back. "That isn't why you're here, is it?"

"No." Hugh looked down at his folded hands. In casual clothes—today slacks, a bright shirt and sweater-vest—he looked more like a professor or journalist, which he had been, than the minister he was. "I've been in with Mr. Crocker since noon."

Giles flinched. "How is he?"

"How do you think? No. That isn't fair." He took a deep breath. "Can you get Father Denton to talk to him? I know he's a lapsed Catholic, but there is something he wants to confess and he'd do better if he has the chance."

"Why can't he confess to you?" Giles was always anxious to avoid religious problems.

"Hell, Giles, I'm a Unitarian. For Mr. Crocker, I barely count as Christian. What he wants is a priest with all the trappings and the Latin and the whole show." He looked steadily at Giles. "He doesn't have a lot longer."

Giles nodded. "There was really nothing anyone could do. A tumor like that . . ." He bit his lip. It was never easy to lose. "Even if Crocker were a young man, he wouldn't have had much of a chance, but at sixty-three, with his medical history . . ."

Hugh's face softened as he leaned forward, elbows on knees. "Giles. You did your best."

"It wasn't good enough, however." As always, when he was tired or upset, his accent was much more English. Unlike many of the British he knew in America, Giles had made no effort to keep the purity of his Cambridge sound. In the twelve years he had lived in California he had learned to flatten his vowels and pronounce all his diphthongs and r's. Now he spoke with BBC perfection.

"You did more than anyone could ask for." His tone was level and reasonable.

"I should have listened to the man. I should have realized that he wasn't trying to be self-dramatizing when he talked about the hallucinations. But that didn't fit the rest of his symptoms, so I dismissed it." He had turned away from Hugh. "Damned medical blindness. I loathe it."

"Why not take a week off, Giles?" Hugh suggested in the same brisk manner. "Get away from here, have some rest, get laid, take some pictures."

"Will Hensell is the only man available to cover for me. Do you know how much he drinks?" Giles shook his head. "I'm depressed, Hugh. I don't want to lose Frank Crocker, and I can't get it out of my head that it's my fault we're losing him. I should have paid more attention. I should have paid more attention to the man and less to his symptoms. I should have . . . Christ! sometimes I hate this work."

"You do it well. Frank isn't angry with you. He's grateful for all you've done."

"He's not aware of what might have been done. He doesn't know the sort of error I've made," Giles said harshly. "I know."

"Would anyone else have done differently?" Hugh asked, meeting Giles' eyes steadily. "You said that the hallucinations were not consistent with his other symptoms. Would another doctor have considered them important?"

"I can't answer for another doctor," Giles snapped. "It's not the concern of another doctor, it's mine. Frank is a good man. He deserves better than what I've given him." He shook his head. "It's no good talking, Hugh. I can't undo the damage now. Whatever happens, I'll have to learn to live with it."

Hugh studied his hands a moment. "Back when I was still a journalist in Nam and Laos, I saw a great many things that I still have to live with. But I've learned not to make those mistakes again."

"That won't help Frank Crocker."

"Then do whatever you can for him, and next time, listen to your patient. The rest is self-indulgence, ultimately." He rose, a man of somewhat more than middle height, dark graying hair, with hazel eyes framed by deep lines. "And you can help Frank. Talk to Father Denton, will you? It's damned awkward if I do it. But it will make a difference to Frank Crocker if he sees a priest. If there's one thing death counseling teaches you, it's humility; humility and pragmatism. Denton knows the formulae that will make it easier for Frank Crocker. And Frank deserves to have those formulae."

"All right. I'll ask. But it's up to Denton." Giles pushed back from his desk, indicating that the conversation was over.

Hugh understood, and broke into a grin. "Denton's a Jesuit. He'll do it." He nodded. "Thank you. It will help."

"I hope so." Giles got to his feet, making it more obvious that he wanted a few minutes to himself. "I have rounds to make in fifteen minutes. And after that, there's a new patient to see."

"Then I'll talk to you later." Hugh never took Giles' abruptness as a rebuke. "I'll let you know how it's going with Frank, if you like."

Giles nodded, unable to answer. "Later, Hugh."

"Good." He let himself out of the office and waved as he closed the door.

Idly Giles picked up Prentiss' letter and skimmed it once again. No, he decided, he didn't like the look of the case at all, but he would see Mrs. Schoenfeld, if only to put his old friend's mind at rest.

Nancy Lindstrom was waiting for him at the nurses' station when Giles finished his rounds. "How goes it?" she asked, giving him a pleasant, cynical smile.

"Well enough. And you?" He was later than usual, and he realized that she had been expecting him.

"Okay. It was sad about Mr. Baggley." She was making conversation. No one was truly sad about Mr. Baggley, who had been in a coma for over ten months and at last had died.

"It was sad that he was ill. It isn't sad that he died." Giles rubbed the back of his neck.

"What about the new one, the man they sent down from Redding?" This was in part an excuse to keep him talking. She was trying to sound out his mood, but Giles was often private and resisted her attempts to draw him out.

Giles shook his head. "Oh, his doctors were right: there's one hell of a malignancy right next to the skull. We'll cut it out, I suppose, but he'll lose certain . . . abilities. You saw the results of the tests, didn't you? And the pictures we've got. There's no doubt." He folded his arms and leaned back against the wall, feeling tired.

"Do you want to come over tonight?" There was an open invitation in her sideways glance, and though Giles occasionally slept with Nancy, sharing deft, utilitarian sexual gratification with her, he resented it when their casual intimacy intruded on their work.

"No. I don't think so. Maybe next week." He had straightened up, and spoke more curtly than he had intended. "I've had a long day," he added, wanting to soften the blow.

Her eyes glittered a moment, then she shrugged. "Well, Dr. Carey asked me out. I guess I'll go with him."

Giles laughed once. "Go ahead. But I warn you, he's got a sadistic streak."

Nancy smiled unpleasantly. "Good. I need some variety."

For a moment Giles was tempted to fight with Nancy, to shake off some of the despair that had been building up in him for several weeks, but the nurses' station was not the place to do it. There was scandal enough whispered around the hospital without adding to it. Or was it, he asked himself, that he really didn't care that much anymore? He had always felt contempt for those doctors who became living scalpels with desiccated souls, capable of seeing the world only in terms of surgery. Now he was terribly afraid that he was becoming one of them. Rather lamely he said, "Have a good time, Nancy. I'll talk to you tomorrow."

She was obviously shocked. "Giles . . ."

He turned to her, devastation in his heart. "Tomorrow morning I've got surgery scheduled for removal of a pituitary tumor. The patient is a Japanese-American male, aged thirty-one. He's an artist, a very good one. His career is just beginning to take off. He's married, with two children and a third coming. There's bloody little chance that the operation will save him—the tumor is fairly large and it's quite likely, judging from the CT scan, that it's metastasized. Anything we do now is probably only postponing the end. But he wants to try, because for him, the alternative is unthinkable. He'll try anything. And I'll use anything, if it will help—really help."

Nancy shrugged. "Well, a tumor like that, it's not going to go away. He might as well have the surgery."

"And his painting?" Giles didn't expect an answer to the question, and did not get one. "Art is alchemy. Any disturbance can throw it off. Change the way the motor responses work, the tracking of the eyes, the perception of movement or color, and the art changes, too. Or it dies."

"Yeah, it's too bad about Gary Kusogawa." She met his eyes and then directed her attention to the three nurses coming down the hall.

Giles watched her as she began to prepare the various records of drug dosages. He thought it was a shame that Nancy should be so excellent a nurse and so uncompassionate a woman. Perhaps they went together. He had seen that particular combination before, but never as clearly as Nancy's case.

"I'll see you tomorrow, Dr. Todd," Nancy said pointedly.

"Fine. Give Dr. Carey my regards," he said, and turned away.

Hugh caught up with him in the many-tiered parking lot. He had called Giles' name twice before Giles looked up.

"Trouble?" Giles demanded as Hugh came to his car.

"No, not precisely. I wanted a word with you before you left." Although he was still vital, there was a subtle fatigue about him, a loss of color in his skin that was not entirely the effect of the poor lighting in the garage.

"What, then?" Giles had already opened his car door, his foot lifted to get into his car, which, to the amusement of most of the hospital staff, was a Land Rover.

"For one thing, I wanted to ask you to come over to Berkeley this Sunday or next Sunday and let me take revenge on you for that trouncing you gave me at tennis last month."

"I thought you were busy Sunday," Giles said, not without irony.

"I am, until two. And then I have a whole day in front of me. Come on over." He smiled and the permanent creases around his eyes deepened.

Giles hesitated. "I don't know, Hugh. I've got my hands full. . . . You know . . ."

"Of what?" Hugh asked pleasantly. "You live alone, you're a long way from anything or anyone. The only recreation you have is walking on the beach." He put his hand on Giles' arm, and though Giles was not comfortable with this familiarity, he accepted it from Hugh. "Do I have to remind you about statistics? You keep on the way you're going, and either you'll crack up or you'll have a heart attack. The only reason it hasn't happened up till now is that you've had the teaching, and it's been a mitigating factor." He stepped back as he saw Giles' face close. "I know. I'm not supposed to notice, and if, by some chance, I *do* notice, I'm not supposed to say anything. Well, dammit, Giles. I work with the dying all day, and I hear, over and over again, how each of them thought it would never happen to them. I don't want you to be one of them. You're too good a doctor and too good a friend." He had folded his arms and he met Giles' glance evenly. "This Sunday or next Sunday?"

Giles capitulated. "Next Sunday. I've got this consultation to do, and it might run into more time than I thought."

"Okay," Hugh nodded once. "I'll hold you to that. If necessary, I'll send Gina over to get you. Since she got her license, she loves any excuse to drive."

But Giles could not help but give one parting shot. "There are times I wish you'd forget you're a minister, Hugh."

Apparently Hugh was not used to such comments, because he grinned. "I've never been known to practice charity on a tennis court."

Before he pulled the Land Rover door completely open so that he could mount to the driver's seat, Giles asked, "Where do you want to play? Junipero Serra . . ."

"Hell, no. That's your turf. Come to my side of the Bay. I'll meet you at the Berkeley Tennis Club. That's the one at the corner of Tunnel Road and Domingo, right near the Hotel Claremont. Give my name if I'm not there yet. How does two-thirty sound?"

Giles nodded. "Sunday after this. Two-thirty, at the Berkeley Tennis Club."

Hugh took advantage of Giles' cooperation. "And afterward, you can come over to dinner. Inga's wanted to have

you over since January. The last time you were over was
Thanksgiving, and that's how many months ago?"

"Sure," Giles said, feeling quite tired. "Why not? It would
be good to see Inga and the kids again." Inwardly he wasn't
sure he wanted to see them so soon. He rarely thought about
his life, the emptiness of it, but with Hugh Audley and his
family, Giles felt a loss within himself. Even as the thought
tugged at his mind he told himself it was foolish, and so he
forced more enthusiasm into his voice than he actually felt.
"I'll look forward to it. Ask Inga what kind of wine she'd
like."

Although he was pleased at Giles' acceptance, Hugh was
guarded in his response, which was unusual for him. "Be glad
to." He looked closely at Giles. "Are you all right? Truly?"

Giles raised his brows. "Why shouldn't I be?"

"You know why," Hugh said, the rejoinder very sharp.

"Hugh," Giles said with weary patience, "don't fret over
me. I'm not trying to commit suicide. I know the risks. I
know what stress does."

"Yeah. But neglect is as bad as stress. Remember that,
too." He caught a fleeting, bleak pain in Giles' face, and
changed his manner abruptly. He spoke lightly. "Here I go
telling you not to take your work home, and I'm pulling exactly that on you. Habit. Well, we'll play tennis a week from
Sunday. I'll check in with you here, from time to time."

Giles tried to smile. "Purely professional?"

At that Hugh laughed. "Now, when am I ever purely professional?" He stepped back from Giles, willing to let this be
his exit line, and satisfied that he had accomplished his ends
with his reticent British friend.

But Giles had one more question. "Hugh, did Father Denton talk to you? He said he would." It was an afterthought,
and as a result, the words came easily.

"Thanks, yes. He did." Hugh was surprisingly humble then.
"Between us, I think we've worked out something that won't
offend anyone's sensibilities too much. Frank Crocker admitted that he couldn't do a real penance, and would refuse a
perfect act of contrition. He's a long way from the Catholic
Church these days, but there are some old needs in him."
Hugh spread his hands wide. "So we've created a provisional
rite that Denton accepts and that won't go contrary to Frank
Crocker's integrity."

Giles had pulled the door wide and now reached in to
touch the steering wheel. "Well, that's good. It makes it easier

for Crocker, certainly. It's good of you to make these arrangements. Crocker doesn't have a lot of time left."

"You can't be sure about that," Hugh reminded him. "You
thought that Jane Merriwell would be dead eighteen months
ago, and she's still going strong."

"Not everyone's a statistic," Giles agreed. "But there are
strong indications in Crocker's case, and you know it." He
was in the driver's seat now, the key in the ignition.

Hugh was about to add something, then changed his mind
and said, "Do you remember that child we had a couple of
years ago, right after the death-counseling program began
here? Shelah McGowan? A kid about fourteen?"

Giles nodded somberly. "I remember her very well."

"I let her down. I didn't realize how important it was for
her to do . . . something. I said I'd arrange it, and I didn't.
Actually, I forgot about it until it was too late. That was very
cruel of me. And until that time I didn't know how little it
took to be cruel. Since then, I've made up my mind that if I
err, it will be from activity. Sins of commission, not omis-
sion." He waved and turned away. "Drive safely. The fog'll
be in soon."

Giles slammed the door and started the Land Rover.

He drove down the hill from Parnassus to Lincoln Way.
The traffic was still heavy, although it was closer to six than
five. At Nineteenth Avenue the cars were bumper to bumper
and Giles made up his mind to take an alternate route home.
He had long ago learned to gauge the density of traffic while
he waited for the light at Nineteenth, and either double back
on Twentieth or continue along Lincoln Way, on the south
side of Golden Gate Park to the Great Highway that ran
beside the beach.

Years ago, when he had first come to California and
settled in San Francisco, he had lived in one of the old, blis-
tered, expensive apartments that looked out to the Pacific
breakers. The apartment had been south of the Park and two
years ago had been torn down to make room for a new mo-
tel. Giles remembered that apartment now, the way the sun
splashed over the faded carpet in the living room on the days
when there was no fog. Prudence had said it was damp there,
but for a year she had liked it, too.

The road climbed gently to the bluffs, moving away from
the fences and trees that marked the zoo and the bulk of the
old, empty Fleischacker pool. Away from the ocean he could

glimpse the outline of Stonestown now, on the far side of Lake Merced. Beyond that the massive buildings of San Francisco State University and the Park Merced towers. These were gone quickly, distantly. He looked along the rising bluffs. Once there had been nothing but wild scrub along this road, and trees sculptured by wind. Now there was row after row of houses, the little houses on the hillside made out of ticky-tacky and looking just the same as the ones Malvina Reynolds had written her song about. Giles had never seen this part of Daly City when it was wild, but the crest of the hill where he lived in Montara still had echoes of that time.

Over the ocean the sky was glaringly white with the approaching fog. The setting sun became a smudge of brightness, and Giles had to squint against it as he drove. The Cabrillo Highway narrowed near Rockaway Beach, and took on the familiar, treacherous form that characterized most of its length. The road turned inland past the bulk of Point San Pedro, then came back to the cliffs at Devil's Slide. Giles smiled. He would be home before the fog came in.

As he turned in at his private road, Giles stopped to open his mailbox and found two letters, his P.G.&E. bill, and three magazines. He dropped these onto the passenger seat and continued up the graveled road he shared with three other neighbors. His own house was the most distant, on the brow of the hill, facing southwest, with Montara Beach and Lighthouse due west, and the gentle curve of Half Moon Bay visible beyond the curve of the hill to the south. The land behind him was protected, in part by the Coastal Commission and in part by the Fish and Game Refuge; a carefully guarded wilderness that guaranteed Giles' privacy as part of its survival.

The house had been designed by Robert Canfield. It was elegantly simple—three stories stepped back from each other, leaning against the rise of the hill. There were two wide decks overlooking the Pacific. At the back of the third floor, behind the master bedroom, was a small Japanese garden and a stand of seventeen young redwoods. The two acres the house stood on were Giles', also, and his most persistent worry was how to keep the poison oak and blackberries from taking over completely. Last year his gardener had planted rhododendrons to flank the driveway, which ended on the shady north side of the house, but these had yet to reach their full size, and so they were spindly and sparse, though a few of them still had huge claret-colored blooms.

As he stepped into the foyer, he thought again that perhaps he should have a dog to guard the house and keep him company. But as always, the thought was fleeting. He reminded himself that he did not have time to give to a pet, and that it wouldn't be fair to subject an animal to deliberate neglect.

The living room was large, the windows covered at the moment with heavy draperies. The walls were natural redwood. Giles had a small collection of paintings, each lovingly selected. The room was comfortable, with low, plump sofas and cozy chairs. With a little effort Giles resisted the urge to drop into one of the chairs and close his eyes. Beyond the living room were two good-sized bedrooms and a bath, ostensibly for children, but used only on those rare occasions when Giles had guests. There was also a recreation room that gave entrance onto the carport. Giles used both the recreation room and the carport for storage.

The kitchen and dining room, along with his library and study, were on the second level. Giles went up the wide, uncarpeted stairs slowly. He was vaguely aware that he should eat, but also doubted that there was much in the refrigerator to attract him. He was too tired to drive into Princeton-By-The-Sea or back to Pacifica for a meal. In the kitchen he looked into his shelves, found some packaged soup and some cocktail crackers. He told himself that he really ought to take the time to do some serious food shopping, but he could not face that prospect with any enthusiasm.

He made a meal of the soup and some cheddar cheese he found in the butter compartment of the refrigerator. He wanted some wine to perk up this dismal fare, but the only bottle in the house was one of '66 Heitz Pinot Chardonnay, and much too splendid a vintage to be wasted on such a terrible supper. He sat in the breakfast nook, a lovely little room with a skylight in the roof and glass on three sides that overlooked the woodsy drop down to San Vincente Creek. Only the flicker of an owl drifting past the window caused Giles to raise his head.

After washing his supper dishes, he went back to the living room and turned on the television. Nothing seemed to catch his interest, not even KQED's current selection of Masterpiece Theater. In less than five minutes he had turned off the set, and eventually he dozed off in one of the comfortable chairs, a book by his side and yesterday's newspaper open in his lap.

Sometime very late he awakened, looked dazedly around, and then reached to massage the kink in his neck. He decided that the discomfort had awakened him, although he had a fleeting impression of a terrible dream in which an ancient stone church had collapsed on him. None of the various interpretations he gave the dream pleased him. Perhaps Hugh Audley was right and he was on the brink of some predictable mid-life crisis. The statistics certainly said so. He went upstairs to the third floor, promising himself a long hot bath to ease the knots out of his muscles.

□ 2 □

The restaurant Prentiss had chosen was justly famous. Its decor was elegant but subdued, the menu excellent and the service remarkable for its very unobtrusiveness. Even Giles, who rarely paid attention to food, liked what he ate and knew it was of superior quality.

After the salad and before the dessert, Prentiss at last got down to business. "Now, about Mrs. Schoenfeld . . ."

Giles laid his fork aside, waiting.

"I realize that this request is somewhat irregular. And I do remember how much you dislike this sort of thing, no matter what you've said in disclaimer." He smiled and leaned forward. Giles remembered the way Prentiss had always had that knack. "But this is a *special* case, because of the nature of my research. I hope you'll understand my position. And do, please, Giles, be frank with me." Prentiss was a tall, square man with a touch of the bluff heartiness that was usually associated with English country squires. In his case the effect was modified somewhat by his professorial look. He had a reputation for being charismatic.

"This has really been an excellent meal, Prentiss, and I've enjoyed talking about the old days"—Giles never referred to England as home now, unlike many others he knew—"but if this was for the protection of the patient, believe me, it was unnecessary."

Prentiss nodded heavily. "Of course. It's so damned unpleasant, having a thing like this happen after such promise. And I do feel myself so . . ."

"Helpless?" Giles suggested, having felt that way himself a great many times. "It's not uncommon, particularly in cases of this sort."

"Not helpless. Not that," Prentiss said in swift denial. "But I am all at sea. I've no idea what I'm dealing with, don't you know? and I hate to blunder about in the dark." Again he gave his wide, charming smile. "It's true, even though it's one hell of a mixed metaphor." Then quickly he altered his manner and was intently serious. "I don't want to do anything that might make it *worse* for Mrs. Schoenfeld. She's a remarkable woman, an amazing woman. To think that she might suffer because of what we've done with her . . ."

"I trust you'll tell me what that is," Giles said, prompting gently.

"I'll explain, of course. But I want you to know that she's taking all of this very well. I *know* that she's very frightened. But she hasn't allowed her fear to paralyze her."

"Good," Giles said, staring unseeing at his plate.

"We've had a certain number of tests run on her already. I've arranged for them to be made available to you. They should be in your hands on Monday. I was hoping you might be able to see her early next week. Tuesday or Wednesday, if possible."

Where there was trouble with the brain, Giles knew that it was important to act quickly. "If I have the test results on Monday, I'd want to see her on Tuesday. We'd want a day of observation, and then our own tests on Wednesday. Can this be arranged?"

"I'm certain it can." Prentiss was completely sure of himself.

"You mentioned that she is a widow, with one child. Is there anyone the child can stay with? I don't want Mrs. Schoenfeld having any more anxiety than absolutely necessary."

Prentiss drank the last of his wine. "No problem there. She lives with an aunt of hers. The boy will be looked after very well. He's quite fond of the aunt, and she's a sensible woman. Not the flighty type. She's been very helpful through all this."

Inwardly Giles hoped that the aunt would continue to be helpful. He had an uneasy feeling about the whole case, and Prentiss' unorthodox procedures had added to that sense. "I will want to talk to this aunt if the tests turn up anything positive."

"Of course." Prentiss let the waiter remove the two butter plates. "We'll have coffee and brandy?" He looked at Giles for confirmation. "And the chef's special torte."

"I'm sorry, sir," the waiter said as if he were informing Prentiss of a calamity. "We're out of that. May I recommend the timbale Grand Marnier?"

Prentiss shrugged. "Certainly." He waved the waiter away and gave his attention to Giles once again. "You'll see Mrs. Schoenfeld before the tests are run?"

Giles recalled that Prentiss had always been slightly overbearing, and had long since learned to accommodate himself to this whenever possible. "I'll try. I want to see her test results that you've got before I make up my mind. I'll arrange the admission with my office at the hospital. Call tomorrow morning for confirmation."

"Thank goodness." Prentiss sighed.

"Why?" Giles asked, sincerely interested. "What is it about this woman that you're taking such pains for her? Are you involved with her?" He moved his hand aside as the waiter put cream-filled pastry shells covered with caramel handles before each of them.

"I suppose you might say that I am involved with her," Prentiss said thoughtfully. "Not physically, if that's what you mean. But you see, ever since her first . . . attack, I've felt that I was responsible for it, somehow." This uncertainty was most unlike Prentiss.

"Why?" Giles ignored the dessert.

"She's part of my program. She came into the ESP program last fall, as part of her master's studies. She was doing her work on external influences and deviant behavior, and thought the ESP lab might have an angle worth following." He scowled suddenly. "She agreed to be a subject for some of our experiments. During those experiments, we found out that she's an exceptionally gifted subject—card predictions of more than eighty-percent accuracy, very nearly consistently. That's damned impressive."

"Indeed." Giles stifled the urge to ask for more information. If he needed it, he would get it later. Now he knew it was important to let Prentiss talk, and to search for clues.

"Of course, the statistics against that sort of thing are quite astronomical," Prentiss said, assuming an air of complacency. "We've had other good subjects in our study group, but Mrs.

Schoenfeld is in a class *all* by herself." As if to buy time, Prentiss picked up his fork. "You should have your dessert. It's really quite good."

Giles covered his disappointment, and did as he was told. Prentiss was right—it was very good. He longed to ask more about Mrs. Schoenfeld, who was suddenly very interesting. He began to understand why Prentiss had been so irregular in his manner of request for help. "And the attacks? When did they start?"

Prentiss didn't answer immediately. "After we began our experiments."

It was not unexpected, but Giles was still unsatisfied. "Tell me some more about her, will you?"

Again Prentiss hesitated. "You mean about the ESP?"

"Preferably." Although Giles finished his dessert while Prentiss talked, the fine pastry and its rich filling had no taste for him: his attention was on his old friend's words.

"At first she gave tests, you know, to gather information. Then she decided she ought to try being a receiver, for more information. She admitted that there were times when she 'knew things' without knowing how. Well, that's damned common. Almost everyone does, but we get trained early to filter it out. But we agreed. It was one more sample." He stopped, and chose his words with more precision as he went on. "So we did a few tests with Zenner cards—you know, the cross, the triangle, the star, the wavy lines, that lot?"

"I've seen them."

"She ran the first test at seventy-two-percent accuracy. We were . . . well, we were so *amazed* that we didn't believe it. We did *another* test, with *another* pack of cards and *another* partner. The results were different, it was true. She was up to seventy-seven percent." He broke off again, and ate the rest of his dessert in quick, large bites.

Giles refused to let his excitement show. "What kind of controls did you have on her?"

"Oh, we're careful. Man, you better believe that we're careful. I'll show you the control system sometime. But we've checked her out so thoroughly. And now this!"

"The poor woman." Giles shook his head, pushing the last of his dessert aside.

Prentiss looked startled. "Poor woman? Oh, yes, that goes without saying. But don't you realize what it could *mean* if it turns out that she has a tumor, or other disease? I can't *believe* that ESP phenomena are the result of brain dysfunction.

I can't and I won't!" There was a stern set to his jaw that Giles had seen many times before. "Don't you understand what that woman can *do?* We have to save her."

Giles smiled ironically at the *we.* "I'll try. You know I'll try. I'll admit that I'm curious about this too, if she can do the things you say she can." He muttered a thanks to the waiter who had brought coffee to their table. "But what if it is a matter of . . . oh, a tumor? What then?"

"But it isn't." Prentiss said it with finality. "Someone with a talent like that . . . It makes as much sense to say that Mozart was the result of brain dysfunction." He drank some of the dark, bitter coffee. "Think of what could be done with that power. If she could channel it, develop it. Think what it could mean. In the proper hands, her impact would be *enormous.*"

"But what would it do to her?" Giles hadn't meant to ask the question aloud, but he was startled at the force of Prentiss' reaction.

"That is beside the point! A talent like she's got, it can't be wasted. It's too important!" His voice had risen so that three diners at a neighboring table looked at them, mildly offended. This was a place of soft voices and good manners. Prentiss broke off and nodded in a conciliatory way toward the others, then turned to Giles once more. "She's got to be saved. Think about it, Giles. Do you remember, when we went up to Cambridge? That lecture we heard by Dr. Godarin? I know it was instrumental in my choice of studies. And it was in yours, too, I'd imagine. Up until that time, you hadn't been that interested in the brain. You were more likely to go into orthopedic surgery than neurological. That opening statement of his: 'The brain is not the mind.' I'm still learning how true that is."

After he drank the last of his coffee, Giles said, "Perhaps you're right."

"Godarin talked about some of the studies being done in Russia. He predicted that whoever held the key to the mind also held the key to everything else. Until Mrs. Schoenfeld arrived, I didn't believe that there *was* such a key. Now I'm certain there is." He picked up the brandy snifter the waiter had just set down and held it in his hand to warm it. "What she has now is a spectacular ability, but it has almost no focus, no direction."

"And she has seizures and moments of amnesia," Giles reminded him, feeling an unfamiliar welling of compassion within him. "Is she that sensitive all the time?"

"Um?" Prentiss was surprised by the question. "No, I don't think so. She has strong flashes of intuition, and isolated bits of precognition, but nothing coherent yet. That's what we're working for." He leaned back in his chair. "You don't know how much I'm depending on you, Giles. This could be so *big.* . . ."

Giles put down the sheaf of records and evaluations that had arrived by messenger almost two hours ago. It didn't make sense. Mrs. Schoenfeld's EMT brain scan was fine. There were one or two irregularities, but nothing significant, nothing that triggered his sense of alarm. The CT scan was inconclusive. There was certainly no evidence of a tumor or the sort of dysfunction that might be expected with her particular history. He went over the cerebral angiogram, reading the evaluation twice. Nagy was a good man; Giles had great respect for him, and if he said that there was nothing significant in the tests, then Giles was certain that the tests were indeed negative.

He put the records down abruptly. Perhaps he was looking at it the wrong way around. Given her behavior and her history, it might be very significant indeed that there were no indications of disease. Not physical disease. He reminded himself that Prentiss was an excellent psychologist, and if the woman were disturbed or psychotic, he must have realized it. As quickly as this thought crossed his mind, it was joined by another. Mrs. Schoenfeld was his particular prize. Where Prentiss Fellkirk would see psychosis in others, in Fayre Schoenfeld he would see it as part of her uncanny abilities.

He hesitated a moment, then picked up his phone. "Mrs. Houghton, will you get me Ferenc Nagy at St. Matis University Medical Center?"

"Of course, Dr. Todd."

Giles waited, and in a moment there was the sound of Mrs. Houghton again. "I'm sorry, Dr. Todd, Dr. Nagy is in surgery at the moment. Shall I leave a message?"

"Yes," he said slowly. "Tell him that I'll call him at home tonight. Tell him it's about a patient of his, one that Dr. Fellkirk brought to him." He was far from satisfied by this change, but he accepted it. He knew his own schedule was difficult, and it was foolish to resent Ferenc Nagy for being equally busy.

"Very good, Dr. Todd," Mrs. Houghton said, and hung up.

In the fifteen minutes Giles had before he met with his class for the morning, he once again reviewed the bewildering, negative test results on Mrs. Schoenfeld.

Giles had been ready to leave the hospital when an emergency was brought in from Daly City. The woman was old, and her strength remarkable under the circumstances. He and his usual operating team worked on her for three hours, but it was a losing battle from the start. Eventually, the old woman slipped away.

"Too bad," Nancy Lindstrom said as they left the operating room.

"Yes," Giles agreed, his voice tight with fatigue and a deep sense of futility.

"But she couldn't have made it," Nancy went on, clearly willing to accept the loss.

"Then why did you scrub for it? Why didn't you just let her die?" Giles had taken her by the arm and it was only by the sudden stiffening of her muscles that he knew he was hurting her.

"Dr. Carey isn't the only sadist around here," Nancy said, and waited until Giles released her. "I scrubbed because it's my job. That's why. Any more questions, Dr. Todd?"

Giles had moved away from her. "No, no more questions." He felt cold with despair, and that feeling did not leave him during the forty-minute drive back to Montara.

It was nearly eleven by the time Giles phoned Ferenc Nagy, and he felt almost guilty making the call. Nagy, he knew, was not a night person, and might well be asleep.

"Another ten minutes, and I was going to bed," Nagy said as he recognized Giles' voice. "I gather this is about Mrs. Schoenfeld?"

"Yes. I got your records on her today. What's going on?" As was his habit, Giles had a pad of paper on the table beside him and three sharpened pencils waiting.

"Nothing, so far as the tests go," Nagy said. "I can't figure it out."

"Perhaps it's a case for a psychiatrist," Giles suggested, listening carefully for Ferenc's reaction.

"No, I don't think so, not now. I did at first, but I've seen one of her seizures now, and whatever it is, it doesn't look like any psychosis I've ever seen."

"Then what does it look like?" Giles asked, the day's buildup of frustration making him sharp. He held one of the pencils so tightly that it nearly broke.

"I don't know. I'd be grateful to see your results. When you have an opinion, let me know." He paused. "I'll tell you something, Giles. When I watched that seizure, I was tempted to believe in possession, like some old peasant."

"What do you mean?" Giles demanded.

"I don't know. It was almost as if she wasn't there anymore, and something or someone else was using her for a channel. It was the spookiest thing I've seen in twenty-three years of practice. I wish I knew what it was."

"All the usual tests were run," Giles said, more to himself than to Ferenc Nagy. "There's no chemical evidence for schizophrenia, is there?"

This time Nagy was short with him. "No. I checked that out before we ran the EMT on her. No schizophrenia, or any other metabolic influence that we could detect."

"No pituitary malfunction?" The chances were slight, but Giles was anxious for answers.

"No. Of course, there was no chance to do tests during her seizure. One of my students down here wanted to run tests on the pineal, but there was no way we could have."

Giles nodded, accepting this for the moment. "Thanks, Ferenc. I appreciate your candor."

On the other end of the line, Ferenc Nagy laughed. "What candor? I'm as baffled as you are. I only hope that you come up with a lucky guess, because for the life of me, I haven't the least notion what's wrong with Mrs. Schoenfeld."

"I'll try to find out," Giles promised him.

"Good. Keep me posted."

"I'll be glad to." He was ready to hang up.

"Giles, good luck." Ferenc's tone was sincere. "In a case like Mrs. Schoenfeld's, she needs your luck."

To his surprise, Giles was touched by Ferenc's good wishes. "Thanks. Truly."

"Anytime. Good night." Without waiting for a response from Giles, Ferenc Nagy hung up.

It was only then that Giles realized he hadn't made any notes. The pencil between his fingers was cracked where he had pressed it earlier, but there was nothing on the notepad in front of him. He thought back over the conversation, thinking to put down a few of Ferenc's remarks, but as he called his colleague's words to mind, he knew that he would not have to make notes. This time he remembered every comment with stark clarity.

Sometime after midnight when Giles told himself firmly he ought to be in bed asleep, he wandered out onto the balcony off his bedroom. He had pulled on a terry-cloth robe, but the night wind off the ocean raised gooseflesh as it touched his skin. The moon was almost full and it rode in a clear sky. There were few trees on the hills near the ocean, but a thick scrub grew there and in the pale light took on the appearance of nubbly carpeting. Giles walked to the edge of the balcony and leaned on the rail there. The darkness tugged at him, and the immensity of the tarnished ocean flecked with spume and moonlight. Two bright lights marked the runway of the tiny airport at Half Moon Bay, and there were occasional lights in the houses farther down the hill, but they were trivial against the magnificent canopy of night.

He turned around and leaned back against the rail, supporting himself on his elbows. Now there was only the line of his house dwarfed by the rise of Montara Mountain behind it. Involuntarily his eyes strayed to the curtained windows beside his bedroom. That was a room he entered rarely now. The piano must be sadly out of tune, he thought. He used to enjoy playing so much, and knew that he played well. For a moment he heard the C-sharp melody of the second Schumann *Papillon* in his mind. Perhaps he would give Tom Baker a call and ask him to come out next week to get the piano back into shape.

The wind increased and Giles felt chilled. He remembered that he had to see Mrs. Schoenfeld in the morning, and if he didn't get some sleep, he would be no good to anyone. Slowly he went across the balcony, no longer seeing the night, and returned to his bedroom.

Mrs. Houghton looked up as Giles moved toward his office. "Mrs. Schoenfeld has checked in, Dr. Todd. She arrived at nine this morning." There was an unstated criticism in her voice, implying that if patients could brave the commute traffic, so could the doctors.

"Good. I'll want to see her in half an hour. Right now, will you see if Hugh Audley is in the building? I've just come from Mr. Crocker's room, and he wants very much to talk to Hugh. He refused to have him paged. So it might be better if you call around to the other floors and find out where he is."

There was a slight softening in Mrs. Houghton's iron face.

"Very well, Dr. Todd." She reached into the neat stacks on her well-organized desk. "Here's the admission information. The lab is doing a blood workup on her right now."

Since this was what Giles had requested, he gave no response. "And call Dr. Carey for me, will you?" In answer to the condemning expression she assumed, Giles said, "One of my students needs to talk to an endocrinologist. You will agree that Carey's the best we've got?"

At once Mrs. Houghton's face was wooden. "Of course, Dr. Todd."

Giles was tempted to say more, feeling, inexplicably, that he ought to explain himself. But Mrs. Houghton was plainly not interested in what he had to say, and he had never developed that casual attitude toward sharing personal convictions which seemed so prevalent among Californians. He went into his office. There were several other matters he had to attend to before he could see Mrs. Schoenfeld.

It was somewhat after eleven when Giles finally walked into the sunny private room on the south side of the hospital. There had been many attempts to make the room as cheery as possible: two bright prints hung on the wall, and turquoise curtains hung over the windows. The drapery around the bed was patterned in soft blues and greens. But nothing could disguise the room effectively. In spite of the pleasant colors and the little cosmetic touches, it was still a hospital room, and that fact rendered everything stark.

Two nurses, one a student, were leaving the room as Giles came into it. The older nurse looked up. "Good morning, Dr. Todd. Mrs. Schoenfeld has just had her bath. We've been a little late with her, on the lab's request."

Giles nodded. "Fine, Waters. Good." He tried to smile, for Ms. Waters was more than usually defensive with him today, but his smile evoked nothing in return, only one stiff nod as Ms. Waters hurried her student away. Giles watched them go, frowning, and turned to draw back the blue-and-green curtain that surrounded Mrs. Schoenfeld.

Fayre Schoenfeld looked up as the light fell across her pillow. She blinked, startled, and then her eyes flew to his. "How sad you . . ." She stopped, embarrassed by the words that had come unbidden to her lips.

If Giles heard, he gave no indication of it. But he stood still, one hand holding back the curtains. "Mrs. Schoenfeld?" he asked in a voice he hardly recognized. He cleared his throat. "I'm Giles Todd." It was only later that he realized he had not used his title.

She nodded, and her pale, smoke-colored hair shimmered in the sun. "Yes. I know. You're Dr. Fellkirk's friend."

"Yes," he agreed, and at last let go of the curtain. "We're . . . we're going to run some tests on you tomorrow, but I have some questions I'd like to ask you now." He had to force himself not to stammer; his English accent was suddenly very strong.

"And will you answer my questions, too?" There was a strain in her voice, but it was still musical, low, very calming to hear.

"Of course," Giles said blandly.

She shook her head, suddenly disgusted. "Christ, you've got that down pat."

Giles was startled, and almost rebuked her for doubting him. "Mrs. Schoenfeld . . ."

"Please . . . please . . . don't take that professional, unctuous tone with me. Dr. Nagy pulled it on me, and told me nothing." There was a challenge in her face. "It's bad enough, going through these . . ."—she faltered, looking for a word—"episodes without having a lot of doctors 'hummmming' over me. I'm not interested in your bedside manner. I want to know what's wrong with me."

"So do I," Giles told her, sensing an affinity to her that had nothing to do with her hostility. "You can believe that, Mrs. Schoenfeld."

"Can I? And if you find out what's wrong, will you tell me?" There was both mockery and desperate hope in her request.

A frown flickered on Giles' brow. "Mrs. Schoenfeld, it's not in either of our interests to have you kept in ignorance. You say you want to know what's wrong. So do I. And the only way we can find out is if we cooperate with each other." He had to resist the urge to touch her, to emphasize his sincerity with nearness. The desire startled him, for he always maintained a strict reserve with his patients, and until now thought it was better that way.

Her hand had moved toward his, but stopped. "Okay. But if I ask you a question, I want a frank answer."

He nodded. "If I can. If I know," Giles said, mastering himself at last. He drew one of the two guests' chairs near the bed.

Fayre Schoenfeld rolled onto her side so that she could

look at him directly. Giles recognized what grace she gave that simple, inelegant movement. "These questions . . ."

"I'm ready, Dr. Todd." Her hostility changed to reserve.

Inwardly he wanted to thank her for this sudden, unintentional aid. He found it much easier to keep his mind on his work now. As he took a pen from his pocket, he flipped open the file he carried. "We've got the name and address and basic history here, of course. You did that at St. Matis for Dr. Nagy. But there are a few things I'd like to know. If you can't answer them, that's all right. The lack of an answer gives important information, too. Please don't be frightened of the questions, and don't assume that a positive answer is necessarily indicative of illness. If you don't understand a question, I'll be happy to clarify it for you. All right?"

"Fine," she said, nodding. "But answer this question for me, first. Then I'll answer yours."

"If I can," he said again. As her eyes met his, he felt their impact again, more strongly than the first time.

"Am I going crazy?" Her voice was a little tighter as she asked, but she had her fear under control.

"There's no clinical indication of it at the moment," he said cautiously.

"Don't lie to me, Dr. Todd. I have to know."

Giles hesitated. "I don't know quite how to answer your question, then."

"It's simple enough. Am I or am I not going out of my mind? Am I turning into a fruitcake, a loony, a nut case, a psycho?" She sounded strangely calm. She had lived with the fear for some time and the words had ceased to bother her. What she dreaded was beyond words. "Well?"

"Don't worry about it just yet, Mrs. Schoenfeld," Giles said, disliking his answer.

She reached out and touched his hand that held the pen poised over his records and her touch went through him like heat. "If I am going insane," she said with intelligent sincerity, "there are certain things I must arrange before it's too late. I've got to make arrangements about my son. I'll have to be sure he's properly taken care of. There's my husband's estate, such as it is. I don't have anyone to look after it, not here, unless I give my aunt power of attorney. You see why I have to know, Dr. Todd. I have obligations and responsibilities. There are things I must do before . . . before I'm too mad to act." She asked, "Well? Am I losing my mind?"

The glib response that Giles had given many times before

would not come. He tried to sound reassuring, hoping that his hesitation would not betray him. "I don't think so. If it were that simple, we would have been able to treat you before now."

She watched him intently a moment, then nodded. "I believe you."

At another time, Giles would have been offended by her attitude, but he could not find it in himself to rebuke her. "Good. We'll get on much better if you'll continue to believe me."

"I will," she said quite seriously. "Unless you start to lie. I'll know if you do." There was a strange expression in her eyes. "I've always been able to tell when people lie."

"Most of us like to think that we have that ability," Giles said, trying his best to be professionally sympathetic.

"That's not the same thing. It's not a question of judgment or assessment. If you lie to me, I'll know. The way I know that two and two is four." She put her head down again. "Ask your questions. I'll do my best to answer them."

"Honestly." This was not a polite question, it was an order.

"Of course. I want to get over . . . whatever this is."

"Then we'll deal quite suitably with each other, I should think." Giles forced himself to turn his attention to the sheet of paper in his hands. "Do your best to answer as completely as possible. The first question: Have you ever noticed if you perceive color differently with your left and right eyes?"

She stared at him, quite incredulous. "Really?"

"Yes." He forced himself to keep his eyes on the paper. "About the color . . . ?"

She gave the matter some thought. "I've never paid any attention. If I do see different colors, it isn't enough to notice. Is that any help?"

Giles just nodded. His hands were clumsy as he wrote her answer. "Do you ever feel you're falling? Not during an actual fall," he amended. "But do you ever get an irrational sensation of falling?"

Fayre closed her eyes, saying at last, "I don't think so. Once in a while, when I'm picking up something, or doing a series of cards for Dr. Fellkirk, I feel sort of floaty. And there's a feeling here"—she touched herself below her breasts where the ribs joined—"almost as if I'm dizzy or nauseated. But it isn't like falling. Maybe I feel that way, though, during one of the seizures. I don't remember them."

Her distress was apparent, and Giles had to struggle

against the urge to take her in his arms and comfort her. He swallowed and cleared his throat. "We'll check that out later." He wanted to sound confident, but realized he hadn't the faintest idea how he could get this information during a seizure.

"Don't lie," she snapped. "Even for kindness."

Giles nodded slowly. "I won't. I wasn't thinking." He moved his chair farther back from the bed. "Do you ever experience sudden changes of temperature perception? For example, have you ever been in a room which you know to have been the same temperature but which seemed to change? I'm not asking about body temperature, but the reaction to external changes."

She spoke very softly. "I feel cold. Like I'm in an envelope of cold. It's a special kind of cold, not really like a temperature change at all." The laugh she tried was unsteady. "I've had that happen every now and then. I know I feel icy before a seizure, but that's all I remember."

This particular reaction disturbed Giles. He tried to keep his face impassive. "All right. Do you experience any visual or auditory distortions?"

"You mean hallucinations?" she asked, challenging him.

"Not precisely. It's not a question of seeing what isn't there, but of inaccurately perceiving what is there."

"That's another kind of hallucination," she reminded him. "I'm not afraid of the word." She sighed and turned away from him. "I see auras sometimes. At least, I think they're auras. They're not these big egg-shaped things I've read about, but a kind of color outline, like being edged in light. It doesn't happen very often. Auditory hallucinations," she said thoughtfully. "Well, sometimes I seem to hear more than one thing. Sometimes it's hard to tell what a person is saying and what they're thinking. If I concentrate I can figure it out. And sometimes when someone is speaking, it sounds like they're talking with a lot of voices, not just one." Her voice quivered. "I hate it when it happens. It's frightening. When it happened the last time, Dr. Fellkirk tried to help me shut it out. He wanted me to turn it off. I couldn't. It was awful."

The auditory hallucination of garbled voices was a common one, and Giles almost passed it by for that reason. But there was something in Fayre's manner—and he was acutely aware of her—that made him consider what she said. "What kind of voices?"

"I don't know. But there were a lot of them, and they

wanted me to do something for them. And I knew if I did it, I would stop being myself." Her eyes filled with tears, which she dashed away impatiently with one hand.

"This happens when? When you're about to have a seizure?" He was beginning to resent his attraction to her. It affected his thinking. She was a fascination, and a distraction. He wanted to get the interview over with so that he could escape from her disturbing presence.

"I'm not sure. I don't think so, but it might be that it happens during seizures and I . . . don't remember." She moved a little farther away from him and drew the bedding around her.

Giles finished scribbling. "Do you suffer from disorientation? Do you lose your balance, or your sense of direction?"

"Not very often," she said, and quite unexpectedly, smiled.

"Can you elaborate on that?" He didn't want her to be uncooperative now.

"It's not important. It's not connected with the seizures." Just as Giles was about to insist, she gave him another of her steady looks. "Believe me. I know."

"I'll have to accept that for the time being," he said with bad grace. "Do you ever experience irrational periods of either depression or elation?"

"Doesn't everyone?" she countered.

"Yes, but usually within limits." He waited for her to give him an answer.

"I don't know what to tell you. You'll misinterpret the truth, and if I don't answer, you'll misinterpret that, too." Her frown had returned.

"You can't be certain of that, Mrs. Schoenfeld." He heard his own voice become noticeably more British. "Why not give me the benefit of the doubt."

"I would, but . . ." Some of her distress was showing again. She twisted on the bed, then, quite suddenly, she sat up. "Dammit! I'm not an invalid."

"No, you're not."

She narrowed her eyes as she studied Giles critically a moment. "I don't want to be. I hate feeling this way." There was the shine of tears in her eyes again, and this time, Giles was irritated by them. At the same instant he admired her courage, he was annoyed that he felt so much sympathy for her.

"It's a good sign that you do," he said, strictly business. "If you were the sort who enjoys illness and indulges in cheap sickroom theatrics, we'd be less able to help you."

Fayre accepted this bluntness with a nod of the head. "Do you see a lot of that, Dr. Todd?"

He relented, feeling oddly shamed by his attitude. "A few. Most of those patients stop short of brain surgery." He was anxious to ask her the last few questions.

She interrupted him before he could speak. "You don't like to operate, do you?"

"Not particularly," he said, shying away from revealing too much to this disturbing young woman. "Surgery is very permanent, you know. It's better to exhaust all the other possibilities first. Occasionally there is no option, but whenever feasible, I prefer to use other techniques." He wondered if his answer comforted her or not.

"And in my case?" She met his eyes in that same calm, steady way.

"We don't know what your case is yet, Mrs. Schoenfeld. That's what all these tests are about. But if you're wondering whether or not I would recommend surgery at this time, the answer is most emphatically no." He smiled reluctantly. "Do you feel better?"

"I'm not sure." She looked away from him. "Do you have any more questions?"

"A few." He readied his pencil for notes. "Have you had any episodes of synesthesia?"

"Which variety?" she asked, then answered without waiting for his comments. "I have had the kind where when one part of the body is stimulated, another responds. Most of the time it's minor and I don't pay much attention to it. Once in a while, when I'm coming out of a seizure and the amnesia associated with it, I have more intense episodes of that sort. But the other sort, where the actual senses meld . . . Well . . ." She made a wan attempt to smile. "Spring smells green to me, and newly turned earth smells brown, but I don't think that's what you mean."

"No," Giles agreed.

"So far as I know, I haven't had that happen. Beyond the usual."

Again Giles felt his curiosity pricked. "You say so far as you know. Would you care to elaborate?"

This time she stared at the mounds of her feet under the blankets. "I think that when I'm having a seizure, I experience a lot of that kind of synesthesia. I think that the ordinary sort of synesthesia I have when I come out of it is a kind of echo of the more complex variety. It's only a hunch. I wouldn't blame you if you ignored all of this. I have nothing to base my conclusions on, just a feeling that I've had that kind of experience while I was in the middle of a seizure." She gave a jerky shrug to her thin shoulders. "It's probably just misleading. Forget I said it, will you?"

Giles had already written down most of her comments. "I think it might be important. It's an indication of how you feel about the seizures you have. That might have some bearing on your treatment later on. Just one more question, Mrs. Schoenfeld, and I'll leave you alone."

She started to say something, and then stopped as a slight flush spread over her cheeks. "Ask away, Dr. Todd."

"Have you ever had any experience that made you think you were not in your own body?" He watched her closely.

"You mean astral travel, or something like that? Out-of-the-body projections?" She was genuinely interested in this question. "Dr. Fellkirk did some studies on it. They aren't finished yet, but they are really fascinating. He doesn't have anything conclusive, so far, but doing the tests is exciting."

"What about your own . . . perception this way, Mrs. Schoenfeld?" Giles didn't want to be sidetracked again.

"My own?" She crossed her legs and rested her elbows on her knees, propping her chin on her laced fingers. "I don't think so," she said slowly. "But sometimes I feel like I've been mashed down inside myself—that I'm getting smaller and smaller, and that something else is running me. I know that sounds . . . not very sane. But I think it's that feeling that frightens me more than anything else. Do you understand at all?" She saw that Giles was about to protest, and added quickly, "I don't care if you do, so long as you don't think I'm making it up. If I'm not crazy, and you say that I'm not, then there's something very odd about this, isn't there?" The way she asked the question, she might have been speaking about the weather or an oddly colored insect.

"That is why you're here, Mrs. Schoenfeld." He started to rise, closing the folder and putting his pen back in his pocket. "Now, tomorrow—"

"Dr. Todd," she cut in on him, "I know it may be too soon to tell, but is there anything . . . unnatural about what's happening to me?"

"Unnatural?" he repeated, faintly puzzled. "If you mean, is there anything supernatural happening to you, you must know that the answer is no. Anything that happens to a human being, no matter how bizarre, must, by definition, be natural. I admit," he said in a gentler tone, "that there are some bloody odd things in nature, and that what they can do to people is damn-all weird and horrible, but even the worse of them is still within the scope of nature."

"I hope you still believe that six months from now," Fayre Schoenfeld said quietly.

"Why six months, Mrs. Schoenfeld? Why not six weeks or six days? Is there something important about six months?" He asked the questions more abruptly than he had intended to, but decided not to apologize.

"I don't know. I just feel that . . ." Her voice trailed off and she turned to Giles with an expression combining worry, puzzlement and friendliness. "Pardon me. I know you can't tell anything yet. I shouldn't be asking you these things. When you know something, you'll tell me." She didn't doubt for a moment that he would not be honest with her. She moved, unlaced her fingers and held out her left hand. "You are left-handed, aren't you?"

Giles very nearly smiled at this odd courtesy. "Yes. Thanks. I will tell you what I know about your case as soon as there's something solid." He took her hand, but released it quickly. Her touch intensified the disturbance she awakened in him. "I'll talk to you tomorrow, Mrs. Schoenfeld."

"Thank you, Dr. Todd."

As he left her room, she waved after him.

"But I tell you, Hugh, I have never—*never*—felt that way about a patient before. It was like walking from a cool building into hot sunlight. It was like being hit with a hammer." He put his lecture notes aside and turned to pull open the second drawer of the filing cabinet in the corner. "I wish I could find the records on Gordon Baxter. One of my students asked about that sort of case today, and I couldn't bring the details to mind."

"Call Medical Records. The transcriptionists must have it down there somewhere." Hugh had put his attaché case on Giles' desk and had opened it. He pulled out a sandwich. "Do you mind if I have lunch?"

"Lunch? It's almost three-thirty," Giles said. "Go ahead. Sure." He had slammed the second drawer and was working on the third. "Baxter. Baxter. Baxter. He had an arthritic condition, the disease attacked the spine, and eventually involved the cervical vertebrae. Where the devil did I put it? . . ."

"Is it in Mrs. Houghton's records? She might have the files on him. Were you the only doctor to see him?"

"Christ, no. We must have had half the neurological staff and a crew of orthopedists in on the treatment . . ." He stopped, and slammed the drawer. "Of course." He picked up the phone. "Mrs. Houghton, this is Dr. Todd. Will you ask Medical Records for the file on Mr. Gordon Baxter?" He heard her efficient response, thanked her and hung up.

Hugh was halfway through his sandwich, but he said, "Take it easy, Giles."

"Stop worrying," Giles snapped. "I'm fine. But I don't, in general, forget the details of cases that held my attention for nearly five months." He sat down and glared at Hugh. "Oh, very well. I'll take five minutes to relax."

Hugh, rather wisely, said nothing.

"You think I'm going to end up like Dawes, don't you? Living on a commune outside of Mendocino, making clay pots for the tourists." Giles had not yet gotten over the shock of Dr. Terrence Dawes' retirement, and the one time he had visited him in that lovely logging-and-fishing-town-turned-art-colony, Giles had been shocked.

"Terry's happy," Hugh pointed out. "And he's alive and over fifty."

"But think of the waste!" Giles protested.

"Would it be any less waste if Terry had died? A second heart attack would have done it, Giles. Would you be more charitable if he were dead? He's a very good potter. He loves what he's doing. Should he come back here and kill himself doing something he'd come to hate?" In the silence that followed this question, Hugh finished his sandwich.

It was foggy in Montara, and Giles didn't bother to open the draperies onto the thick whiteness. For the first time in several months he had had trouble driving up his private road, since the fog and the darkness distorted the shape of the road and the familiar twists became dangerous. He had been grateful to get home.

The chill of the fog permeated the house, and at last he lit a fire in the huge stone fireplace. He had not planned on using it until autumn, but spring had fooled him, as it did occasionally on the California coast, turning clammy before the coming of summer. He sat in front of the fireplace, a book open in his lap, and found his thoughts drifting back to Fayre Schoenfeld. What was it about that woman? he asked himself.

Why should she, of all the patients he had seen over the years, disrupt him so? She wasn't particularly beautiful. It was true she had the most extraordinary hair, and her steady eyes were quite attractive, but he had seen lovely hair and cool eyes before. Perhaps it was the puzzle, he thought. She interested him because her case was so unfathomable. He was caught up in what was wrong with her. Immediately he rejected the idea. He refused to be one of those doctors who saw people only as a collection of diseases. That was not acceptable to him. He had to have more humanity than that.

Slowly the fire died, and when it was quite cold, Giles left the living room and climbed to the third floor. He had intended to go to bed, but, on impulse, he opened the door to his music room and went inside.

The room had a musty, unused smell, and there was a film of dust on the closed piano. Carefully he lifted the lid and looked down at the keys. Tentatively he fingered an E-flat-major chord, and winced at the jangle the untuned strings made. He really ought to have it tuned, he knew he ought. He sat down on the dusty bench and played a few scales, badly at first, and then with increasing ease and skill. He ignored the out-of-tune keys, and put his mind into his practicing. There was something truly grand about a grand piano, even one so dreadfully flat as this. He remembered how much he had enjoyed *I Peccati di Vecchiaia* by Rossini, and tried to recall *Quelques Riens* from that collection. As he played, he realized once again that Rossini's idea of little nothings and his own were vastly different. He gave his attention to the keyboard and his fingers.

It was well after midnight when he finally closed the piano and left the room. As he drifted to sleep, half an hour later, he was still thinking on the fingering of the *Passacaglia* in B minor he had attempted last.

□ **3** □

"How's it going?" Giles asked the young technician who was monitoring the computer display. "Anything conclusive?"

"Nothing so far," the technician said. "I've double-checked

the program and we've followed your instructions on it. But there's no sign of any pathology. From what I can tell, Mrs. Schoenfeld is a perfectly healthy brain."

Giles was shocked by the young woman's casual attitude. "If the brain were the only thing we're concerned with here, I'd be delighted to hear this. Unfortunately, she's a woman with very alarming and baffling symptoms. She deserves more consideration than this. She is not an insect." He realized he had raised his voice more than usual, and he forced himself to be cooler. "I'm sorry, Ms. Loomis. I don't mean to upset you. But if any of us are going to do that woman a jot of good, we must think of her as a person, someone who is enduring fear and pain." He stopped and turned away. How many times had he told his classes that it was unwise to think of a patient as another human? Yet here he was saying the very thing he felt was most dangerous. If he thought of them all so personally, with such reality, he would have to join Terry Dawes on his Mendocino commune.

"Anything else, Dr. Todd?" Ms. Loomis asked, an edge of sarcasm in her voice.

"No. Not now. Send your results up as soon as you have them." He left the monitor quickly, suddenly wanting very much to shut Fayre Schoenfeld out of his life.

At the end of his lecture, he gave a summary of the Baxter case to the student named Soldat, who had asked for it. He answered a few questions, and was almost ready to start on rounds when he heard a familiar voice behind him.

"Giles, do you have a minute?" Dr. Veronica Beaufort called out. "I've been looking for you. Your office said I might catch you here." Dr. Beaufort was so entirely average-looking that she was practically invisible. "It's about Mr. Limmer. We're having trouble again."

"Trouble? What kind of trouble?" Giles had not lingered. "I've got to start rounds. Come with me, why don't you?"

"A psychiatrist on neurology rounds?" she asked, amusement in her surprise. "I'd like to see how the other half lives. Okay. I don't have a patient until five. And he's a dilly. I wish we could get him into an institution—a remote institution—until we get his behavior under control."

Giles had got to the elevator. "Sounds just wonderful. What is the trouble with Limmer?"

When the elevator doors had closed behind them, Veronica said, "Well, he was your patient first, and I wanted to know if you think he might be developing a home-grown. I know you said last year that there was no trace of such a thing, but he certainly isn't responding to analysis the way I'd expected."

"Maybe it's something in the water," Giles said, smiling a little. "What's his living situation like?"

Dr. Beaufort shrugged. "He's got some strange friends, from what I understand. You know, the group that hangs around Alan Freeman, the witchcraft-and-occult-and-such-nonsense man at St. Matis. They're doing their level best to bring back Beltane and Lammas. You know what those are?" she asked in a less scornful voice.

"Pagan holidays. They're associated with Black Masses. We all knew a little about them back in Gloucestershire, what with one thing and another." He stood aside for her as the elevator doors opened. "It sounds rather simpleminded to me. Most people who are playing with that today are after thrills. I wouldn't take it seriously."

"I don't. But Limmer does. He's taken to wearing an owl's claw on a leather thong around his neck. And his temper has become very unstable. He claims that someone has put an evil spell on him, and that it's causing all his troubles. Honestly, Giles, if it were ethical, I'd give him a good swift kick where he'd pay attention." She stopped as he picked up his files for rounds.

On the other side of the nurses' station, Nancy Lindstrom made a point of turning away from Giles.

"Finally gave her up?" Dr. Beaufort asked as they walked away from the station. "It's none of my business, but it's my profession to be nosy."

Giles had decided not to answer her, but said, "It's more the other way around."

"Thus the affectionate greeting back there?" Veronica Beaufort didn't push the matter. Instead she fell into step beside Giles. "Well, what do you think? Limmer has me worried. I haven't ever had to combat spells before. Schizophrenia, paranoia, depression, megalomania and all the rest, yes, spells, no."

"Find a shaman and counteract the spell. Then Limmer won't have the excuse anymore." Giles had said it flippantly, but Dr. Beaufort grinned.

"It just might work! I should have thought of that, myself. Do you know where I can find a shaman?" The question was teasing, but Giles gave it a little thought.

"Ask Hugh Audley. A Berkeley Unitarian ought to be able

to dig one up for you in no time." He wasn't entirely serious in the suggestion, but as he said it, he decided it might be a workable idea.

"Hugh! Of course!" She gave him an affectionate pat on the shoulder.

Giles had to fight the formal reserve that took hold of him. Despite the years in California, he still found it difficult to be so much at ease with people. With considerable effort he forced himself to return the touch, and with a nervous chuckle said, "It's my English pragmatism, my dear."

They had come to the first room, and Giles said, "This is Miss Wallace. She's eighty-two, and has had a series of very minor strokes."

"Is she still functional?" Dr. Beaufort asked.

"Oh, for the most part she is. She's lost some motor control, which is hardly surprising. There isn't a lot we can do for her. Surgery is out of the question. If she had someone to look after her at home, we would have released her last Friday, but as it is, we want her to be a little more stabilized before she goes to a nursing home." This was said carefully neutrally, but Giles felt a great deal of sympathy for the old woman, having spent so many of his early years alone. To have no place to go was a terrible thing at any age. For an old woman whose life was draining away, it was pitiful.

"No relatives?" Dr. Beaufort wondered aloud.

"Two nieces, one in Boston and one in Minneapolis. Neither of them are in any position to take on Miss Wallace, even if she were in any condition to travel."

"I see," Dr. Beaufort said, and followed him into the room.

The fifth room was Fayre Schoenfeld's. Giles stopped outside the door, reluctant to enter. But with Veronica Beaufort beside him, he could not avoid seeing the disturbing young woman again. He scowled as he said to Dr. Beaufort, "This woman is in for a special neurological study. All her tests have been negative, and there is, apparently, no psychiatric component of her . . . problem. We don't have all the data on her yet, and there are two more tests to make."

"What are your data like so far?" Dr. Beaufort asked casually.

"Inconclusive," Giles snapped, and opened the door.

Fayre had been looking toward the door, the beginning of a smile in her eyes. She nodded to Giles. "Dr. Todd."

"Mrs. Schoenfeld. This is Dr. Beaufort. She's doing rounds

with me." He tried not to look at her, but realized that she was as disarmingly attractive as he remembered. He had hoped that it was an accident, his earlier reaction to her, but now that he was once again in her company, he knew that the pull was there, stronger than before.

Veronica Beaufort gave Giles a swift, quizzical look, then went over to the bed and shook hands with Fayre Schoenfeld. "You seem healthy enough," she said briskly.

"I am, I hope. My body's fine. It's the mind that gives me the most trouble." She tried to give Dr. Beaufort an appreciative smile, and almost made it. Only the curve at the corners of her mouth quivered.

"Dr. Todd tells me that your tests have been negative so far," Veronica Beaufort said in her most bracing manner.

Ordinarily this would have reassured the patient, but Fayre Schoenfeld closed her eyes a moment as if in sudden pain. "I know."

Now Veronica Beaufort was curious. She looked swiftly, archly at Giles and then turned back to the patient. "Mrs. Schoenfeld, I don't think you should doubt what Dr. Todd has told you. If he says your tests are negative, he is telling you the truth. You don't have any reason to doubt him."

"I know that," she agreed. "He's a terrible liar." At last she looked at Giles. "But you don't know what is wrong yet, do you?"

Chagrined, Giles said, "No. But that doesn't mean I can't find out."

"Do you want to?" Fayre asked, hearing a new determination in his voice.

"Yes. I think I do." Then he let himself meet Fayre's candid gaze. The force of her eyes shook him afresh; his throat tightened and his legs tensed. He was committed now, he thought with mild self-mockery. Perhaps committed in both senses of the word.

"It isn't capricious, is it?" Fayre asked, breaking into his thoughts. "You don't have to do anything more. You've run most of your tests."

"But I don't have any real answers, not yet. Don't you want to know what's been happening to you?" He caught the knowing look from Veronica Beaufort.

"Yes. And I don't want it to happen again." Fayre looked at Dr. Beaufort, then back at Giles. "May I talk to you alone, Dr. Todd?"

Giles was startled. "But Dr. Beaufort is my respected colleague," he began in protest. "If there is anything to—"

Veronica Beaufort interrupted him. "Don't be an insensitive clod, Giles. Mrs. Schoenfeld is upset. She wants to speak to you in confidence. And you, as her doctor," she added with a touch of irony, "should be willing to hear her out." As she crossed the room to the door, she added, "I'll see you tomorrow. Let me know if you'd like my opinion on the tests."

"Thanks," Giles said, glaring after her. Then he went and stood at the foot of Fayre's bed. "What do you want to say to me, then?"

Fayre hesitated. "Don't be angry. It *is* important." She had been sitting up, but now she slumped and lay back against the pile of pillows.

A twinge of worry made Giles move around to the side of the bed. "Mrs. Schoenfeld? What is it?"

Now she could not meet his eyes. "I'm frightened. I'm scared that when I leave here, the whole thing will start all over again."

"But your tests . . ." Giles began, and then his tone changed, grew tender. "Mrs. Schoenfeld, you needn't be afraid. I know that you have alarming symptoms, but you also have alarming gifts."

"And if they're connected?" Fayre asked in a small voice. "What if this talent of mine leads straight to the mental ward?"

"You don't know it will happen," Giles said, trying to reassure her.

"I don't know it won't, either." She sat up slowly. "Night before last they gave me a sleeping pill, you know? And I took it. I was jittery. It seemed like a good idea. But it was awful." Now she put her hands to her face. "I thought it would happen again. I felt as if I were being drawn far back from myself."

Giles reached out and took her hands in his. "Why didn't you tell me?"

"It . . . it didn't seem important. It had happened before, when I first had the seizures, they put me on tranquilizers and I had a reaction something like it. I didn't take the pill last night, and everything was okay." She stared up at him. "But I'm going home tomorrow, and I'm scared. What if it happens there?"

It had always seemed to Giles that to sit on the side of a patient's bed was the height of unprofessional behavior. The thought barely crossed his mind as he sat down, facing Fayre. He salved his conscience by reminding himself that she was not, in the technical sense, ill. "Don't assume anything, no matter how trivial, is unimportant. It may be silly, but if it makes you worry, tell me about it. This reaction to the sleeping pill, now. What was it like?"

Her color heightened. "It'll sound foolish to you."

He was about to deny it, then said, "Just because it sounds foolish doesn't mean that it is. Tell me."

She gulped, as if her mouth was very dry. "It was . . . so unreal at first. It was like being drawn out into a long, fine wire. Away from myself. I know this isn't sensible," she added fiercely. "It's not a sensible feeling."

His hands tightened on hers. "Shush-sh. Tell me what you feel. Don't worry if it's sensible. That's my field."

"And you'll tell me?" she demanded.

"Yes. Yes, Fayre. I'll tell you." He was not aware that he had used her first name, he only knew that he wanted to save her from more fear.

She nodded. "Okay. I believe you." Her body was not so rigid now. "Thank you."

"About being drawn into a wire," he prompted her.

"Yes. Into a wire. It's . . . it's as if I were transmitting messages. Just being a channel for messages to use. Like a violin string. And it's terribly, terribly wearing. I feel I'm at the limit of myself, and that nothing I say can be heard, only the messages running along me." Her clear eyes never left his, but there was a faraway tone to her voice. "When I took that sleeping pill, I could feel it start again. I was pulled out and out and out."

Giles was never certain why this disturbed him so much. He tried to conceal his anxiety, but there must have been something in his face, for Fayre said, "What is it?" quite sharply.

"Nothing," he answered after a moment. "I don't know. You say the sleeping pill triggered this?"

She regarded him. "Why? What does it mean?"

"I told you, I don't know. And that," he added, "is just as important as what I *do* know." His expression was surprisingly self-effacing. "Your particular problem may be something brand new. There's no way to fit you into a handy category. So it's necessary that we investigate everything. The key may be in the smallest, silliest thing." At last he released her hands.

"I see." Her voice was still. "Well. What now?"

"You're going home," he said with false cheer.

"And what then?"

"Then we'll see. Dr. Fellkirk will keep an eye on you, of course . . ."

"And you?"

Giles had intended to stay in the background of the case, but looking down at Fayre, he said, "Oh, I'll check on you regularly. If there's the slightest hint of a recurrence, then we'll get you back here for more studies."

"More studies," she echoed, and turned her head away.

Again he touched her hands. "It's all I can do, Fayre, until we learn . . . something." He knew she was frightened still, and he felt his own chest grow tight in sympathy. "Look, if you need help. For any reason. *Any* reason. Call me."

She said nothing, but she faced him once more, a certain questioning in her eyes.

"I'll make sure you get my number, both here and at home. I live in Montara. It takes me about forty minutes to get from here to there, sometimes more if there's fog on the coast. If you miss me here, call me there."

"In Montara?" The worry in her face lessened. "It's pretty there, but Montara?"

"I don't like cities," Giles said brusquely.

Fayre was about to say something, but changed her mind. "You're sure you want me to call you?"

At that moment he wasn't sure at all. "I hope you won't have to, but if you do, I don't want to lose any time reaching you."

For a moment she was silent. "Thank you, Dr. Todd."

Giles had long since picked up the American habit of saying "You're welcome," but this time he responded differently. "I haven't done anything yet. When I do something . . ."

"You've helped me, Dr. Todd." At last her hands answered his touch. "If you do nothing else, you've made me feel less a freak. That means a great deal to me."

There was an instant when Giles saw her vulnerability and courage, and he remembered, when he was a child, during the Blitz, how his parents had talked of preserving a decent fortitude, that steadfast refusal to accept fear or pain. What he saw in Fayre Schoenfeld's face went beyond that, for she did not—she could not—refuse her fear and her pain, for they were within her. But she would not be crippled. With difficulty he said, "You humble me, Fayre."

"But you've borne so much . . ." she said impulsively, then stopped.

His smile was distant and sad. "That was a long time ago."

"More recently . . ." Once again she stopped.

He pulled his hands away and stood up. "I'll check on you tomorrow before you leave. And I'll see you have my phone numbers."

Fayre was staring up at the ceiling. "So I'm a freak, after all."

Giles had turned away and was moving toward the door when her words stopped him. He looked back at her. "No." When she gave him no response, he took a step toward the bed. "No, Fayre. Anyone who thinks so deserves to be flayed."

"But you think so," she pointed out, still unwilling to look at him.

"No. If anyone is a freak, I am. I've forgotten . . . myself, I guess." He tried to shrug this off and failed. "Don't worry about it. I'm a good doctor, and you have my word that I will do everything I can for you."

Now she was looking at him closely and he found it uncomfortable to have her eyes on him. "Arrogant, aren't I? It comes with the job. How else would we have nerve enough to cut into a brain?"

"You're not arrogant," Fayre said gently.

"I . . ." Giles could not speak. He took one involuntary step nearer to her. Then he gestured helplessly. "I can't." At that moment he did not know why he said it, but it brought tears to her eyes.

Her next words startled him out of the strange attraction that drew him to her. "Do you know if the book lady has been around yet? I've read everything I brought with me, and television bores me. If you could get me a couple paperbacks. Mysteries, good historicals, anything readable. I've got to do something with my mind other than worry."

"Of course," he agreed quickly. "When I see Sylvia, I'll send her in. In the meantime, I've got half a dozen paperbacks in my office. I'll have someone bring them down to you, if you like. One's about famous historical frauds. I've got a couple Thomas Hardy novels . . ."

"Are you homesick?" Fayre asked, obviously surprised.

"No. But I like Hardy. What he writes about is so unlike all . . . this." He gestured once, as if to take in the whole hospital.

Giles knew he was looking for excuses to stay with Fayre a little longer, and he mentally reprimanded himself. But the sight of her, a green robe drawn around the ugly hospital gown and her splendid smoke-blond hair in disorder around her shoulders, tugged at him again.

"I'm sorry, Dr. Todd. I know you're busy. I shouldn't keep you." She held out her hand to him. "Thank you for everything. Half an hour ago I felt like a specimen on a slide, and now I think I'm human once again."

He took her small, firm hand in his and stared as his own long, straight fingers closed around it. Her skin was cool on his, the flesh firm. His own hand felt hot now, as if he had laid it on warm metal. How strange it was, the contrast between their two hands, his square palm with long, big-knuckled fingers and big thumb; hers small, with pronounced pads on the palm and short, slightly tapering fingers. He rarely noticed hands. Now he felt his world contract to that spot where they touched. He knew now that he was too much involved with Fayre Schoenfeld, and he ought to recommend another surgeon. But with it came the fear, unreal but persistent, that another man might not understand what he was dealing with, might tamper with her remarkable abilities, might, in some way, harm her. He was silent, so intent on her hand in his, that he was surprised when she said nothing. Finally he forced himself to speak. "I shouldn't be saying this. But perhaps, when you're feeling better, you might like to come out to Montara. You'd find it relaxing. Maybe away from here, we could find out more about what happens to you . . ." He broke off and tried to laugh. "No, that's not it. I want to see you again. And this is as good an excuse as any." His face felt hot and he wondered if he, at age thirty-nine, could still blush.

Fayre nodded. "I'll come. Whatever your reason."

"You can bring your son," he added quickly, wanting to assure her that he was not forcing an unwanted intimacy on her. "And your aunt, the woman you live with. We could picnic, or go to one of the Sunday jazz concerts in Half Moon Bay." Was it this weekend or next weekend that he was to play tennis with Hugh Audley? At the moment he couldn't remember. "I'll call you, all right?"

"I'd like that."

"And we might learn something more," he added, by way of encouragement.

Although her voice was tinged with irony, there was no trace of it in her smile. "So we might."

On the other end of the line, Prentiss Fellkirk sighed. "Well, I suppose you're right, but Nagy was half-planning to monitor the case. He's right here, of course, and he's familiar with the case. I don't know, Giles."

It wouldn't do to sound too eager, so Giles said, quite reasonably, "Ferenc Nagy's a fine surgeon. You couldn't do better. But he wasn't in on the studies we've just completed, and I don't know if he can spare the time to go over the results we've got. There's a lot of material here, and, to be candid, I haven't figured out the half of it yet. I admit that my curiosity is piqued." He leaned back in his chair and tried to think of how he could persuade his friend to keep him on the case. "I can see why you're so fascinated by Mrs. Schoenfeld. She's quite a challenge."

This got somewhat unexpected results. "A challenge? I never thought of it that way, but I suppose you're right." There was a pause while Prentiss cleared his throat to indicate he was thinking. He had done it for as long as Giles could remember. "Giles, between us, do you think her condition is deteriorating?"

Giles could hear the apprehension in Prentiss' voice, and he answered honestly. "No, I don't. But I'm certain that there is something going on. She has a lot of anxiety, which is normal, and I'm willing to bet that it's having an effect on her . . . abilities. I'd like to keep an eye on her for a while. If there's no more seizures, and she is less worried, then let Ferenc handle it."

"How often would you have to see her?" Prentiss had already accepted the idea, Giles knew, and he decided not to press his advantage too far.

"Twice a week for a month, say, and if her condition seems stable, then once a week, with a phase-out if nothing new occurs." He allowed himself to sound reluctant. "If there's a serious problem, I suppose I could come down to Palo Alto once a week, if she can arrange to be up here the other time."

Prentiss chuckled. "So you're as hooked as I am. It *is* a landmark case, isn't it?"

"Well, I'd like to stay on it, just to see what happens. You dropped this into my lap, Prentiss. I'd like to see it through." Giles paused, as if the idea were new to him. "Do you think there's any way we could work together on this? Perhaps we could coordinate studies, or compare results . . ."

Again Prentiss hesitated. "I'm not certain she should go back into the program yet. You say there was nothing conclusive in your tests, and Nagy came up with nothing, but there is still the danger of another seizure and perhaps a psychotic episode."

Giles knew now what it was that Prentiss wanted from him. "I'll take responsibility for that, Prentiss. It's probably wise to give her a little time off, but don't rule her out completely. If anything happens, I'll handle it as best I can. If you like, I'll give you a letter to that effect." He waited, guarding his hopes.

"The administration would probably prefer it," Prentiss said heavily. "Ever since that student of Alan Freeman's killed himself last year, there's been a lot of worry about lawsuits. I hear the boy's parents got a substantial sum." There was anger in Prentiss' voice now, and contempt. "Damn Alan Freeman. He's been a regular millstone on my research. And he's in the *English* department, for the love of . . . ! Since he came out with that dreadful book on demonology, it's all I ever hear about. No wonder parapsychology has so much trouble getting taken seriously when twits like Alan Freeman turn out such sensationalistic, credulous material. He uses Montagu Summers as an academic expert, and never mentions Summers' religious background, or his biases!" Prentiss stopped abruptly, and added in another tone, "Sorry I got started on that. I had a run-in with Freeman on Monday and I'm *still* seething."

"I read his book," Giles admitted. "I don't know much about the field, but it seemed pretty sloppy to me."

"*Sloppy*? It was unmitigated nonsense from one end to the other. . . . No . . ." Here Prentiss cleared his throat again. "Never mind Alan Freeman. I would appreciate a letter from you, something I can show the administration to make this all more legitimate. And also, to assure them that the ax won't fall on their heads this time." There was an embarrassed silence. "I hate to do that to you, Giles. You've been more helpful than I had any right to hope for. I wish there was something I could do in return."

"Just let me stay on the case," Giles said quickly. "If you get a parapsychological plum from this, I want the medical one to go along with it." He had learned long ago that Prentiss respected ambition, and now he used this knowledge without a qualm.

Prentiss laughed outright. "Okay, okay, Giles. Whatever you say." The laughter tapered off, and Prentisss added, "When do you think it would be safe to return Mrs. Schoenfeld to the program?"

It was a question Giles feared, but he answered with an assumed ease, "Oh, I don't know. Give her a couple of weeks, after I've seen her a few more times. We'll see how she's coming along and then make changes, if we have to." He was toying with a pencil, standing it on one end and sliding his fingers from the top to the bottom and then turning the pencil over again. "Let's play it by ear until there's more to go on."

"Fine with me. I'll look for your letter and then go bludgeon the administration."

"Great." Then, as a kind of afterthought Giles said, "I'm thinking of having Mrs. Schoenfeld out to my place in a couple of weeks. I want to see what she's like informally. If that's okay with you."

"Have her out?" Prentiss asked, puzzled.

"Her son and aunt, too, of course. The trouble is that the environment around here is so artificial, I'd like to see what she's like away from formalized situations. If there's a great deal of behavior change, it might mean something."

"You mean, you think there may be a greater psychological component in this than we thought at first?" Prentiss sounded annoyed and Giles did his best to placate him.

"I don't know what to think. It's possible, and for that reason I want to check it out. If there's no change, then we can eliminate that possibility and try something else." His fingers slipped and he dropped the pencil.

"Why not?" Prentiss thought aloud. "Give me a full report, then. And tell me if she looks good in a bathing suit." He laughed indulgently, and Giles hated himself for echoing the laughter.

"Sure," he promised, his teeth set. "Thanks, Prentiss. This is one bloody hell of a case, but I'm glad you brought me into it." He was ready to hang up now, feeling confident that he had done his best with Prentiss Fellkirk.

"It's good to have you taking an interest. Drop by my office when you come down to see Mrs. Schoenfeld. I'll give you a tour, if you like."

There was little that Giles wanted to do less, but it occurred to him that he should know what was happening in that laboratory, since that was where Fayre had first used her abilities. "I'd like that. I'll look forward to it."

"Good. I'll see you later then."

"Right." Giles agreed, and hung up. Then he sat staring at the poster on the wall. It was one of Roger Dean's posters, showing two badgers in the snow. Giles had bought it on impulse in a bookstore, and found that it didn't look right anywhere in his house. The gray-white walls of his office showed the work to advantage, and the thin black matting Giles had found for it gave it a pleasant accent. He liked the look of the badgers, and wished he could concentrate on something else. His mind seemed to be drifting, and it took the full force of his will to drag his attention away from the poster. Rather unsteadily he rose and moved away from his desk, rubbing his eyes. He was tired, he told himself. He had two more patients to see, and then he would be through.

Taking care not to look at the poster again, he left his office.

Giles was almost ready to leave when one last phone call came. For a moment he debated answering the insistent ring, but habit won out and he lifted the receiver. "Dr. Todd," he said impatiently.

"Hello, Giles." The voice on the other end was cool, self-possessed and faintly cordial.

As always, when he heard his ex-wife's voice, Giles saw a ghost of her, tall, competent, aloof, before him. He sank into his chair. "Hello, Prudence," he said, filled with an emotion somewhere between eager suspicion and affectionate regret.

"I'm going to be in San Francisco tonight, and I thought perhaps we could have dinner." There was that faint, underlying whisper of apology in her suggestion, and Giles was nudged by the old sense of failure that was the legacy of his divorce.

He made up his mind quickly. "Where are you staying?"

"I'm at the St. Francis. But I could meet you wherever you like."

There had been several restaurants they had patronized often when they were married, but Giles could not bring himself to suggest one of them. "There's a good restaurant in the hotel, isn't there? I'll come there, if you like."

If Prudence was disappointed by this there was no indication of it in her reply. "That will be fine. I'll call for reservations. Would an hour be unreasonable?"

"No, I can do that," Giles said, wondering if he sounded as inane to her as he did to himself. "An hour, then. In the lobby? Isn't there a lobby bar where I can meet you?"

"Yes. I'll see you there. In forty-five minutes?"

"Fine. That's fine, Prudence." He wanted to get off the phone. He hated talking to her on the phone, for he could not read her face then. "Forty-five minutes."

"It will be good to see you again, Giles," she said, and hung up.

Giles glared at the phone. Why had he done that? he asked himself. Every time he saw Prudence his conscience felt raw with guilt. He had been stupid about the divorce—he knew it now and he had known it then. And since that time he had been afraid to refuse to see Prudence as much as he disliked the self-condemnation she awakened in him.

There was a minuscule coat closet off the receptionist's office, and Giles always kept a change of clothes there, a suit and tie, in case he had a change of plans, or an emergency ruined what he was wearing. The suit was dark navy blue, a color he did not like particularly and that did nothing for his light brown hair and somber gray eyes. He dragged the suit off the hanger and went to change.

Dinner had been awkward, full of unfelt pleasantries and polite comments. Giles watched Prudence carefully, trying to discover what she wanted of him this time. They were onto coffee before she told him.

"I wanted to ask you a question," she announced rather abruptly as the waiter refilled their cups for the second time.

"Yes?" Giles paused in reaching for the cream and sugar, which he rarely used.

"I wanted to talk to you before I made up my mind." She was staring across the room at the huge windows and the lights on the hills beyond.

"Is anything wrong?" Giles asked quickly, fearing that perhaps she was ill, that she had left her job at the university, that she had left Dario Ramos, with whom she had lived for six years. "May I help?"

"Oh, nothing is wrong, exactly. It's actually very nice." She stirred her coffee and refused to meet his eyes. "Dario wants to get married."

"Married?" He frowned. "And do you want to?" Now that

he knew what Prudence wanted, it was almost a letdown. It was a simple, ordinary question, one that required little from him.

"I've thought about it a lot. I think I do want to marry him."

"I'm happy for you," Giles said, inwardly surprised that it was so.

At last Prudence looked at him. "You are?"

"Yes. Dario is obviously very good for you and you are for him. I think marriage is right for you. I have for some time." He read a certain disbelief in her face. "I mean it, Prudence. If my . . . blessings mean anything, you have them."

"Well, that was part of it," Prudence began, rather confused. "I wanted to tell you myself, so you wouldn't be hurt, or angry." She fumbled with her napkin. "I wasn't expecting this."

"Why not?" Giles found he could smile easily. "It hurt when we broke up. And for a long time after I was . . . numb, I guess. Numb," he repeated, as if the word were unfamiliar. "But it's been a while. Time might not heal wounds, but it changes things."

"But Prentiss said . . ." She stopped, and drank some of the hot, bitter coffee.

"What did Prentiss say? And when?" He recalled that Prentiss had been opposed to the divorce when it had happened, but a couple years before, he had changed his mind.

"I saw him at a conference in Seattle last year. He said then that you were isolating yourself, cutting yourself off from everything except work. He was afraid you were trying to live in the past." She half-smiled reminiscently. "Prentiss had a terrible time at that conference. Nobody took his results seriously. It was just after that Freeman book came out, and there were a lot of very cutting things said to Prentiss. He was rather soured by the end of the conference."

"But not permanently," Giles said, glad now that the worst of the evening was over. "He's got a fine lab and a reasonable number of grants for his study. And I think next time he gives a paper, there might be a different reception."

Prudence, too, seemed pleased to be able to talk about someone else. "I'm glad to hear that. Prentiss has worked so hard, and for so long."

"He certainly has," Giles agreed, and signaled the waiter for more coffee. "I saw him a little while ago. He was in good spirits. In fact, I talked to him today, about . . ." He stopped, wondering if it would be wise to talk about Fayre Schoenfeld.

Prudence had picked up his hesitation. "About?" she prompted.

"About a subject of his. They were doing some brain-pattern studies and there were some puzzling results." It was approximately the truth, Giles told himself.

"Um." She finished her coffee. "You don't seem to be as alienated as Prentiss suggested you were."

"Well, last year was pretty hard. One of the surgeons at the hospital had a very bad time of it. He had to stop practicing, and the rest of us tried to take up the slack. For a couple of months, it was murder." That was not the real reason, he reminded himself. Even two weeks ago, long after the crisis of Terrence Dawes, Giles had felt himself a complete stranger in the world. But not now. "You remember Terry Dawes, don't you? He was the one who became ill. You can imagine what it was like."

"I certainly can." Prudence shook her head. "Poor Terry. Is he all right now? Is he going to be all right?"

"Well, he's retired, of course," Giles said, still feeling uncomfortable about it, then added, unknowingly repeating Hugh Audley's sentiments, "It's a good thing, really. If he stayed on the job, it would have killed him. He's alive, fairly well, and . . . happy."

"Good." Prudence nodded, not really caring. "I liked Terry."

"So do I." He signaled the waiter to ask for the check.

She put her napkin back on the table, a signal that Giles remembered well. Now dinner was over, and so was the important conversation. From now on, it would be social talk only. "I was in England last fall," she remarked. "I made a point to see your cousin Roderick."

Giles hated the way Prudence always referred to Roderick Hallioll as your-cousin-Roderick. He concealed his irritation to ask, "And how was he?"

"Very pleased. He's finally got some sort of grant to restore Stormhill. Ever since they authenticated those Plantagenet manuscripts, there's been increased interest in the place." She sipped delicately at her coffee. "I gathered you haven't seen him recently."

"I was over in seventy-four," he said, remembering for a moment the prettiness of the Cotswolds in spring. "They hadn't found the manuscripts then, of course, and Roderick was fairly depressed."

"Don't you miss Stormhill?" Prudence asked rather wistfully.

"Well, I only lived there two years, after my parents were killed. It doesn't mean a lot to me. I'm happy for Roderick, because it's his home." He made a simple gesture with his hand. "You know it's never mattered to me as much as it has to you."

She pretended not to hear this last. "His father was very kind to you."

"Was he?" Giles said, desolation in his memories. "Well, he took me in. That's something. On behalf of his martyred sister." He wanted very much to change the subject, but he knew that Prudence had always been fascinated by Giles' titled relatives, with that particular snobbery that only Americans seemed to have. "It really wasn't anything like what you imagine, Prudence. That's why I left. There was no reason to stay."

"There are traditions, and ties," she insisted.

"I suppose so. Let's not talk about it anymore. How's your brother? Is he still commuting into Boston every day?" Giles had very little interest in his former in-law, but knew that Prudence took great pride in her brother's success.

"He only goes in three days a week now. And he's adding an office onto his house." Prudence's brother was an architect who had recently developed an enviable reputation.

"Good. Give him my regards when you talk to him next." As the waiter appeared at his elbow, Giles handed him a credit card.

"You don't have to pay for this. I invited you; I'm willing to pay," Prudence said, frowning at Giles.

"I know. Call it an engagement present." This time his smile was quite wide. He wished he had the courage to ask how her family felt about her coming marriage to Dario Ramos. "I'm sure you and Dario will make a success of it. And I am glad you told me before you made a general announcement."

"So am I," she admitted. "I was afraid, well, that you'd object. I see I was wrong."

"Thank goodness," Giles added for her.

"Yes." She started to rise, then her eyes narrowed as she looked at Giles once more. "You're different than you were."

He shrugged. "It's been a while."

"No, that's not it. The change didn't happen because of time. It's happened some other way." She shook her head as she got to her feet. Giles stood beside her and watched for the waiter to return with his credit card. "What's happened to you, Giles?"

"Nothing." He took the small tray the waiter held out for him and reached for a pen to sign the receipt.

"I don't believe that." The words were not sharp, and there was no anger in her, only a slight perplexity.

"Maybe I'm getting a second wind," Giles suggested lightly as he put his credit card back into his wallet. "Thirty-nine's about the right time for it."

"Okay, if you won't talk about it," Prudence said, still not satisfied.

"Prudence, there's nothing to talk about. Truly." He stood aside so that she could precede him out of the room.

"Perhaps," she agreed. "Whatever it is, though, it's very pleasant. I like you better this way."

Giles had an idea then. "You're probably more relaxed around me now that things are settled between you and Dario," he said, and after a moment added, "I'm probably more relaxed now, too. It's good to see you so happy again." His conscience told him this was a cheap shot, but he refused to feel guilty. He walked to the elevators and waited for them to arrive. Prudence had a few pleasantries for him, and an oddly affectionate farewell, but Giles only responded mechanically, for he had other things on his mind.

□ **4** □

A brisk wind rushed over the court at the Berkeley Tennis Club, bringing with it the first high streamers of fog to veil the intensely blue sky. The afternoon had been beautiful, but the wind had kept away the drowsy warmth of spring, and all the courts were filled.

On the far side of the net, Hugh Audley stretched for the serve and chuckled as Giles scrambled for the ball. It was their third game of the afternoon and Hugh had won the first two easily. "It's a crime to keep score!" he shouted.

"You insisted on this game," Giles called as he returned the ball. He had been a good player once, but that was many years ago, and he found he no longer had the deep ambition to win at all costs. He loped across the court and used his racket with skill, but not with his former drive. He had discovered, to his surprise, that he enjoyed the game more now when he no longer felt the uncompromising hunger to beat his opponent.

"Come on, you can do better than that," Hugh insisted as he drove the ball into the far court.

"It's more fun this way," Giles said without rancor as he chased after the ball and with a smooth backhanded stroke sent it skimming the top of the net to fall a few feet beyond as Hugh raced forward, just missing the return.

"Dammit, Giles! That's sneaky."

Giles laughed, shrugged, and took up his position once again.

This time their rally was a long one, and ended when Giles mistimed his stroke, cursing gently as the ball bounced off the edge of his racket. "I'm getting tired," he said, hoping that it might evoke some sympathy from Hugh.

"Let's see if we can finish this game before the fog blows in. Inga isn't expecting us for a couple more hours at least." His racket met the ball solidly, echoing the other sounds from the adjoining courts. "Get that one!"

"My pleasure." Giles felt the pull of the racket as it moved through its swing, and thought that he needed more exercise. His shoulder was beginning to ache already, and he knew he'd be sore the following morning.

"Good. Hit it harder next time!" Hugh shouted as he slammed the ball.

Giles paid no attention to this, but continued to pace himself, playing competently, without flair, and losing gracefully. The game did not excite him any longer, and in the back of his mind, the image of Fayre Schoenfeld distracted his concentration. He had seen her on Friday afternoon, and would see her again on Tuesday in Palo Alto. He had given up trying to convince himself that it was only scientific curiosity that motivated him. He was aware of much stronger and more conflicting emotions. He faltered as he crossed the court and the ball bounced past him.

"Pay attention! You're woolgathering!" Hugh was flushed and took advantage of this lull in the game to untie the arms of his sweater from around his waist and drag it over his head. The high, shimmering fog was beginning to touch the afternoon with its chill, and in the adjoining court, play had stopped.

"Sorry!"

Again the serve, and Giles wondered if he should play badly enough to end the game quickly. It was not fair to Hugh, who was enjoying himself tremendously. When they had first come onto the court, Hugh had admitted that he was glad to play with someone who did not look to him for guidance, in matters either of life or of tennis. Giles had understood, and now did his best to maintain his flagging interest. Would he, he asked himself, feel so bored by the game if he were playing with Fayre instead of Hugh? He did not know if she played tennis, but hoped that she did. Perhaps she skied. Giles hadn't been skiing in three years, but found that the thought of Fayre in the snow held his attention.

"Hey! Giles!"

At the very last moment Giles managed to return the ball, and sternly reprimanded himself for wandering thoughts.

"That's better!"

"I hope so!" Giles shouted, and moved back a few steps as the ball arced over the net. He met it in near-perfect form and watched as Hugh ran to return it. Narrowing his eyes in concentration, he forced himself not to think of that strange, haunting worry that possessed him every time he thought about Fayre Schoenfeld. It was only that she had a very special talent and it was disrupting her life, he told himself again. How could she be in danger from anyone? It was ridiculous. She had let herself become oversensitive, and it had made her frightened. That was quite understandable. He would probably feel the same way himself. And she was dealing with the difficulties ahead with more courage than he had seen before. He would have to help her get over her sense of danger. He had mentioned it to Prentiss, of course, but he wanted to talk to her about it, as well. Prentiss had suggested that they work together on that...

"For Chrissake, Giles!" Hugh laughed in exasperation as he lobbed the ball almost directly over Giles' head. "Wake up!"

Chagrined, Giles apologized to Hugh and added, "I'm pretty worn out," by way of excuse.

"Worn out? You weren't paying attention in any way. One more and I've got you." He smiled broadly. "But let's make it a contest, okay?"

"Sure," Giles said, meaning it. "I was a thousand miles away. Ready?"

This time the rally was fast, intense, as if to make up for the offhand play earlier. Giles, goaded by his own irritation, slammed his racket into the ball and sent it hurtling into the far end of the court.

Hugh had already started to run forward to intercept the ball, so that the high, fast return took him completely off guard. He started to turn and came down on the side of his ankle. Hurt, startled, he tried to lift his twisted foot, and instead fell onto his side, sliding.

"My God!" Giles shouted, dropping his racket and sprinting around the net. "Hugh! Are you all right?"

Hugh had rolled to his other side and was now pulling himself onto his knee. "Skinned my shin. And probably sprained my ankle. It sure as hell feels like it," he said through clenched teeth. "Damn!"

Giles knelt to examine the ankle and the long scrape. "It's superficial," he said in relief. "But you ought to clean it right away and get a bandage on it."

"But I'm winning," Hugh objected, attempting to laugh off the long, bloody abrasion.

"Then you can't blame me for seizing this excuse to stop," Giles said, his face severe.

"You're out of your territory, Giles. It's my shin, not my brain that's affected." He tried to get to his feet and almost fell. "Yep, that's a sprain," he said matter-of-factly. "If I were a Catholic, I could offer it up."

Giles recognized the feeble joke for the distraction it was. "Convert, then." There was a welling of blood down Hugh's leg, and his face had gone pale under his tan. "If you'll lean on my shoulder, we'll get you off the court."

Hugh drew away. "It's okay. All I want's a hand up. Then we can clean it off, put some antiseptic on it, and if the sprain doesn't get any worse, maybe we can finish the game." He had taken Giles' proffered hand and now pulled himself to his feet. "I can make it," he said as he started limping toward the clubhouse, talking over his shoulder. There was a patch of blood on the court where he had fallen.

"Back to the clubhouse, maybe, but no more tennis today. For one thing, it's getting cold." He looked up at the sky, which was shining with glare as the fog grew thicker. "For another, you've already taken me apart twice. Show a little kindness and give me a breather. I don't think I could finish another game. I'll concede you the match, how's that?"

Hugh was through the gate that closed the court, and on the way to the clubhouse. He stopped long enough to be sure the gate was latched. "I'll think about it. But I'll want a rematch."

In the locker room Hugh at last allowed Giles to examine the scrape. "It's not too deep, but nasty, all the same. The bleeding hasn't quite stopped." With gentle fingers Giles cleaned the wound, then looked about for antiseptic and dressing.

"It's in my locker, there, by the shower." Hugh was still pale and his breath was rather shallow. "It's open. Just take the lock off."

Giles did this, and brought back the antiseptic and an Ace bandage, as well as sterile gauze. "It's a good thing you have this."

"Oh, yeah. I don't know why it is, but I've got a knack for twisting my ankle. Not this badly, most of the time. This"—he gestured to the puffy flesh at his ankle—"isn't typical. This is much more ambitious than I usually am. Last fall I got a moderate sprain. Since then I keep an Ace bandage here, just in case." He looked down at his scraped shin and then pulled at the cuff of his shorts. "Dammit all anyway! I've got blood on my whites. Inga'll be furious."

"It'll wash out."

"Maybe. I must have done it when I fell." He steadied himself as Giles applied the antiseptic and expertly wrapped the gauze around the leg after putting a small pad of it directly over the abrasion. Hugh watched critically. "Very neat, Dr. Todd," was his verdict.

"Thanks," Giles said dryly. 'Do you want some aspirin?"

Hugh thought this over a moment. "No. I don't. I want a drink. Let's go up to the Claremont."

"That's the first sensible suggestion you've made all afternoon," Giles said with alacrity.

The huge white hotel sprawled over the hillside, a wooden Victorian interpretation of a medieval castle. The wide glass windows in the bar gave a splendid view of Oakland and part of Berkeley as well as San Francisco and the Bay. At the moment the bridges were obscured by fog and the skyscrapers in San Francisco loomed like ghosts on the horizon.

Hugh had ordered his second gin-and-tonic and had begun to relax. "I feel like an ass, falling that way."

Giles laughed, slightly preoccupied. "It's not important. You're lucky the thing was superficial. You could have broken your leg."

"Next you're going to tell me that sprains can be fun." Hugh glared a moment. "I was winning and this had to happen." The gentle irony in his smile belied the tone as he set his glass aside. "You're not paying attention, Giles."

"Sorry. I've been like that all day."

"I noticed," Hugh agreed. "Is it anything important? Do you want to talk?"

Giles forced himself to shrug. "I don't know. I don't think there's anything you can do. Thanks anyway."

"Okay." He waited in silence, then said, as if it were only an idle thought, "I talked to that special study of yours, the one who was discharged on Thursday."

Although Giles knew precisely whom Hugh meant, he hesitated. "You talked to Fayre Schoenfeld?"

"Who else are you doing special studies on? She told me there were no sure indications in the tests. Is that true?"

"As far as it goes, I guess so." Giles did not want to ask the next question. He was startled how anxious he was to keep their relationship private. "Why? Is she worried?" The thought that she might have confided her fears to Hugh rather than him made Giles snap at Hugh, an unexpected spurt of anger in his heart.

"Of course she's worried. Wouldn't you be?" He stopped talking as he stared out the window. "Fog's getting thicker. You can stay over tonight if you don't want to drive back in it."

Giles had been marginally aware of the fog but now he gave it a dismissing wave of the hand. "I drive in fog half the days of the year."

There was another moment of silence. "Okay, Giles. But if you change your mind, you're welcome."

"What did Mrs. Schoenfeld say?" Giles asked uncertainly as Hugh finished his drink.

Hugh turned to look at Giles now, examining his face. "Why? A moment ago you acted as if you couldn't remember her."

"I remember her." The words were softly spoken and Giles could not meet Hugh's eyes as he spoke them. "What did she want?"

When he responded, Hugh's manner was entirely different. Now he was compassionate, his hazel eyes intent. "She wanted reassurance, I think. She was very frightened, you know."

"Why didn't she talk to me?" Giles had not meant to say that aloud, and his outburst startled him more than it did Hugh.

"She *did* talk to you. She told me how much talking with you helped her. But . . ." Hugh leaned forward. "Look, Giles, don't take me wrong. I am not trying to mess with your life. But you said yourself that she had quite an effect on you. She knows it. And she knows that you'd protect her if you could."

Giles looked away, shaking his head in denial of something, but of what, even he was not sure.

"Giles, for God's sake, don't do this to yourself. Let yourself care for once, won't you?" The bright hazel eyes were piercing, but Giles refused to meet their challenge. At last Hugh moved back in his chair again. He shook his head and remarked flippantly. "You damned clam-souled limey bastard."

Giles insisted on paying for the drinks, and it was only when he was helping Hugh make his painful way from the room that he mentioned seeing Prudence on Wednesday. "She's getting married again," he said nonchalantly.

The news stopped Hugh. He leaned on the low railing that separated the bar from the small tables on the lower level. "How nice for her," he said dryly.

"It is," Giles insisted defensively.

Hugh resumed his slow limping toward the door. "Sure."

Inga Audley was an excellent cook. The large oak dining table was beautifully set and there was a lovely, low centerpiece arranged with ferns and tiny fuchsias.

"I've sent the kids off for the evening. Gina's over at Nancy Stephens' place and Cory's off with the Mastersons. We'll have a peaceful, uninterrupted dinner." She made no comment on her husband's laborious progress up the long, shallow steps into the living room.

"I twisted my ankle," he said as he dropped into a chair. "The dumbest thing."

"Not again, Hugh," she exclaimed in mock dismay. "There are times I think you're worse than Cory." She turned to Giles. "I suppose I should be grateful that you were around.

Knowing Hugh, he would have gone on playing until he swelled up like a beach ball."

"I'm not that bad," Hugh protested from the depths of his overstuffed chair.

"Of course not," Inga agreed. "But, Giles, I'm afraid I'm going to have to ask you to lend me a hand for a moment in the kitchen. I'm certainly not going to risk my canapés to Hugh's sprain." She tucked her fingers around Giles' arm and led him toward the back of the house.

It was comfortably large, comfortably rambling, one of many that were built in the decade following the First World War. The kitchen was like the rest—spacious, warm, with large windows over the sink giving a view of the hedged-in backyard.

Inga smoothed her hair as the kitchen door swung closed behind her. "Giles, thank you for making Hugh stop. I know what he can be like. Give me a moment and I'll have the tray ready."

Giles had to fight down the odd sensation that he had entered into a conspiracy with Hugh's wife. "It wasn't anything. I wanted the excuse to stop, anyway."

But Inga was busy with setting the canapés out on a tray. "There's sherry and glasses in that cupboard." She waved one hand toward the far wall. "Just choose what you'd like. And if you'll put the bottle and the glasses on the tray with these . . ." She had already turned her attention to the oven.

Sighing, Giles got the sherry and the glasses. The warmth of the kitchen, the friendliness of the house depressed him, as if his own life, in comparison, had lost some of its value. He wanted badly to break out of the shell that threatened to overcome him. "How are classes this quarter?" he asked rather inanely.

"Classes?" She closed the oven door and stood up. "Oh, about what you'd expect. History is not the most popular subject at the moment, not even at Cal. And the history of pre-Christian Europe, well . . ." She smiled philosophically. "I have seventeen students in my advanced class. I suppose I should be happy."

"How many courses are you teaching?" He had put the glasses on the tray with the canapés and was trying to fit the bottle onto it as well, without much luck.

"Three. And I'm doing a little advising. I've got three classes and four master's candidates to take care of. You know, when I started, ten years ago, I had more students and more grad advisees than I do now, and that's in spite of two books and another coming out this fall." She had turned her attention to the refrigerator. "Do you prefer blue or Russian?"

Correctly interpreting this as salad dressing, Giles asked for the Russian. "Unless it won't go with the rest of the dinner."

"No trouble." She closed the refrigerator door. "Now, let's get back to Hugh before he decides he's fit enough to dig up the back lawn." She pushed through the door and held it for Giles.

Hugh was still in the overstuffed chair, but he held an open book on his lap, which he lifted up. "Have you ever read this?" he asked. The book was a recent study of the history of the worship of the devil in myriad forms. "Fascinating stuff."

Giles was surprised to see the book here, knowing that Hugh had very little patience with the traditional theological concepts of the devil. He put down the tray and pulled the coffee table nearer Hugh's chair. "I haven't read it."

"And you're surprised that I have?" Hugh chuckled as he put the book aside. "Oh, you know I have about as much use for devils as angels. Silly, demeaning critters, all of them. But the systematic worship of destruction, that's something else." He looked at the tray and reached for one of the canapés. "Hey, Inga, why don't you cook like this for me?"

It was an old, affectionate joke with them. During the week, the cooking chores were divided between them, and often quite simple. Inga poured the sherry and held a glass out to Giles. "I made a vat of lasagna for you just last week," she protested.

"Lasagna. Lasagna! Inga Bjornsten's lasagna!" He accepted the sherry.

"I don't know whether you should have that," Inga added. "Does sherry mix with whatever you had after tennis?"

"Gin-and-tonic," Hugh said promptly. "Of course it does. And besides, it's for the pain." He clapped his free hand to his brow. "It's cruel to deny me."

Inga laughed again and shook her head. "You're incorrigible, Hugh." She pulled a hassock nearer and settled onto it, and at last poured her own sherry. Smiling, she raised her glass. "To you, Giles. It's been too long."

Giles shifted awkwardly in the leather-backed chair as his hosts drank the toast. "It's good to be here," he said, almost embarrassed. "It has been too long. Thanks for having me."

He lifted his glass. "To you. For insisting." He almost emptied the small glass, and this flustered him, as well.

"Refill?" Inga asked, and poured more sherry. "Have some of the cheese and crab. It's a specialty of mine."

"Dammit, Inga," Hugh said with mock annoyance, "*I* was going to eat them all."

"Thanks," Giles said, taking the little appetizer. "It smells wonderful." It tasted good, too, he thought as he bit into it. Again he wondered if he should be here with these kind, well-meaning friends. He told himself that he enjoyed his remoteness, his isolation. But now he was not certain it was true. The day before he had arranged for Fayre Schoenfeld to come out to Montara on the following Saturday with her aunt and son. Looking at Hugh and Inga, he felt a twinge of—jealousy?—envy?—or was it regret? He took another canapé and tried to concentrate on what Hugh was saying.

". . . So next week we told them they could have a Goddess celebration after regular service. They've got all those fake Neolithic statuettes they're so fond of. Now, I go along with the round lady with the big breasts being female, but it is just ridiculous to call those sticks with the two knobs female. Those are artificial phalluses. I don't care who says different. I know a dildo when I see one, and those things, believe me . . ." He nodded toward Giles. "Well, it's faddish. They believe Graves about Claudius, too."

"Faddish?"

"This Goddess worship. I'm delighted to give equal time to women. It's long overdue in church. But the Goddess, Graves or no Graves, is bunk." Hugh finished his sherry. "Not a bad myth, and a very acceptable alternative to Jehovah, believe me. But neither of them are valid. If there is any Deity . . ."

"If?" Giles asked, somewhat startled.

"Yeah, if. If there is one, it sure as hell doesn't have any kind of gender. Gender, dammit, is physical, and I refuse to believe that any valid Deity would be so anthropomorphic as to have human sexual organs. Come on, Giles. It's absurd."

"Well," Inga said carefully, "there's plenty of evidence that Neolithic Europeans worshiped fertility."

"Fertility, sure. That's why I say those long skinny things with matching knobs are male. It figures that about the time good old humanity figured out that men and women together made babies, that the phallic cults arose. Before then, fertility was very mysterious, but there were a lot of rituals having to do with sex, and you can't tell me that they didn't come up with some sort of magic implement for the rituals that was male as well as those they had that were female. I mean, think about it. Most of those rituals were orgiastic. The officiating priests, or whatever, were likely to use symbolic copulation to honor the occasion. Hence the round slit rocks where the alpha male could jerk off, and the phalluses for the officiating woman. She may have been more important in the ritual, since only women got pregnant. And it was important to do everything possible to create the circumstances to bring that pregnancy about. For them, pregnancy was magic, and it was absolutely necessary to do everything required to create the proper atmosphere for the magic. Orgies, diet taboos, rituals, prayers, the whole works."

"I knew you shouldn't have had that sherry," Inga said with resignation. "Honestly, Hugh."

But Hugh was enjoying himself. "We haven't come that far from it, really. Think about the Mass, right? Now, the only important part of the Mass, the only thing it is really about, is the elevation of the Host so that transubstantiation can occur. You can take everything else out of a Mass—the music, the theatrics, the recitation and responses, the sermon, all of it—and as long as the Host is elevated and transubstantiation occurs, it's still a Mass. Let me tell you, lay Catholics don't like to hear that. Neither do most of the clergy. So what is the rest of it? Why, it's a kind of magical ceremony, a guarantee that the magic will work. It's also a beautiful show, but that's another matter." He took the last of the crab-and-cheese canapés and popped it into his mouth. "The thing," he said, his words muffled as he tried to chew at the same time, "the thing is, we keep forgetting that when all that attention gets focused, something *does* happen. That's what the ceremony is about really, a way to get everyone to keep their mind on the magic. It has very little to do with faith. But it has a lot to do with concentration. That's where a lot of religions go wrong. They get all caught up in repeating ritual, and they forget to concentrate on what's important. So the magic doesn't happen anymore. And that's when they start copping out, talking about faith. Faith! That's a piss-poor substitute for magic. You see, I think Jesus was dead right when he said that the Kingdom of God is within you. I mean, where else? He was talking about magic, and concentration, and those mealymouthed Roman bureaucrats took that and turned it into faith. No more questioning. Acceptance only is tolerable! If you're going to be religious, at least do it the respect of examining it, questioning it, concentrating on it. Most people let their religion wash over them like bubble bath, and choose only those parts that support their own particular bigotry. That, my friend, is what most people mean by faith!" He tried to stand up and winced as he incautiously put too much weight on his sprained ankle.

Giles half-stood. "Hugh . . ."

Inga was not as disturbed. "You know, Hugh, Abelard said the same thing. Remember what happened to him?"

"Sure. He was castrated and there were attempts to poison him. But he, at least, was courageous. He examined his religion. For him, the price was enormous, but he paid it. And for what little merit there is in it, he is honored to this day." He had steadied himself against the chair and suddenly looked at Giles rather sheepishly. "I'm sorry, Giles. When I get a little loose, I tend to lecture. If I put something solid in me, I'll stop. I promise."

"Thank goodness," Inga sighed. "Another ten minutes of this and dinner would be ruined. We're five minutes past done as it is." She reached for the tray, which still had one lonely stuffed mushroom on it. "Giles?" she said, offering the last to him.

"Thanks." He took the canapé, but stood a moment, watching Hugh through narrowed eyes. He had never thought to ask why Hugh had given up his prestigious career as a journalist to become a minister, but for the first time he began to understand how great the force had been that had changed his friend.

It was quite late when Giles left the Audleys' house, and the fog had thickened. He drove slowly to the freeway, and more slowly across the Bay Bridge. His thoughts were still abstracted, disturbing, and he wished he could ignore the questions that rose in his mind.

On impulse, he got off the skyway at Ninth Street and pulled into the nearest service station. The lights over the pumps were dark, but in the far corner two phone booths shone in the greenish light. He got out of the Land Rover and pulled a notebook from his jacket. Checking the number, he dropped a dime into the slot and dialed.

"Who is it?" asked the sleepy voice after the fifth ring.

"Nancy? It's Giles." Hearing her voice had an instant effect on him. His need was sudden, urgent, and clinical. There

was no question of affection, and no desire for intimacy.
"Are you . . . busy?"

"Giles?" Nancy Lindstrom sounded surprised, and certainly
more awake. "I didn't think—"

"Is anyone there?" he cut in sharply.

"No. Not now." Her voice changed subtly. "Are you
horny?"

It was an expression he loathed. "Yes."

Nancy's laugh was low, subtly mocking. "Okay. Where are
you now?"

He calculated the distance and the fog. "It'll take me about
fifteen minutes to get there. All right?"

"Fifteen minutes? I'll be ready. Do you want anything . . .
special?" This time the provocation was blatant.

"No," he said angrily. "Nothing special. I leave that to Dr.
Carey." He almost slammed the receiver down, but Nancy's
voice stopped him.

"There are other kinds of special, Giles. Think about it on
the way over, lover." And she had the satisfaction of hanging
up on him.

As he got back into the Land Rover, Giles felt a kind of
fury welling up in him. If his need had not been as keen, as
demanding as it was, he would have got back onto the skyway and driven back to Montara. But the tug in his groin
was too pervasive. Irritated with himself as much as with
Nancy Lindstrom, he started the car and drove along to the
next corner, turning right. Nancy's last, taunting suggestion
echoed in his mind as he crossed Van Ness.

"Oh, shit, Giles," Nancy said as he rolled off and away
from her. He had been abrupt with her, with only the most
superficial of preliminaries. Now that he was spent, he was
disgusted with himself. Part of him wanted to castigate
Nancy, but he knew that she was not the cause of his feeling.
He said nothing.

"What a rotten thing to do," Nancy said as she got out of
bed and started toward the bathroom. "I don't like that kind
of fucking."

"Neither do I," he muttered.

"What?" she called over the sound of running tap water.

"I said," he repeated, "that I don't like it either." He sat
up, his feet over the side of her large bed. He thought he
must have been crazy to come to Nancy. His head ached and
he felt queasy.

Nancy appeared in the lighted bathroom door. "Then why'd you do it?" she demanded. She had pulled a terry-cloth robe around her. "For all his kinks, I like Tim Carey better than you. He's not lying when he hurts me. He's honest."

"Great," Giles said, tasting something metallic in his mouth. "Is he the one who gave you that bruise on your hip?" He felt a certain responsibility toward Nancy now, knowing that he had used her unkindly.

"I don't want to talk about it." She turned away and almost closed the door.

"You brought him up. Does he beat you?" He wondered why it was that Nancy Lindstrom wanted Dr. Carey. For she obviously did. He had seen her look at him a week ago, and there had been the same terrible hunger in her eyes that he had seen in some of his patients, a hunger for ruin and disaster. Perhaps that was what Hugh had meant earlier that evening, about the devil. . . .

"Sometimes," Nancy admitted, not without a flicker of both pleasure and shame. "He does other things, too. Why?" She appeared in the door again. "Do you want to hear about them? Will that turn you on?"

"No. It won't." He rose and looked about for his trousers. "I'm sorry, Nancy. Truly."

"Sure," she said, plainly not believing him, and not wanting to believe.

He gathered his clothes and dressed in silence. He recalled the old Latin phrase, *Post coitum totum tristum est.* He was pretty sure that he had the Latin wrong, but the sense of it was still true. After having sex, everyone is sad. He wondered why that was.

"Leaving?" Nancy asked as she came back into the room.

"Yes."

She cocked her head to one side and considered her next remark. "I don't know what's wrong with you, Giles, but until you straighten it out, don't come back, okay?"

He had expected this from her. He could not blame her. And he felt a certain relief to have ended things between them. Yet his throat seemed tight as he answered. "Okay. If that's the way you want it."

"It sure is," she said, and went to her apartment door with him. They did not kiss, and she refused to shake his hand. And when she closed the door behind him, he heard the snick of the lock and the slide of the chain latch behind him.

□ 5 □

Giles pulled off Sand Hill Road and into the parking lot beside the neatly functional single-story building that lay along the crest of a gentle knoll. The large, carved wood sign near the entrance announced that this was the Monroe H. Farris Center for the Study of Parapsychological Phenomena, East. As Giles strode up the wide curve of the walkway, he noticed that there were dense hedges on both sides of the building, and, oddly, no path around it. He went up the steps and into the reception area.

Behind a wide desk sat a pleasant-faced receptionist. He looked up as Giles came in and said, "May I have your name, please?"

Giles was somewhat startled. "Dr. Giles Todd."

The young man consulted his list, and looked up at Giles, rather baffled. "I'm sorry. When were you scheduled? I don't have you down here. . . . Are you sure you were supposed to come to the East side?"

Although Giles found the questions mildly confusing, he said, "I'm supposed to see Dr. Fellkirk. He told he to come in this way."

"Are you one of his subjects?" The young man was becoming upset.

Giles laughed. "No. I'm an associate of his. I'm consulting with him on a particular case."

Relief was plain in the receptionist's face. "Oh. Well, let me ring through. Just go down that hall"—he pointed behind him, away from the doors that gave easy access to the reception area—"and wait until the door is opened for you. It can't be opened from this side without a key."

"Thank you," Giles said, and went past the desk, down the short hallway. The door was solid, and there was not so much as a knob on this side. He waited until there was a sound and the door opened.

"Giles! How good of you to come." Prentiss beamed at him and held the door wide as Giles came through it. "You'll have to excuse this rigamarole we put you through. It's part of the procedure to keep the experiments pure, if you want to call it that." He led the way down the corridor, pointing out various things on the way. "That's the monitoring room, right there. We're running only one set of subjects at the moment. That's the men's room, if you need it later on. And this," he said as he flung open the door, "is my office. Not bad for a maverick psychologist like me."

"Very nice," Giles said, with honest appreciation. Two of the walls were wood-paneled, and, as the room was at the end of the corridor, it had four tall, narrow windows looking out on the greenery and the hill that sloped away toward the main bulk of St. Mathis University. The wall beside the door was entirely bookshelves, and these were filled to overflowing. Prentiss dropped into the well-made revolving chair behind his wide desk and motioned Giles to one of the other two chairs on the other side of the desk.

"Sit down, sit down. Nagy called over a few minutes ago and said you were on the way. I'm delighted you could spare the time to take the tour of the place. I think you'll find that we're making some important advances in the techniques of parapsychological research. Stanford Research Institute helped, of course."

Giles was somewhat put off by this grand manner, so he said, "I'm curious, naturally, but I thought you'd prefer to discuss Mrs. Schoenfeld, first."

Prentiss instantly sobered. "Yes. How is she? Nagy said you'd spent about forty minutes with her. I hope that isn't a bad sign?"

"Well, no," Giles said, and hesitated. "She's still very apprehensive. That's one of the reasons I decided to take some extra time with her. In cases as baffling as hers, it's very important to avoid stress. And she had had a few . . . oh, I guess you'd call them impressions, and I wanted to help her with them."

"Oh?" Prentiss said, with an inflection that demanded a fuller explanation.

"It's her son. Now, I think this is probably a case of the most simple transference, but she's worried about him. She thinks that someone may try to harm him as a way to hurt her." Giles saw the scowl begin to cloud Prentiss' handsome features. "Don't let it bother you. I'm having her and the boy and her aunt out to my place next weekend. I think I can do something about her apprehensions then. But in the meantime, if she talks to you, you might do your best to reassure her."

"Umm," Prentiss said, and reached for his pipe. "Anything else you feel I should know about?"

"Not so far. She seems to have stabilized. It'll take more time to be sure, of course, but she's coming along very well."

Prentiss sighed as he lit his pipe and began to draw on it. "Good. I'll be honest with you, Giles. I need her back in the program. Our other results have been good, but nothing like hers. If we're going to expand our studies, we'll need more grant money, and for more grant money we'll need some pretty impressive results. Having Fayre Schoenfeld in the project would help immeasurably." He raised an eyebrow and waited for Giles' response.

"How soon would you want her back in the project, then?" He felt a certain misgiving about the question, as if he and Prentiss were somehow in collusion against Fayre.

"As soon as possible. We'll have to have the grant request in before classes start in the fall. If we had another six weeks of study with Mrs. Schoenfeld, it would be very beneficial. And," he added, as Giles hesitated, "I must say, if it turns out that she's able to do this, it's probably a good idea for her to get back to it as soon as possible. I'm certain it would be a mistake to make her feel more apprehensive about her abilities than is absolutely necessary." He held his pipe out and chortled. "And, naturally, I'm very anxious to have her back with us. She's the most exciting subject we've had, and by a *considerable* margin."

"So you said when you brought me into this case," Giles agreed. He smiled at Prentiss, remembering how he had always been the one at school to work harder and longer for his successes, and was justifiably smug when he repeatedly outstripped his classmates. Prentiss had not changed much in the intervening years, Giles realized. He still wanted to be first in the class, and was still willing to work harder and longer to achieve his superiority. He shook his head once.

"What is it?" Prentiss asked.

"Nothing, really. I was thinking about being at school; what an ambitious student you were. You still are."

Prentiss shrugged. "Well, there's rather more at stake here than there was at school, after all." He put down his pipe. "When do you see Fayre Schoenfeld again?"

"Thursday. She's coming up to San Francisco and I'll check her out. And I'll give you a report on the weekend, if there's anything worth reporting. My guess is that the change of scene will be relaxing, and that might speed her recovery." Recovery from what? he asked himself, and still had no answer.

"Good. Good. I can't tell you how *grateful* I am that you came into the case. Nagy's an excellent man, really *excellent,* but you and I, well, it's been almost thirty years. There's no substitution for that experience." He stood up rather abruptly. "Come on. Let me show you the plant."

Giles rose and followed Prentiss out the door. Prentiss led the way back down the corridor, his speech animated. "You saw those doors opening onto the reception area when you came in, didn't you? Those are the subject rooms. There's an identical set on the other side. There's separate approaches to the building, and you can't get from one side to the other without going through this central core. The rooms are monitored with closed-circuit TV as well as some fairly sophisticated systems that pick up pulse and breathing rates. We don't put anything on the subjects, of course, because it might interfere with their concentration. They're provided with a table, chair, and a chaise, as well as writing paper. Each room comes equipped with what is euphemistically called a washroom, about the size of a closet. I've often wondered why it's called a 'john' over here and a 'loo' in England. Haven't you?"

"I never thought much about it," Giles said, although he had a sharp recollection of a few terribly embarrassing moments when he had first come to California, before he had become familiar with the new term.

"Yes. Um. Anyway, we've got computers to store all the monitored information. The sender and the sendee never see each other. They are told to arrive at opposite sides of the building—you've probably noticed there's no easy way to walk around it—and their arrivals are scheduled twenty minutes apart, to avoid the possibility of them arriving together, and therefore seeing one another." He tapped at a door, and a woman answered. Prentiss pulled the door open. "This is Leslie Yamada, Giles. Dr. Todd, Dr. Yamada." He stood aside so that Giles could shake hands.

"Dr. Todd," she said in her pleasant voice. "Dr. Fellkirk has spoken a great deal about you."

"Don't believe the half of it," Giles said, thinking of Prentiss' larger-than-life style.

"Oh, I always reserve judgment," she said gently.

"Dr. Yamada is our medical monitor. She keeps track of all the data we get on the physical reactions. She was the first one to witness one of Fayre Schoenfeld's . . . seizures."

Immediately Giles was interested. "Will you tell me about it?" he asked the Japanese doctor.

"Of course. It's all in my records. If you like, I'll have a Xerox made and sent to you." She paused for a moment. "I'd have thought it was already in Mrs. Schoenfeld's folder, though."

"Perhaps I overlooked it," Giles said, knowing full well he hadn't. "I'd appreciate it if you'd send me the copy, Dr. Yamada."

"My pleasure, Dr. Todd." She looked at Prentiss a moment. "I'm sorry, Dr. Fellkirk, but we're about to start testing the Roshananda woman. I've got to get my equipment ready."

"Oh, by all means. Certainly." Prentiss opened the door again. "Thanks for letting us come in."

Giles echoed this, then said, "I do appreciate your help on Mrs. Schoenfeld's behalf."

There was a slight thaw in Leslie Yamada's formal manner. "I'm glad to do it, Dr. Todd." Then the door closed.

"Wonderful woman," Prentiss said, somewhat perfunctorily. "A most precise physician." He opened another door. "This is the machine room. You see the monitor screens for the TV. Yes. Hello, Richard. Hello, Elenore. I'm just showing Dr. Todd around. He's the one who's looking after Mrs. Schoenfeld for us."

The people seated before the screens glanced up a moment, murmured a few polite words, then returned their attention to the screens.

"Everything is studied," Prentiss said. "Chadri Roshananda, the woman we're testing this afternoon, is quite good as a scryer," he went on with more enthusiasm. "She gazes into a bowl of water—gazing into things for purposes of divination is called scrying—and fairly consistently picks up what her sender is sketching. We've found she works best with sketches and photographs, less well with thought or words."

On one of the monitors a slender young woman appeared. Although obviously Indian, she was dressed in a neat pantsuit and her heavy dark hair was cut short to frame her face.

"You should see her in a sari," Prentiss said, his eyes brightening. "She's absolutely stunning. She comes from a very progressive, Westernized family, of course, or she wouldn't be dressing like that. Her father's a very learned man; quite an expert on the occult, in his own way." He motioned toward the other lit screen. "That's the sender. He's proven very effective before." He nodded toward the screen where a young man sat, apparently rather bored. He was reading a paperback book. "That's George Brenner. He's getting his Ph.D. in, of all things, physics. He came into the project hoping to find out the laws of this sort of thing."

"How do you feel about that?" Giles asked.

"I agree with him completely." He leaned forward. "In a moment we'll signal George and Chadri, and you can watch us run a series, if you like."

Giles glanced at his watch. "Some other time, Prentiss. I have to do rounds yet, and at this rate I won't be back in the city until almost four, just ahead of the traffic."

Prentiss did not object. "Well, perhaps next time, then. I think you might find it very interesting." He turned away with Giles and was about to leave the room when another man entered.

"Oh, Sam." Prentiss beamed at the newcomer. "This is Giles Todd, my old friend I've mentioned to you. Giles, meet Sam Weintraub."

Sam Weintraub shook hands grudgingly. "Glad to meet you."

"We're very fortunate to have a surgeon as responsible as Giles on Mrs. Schoenfeld's case, Sam. He's the best there is, and no one could give her better care."

"Great. That's great. Do you mind if I keep an eye on Chadri?" He turned away abruptly, not waiting until Prentiss and Giles had left the room.

"Charming," Giles said under his breath.

"Who? Sam? Don't mind him. He's been having bad luck with one of his sendees. Nothing like Mrs. Schoenfeld, just plain bad luck. I'm afraid," Prentiss said with a slight smile, "that he's somewhat jealous of my success."

Giles felt himself smiling in return. "Which, of course, you do nothing to encourage. I remember how you used to crow when you placed first at school."

"Oh, come, Giles. I'm not as bad as *that*," he objected. "But I do admit I was overjoyed when Mrs. Schoenfeld turned out so well. You can't *imagine* what a difference it made. I was even pleasant to Alan Freeman."

"Remarkable." They had reached the door where Giles had come in. "Well, thanks for the quick tour. I'm quite impressed. You seem to have taken almost every reasonable objection into account and guarded against it." Giles was sincere as he spoke, and he found himself even more impressed with the ability Fayre had displayed. "Do remember about Mrs. Schoenfeld's son, will you? She really is concerned, and the sooner we quieten her on that front, the sooner she's apt to be back in one of those rooms."

"Oh, yes. The son. Very well." He started to open the door. "You know, Giles, I *do* appreciate everything you're doing for me. I did impose, I know. It may have been dirty pool holding our friendship over your head, but I have to admit, I'm glad it worked."

Giles shook his head. "You don't have to thank me. Just let me stay on the case. It's absolutely fascinating. I can see why you're so caught up in it." He reached down and turned the handle. "I'll talk to you after I see Mrs. Schoenfeld this weekend."

"*Marv*elous," Prentiss said as they shook hands.

Frank Crocker died on Wednesday, and Hugh came to Giles' office when it was over.

"You did everything you could," Giles said emptily. "So did I, but it couldn't stop him dying."

Hugh nodded. His eyes were fixed on the middle distance, almost mesmerized. "I know," he said slowly. "But I wish I had made it easier for him. Even Father Denton . . ."

"Yes?" Giles said when Hugh had been silent awhile.

"Oh, nothing." He got up. "It doesn't matter now, anyway. I've got to see this new admit of yours. What's the name? Pearce, I think."

"That's right. Wilma Pearce. She's fifty-five." Giles kept his voice very carefully neutral.

"That bad?" Hugh asked, knowing what that noncommittal sound meant.

"Oh, yeah. She should have come in six months ago." He sighed. "I'm not sure we could have done anything then, but we might have given her a little more time. Well, that's academic. How's the ankle?"

"Getting better." He shifted his weight from foot to foot. "See."

"I had a wonderful time Sunday night," Giles said, thinking it was almost true. The time he had spent with the Audleys had been wonderful. He preferred to forget the ghastly hour at Nancy Lindstrom's that followed.

"When do you want to do it again?" Hugh asked quickly.

"Oh, a month or so. Why don't you come out to my place?" He gave a tired smile. "I promise not to cook this time."

"Good." Hugh studied Giles a moment. "Are you okay, Giles?"

"Yes. I am." He met Hugh's eye. "I promise you, Hugh. I am okay."

"If you say so." Hugh nodded. "I think you might be on your way to it, myself. That's good." He turned toward the door, and Giles noticed he had very little limp left. "Inga told me to thank you for the flowers, by the way, so thank you."

Giles had ordered flowers delivered to Inga from a Berkeley florist the morning after their dinner. "My pleasure. I thought the color would go with the draperies in the dining room."

"You were right." He changed his tone. "What's on your agenda now?" Hugh had started to open the door, but he waited for an answer.

"Oh, I'm running some tests on one of Veronica Beaufort's patients. He's either got one hell of a psychosis or there's a major brain dysfunction. He's not coherent enough to give us any real pointers."

"It could be both. What a business to be in," Hugh said solemnly as he left Giles' office, closing the door behind him.

Giles got to his feet and picked up the folder that lay open on his desk. "What a business," he agreed.

The sun was warm but the wind that nipped off the ocean made sweaters necessary for comfort on Montara Beach. The narrow strip of sand was fairly smooth and almost deserted, most of the beach users preferring hotter weather and either the gentle swath of the beach at Half Moon Bay or the more accessible Rockaway. At two in the afternoon the sky was clear and no hint of fog hung toward the horizon. The Pacific gleamed like watered silk.

Giles had cleared away the picnic basket and had left Anna Dubranov sitting on the huge beach blanket, her sketchpad open on her knees and an improbably wide straw hat shading her round, weathered face. "That's all right, Fayre," she said to her niece. "Don't bother about me. I've been wanting some time to myself since we got here. One of the reasons I divorced Vasilyi was that he wouldn't leave me time to draw. You know I can't keep my mind on what I'm doing with people around me."

"If you're sure," Fayre said, bending down to glance over her aunt's shoulder. She gave the older woman an impulsive hug before she straightened up and called to her son. "Kip!"

"Here, Mom!" he shouted from almost a hundred yards up the beach. "I found some seaweed! Look!" He held a bedraggled bit of kelp up and waved it excitedly.

"Do you want him to have that?" Giles asked as he came up to Fayre. He was wearing an Irish fisherman's sweater and his jeans were rolled above his calves. His shoes were on the blanket, keeping one of the corners from flapping in Anna Dubranov's face.

"It's fine. It *can't* eat him, and he *won't* eat it." She bent to roll the cuffs of her slacks up farther and the sun made a pale halo of her hair. "Okay. I'm ready."

"North?" he asked, pointing toward Kip, who was squatting in the sand.

"Fine." She fell into step beside him, stretching out her stride to match his. "Don't walk too fast," she said as they walked onto the cool wet sand where the spent waves rushed against their feet as they went.

"I'm glad you thought to bring chicken," Giles said when they had gone a little way. "I love it, but I can't cook it worth a damn."

Her only answer was a laugh. It was a delicious sound, free of all the tightness and restraint she had shown on their previous meetings. She walked easily, her hands tucked in her pockets, her loose, dark green sweater hiding the curve of her body. Giles tried not to look at her too long, knowing how much of an effect she could have on him. He reminded himself sternly that this was for observation, an evaluation period, nothing more. And he knew he did not believe it.

"Isn't an afternoon like this something more than the usual treatment you prescribe?" She did not sound entirely serious, but she had caught him off-guard.

"Well, it depends on circumstances." He looked away, out to sea, the lines settling back into his face.

"Hey, Giles," she said gently as she stopped beside him. She had not used his first name before, but there was no strain as she spoke it. "Don't be afraid."

"Afraid?" He turned on her.

"I don't mind if this is just social. In fact, I'm very flattered. Someone as closed as you are . . ." She stopped, reading the expression in his eyes. "Okay. I won't say anything."

He was about to rebuke her, but forced the words to remain unspoken. He looked down as the cold foam splashed around his toes. "Perhaps I am afraid," he said, as if addressing his feet.

"You don't have to be," Fayre said lightly, and began walking toward Kip again.

Giles turned and followed her, frowning a little, and telling himself that he was being foolish.

"Kip!" Fayre called. "What have you got there?"

The boy, who had been squatting in the sand, held up what seemed to be a bit of waterlogged driftwood. "Look what I found!" He waved it excitedly and then began to brush the sand off it.

Fayre had come up to him and dropped to her knee beside him. "Just be sure you don't let it give you splinters," she said, wrinkling her nose in disgust at the half-rotten wood.

"I'm gonna take it to school," Kip announced. "Boy, you just wait till Jerry Gotendag sees it. Him and his rat skeleton. This is lots better than any rat skeleton." He looked up as Giles stopped beside Fayre. "What d'you think, Dr. Todd?"

"It's better than a rat skeleton," Giles said.

"Ms. Bridgestreet will like it," Kip said, not quite as certain of himself. "She likes all kinds of weird things. You should see the beads she wears. Jeez." He put the old driftwood aside and renewed his digging in the soft, moist sand.

"Are you looking for more?" Fayre asked, obviously glad that Kip was enjoying himself.

"Maybe there's monsters. Boy, what if I found a Godzilla egg! That'd be something!" He dug more eagerly.

"We don't have any place to put a Godzilla egg. Let alone a Godzilla," Fayre reminded him.

"Oh, sure," Kip said, pausing in his digging a moment. "We don't use that upstairs bathroom very much. We could put it in the shower up there and put a lightbulb in there to keep it warm, and wrap it up with pillows. It'd work fine."

"I see you've thought it all out," Giles said, amused.

" 'Course, there's no saying if I *will* find a Godzilla egg," Kip said darkly, "but it'd be great if I could." He went back to work, humming a little as he tossed the sand aside.

Fayre shook her head, then held out her hand so that Giles could—quite unnecessarily—help her to her feet. "Thank you," she said as she brushed the sand off her slacks.

"Glad to." He looked down at Kip. "Do you need any help there, Kip?"

"Naw. I'm fine." He hadn't stopped to respond.

Giles touched Fayre's arm. "Come on. We'll walk a little farther. Kip's fine."

In response to hearing his name, Kip looked up once again. "Hey, Dr. Todd, how come you don't call me 'son'?"

Somewhat taken aback, Giles gave him the first answer he had, which was the truth. "Well, you're not my son, Kip. You're a good kid, I think, but you're not mine. Why?"

" 'Cause that Dr. Fellkirk always calls me 'son.' Sometimes I could puke! Only my dad could call me son, and he's dead." He looked down into the hole he had dug.

"No Godzilla egg?" Giles asked.

"No. Godzilla isn't real, anyway. He's just a fancy model. Mom, can I go climb on the rocks?"

Before Fayre answered, Giles said, "You're not supposed to, Kip. They're very dangerous. A lot of people get hurt on them every year. The thing is, they are loose and they break away if you climb on them."

"Heck." He stood up, obviously annoyed and ready to argue.

"But," Giles went on, "there are a couple tide pools out at the end of the rocks. The tide's far enough out so that you could walk out and look at them. If your mother says it's all right," he added, with a swift glance at Fayre.

"Fine," she said. "But be sure you stay off the rocks. And come back from the tide pools when I call you."

"Good!" Kip was prepared to run off to the edge of the surf, but he cast a look back at his driftwood. He hesitated a moment, then thrust the thing toward Fayre. "Keep it, Mom, will you? I want it for school." Without waiting to hear her response, he raced away down the beach.

Fayre held the soggy wood at arm's length. "Perfectly hideous," she said with a shake of the head.

"Just what I was thinking," Giles agreed. "But you'd better keep it. After all, he wants it for school. To show up Jerry Goten-something." Giles smiled rather sadly.

"You didn't like school, did you?" She held the driftwood gingerly in the crook of her arm.

"No, not particularly. It was very . . . lonely." He forced himself to put aside the unpleasant memories. "Well, that was a long time ago. It's over." He started to walk very slowly. "Tell me about you, Fayre. I have a case history, but that's, well, nothing but symptoms and tests." He let the back of his hand brush hers. He wanted to touch her, and he remembered with sudden clarity the way her hand had lain in his.

Her fingers curled around his, small, cool and slightly sandy. She didn't say anything, but when he tried to pull his hand back, her fingers tightened.

"Fayre . . ." He stopped then, and said something to her he had never told anyone before. "The first human brain I ever saw was my mother's. It was splattered all over the wall in our flat. A flying piece of cement had hit her. I was four. I kept trying to put the bits back into her skull, as if that would bring her back to life. I don't think I've ever cried as I cried then." He was looking out to sea, his light brown hair ruffled by the wind. When the weight of the words was off him he looked at her. "That's why I'm a brain surgeon, you know."

"Oh, God, Giles." She was standing quite near him, her hand in his, and her voice was so soft it was almost inaudible above the sound of the ocean.

His face was set and he looked at her in puzzled anger. "I don't want you to misunderstand about me. I *do* care about you as my patient. I *have* to care."

Fayre still said nothing.

"But that's not why I wanted you here, not really," he said, the anger suddenly evaporated.

"You don't have to say anything to me." She spoke more loudly this time, and the pressure of her hand in his brought him around to face her. "I told you when I met you, I can tell things about people. I like your concern." Her face softened. "I like *you*, Giles."

He stared at her. "What?"

"I like you." She smiled and her eyes danced. "Didn't you know that? If I didn't like you, I wouldn't have come out here with or without Aunt Anna, particularly on the really flimsy excuse you've got. Response to relaxed surroundings. Honestly!" She leaned her head against his shoulder. "Giles Todd, you're so damn transparent."

Should he kiss her? he wondered. Should he take her in his arms, or what? He wanted so much to touch her. If they had not been on a beach, at midafternoon, with her aunt and her son in plain sight, he might have held her, or tugged off her sweater and explored the body beneath it.

"It's all right. Aunt Anna won't mind." She had moved a little so that she was standing in front of him.

He could find no words as he drew her gently into the circle of his arms. Little waves lapped and rustled at their feet and the sand slid around their toes. Fayre was not particularly tall, and only the top of her head brushed against his jaw. Her arms were around him, her hands pressed tightly against his back. He wanted to shout or throw things into the air. Instead he stood very still, so that he would be able to remember the most minute detail of this for all the days of his life.

Kip's driftwood lay on the wet sand beside them, and occasionally the wet finger of the tide would pluck at it.

"Hey, Mom!" There was real alarm in Kip's voice. "Mom!"

Fayre stood back from Giles slowly, held by the emotion in his eyes as much as by the strength of his arms.

"*Mom!*" Kip's voice was much higher, and filled with near-panic.

It was Giles who spotted him, at the end of the point, far beyond the safe area. He was clinging to a rock as the waves splashed greedily around him. "There," Giles said steadily. "He went too far out."

Fayre had put her hand to her mouth. "Oh, Kip. Stay calm. Hold on. Hold on." She did not speak loudly, but there was a terrible intensity in her gaze.

Almost as if he had heard her, Kip tightened his grip on the rock and stopped trying to scramble farther up it.

"The tide's turned," Giles said, knowing he could not keep it from Fayre. "If we're going to get him off that rock, it had better be now." He scanned the beach. There were very few others on it, and the nearest couple were very obviously leaving. "I'd best go after him. It would take about ten or fifteen minutes to get help, and the waves might build up too much . . ." He could not finish. Instead he pulled off his sweater and handed it to her. "I'll want that warm when I get back. You'll need the beach blanket for Kip."

"Giles, can you?"

"I can certainly try. If I get into real trouble, you go take the Land Rover and drive down to the lighthouse. They've got some rescue equipment there." He had already started into the water. As always, he was startled by the cold. "Get moving, Fayre."

She nodded dumbly, then turned and headed down the beach.

The drop-off here was fairly gradual, and Giles was more

than two-thirds of the way to Kip's rock before the first wave broke over his head. He kept his footing, but began to sputter as the cold filled him. He could see Kip clearly.

The boy still held onto the rock, but it was certain that he was frightened. Giles had tried to call to him, but the noise of the surf was greater as the tide came in, and Kip could not hear him.

Another wave almost threw Giles off his feet and he flailed about, certain that if he could not stay on his feet, he would be dashed against the nearby rocks. Carefully, determinedly, he kept on.

He was almost at the rock when a wave caught him and knocked him against one of the submerged boulders. Giles shouted with frustration and pain, but managed to grab onto the boulder and to cling to it until the first effects of the battering had passed. It was less than five yards to Kip now, and Giles went toward the boy with a purpose that seemed almost ludicrous. Foot by difficult foot, Giles worked his way along the tongue of rock to the last upthrust point where Kip hung.

Giles was burning with cold as he finally came abreast of Kip. The boy was rigid, his fingers gripped the rock with deadly tenacity, and his eyes were set, staring.

"Kip!" Giles had to shout to be heard over the surf. "Kip! You've got to let go of the rock!"

Blindly Kip shook his head. "Mom said . . ." he said, and the words ended on a sob.

"It's okay," Giles yelled. "She sent me to get you. You can let go." His side was beginning to ache where he had struck the boulder and his legs were tingly. He had to get Kip away quickly, or the rocks would claim them both.

"I don't know . . ." He tried to turn to look at Giles, but another wave broke and the salt water splashed his face.

"Kip, listen to me!" Giles kept his voice loud but calm as he moved around behind the boy. "Kip, I'm going to climb onto the rock behind you. I want you to turn around and take hold as soon as I tell you. Put your arms around my neck and your legs around my waist, okay?" He didn't wait for an answer, but began laboriously to climb so that Kip's body was masked with his own. "Now! Turn!"

With a shriek, Kip scrambled on the rock, and reached desperately for Giles. The force of the water buffeted him, but he was too frightened to fight it. Knowing how great a risk it was, Giles released part of his hold on the rock and pulled Kip back to him. "Hang on!"

Kip nodded, and his arms went around Giles' neck.

When the next wave had surged over them, Giles stepped away from the rock, slipping toward deeper water.

"Hey . . . !" Kip screamed, and tightened his hold on Giles' neck.

"It's okay," Giles said, and pulled at the boy's panic-strong fingers. "We're going to swim now!" He pulled himself onto his side and began to draw away from the rocks. His strokes were powerful, and he timed them with the waves so that only once did he find the curl of a breaker above him. Kip, terrified now, clung to him but made no sound.

When Giles was certain they were free of the rocks, he turned toward the shore and willed new determination. His body ached with the cold, his hands and feet felt like stumps and his face seemed to have been rubbed raw by the icy waters. "Hang on, Kip," he panted as he at last neared the beach.

There was the scrape of sand under his toes. Giles stood up, more than waist-deep in the chilly Pacific. He held Kip close to him and began to walk through the hissing surf. Ahead he could see Fayre and her aunt Anna waiting, the blanket ready. Fayre had Giles' sweater tied around her neck. It sent an odd spurt of pleasure through him and he lifted one hand in a tired salute.

A few minutes later and he had lifted Kip into his mother's arms and watched while the boy was bundled into the beach blanket. Only now, safe on the blowing sands of the beach, did Giles begin to feel the full weight of his ordeal. His teeth begin to chatter, and no matter how he willed them to be silent, they continued the nervous quivering. His hands were stiff, unwieldy. He tried to talk but achieved only a hoarse croaking.

"Giles, Giles, thank you," Fayre said as she turned from Kip. "Without you . . ."

Giles forced himself to speak clearly. "Without me, he would not have been on that rock."

Fayre looked shocked. "That's not what I meant. If you hadn't been willing to help him, we probably would not have got him off in time." Her eyes were moist, but a quick motion of her hand banished the tears. "Good Lord, look at you. You're soaking. You've got to get out of those clothes."

His spurt of laughter startled Giles. "Not on a public beach, thank you." He reached for his sweater and rubbed it briskly over his chest, and winced as he touched the place where the rocks had struck him. "My home is just over five minutes away from here."

"You don't have to—" Fayre began.

"Nonsense," Giles cut in. "I have to get cleaned up, anyway. Bring Kip along. Likely as not, he'll want something hot in him and a long soak to get the knots out of his muscles." Without waiting for an answer, Giles turned away from her and started toward the parking area.

□ 6 □

"How is he?" Giles asked from his place by the fire as Fayre came into the living room.

"All right, I think. Exhausted more than hurt." She settled into a low chair opposite him. "Aunt Anna is going to keep an eye on him for half an hour. If he's asleep by then, we'll take you up on your offer for the night."

"You don't have to wait that long," Giles said. He was still in his long robe and slippers, having decided that a change would be useless. "How are you? is the question."

Fayre was staring into the fire. "Giles, he said that a devil-man had led him out onto the rocks. He insisted that he saw the devil-man."

"Probably just a couple scuba divers. We get them around here." He moved to put another log onto the fire. "Don't let it worry you, Fayre. He's safe. Frightened, but no real harm done, I think." He watched while the low flames began to lick tentatively at the log, wishing he could recapture the intimacy of that afternoon.

"No. He's not making it up. I think he might have seen someone he thought was a devil. But who? Who'd want to frighten a child? Who'd want to hurt him?" Her voice had risen and her hands worked against each other in her lap.

"But Fayre . . ." Giles said, then stopped. With her particular talent, there was little he could say that would change her mind. She sensed the reality that her son had made and he knew better than to try to argue with her. He didn't want to argue with her. Satisfied that the log would burn, he moved away from the fireplace and reclined against the hassock once more.

"You think I'm being foolish, don't you?" She did not make the question an accusation.

"No," he answered slowly. "Not foolish." He remembered that she had expressed apprehension about Kip earlier that week, and he was determined to lessen her fears.

"I am not making a transference," she said sharply. "I know what's happening in myself, and I know the difference between that and what goes on in my son's life." Her chin tilted upward with defiance. "And don't you dare coddle me, Giles. I don't need that. Especially from you."

It was so tempting to ask her what she did need from him, Giles thought as he looked at her. But he was not sure he wanted her answer, not yet. "Fayre."

The tone of his voice had changed sufficiently to hold her attention. "Yes."

"Will you see me again? Not professionally, socially." He watched the log as it crackled in the fire. "Think it over, if you like. With things the way they are, you—"

"I said yes," she interrupted him gently.

"Next Thursday?" he said. "After I check you over, we could have dinner, if you like, or go to a movie. Maybe I can get symphony tickets." He had no idea what was on the program, or if tickets were still available, but if she said yes, he knew he would find a way to get them.

"Dinner would be fine. Let's just talk. No movies, no music, not this time." She was about to say something more, but then her attention shifted as she turned her head.

Her aunt opened the door that led to the guest rooms. "I'm sorry to bother you," she said, "but I thought you ought to know that Kip has fallen asleep and seems to be resting soundly. If it's all right with you, Dr. Todd, I think it might be wisest to accept your kind offer."

Fayre started to say something, but Giles cut her off. "I'm delighted you'll stay. I hope you'll let me take you all out to breakfast in the morning. It's been too long since I've had guests." He shifted his weight against the hassock and felt the ache in his side ease a bit.

"Aunt Anna," Fayre said after shooting a quick look at Giles, "did Kip say anything more about the devil-man?"

"Nothing much. He's quite worn out, poor boy." The older woman came into the room and looked down at the fire. Her matter-of-fact sympathy pleased Giles. Anna Dubranov was not the sort of woman to be easily panicked, and her stern good sense would be a great deal of help to Fayre.

"I know Aunt Anna has been tremendously helpful," Fayre said, not quite kindly. "But she doesn't have to be my nurse-maid."

"Well, of course not," Anna exclaimed mildly. "A woman your age . . . I must say, it's been much pleasanter having you in the house than it was having Vasilyi. That man would have driven a saint to murder." There was a twinkle in her heavy-lidded eyes. "Besides, Fayre does half of the house-work, which my ex-husband refused to do. Not," she added thoughtfully, "that either of us like it much."

Fayre laughed and got up from the chair. "Well, if we're staying here for the night, I'm going to take a shower and find my bed." She turned back and there was a warmth in her face that held Giles as surely as her arms had held him on the beach. "Thank you. I mean it, Giles."

"You're welcome" sounded so banal, so inane that he could not speak the words. He nodded and tried to smile. "Sleep well."

"You don't have to leave so early," Giles said to Fayre when they had come back from breakfast. The morning was foggy, wet-smelling, and the little restaurant in Pacifica where he had taken them to eat had been virtually empty.

Fayre shook her head. This morning her splendid hair was confined at the back of her neck with a dark green scarf and her sweater seemed wholly misshapen. "No, I think we'd bet-ter get him home. He's still pretty shaken up."

Giles tried to take this lightly. "Well, if it's a doctor you need, you've got one right here."

Impulsively Fayre touched his arm. "Oh, Giles, you know I wouldn't go if it were just me. But Aunt Anna is still sleepy, and believe it or not, I do have studying to do."

He had already begun to walk with her toward her bat-tered old Volkswagen. "But you'll come again?"

"Aren't we having dinner on Thursday?" They spoke al-most at the same time, and Fayre's laughter put Giles at ease once again. "After you check me out, isn't that right?"

"That's right. I know a very nice restaurant in Belmont. We can go there, unless there's some place you'd prefer?"

"I'll trust you," Fayre said. Her hand was still on his arm, the most gentle touch. "Thursday, then."

Anna Dubranov was driving, so, she explained, "Fayre can

deal with Kip. He's a good kid, but he can get carsick, and after the trouble he had yesterday . . ." She shook Giles' hand in a hearty way. "It's a beautiful home, Dr. Todd, and you've been such a nice host."

"But I didn't do much of anything," Giles protested.

"That's exactly what I mean. There's nothing worse than a host who hovers and directs and tries to be a traffic cop. I hope to see you again." She started the car as Fayre went around to the passenger door and got in, climbing into the back so she could sit with her son. As the car moved forward, she turned and waved, and her mouth moved with words that Giles could not hear.

"Well, what do you think?" Veronica Beaufort asked as she and Giles studied the report on the tests Giles had run on her patient.

"I'd give it a little time. This pattern here"—he indicated an area of tracing on the second chart, frowning as he studied the lines—"I've seen something similar in psychomotor epilepsy, but this is certainly inconclusive here. There are no other indications to support that diagnosis. Have you tried drug therapy yet?"

"A little. We're not getting any sort of predictable response."

"Look," Giles said as he fingered the various charts and reports from the tests, "I know this sounds unlikely, but do you think you might be dealing with a very peculiar allergy?"

"Allergy?" Veronica stared at him. "To what?"

"I haven't the vaguest idea, but when I read the preliminary notes you had on the case, and considering what little we've come up with here, I don't know. It's just a hunch, but it might be worth checking it out." He dropped the papers onto her desk, his face still thoughtful.

"I suppose we could run a series on him, but that gets very expensive. He might not be able to afford it." Veronica sat down and checked through the Rolodex. "Excuse me a moment, Giles. You've given me an idea." She dialed an extension. "Dr. Passavoy, please," she said, and while she was waiting, looked back at Giles. "If there's anyone who might take Mr. Jenkins on for study, it's Jack Passavoy. I wouldn't have thought of it if you . . . Hello? Jack? This is Veronica Beaufort. Look, I want to talk to you about a patient of mine. He's got some very unusual symptoms that might be more in your field than in mine." She nodded and made a complicated gesture as Giles left her office.

He was on his way to a meeting with some of the interns when he almost ran into Nancy Lindstrom.

"Oh. It's you. Good morning, Dr. Todd," she said in a tone that bordered on the contemptuous.

"Good morning," he said, feeling a rush of embarrassment from their last meeting.

"How's the lobotomy business today?" She was deliberately setting out to wound Giles, for she knew he had refused to do any lobotomies after seeing the particularly tragic results of one such operation.

Giles refused to be angry. "Are you okay, Nancy?"

"Ask Tim Carey." She was about to push past him, but he grabbed her elbow. "Listen, Nancy. I am terribly sorry about the other night. I should never have done that to you. If you can't forgive me, I understand, but believe me, I didn't mean to be that way."

Her eyes were very angry now. "And that makes it all right, doesn't it? You turn me into a thing, an appliance, like one of those big plastic dolls you fuck, and then you say you're sorry, and I'm supposed to understand. Pity the poor, lonely brain surgeon. It's bullshit, Dr. Todd." She stared at his hand on her arm. "If you touch me again, for any reason, I'm going to the administration and file a complaint. Do I make myself clear?"

"Yes." Giles released her, a coldness taking hold of him. "You certainly do. All right. Except for the demands of our professions, I'll endeavor to stay away from you at all times. Will that suffice, Ms. Lindstrom?"

"Thank you, Dr. Todd." She gave him a wide, malicious smile and went down the hall away from him.

"How was the weekend?" Prentiss sounded more hearty than usual. "I talked to Mrs. Schoenfeld this morning, and she said it was lovely, except for some trouble with her boy."

Giles' head ached, his feet were sore and his lunch had not agreed with him. He was due to run another series of tests on the young artist, Gary Kusogawa, whose recovery from surgery had not been going well. "Well, I mentioned she was apprehensive about Kip," Giles said slowly. "There was one unfortunate thing: the boy went out too far on the rocks and it was a little difficult bringing him back when the tide turned. Mrs. Schoenfeld is still concerned for him. I think you can be of help there."

"Oh, I'll do what I can, Giles. How did she seem to you? Do you think she'll be able to return to testing soon? I'm sorry to lean on you like this, but frankly, we're in a bit of an uproar here. There are two conflicting studies competing for grant money, and we'd be in a much stronger position if we had Mrs. Schoenfeld back in the program." He sighed. "I mentioned this to you the other day, but it's getting more difficult."

"Prentiss, I'm not sure this is the sort of thing that ought to be pushed. If she goes a month or two without any recurrence of a seizure or any episodes of amnesia, then it might be a good idea to resume testing, but on a reduced schedule. . . ."

"I was afraid you'd say that," Prentiss said with an indulgent chuckle. "Very well. I'll keep this in mind. But, Giles, if you decide that she's able to resume testing here before then, will you let me know? It's very important, or I wouldn't ask. I'd hate to do anything that would harm her—gifts like hers are so rare."

"Yes," Giles said quietly, then cleared his throat. "I'll keep your problem in mind, Prentiss, but Mrs. Schoenfeld, as my patient, deserves my greatest concern."

"Naturally," Prentiss agreed quickly. "I didn't mean to imply anything else. Giles, you know what I'm like. And there's so *much* we could do, if only we get the chance. Imagine the *knowledge*, the *power* we could achieve if only we're allowed to keep on with the experiments."

"Do you mean there's a chance the project won't continue? You have such a fine setup there, I would have thought . . ." Giles scowled at the phone.

"Oh, no, nothing that drastic. But, dammit, Giles, we're so *close*. Any delay is difficult, and the politics, well, to be candid, there *is* a lot of politicking going on right now. If we were in a slightly stronger position, it would make all the difference. But there. That wasn't really what I wanted to know. So long as Mrs. Schoenfeld is recovering, it's good news." He paused a moment and Giles imagined Prentiss loading his pipe as he bought time for his next move. "She's a remarkable woman. I hope we are able to do more with her, perhaps develop better ways for her to focus her talents. Well. That's for later. You take good care of her. I know you will, but I feel I owe it to her to be certain that everything possible is being done. . . ."

In spite of himself Giles laughed. "Yes, I assure you it is. It would be easier if I knew what exactly had happened, but whatever it is, it hasn't happened again. Don't worry. As soon as I think she can come back into your study program, she will." He glanced at his watch. "Prentiss, I have to go. I'll talk to you after I have another week of observations to compare with this one. Unless," he said suddenly, "you're free one afternoon this weekend. We might get together for a meal. . . ."

"It's unfortunate," Prentiss said, and by the sound of it, he meant it, "but I've got . . . commitments for the weekend. I've got a debate at Dinklespiel on Saturday evening with that twit Freeman, and Sunday a very attractive young doctoral candidate is spending some time with me." There was a playful lasciviousness in his voice now. "It will certainly make up for that unpleasant time with Alan Freeman. But we might be able to do something the week after?" He didn't wait for a response. "Think about it, and let me know later. Have a pleasant evening. I'll talk with you again soon." The line went dead and Giles was left with the uncanny feeling that Prentiss had not wanted to prolong their talk and was glad of the excuse to cut it short.

But then Mrs. Houghton came into the room with the records Giles had requested, and he was busy again. His disquieting conversation with Prentiss was forgotten.

On Wednesday Gary Kusogawa took a turn for the worse, and Giles was forced to call Fayre and ask her if she could manage Friday instead of Thursday.

"I'm sorry things are going badly," she said with genuine sympathy that was untinged by jealousy. "Friday should be all right, but we might have to make an early evening of it."

Giles thought that if he had not had so difficult a time, this qualification would not upset him as much as it did. "Why?" he could not stop himself from asking.

"Well, you see, I've promised Patrick and Marian that I'd bring Kip out for the weekend. Harold's parents, Kip's grandparents," she explained. "They don't get to see him very often and he's the only link they have with Harold. I promised them, weeks ago, that they'd have a weekend with him." There was an air of apology. "Do you mind?"

It was useless to lie to her. "Yes. Not because of the grandparents, I understand that. But I've been looking forward to seeing you so much . . . this delay aggravates me as it is. But if that's the way it is . . ." he said through a sigh. "There will be other times, won't there?" He had not planned to sound wistful, but he must have, because Fayre said, "Certainly. Giles, if it weren't for Kip, I'd much rather spend the time with you."

"You're welcome anytime," he said quickly as unbidden images rose in his mind, moments recalled from that Saturday before Kip had been trapped on the rocks.

"I'd like to walk on the beach again," Fayre said, almost as if she were agreeing with him.

"Friday then. I'll see you at the Medical Center at four, if that's okay? And we'll have an early dinner, say, five-thirty." That way he would have an extra hour with her, and suddenly that hour seemed precious.

"Fine. Four. Don't be too upset that we had to rearrange it. It's part of your conscientiousness, and I like that about you."

Giles felt deeply pleased. "Thank you, Fayre." He was glad she said nothing. "Good-bye for now. Call me if anything worries you."

"I will. Good-bye, Giles."

Ms. Loomis left the hospital at six and was replaced by Ms. Profida, who would be on until midnight. The various instruments monitoring Gary Kusogawa were being carefully watched, as the hope of a stabilization of his condition faded.

Dr. William Hensell saw Giles in the hall just before ten. "You still here, Giles?" he asked, plainly on the way out himself.

"Yeah. Why are you here so late?" There were times Giles wished he smoked, and this was one of them. "That Lasker boy?"

"What else? We're past the worst of it, of course, but I'm afraid that his parents aren't going to be very pleased. And I won't be the one to tell them that it was their own ambition that did this to him. Chambers was all for jumping on them with both feet and cleats, but considering what's happened to the boy, there's no point. It isn't as if he'll ever have the chance to do it again." William Hensell was a handsome man, the sort worthy of the myth that was perpetuated about doctors. He was lean, his face falling somewhere in the aristocratic-priestly stereotype. His expensive blue suit was conservatively elegant, his tie the right width. Only the heavy pockets under his eyes and the first suggestion of broken veins in his cheeks and nose revealed his weaknesses. "Say, I'm going out for a drink. Can you spare a minute? You look like you could use a touch of the good stuff yourself."

Giles was aware that with Will Hensell, one drink was not possible. "Sorry, Will. I've got a patient here I'm very worried about. I'd go home, but it takes forty minutes from here to there, and that's too long. So I'm staying here. Some other time?"

"Sure, sure. Say, is the case that artist? I heard a couple of the nurses talking about it. It's a shame, considering. What is your prognosis? The nurses weren't very optimistic." He had shifted his fine leather attaché case from one hand to the other.

"I wish that nurses would learn to keep their mouths shut," Giles said. "And doctors, too. The gossip that goes on around here . . ." He stopped. "I didn't mean that. I'm edgy. And if you want to see my prognosis . . ." He went through the door into the monitoring room that adjoined the intensive-care room where Gary Kusogawa lay. "Look for yourself."

Ms. Profida looked up. "Nothing new to report, Dr. Todd. He's unstable, but there's nothing very negative."

"The instability is negative enough," Giles said. "That's what's worrying me." He turned to Will Hensell. "Do you see what I mean?"

Hensell was studying the tracings that were stacked on the typing table next to the machines. "Holy shit. Are you going to operate?"

"What for? We've got the malignancy. This is something else. And with his condition seesawing, would you operate?" Giles felt weary, very weary. His eyes ached and he thought perhaps he ought to have them examined in case he needed glasses.

"Maybe you're right," Will Hensell conceded. "Still, there might be something worthwhile in going in." He looked at the tracings once more, then set them aside. "Glad it's your case and not mine."

"Thanks," Giles said without rancor, and did not turn his head away from the monitoring machines as Will Hensell left the little room. "I'm going out to talk to Mrs. Kusogawa, to see if I can arrange for a place for her to sleep tonight. Nurse Waters said she wouldn't go home. You know where to reach me if you have to."

"Of course, Dr. Todd." Ms. Profida hardly looked away from the monitors. "It's going to be a long night."

"It is." Giles nodded as he left the room.

Shortly before dawn Gary Kusogawa's condition began to deteriorate. Giles, called in from the cot in the nurses' lounge, studied the monitors, his eyes becoming grimmer as he watched the graphs. "I see."

Ed Franks, the third monitor technician, nodded. "It's not just brain patterns now, Dr. Todd, it's everything. Dr. Carey was in ten minutes ago, and he said he'd give it up."

The thought of Tim Carey looking at one of his patients gave Giles a moment of rage, but it was a luxury, and he forced it from his mind. "I'd better talk to Mrs. Kusogawa," he said reluctantly. "She may want us to take heroic measures. Not that they'll do any good. But it's her choice now."

It was almost four in the afternoon when Gary Kusogawa died. His wife had been with him, and although Giles very much doubted that her husband was aware of that, when she asked him, he said he felt certain that Gary sensed her presence and was comforted.

"You have a new admission and I had to cancel your lecture," Mrs. Houghton accused Giles as he came back to his office.

"That's regrettable," he said, too fatigued to speak sharply to her. "What about the admit? Is it serious?"

"Not immediately," Mrs. Houghton admitted. "It's a second CT scan. You did one on this woman about five months ago. The lecture is rescheduled for tomorrow afternoon."

Giles was about to agree when he realized that was when he would see Fayre. "No. We'll have to do it Monday. I'm sorry, Mrs. Houghton. I know you've done an excellent job. I appreciate it. I forgot to tell you," he went on, knowing that he had told her and that she had not marked it in her books, "that I've changed the Schoenfeld examination to tomorrow. I've already got the provision at St. Mathis Medical Center, and it would be unwise to change the requirements a third time." He was improvising, but he knew how much Mrs. Houghton hated altering plans, and knew that this explanation would be acceptable to her.

"Oh. In that case . . . I'll tell the students to meet with you at nine-thirty on Monday, before you scrub to assist Dr.

Hensell." It was a subtle punishment, and Giles recognized it
as such. He decided it wasn't worth fighting about. "That's
fine. Just fine."

"And Reverend Audley called. He asked that you return
his call at your convenience." It was her parting shot, and
Giles closed the door on it.

Reverend Audley had not left the building, and said, "It's
nothing. I'd heard you'd been here all night with the
Kusogawa case. I was sorry to hear he'd died. I know how
hard you worked to save him."

"Not hard enough, Hugh." Giles felt depression settling
onto him like a dark cloak. "There just wasn't enough to go
on, and he was so weak . . ."

"Can you leave now? You sound like you could use some
rest." Hugh made no attempt to mask his concern. "If you
try to practice medicine in the state you're in, you'll be lucky
if you don't get yourself sued six ways from Sunday."

"And deserve it, no doubt," Giles added. "You're right, but
I have one more patient to see. Then I will go home, I
promise you. I don't have to be here until eleven in the morning, and I won't be. I won't even get up until nine-thirty.
Does that meet with your approval?" He debated whether he
should have some strong coffee before driving down the coast
highway, but decided it would only make him jittery, which
he most emphatically did not need.

"You're the doctor. And a stubborn one," Hugh said, then
added casually, "You're going down to St. Mathis tomorrow,
is that right?"

"To check Mrs. Schoenfeld, that's right."

"Well, Inga and I have an extra ticket for ACT, if you'd
care to join us."

"You never give up, do you Hugh?" Giles managed a fatigued chuckle. "Sorry to disappoint you, but no."

"No? You aren't going to be on the Peninsula all evening,
are you?"

"As a matter of fact, I am. I'm taking Mrs. Schoenfeld to
dinner. If, of course, that meets with your approval." He did
not sound as sarcastic as he had intended, but it didn't bother
him.

"Meets with my approval? I'll give thanks and sing all the
even-numbered psalms. Have a wonderful time. Do it up
right. You have made my day." Hugh stopped his enthusiastic outburst, and said far more seriously, "She's not the kind
of woman to be taken lightly, Giles."

"I don't take her lightly." He was stung by the implication.

"I didn't think you did. But you're so private . . ." He had the grace to sound abashed. "That wouldn't work too well with her, though, if what I've heard is true."

"I don't know what you've heard," Giles snapped. "And whatever it is, I will thank you not to repeat it."

"Certainly. As if I needed the warning." There was an edge to Hugh's voice.

"Christ, I'm sorry, Hugh. It's the fatigue, and a lot of other things." He put his free hand to his eyes and wished that he could cry. There would be relief in tears. It had been, what? ten years? twelve? since he had wept. He could not remember the last time he had allowed himself to cry. He had kept that decent fortitude which his parents and his uncle and cousin so admired. And now, with frustration and anguish filling him, he discovered he no longer had the key to free himself.

He drove carefully; he knew he was too tired to think quickly. There was, luckily, no fog on the road, but the wind was brisk and swiped at the Land Rover as he made his way toward Montara. He drove through Pacifica without stopping for groceries, although he had planned to get them. That would be for later, when he was less fatigued. He remembered he had some eggs and cheese, enough for a light meal, which, he knew, was all he wanted.

The dark, almost lunar desolation of Devil's Slide bothered him, although he had long since learned the road. Now he was glad to be past the forbidding dark rocks and on the long, gentle curve into Montara. He made his left turn away from the highway with deep relief. In five minutes he would be home.

The phone was on its fourth ring before Giles was awake enough to recognize it. He turned slowly toward the phone on the stand by his bed, and as he fumbled for the receiver, he looked at the clock. "Seven-thirty," he muttered and dragged the phone nearer. "Hello?"

"Giles? Sorry to wake you. This is Prentiss. I wanted your advice on a matter concerning Mrs. Schoenfeld." The voice was very hearty, and Giles knew by the sound of it that Prentiss had already made up his mind and wanted only Giles' approval of his idea.

"Tell me," Giles muttered.

"Did I wake you?" Prentiss asked solicitously. "I'm very

sorry." There was a certain contrition in his voice, but it was for form's sake.

"I had an emergency and I haven't had much sleep," Giles said, thinking that it was not entirely accurate but philosophically correct. "It's time I was up. Tell me about Mrs. Schoenfeld."

"Yes. That. I spoke to her yesterday, just keeping her abreast of developments, of course. She mentioned that she was planning to take her son to visit his grandparents in Manteca."

"And?" Giles lay back, the phone set on his chest. He stared at the beamed ceiling and listened to Prentiss talk.

"Well, that anxiety of hers we discussed, this transference of worry to her son: I've told her that I think it would be better if she let her aunt take the boy to visit the grandparents, and she can spend the time studying. It's healthy for her to let the child off the leading strings, don't you think?"

"You're the psychologist. But if she's seriously concerned, she might do better if she stays with Kip." Part of Giles' mind urged him to support Prentiss. If Fayre did not have to go to Manteca, she could spend more time with him, perhaps even come out to Montara again for the Sunday afternoon. The weather had been good, it was May, a pretty time. They'd be at leisure, and she would not be preoccupied with thoughts about Kip.

". . . And when I called the aunt and explained, she said that she was willing to drive the boy to Manteca and stay with him. In fact, she seemed to think it was a good idea. She told me that Mrs. Schoenfeld needs more time to herself, to follow her own interests."

"Well, Prentiss," Giles said, fighting down the absurd hope that Anna Dubranov was promoting his suit with Fayre, "I can't say one way or the other. If Mrs. Schoenfeld brings the question up when I check her over this afternoon, I'll try to draw her out, but I don't feel quite . . . honest, I guess, telling her to leave Kip for the weekend if she truly doesn't want to." He considered telling Prentiss that he was going to have dinner with Fayre, but apparently neither she nor her aunt had, and he decided to wait until the evening was over before saying anything. Besides, he reminded himself, Prentiss found most of the trappings of affection laughable. Giles could still remember the first time Prentiss had told him about his current affair. "Absolutely made to be plowed, I must say. You know, it's *amazing* what seven hard inches can do to a woman. She's got to be the most *boring* female in three counties, but put her on her back and she's eager as a derby filly." Giles was not certain that Prentiss still felt that way, but found he did not want to press the question.

"But it's a *foolish* attitude. She's using it as an escape, and if she doesn't come to grips with it now, she'll have to do it later and it will be so much more difficult."

"And besides," Giles said with an indulgent chuckle, "the sooner she gets over her fear, the sooner she can come back into your study program."

Prentiss returned the laugh. "There *is* that, of course, and there's no point in denying it. What the hell. If you think you can talk to her, do. If you can draw her out, do. You and your damnable noncoercion. You're absolutely incorrigible. You always have been." The chuckles decreased. "Do you remember that time when we'd been out after-hours and we had to try to get back into Corpus through the gate? I was all for stripping and soaping but I couldn't have made it. *You* were the one who insisted that we go along to the porter's window and make a clean breast of it, and hope that we'd get off with a glass of sherry and a lecture. And when I said that we'd been delayed because of a flat tire on your cousin's car, *you* had to go and tell them that we'd left late because of a party at Stormhill and no one had been willing to drive us back until it was over. Your *honesty*, Giles. Oh, I give your integrity its due, absolutely. But there are times you dismay me."

Giles nodded. "It wasn't too bad, Prentiss. And they did give us really excellent sherry." He held the phone so he could roll onto his side. The bruise there had almost faded and most of the stiffness was gone. "I appreciate how much Mrs. Schoenfeld's abilities mean to you. And I'll do my best to put her back into your program as quickly as I can. You have my word. You may be right about the boy, but for the time being I'll have to reserve judgment on it." He rubbed the stubble on his chin. "Look, Prentiss, it's time I was up. I'll let you know how it goes with Mrs. Schoenfeld."

"Excellent. I'll be seeing her this noon, before I go to Freeman's lecture on *La Bas*."

"You're going to one of his lectures?" Giles was surprised. "Why? I thought you had no use for the man."

"I haven't. But I want to get material for our debate, of course. What better way to demolish him than with his own weapons?" He paused, and added with relish, "To tell you the truth, I'm very much looking forward to the debate. The man's a bloody incompetent and it's time he was shown up for it. This isn't the medieval period anymore. We're *scientists,* not ruddy, mumbling sorcerers. We're after provable, demonstrable, repeatable, *usable* results, and along comes this blathering *English* professor, and starts talking about *horror* and the *supernatural,* and *interfering* with my *legitimate* experimentation." Prentiss' voice had risen almost half an octave and he was speaking much louder.

"You don't need to convince me," Giles said quite calmly, knowing how excited Prentiss could become about his work. "But don't yell like that when you debate Freeman, or he'll use it as evidence that you're one of those typical insane professors."

"Like poor old Baron von Frankenstein?' His laughter cracked ominously, like the sound of a pistol or a whip. "Freeman is much more the type than I am. Oh, don't be concerned. I'll be the utter epitome of the bloodless scientist. And to hell with Alan Freeman and his catalog of folkloric demons!" There was a pause again, and this time when Prentiss spoke he was truly much less agitated. "It was good of you to remind me."

"What are friends for? After a quarter-century, I should hope I know you well enough for that."

"Yes," Prentiss said slowly, enigmatically. "I should *hope* so. Well, perhaps I shouldn't anticipate difficulties, but I always do."

"But they've never stopped you," Giles reminded him. "I must get going, Prentiss. I'll give you a call on Monday or Tuesday, in the evening, if that's all right?"

"Yes. Yes. Fine. I look forward to it. Thanks." He hung up without saying good-bye or waiting for Giles' response.

In another person, this abruptness might have disturbed Giles, but he knew Prentiss well enough to be aware that his mind was elsewhere. Considering the pressure on his old friend, Giles could not blame him for his short manners. As he dressed, Giles thought that perhaps he would pick up a copy of Freeman's book, just to find out what it was that put him at such odds with Prentiss. He had read the book when it came out, and it had not impressed him, but he felt he owed Prentiss that much attention. This way he could refute Freeman with some authority. He wished he had kept the book now, instead of giving it to Mrs. Treuhoff, who cleaned his house twice a week.

By the time he left his house, he had put the thought of Alan Freeman and Prentiss Fellkirk out of his thoughts. Even his class seemed unimportant. What was uppermost in his mind was that that evening, he would have dinner with Fayre. For the first time in several years, he hummed as he drove.

□ 7 □

Their conversation faltered the third time about halfway through the entrée. Fayre sat with a fork in her hand, poking at the asparagus, and Giles found himself staring at the bottle of Pinot Noir.

Fayre took a shaky breath. "I had a talk with Dr. Fellkirk today," she said, attempting to get talk started again.

Giles was grateful. "About what?" He knew, of course, but did not want to take the risk of stopping their words again.

"He talked to me about Kip. He said I shouldn't be so protective of the boy because I was afraid for myself." She was dressed in a soft green sleeveless dress, and she looked chilled as she spoke. "I felt the fear while I talked to him. Just saying the words brought it out. I guess he was right. Anyway, Aunt Anna is taking Kip to see his grandparents, and I'm going to stay here. And considering what I've been going through, it might be good for Kip to get away from me for a while. I talked to him about that before Aunt Anna and I made our arrangements." She stopped and had some of the wine. "He didn't say it, but I knew he wanted the time away from me. I guess all parents go through this eventually. Maybe it's harder for me because Harold's dead."

"He died some time ago, didn't he?" Giles had to resist the irrational gladness he felt at the thought of more time with her. "I believe Prentiss said he was killed in Vietnam."

"He was." She stared across the restaurant, unseeing. "I knew when it happened. It wasn't frightening. It wasn't particularly depressing. But I knew, the way I know what day of the week it is, or that nine goes into twenty-seven three times." Her hands were steady as she took the glass and drained the last of the wine. "Don't remind me that wine is a depressant. I'm not worried about that tonight."

Giles had, in fact, almost told her to avoid the wine, and so he nodded. "Okay. I won't." Giles refilled their glasses. "Go ahead." He lifted his glass in silent toast to her, but put it down as soon as he had taken the sip. "Fayre . . ."

"Yes. I know. Let me think about it." Her hair was done up this evening, in a kind of knot on the back of her head. Giles wanted to pull the pins from it and spread it . . . spread it?

"Do you want to leave now?" The suddenness of her question surprised him.

"I want to stay with you. I know it's been an off night for me. But, truly, Fayre, I'd rather spend the time with you if you'll have me." Just saying the words aloud seemed more of a risk than he wanted to take, and to be thinking at the same time of her splendid smoke-blond hair spread on the pillow beside him, beneath him . . .

"I meant," she said with longing and irritation in her face, "I meant we should go back to your house. That's what you want, isn't it?"

Giles swallowed hard, although there was nothing in his mouth now but a sudden dryness. "Yes. It's what I want. And you . . ."

Her eyes glittered. "Why do you think I asked? Giles, I want you. Do I have to beg to make you believe me? Are you that far away?" Her hands were clenched on the white table linen.

For one terrifying moment, Giles could neither speak nor move. "I thought it was just me." The confusion that filled him was as distracting as her loveliness. He managed to sort out his thoughts enough to signal the waiter as he rose, leaving thirty-five dollars on the table. It would pay for the meal, the wine and the indignity, he hoped. He held Fayre's chair for her, and draped her lace shawl around her shoulders.

It was dusk now, and as he opened the car door for her, her nearness overwhelmed him. His arms went around her, before he had the time to resist the impulse. Her mouth was warm against his, slightly open so that their tongues could touch. It was like being licked by an inner flame. He pressed closer to her, wanting to merge with her, to feel what she felt, share her responses.

When at last they moved apart, Giles was too shaken to

say anything. He held the door as she climbed into the Land Rover, then went quickly to the driver's side.

He had never driven that road as fast as he did that night. The winding, narrow asphalt track twisted up and over the coast range and down the long gullies to the ocean. Only his familiarity with the curves and rises of the little state highway allowed Giles to drive it at over fifty, rather than the usual forty. Beside him Fayre said nothing, but she was obviously not afraid.

As he turned up the private road to his house, Giles did not stop to get the mail, although the flag on his box indicated that there was some. The headlights of the Land Rover lanced through the darkness as he made the last long turn toward the edge of the knoll where his house stood. He parked quickly, still saying nothing. In seven determined strides he was around the car and holding the door for Fayre. He felt the movement of her body as she left the car, but he only took her hand as he led her toward the house.

The bottom floor was dark, and he did not pause to turn on the lights. Giles went quickly to the stairs and drew Fayre with him.

"But . . ." she protested and tugged at his hand, as if leading him toward the guest rooms.

"No. I want you to come to my bed. You're not a guest." He continued up the stairs. There was a light on in the dining room, as there always was. He paid it little attention as he climbed the next flight, Fayre behind him, as quiet as he.

His room was as he left it—the bed unmade, two jackets thrown over the back of one of the chairs, the curtains still open where the tall windows faced the ocean. Giles had forgotten the disorder he had left behind that morning. It had not occurred to him then that Fayre would be returning with him. He started to explain, but Fayre stopped him.

"It doesn't matter, Giles. You're here, that matters." She went toward him, into his arms, and this time their kiss was roughened by urgency. It was a complicated kiss, filled with desire and uncertainty, with immediate need and old longings. Her lips were firm, responsive. Giles tightened his hold on her with one arm and with the other reached to pull the pins from her hair, as he had been wanting to do all evening.

They separated only long enough to take their clothes off themselves and each other. Jacket, dress, hose, trousers, shoes, all were tossed aside without regard.

Yet as he drew back the rumpled sheets, Giles looked questioningly at Fayre. "You're certain?" He had no idea how he could stop now. His groin was so tight with desire that he thought his testicles would pull up inside his body.

"Oh, Giles." She held him in her arms and leaned so that they fell, almost laughing, onto the bed.

He knew there should be preliminaries, time devoted to stroking and kissing and touching, time for sweet words and exploring caresses. And he realized he wanted those things very much, but his need now was too great. Her breasts were high and full, slightly pendulous, and the nipples like small hard pennies at the centers of dark aureoles. The scent and taste of her filled his being, salty, warm, with a tang, bitter and sweet at once, like sage. He entered her quickly and deeply, and felt her pulse around him.

The light by the bed was still on, and he watched her face as her body moved with his. Her hair, as he had imagined it, spread over the pillow, and slid like waves as she rolled her head back. He had never seen a face so changed by passion. Her features were suffused, her mouth open, her eyes almost shut. As he moved into her, into her, into her, her heartbeat strengthened, grew more rapid, as demanding as her hands that strained him to her.

The end came quickly, shattering as lightning, so consuming that he heard neither the sounds that she made nor those that came from himself. And when it had passed, he could not bear to release her, but rolled to the side, his arms still around her, the smell and taste of her flooding his senses, her mouth against his shoulder, her legs tangled with his.

When they woke again, it was far into the night. The wind was still and a pale moonpath lit the distant ocean. And now, there was time for stroking and kissing and touching, for discovery and sweet words and caresses, for slowly building desire, for tender fulfillment arrived at through all the senses, joyously varied, endlessly new.

Giles was splendidly sore. He reached out and touched Fayre, tracing the lines of her face with gentle fingers as she slept. He had looked at the clock once and discovered, without much surprise, that it was almost ten-thirty. As he traced the curve of her mouth, she followed his fingers with kisses.

"I didn't want to wake you up," he said, moving nearer to her.

"Why? Do you need more time?" Her smile was genuine.

She slid into the crook of his arm. "I could lie here all day, I think, just being close to you."

"Feel free. Unless you get hungry." He remembered he had not gone shopping. "In which case, we'd have to go out."

"Are you hungry?" she chuckled.

"Of course not," he said staunchly, and realized that he was famished.

"You are the most terrible liar." She laughed, and turned so she could lay her head on his chest. "What's troubling you?" There was no accusation in the question.

"Nothing much. I wasn't prepared for this. I wanted it, I think from the first time I saw you, but it never seemed possible, only one of those beautiful wishes we all have. It's not the way you feel about, oh, a movie star, because no matter how glamorous they are, you can't help but recognize, somewhere deep inside, that what they're doing is a job. The wishes are like lives. You don't ever expect to have the chance, let alone the inclination, to make love to a person you only see on the screen. But someone you see, a real person, whose life touches yours, that's different. I remember," he said suddenly, as the image came back to him, "a friend of mine in medical school. He knew a woman who's very famous, very fascinating. They'd been friends for years and years. They didn't see much of each other, her schedule being the kind that took her all over the place, but they did write. Tony used to say that they knew each other better than either of them knew anyone else. He was never impressed with her fame, but his love for her seemed to me then to border on the idiotic. Now, I think he was one of the most fortunate men I've ever known."

"When did you decide that?" She was sliding her hand over his chest, and the effect was more affectionate than erotic.

"About eight years ago. When my marriage failed." He said it flatly, but there was still an element of pain to the words. "Prudence is getting married again. It's taking a lot of courage to do that."

"Why?" Fayre demanded. "You can't have been that bad a husband."

"No. I don't think so. Aloof and unreasonable and insufferable, but not that bad." He caught her hand with his. "The man she's marrying is a very long way from her New England, old-money background. He's an aggressive, outspoken, brilliant Chicano, and just as old-blood as her family. His people came to California with Serra." He turned his head to look at her. "I still don't believe you're here."

"Good Lord, what would it take to convince you?" She pulled one arm free so that she could prop herself on her elbow and stare at him. "The Hindu literature recommends scratches and bites as evidence, but that really isn't my style. Besides, you might think they're psychosomatic." She kissed him. "That will have to do, Dr. Todd."

Another thought occurred to him. "I should have thought of this last night. Shit." He knew he should not be so acutely upset, but still the words came out badly. "I didn't use anything."

"I know," she said, and kissed the arch of his brow. "But I did. I have an IUD." She hesitated, then answered his unspoken question. "About a year and a half after Harold died, I met a man. He wanted to marry me, or he said he did. Now, I don't know." There was a sad, distant look to her face. "I was very lonely, and I thought he'd be an end to it. And he was, for about ten minutes. Then it was much, much worse. I got the IUD while we were having the affair, and after it was over, I never bothered having it out. I think I didn't want to believe that my sex life was over. It doesn't give me any problems and . . ." She looked at him for a long moment. "It wouldn't have made any difference, though. I wanted to make love with you. I wouldn't mind the risk."

"I would," Giles said slowly. He rolled onto his side and pulled her nearer. "After what you've been through, I wouldn't ask you to . . . expose yourself to more hurt." He kissed her slowly. "Do you really want to stay in bed all day?"

"Yes. But we'd better get up. I've got to get back to Palo Alto. I have studying to do." She made no attempt to get out of his embrace.

"May I help you?" His arms tightened a little at the thought of having to let her go.

"You mean come along? You'd distract me completely." She seemed to sense his concern. "And I don't want this to happen too fast. I want to be sure I'm not escaping from other things to you. It's very important to me that this be real, and strong. I've had more than enough of false intimacy. It makes me cautious, no matter what you think of last night."

" 'Cautious' would not be the first word I'd choose to describe it," he admitted as he pulled the ends of her pale hair toward him. "I love your hair. When I first saw you, your hair was all around you. It's soft and shining. If the moon were gold instead of silver, it would be this color, I think."

"But I am cautious," Fayre said. "There's so much happening in my life right now. Let me have growing room, Giles. I won't desert you, I promise you." Then she added in a low voice, "But I never thought that anyone would love me the way you do."

The words shocked Giles. He had not spoken of love to her—of need and desire, perhaps, but not of love. Recognition seemed to overwhelm him, filling him with conflicting emotions. He tried to sort the feelings out, and found himself baffled. "Is that what it is?" he asked aloud.

"If it isn't, I don't know what else to call it," she said, touching his face.

"Very well then. It's love."

By four o'clock Fayre was back in Palo Alto, and by five Anna Dubranov had also returned with an almost hysterical Kip. Giles had been lingering over a cup of coffee when Fayre's aunt came into the house carrying the boy in her arms.

Fayre, who had fallen into a moody silence, had jumped up even before the door opened, and when she saw who it was, she ran to her aunt. "God, what's wrong? Is Kip . . .?"

"He's all right," Anna said with stolid good sense. "He's had a little scare, that's all." She put the boy into a chair, where he huddled, staring at his mother with huge, frightened eyes.

Giles had come into the living room, and stopped in the archway. "Fayre. . . ?"

"Oh, it's you, Dr. Todd," Anna said, and gave him an approving nod. "I'm glad you're here. You can make things easier for the child and for his mother."

Fayre had taken Kip in her arms and sat without moving while the boy hid his face against her shoulder. "What was it?" she asked, choking the words out.

"He went out playing with the Thompson children, you know, the ones down the road. His grandparents," she explained for Giles' benefit, "live about three miles outside of Manteca. They have two hundred acres there, and the Thompsons live about a quarter-mile away, on the other side of the road. They've got seven children, and Kip's played with them a good deal over the years."

"But what happened?" Fayre demanded, her voice rising.

Giles crossed the room and put a hand on her shoulder. Although she did not appear to notice it, some of the brittle shine went out of her eyes. Giles remained beside her.

"Well, from what he said, he and the Thompson kids, two or three of them, anyway, went out to play. They were in one of the orchards, apparently. Kip claims that they were playing tag or ambush or something of the sort when a devil-man came after him and tried to catch him, or hurt him—"

"He said he'd fill me with maggots and bury me, so they'd eat their way out of me alive!" Kip fairly screamed the words and started once more to cry with high, convulsive sobs. Fayre held him tighter and murmured to him, but there was a hard anger in her face.

"I tell you what I think happened," Anna said. She was not quite as steady as she had been and her mouth had turned down at the corners. "It distresses me to say so, but I think that that next-to-youngest Thompson child, Jamie, I think he probably started telling about that kidnapping that happened there, when all those schoolchildren were buried in the bus. And he may have made a few threats. You know that Kip's a very imaginative child, and it doesn't take a great deal to upset him. That Jamie has a mean streak in him. You've said it yourself, Fayre. He wouldn't have to say a lot to make Kip believe—"

"No! *No!*" Kip shrieked. "It was a devil-man! Like before! He was all black and he had one big eye in the middle of his head. He didn't have a nose at all, just the big, big eye!" He kicked angrily, as his crying increased.

Giles looked down at Fayre. "I have an emergency kit in the car. If you'd like him calmed down, I've got a couple very mild sedatives that would do it." He looked at the child. "I don't ordinarily favor giving tranks to kids, but it won't do him any good to keep on like this." His voice was level as all the years of his profession took over, but inwardly he was deeply concerned. With Fayre's sensitivity and her fear about the boy, this would cause her a great deal of unnecessary anguish. It infuriated him to think that anyone would deliberately, cruelly frighten a child, but what lent coldness and implacability to his rage was the hurt and fear that Fayre felt. The intensity of this feeling was oddly satisfying.

Whoever was responsible for harming Fayre Schoenfeld, Giles knew he would never forgive.

"If you think it wise," she said, her attention still on Kip, who was struggling in her lap. "No, honey, don't do that. Be calm, Kip. It's fine. There's no devil-man here. We won't allow it."

Giles heard the "we" and knew it was intended for him. "I'll get the kit." He went out the door and to his Land Rover quickly, for his many years of practice told him that Kip was working himself up into a fit, and if there was one thing Fayre did not need at the moment . . . He took the small case from the back seat, opened it for a quick check. Yes, the packets were there. He slammed the door and locked it, and returned to the house.

Kip had begun to scream with a kind of systematic determination. His legs were drawn up to his chest and his hands were closed into fists. Fayre was trying to hold him, but he was not responding to the soft words she said.

"What should I do?" Anna asked as Giles came back into the living room.

"Get me a large glass of water, and if you have a plastic or heavy ceramic cup, fill it about half full of water." Giles had opened the kit, and as he removed one of the packets from it, he said to Fayre, "As soon as your aunt brings the water, I'm going to throw some on Kip. We've got to break the cycle before I can get anything into him. Be ready. And then, this capsule should do it. What does he weigh? About seventy pounds, I'd guess."

"Closer to sixty." Her words came in spurts as she worked to keep a hold on her son. "Is the water necessary?"

"Something is," Giles said, rising. "But I don't think that hitting him, in this mood, is a good idea, Fayre." He said it lightly and saw her nod.

"Okay. Just give me warning." She changed her grip. "I suppose this will keep him in line for you." She was thinking quite calmly now, catching her composure from him.

Anna was back in the living room now, a twelve-ounce tumbler filled almost to the brim in one hand, and a squat ironstone mug in the other. "Where do you want me to stand, Dr. Todd?"

"Beside me, away from Fayre. Give me the things as I ask for them. Make sure they're in my hand, because I won't take the time to look." He gave her a quick smile that he hoped would reassure her. "Are you ready?"

Both Fayre and her aunt Anna said they were.

"Now!" Giles held his hand for the glass, which Anna pushed at it. He had put his free hand on Kip's shoulder, touching him lightly. Then his fingers tightened and he held the child still. In the next instant he poured the water over Kip, wetting the boy, Fayre, the chair and a patch of the rug.

Kip yelled with indignation and shock, but the repeated screams were stopped.

"Hold him, hold him," Giles said quietly as he reached for the mug. Anna put it into his hand quickly and efficiently. He was glad of her sensible attitude, and told himself he should compliment her later. He took the capsule from his shirt pocket, letting go of Kip long enough to do it.

"He isn't fighting me now," Fayre said as her hold relaxed.

"Then tell him to open his mouth. We'll get this down him quickly." Giles leaned nearer.

"Kip, open your mouth. I want you to take a pill. You'll feel better if you take a pill."

Kip's answer was a high, protesting yelp, but Giles was ready for that. As soon as the boy opened his mouth, Giles thrust three fingers into it and slid the capsule along the fingers, and followed immediately with the water in the mug. He kept his fingers in Kip's mouth until he felt there was enough water in it to force the boy to swallow. He pulled his fingers free and watched intently.

With a sputtering sound, Kip swallowed and then started to scream again, this more from outrage than fear.

Fayre had been contained and self-possessed, but this new outburst was apparently more than she wanted to deal with. "Kip! Stop at once!" The sharp words had some effect, but not very much. She stared up at Giles. "I don't know what to do. And he's so . . . different."

"Here." Giles reached down and lifted the shouting, screaming child into his arms. His shirt was suddenly quite wet and he found Kip hard to hold. "Kip, you're okay. It's okay. No devil-man can get you here. You need to rest. Wouldn't it be nice to get into something dry and have a bit to eat and then go to bed?" He was saying the words more to have something to say than to persuade Kip of anything. "You can dry off, and watch TV or read a story. You'd like that, wouldn't you?"

"*No!*" Kip lashed out with arms and feet, and Giles nearly fell as he strove to hold Kip and stand upright. He felt encouraged, though, because Kip had used a word to protest,

instead of incoherent screams. He was more concerned about
Fayre, who was almost white in her face, and as she rose to
help Giles with her son, he could see that her hands were
trembling.

Anna, who had left the room after Giles had got Kip to
take the capsule, now returned carrying two large bath towels. "I figured you'd need these," she said as she gave one to
Fayre.

"Aunt Anna, thank you. I'm so sorry about the chair."

"Don't be silly," she said to her niece. "We'll sop up as
much of it as we can, and then, if that isn't enough, I'll stand
it out in the backyard to dry it out. It's not a valuable chair.
I've had it for over fifteen years and I got it at a clearance
sale. Dry yourself off."

Giles had a fleeting impression that in spite of her protests,
Anna Dubranov liked the chair, but was too kind to upset
Fayre with any additional concerns. Kip had got to the hit-
ting stage and was striking out at Giles' arms and chest, and
Giles wanted to restrain him without hurting him. "Stop it,
Kip. This is so babyish."

The word was magic. Giles had forgotten the terrible pride
of young children, when each year, each portion of a year,
had its own strict code of honor. Kip was so stung that he
stopped and glared at Giles with full recognition. "I am not a
baby. I'm seven years old." The announcement was made
with great dignity and Giles knew it would be unkind to
laugh.

"Then you should not act like a baby," Giles said, taking a
very reasonable tone. "If you're seven, you ought to stop
kicking and screaming. It was one thing when you were
frightened, because all of us do strange things when we're
frightened. But after that, you didn't behave very well for a
young man of seven."

Kip looked abashed, and with considerable difficulty admitted he knew that. "But I didn't know how to stop."

As Giles put Kip down, he smiled ruefully. "That, my dear
boy, is a problem we all have." He looked at Fayre and held
out his hands. "Are you all right?"

"Yes. Yes. I'm better. For a moment there . . ." She shuddered and could not meet his eyes. "Thank you, Giles. I
couldn't have managed on my own." Her fingers tightened on
his.

"You did very well. I've seen doctors do worse than you
did just now. You have nothing to be ashamed of. Nothing."

He wished he could take her in his arms, to comfort her, to shield her.

She took a step toward him, then hung back. "Giles, I'm sorry you had to deal with this."

"I'm not," he said promptly. "It's not what I'd call the perfect end to an afternoon, but I think it was a good thing I was here." He looked down at Kip, who was now sitting on the floor, one of the towels dragged around his shoulders. "He's a good kid, Fayre. You don't have to worry about him. He'll get over this."

"I hope so," she said, not sounding very confident. "He really believes that he saw a devil-man. I wonder what it was, and why it frightened him so much?" She put her hand on Kip's head. "Are you okay now, Kip?"

"I guess. Mom, why'd it happen?" He was not particularly scared now, and his curiosity had an edge of anger in it. "It was a really rotten joke."

"Yes," Fayre agreed. "Some people don't know how to make jokes." She turned her eyes toward Giles. "May I talk to you a moment, in private?"

"Certainly." He knew he ought to leave, but he was still reluctant to do so. "Come out to the car, if you like. Kip will be safe with Anna."

Anna had gone for more towels to put on the chair, so Fayre called to her, "Aunt Anna, can you come in here with Kip? I'm going to see Dr. Todd to his car."

"Certainly," Anna answered, and came back into the living room, a stack of hand towels in her arms. "You go out, and Kip and I will have a chance to talk. Okay, Kip?"

"Sure, Aunt Anna." He was starting to sound drowsy, and Fayre gave Giles a questioning look as he held the door for her.

"Don't worry about it. He's bound to be tired after a prolonged session like that one. The trank will keep his anxiety from kicking over and let him relax a bit. If he doesn't seem to be feeling better when I see you on Monday, bring him along and we'll have him checked over. All right?" He had taken her hand again as they neared his car. "I don't like to think of you getting so worried. It's not a way to get over . . . whatever it is you've got." He touched her hair with his free hand. "Is there going to be another time, Fayre?"

"Of course. We'll talk about it Monday, after I've had a chance to think, and when I'm certain Kip's okay." She tried to smile, but her mouth was unsteady and she sighed.

"Oh, Fayre." He looked into her face. "I wish I could tell you. I can't."

"On Monday. We'll work out a time, somehow. I want to see you. There's a lot we haven't said yet, or done." She reached forward and pulled his head down so she could kiss him. "Don't worry. We'll have time."

"Good." He glanced back toward the house. "You'd better get back in now. And if anything happens that worries you, no matter how trivial or small, you'll call me, won't you?"

"I'll call you," she said, and he was sure it was a promise.

Sunday evening was pleasantly warm and Giles had sat out on the balcony off his dining room, looking toward the ocean and the lights at Half Moon Bay. He hardly heard the phone the first time it rang, and then had to race to get it. "Hello?" he said rather breathlessly.

"Well, you're home," said Hugh Audley. "I called twice this afternoon and no one answered."

"I was out shopping. I didn't get back until half an hour ago. What's the matter?" He had dropped into one of the chairs at the dining-room table.

"Does something have to be the matter? I just found out that a couple of Inga's cousins are coming into town next weekend and I've got tickets for the symphony on Saturday. Mozart and Mahler, if you like them. I'd be happy to let you have them. Or, if you're feeling virtuous, you can pay for them."

Giles laughed. "You are the most persistent . . . Hugh, where did you come up with this farradiddle?"

"Farradiddle? Inga's cousins won't like being called that. And what the hell? You're the one who might have the most use of them. Think of them as bait," Hugh said.

"Bait?" Giles had been about to refuse, but the word caught him. He did not know if Fayre liked symphonic music, but it would be a good reason to see her again. "Okay. I'll take them."

"Great. I'll tell Veronica. She had second refusal on them, but she doesn't like Mahler." He hesitated. "She said you were the one who told her to contact me about a shaman. Is that right?"

"You seemed the likely choice," Giles said. "Have you found her one?"

"I think so. There's a woman in the South Bay, and everyone speaks highly of her as a white witch. Alice Hartwell, I think she's called. She's agreed to do a counterspell for that patient of Veronica's, Limmer, his name is. She told Veronica that it might not do any good, but if Veronica understands that, she's willing to give it a try. A respected neurosurgeon and a psychiatrist advocating witchcraft. Scandalous!"

"Coming from you, it's a compliment," Giles said, unwilling to trade insults with Hugh. "I'll get the tickets tomorrow, before I leave. Come by my office about five-thirty and I'll give you a check." He stared into the kitchen, enjoying the sight of the newly stocked shelves. Fayre and he could spend the time alone, with nothing to take them away from the house. He would see her at two the next day and he'd tell her then about the groceries. It would amuse her, he decided. "Thanks for thinking of me."

"Glad to do it. But think of me, surrounded by cousins from Indianapolis. The things I do for friends." He gave a low chortle. "See you tomorrow."

"Yeah. My regards to Inga." He hung up and went into the kitchen, trying to make up his mind what to have for supper.

"How's Kip?" Giles asked as he finished the examination.

"He's fine. He keeps talking about devil-men, but it's turning into a game with him. You did so well with him." Her face had lost the tightness it had had when he saw her last.

"What about Saturday? Will you come to the symphony with me? And perhaps come back to my place for the night?" He was anxious to have her answer, but tried not to press her.

"Someone's got to help you get rid of all those groceries, I guess. And I'd like to spend the weekend with you, Giles. If it's okay with Aunt Anna, and Kip is still doing well on Friday, I'll call you and we'll make arrangements." She had put one hand on his shoulder. "Will that be soon enough?"

It would have to be. "Fine. Now, let me walk you out to your car. I've got to be on rounds in fifteen minutes." He kissed her quickly, fondly. "You've made my day."

"And the same time Thursday, at St. Mathis Medical?" She had pulled on her jacket and was slipping on her shoes.

"I'll be there. You're doing very well, you know. I'm not saying that just to reassure you." He put both hands on her shoulders.

"I know. You lie so badly." At last she broke away and started out the door toward the stairs. "I'm feeling better.

There's lots of reasons, but you know what the most important one is."

He smiled broadly. "I had hoped it might be. Fayre . . ." He stopped in the door as he held it for her.

"Yes?" Those clear, direct eyes of hers shone into his.

"I . . . I'd rather lose an arm than lose you. No, that's not what I mean. I want you in my life. It's not a very romantic way to say it, but I don't know how else . . ."

She touched his cheek. "I know what you mean, Giles. Truly." She was out the door then and she turned and waved as she started down the street.

"Dr. Todd, Dr. Todd. Paging Dr. Todd," the PA system said in its electronic nasal voice. "Dr. Todd, you have an emergency call. Dr. Todd, you have an emergency call."

Giles looked up from the patient and turned to Will Hensell. "I've told you what I think, Will. It's your case, of course, but I'd make another series of X rays before I made up my mind."

The paging went on and Will Hensell nodded toward the door. "They want you for something. They said emergency call."

"Yes. I'll get it." He went to the door and looked back at Will Hensell once. He had grave doubts about Will's handling of this case, but he had done all that he could without making a formal issue of it. That question was still foremost in his mind as he picked up the emergency phone in the hall. "Todd here," he said, a trifle distantly.

"Giles!" It was Prentiss Fellkirk and the sound of his voice brought Giles' full attention. "You've got to come down here."

"My God! Is it Fayre?" Was she hurt? Ill? He had seen her the day before and she was fine.

"I didn't think it would hurt her, just coming to the lab. She'd said she'd wanted to see what we were doing. I doubted there was harm in that. She's been so much a part of the project, and it wasn't as if we were going to do any *testing*—"

"What's happened?" Giles almost shouted into the receiver, and one of the nurses passing in the hall gave him an annoyed look.

"She didn't even go into one of the testing rooms. She was only in my office and the monitoring room. Everything seemed fine. She said she was okay. She *looked* okay."

"Prentiss, stop this babbling!" Giles said, controlling his

worry and his temper with an effort. "What's happened to Fayre?"

"She's had another seizure. We can't bring her out."

Giles felt his chest tighten and his hands grow cold. "Of what? What is it?"

"She's . . . it's as if she's gone . . . somewhere else. She doesn't respond. It isn't catatonia. It's . . ."

"I'll be there in an hour. Have Nagy take over and tell him I'll meet him at St. Matis Medical as soon as I can get there. Do it!" He hung up before Prentiss could say anything more. Then he stood still a moment, forcing himself to think rationally, calmly. But Fayre couldn't be harmed. He would not allow it. It wasn't possible. It made no sense. He picked up the white phone again and when the operator answered, he said, "This is Dr. Todd. I've had an emergency come up in this special case at St. Matis. Is there anyone here who can cover for me? I'll have to leave within ten minutes."

He waited impatiently, his ear to a hold tone while the hospital operator made a few calls. He refused to think about Fayre until he saw her. Anything else would endanger her, for it would distort his thinking. Instead, he turned his mind to practical matters. He would call the Highway Patrol as soon as he had arranged a cover here, and it would be possible to get emergency clearance from Daly City to Palo Alto. If he could travel at more than fifty-five, he could take, perhaps, ten or fifteen minutes off his travel time. Those minutes could be very important. . . .

"Dr. Todd?" the operator said crisply. "Dr. Hensell has said that he'll cover for you. Is there anyone else who should be notified? Do you have patients or students to see this afternoon?"

It was an effort of will for Giles to think of such things. "No. There's one patient, but Mrs. Houghton has time enough to reschedule. Please have her do that. And tell Hugh Audley where I've gone. Thank you." He hung up, then went to the nurses' station at the end of the hall. "I have to get an outside line. May I use your phone?"

Nurse Waters looked up. "Certainly, Dr. Todd. Punch nine."

Ten minutes later Giles left the hospital. He had cleared speeding with the Highway Patrol and had got the results of all the special study he had done of Fayre. He drove fast, twice with a Highway Patrol car for an escort, and he kept his mind on his driving. Over and over he told himself it was folly to attempt to deal with Fayre's case now, but the fear of losing her was a specter that drove with him all the way.

□ 8 □

Ferenc Nagy drew Giles to the far corner of the room. "Well?" he said softly.

In the bed Fayre lay, quiet, somehow distant. Her breathing was shallow but regular, her pulse slow, her temperature depressed. She seemed unreal, almost doll-like, her face curiously without expression, not even the expression of sleep.

"I don't know," Giles admitted, rubbing his hands on his jacket pockets. "There's nothing in the tests we did on her that would explain this."

The craggy old Hungarian gave Giles a narrow look. "Care to venture a guess? I agree that there is not much to go on."

"I haven't a clue," Giles said, hating to say it. "I wish I did. How long has she been this way, did you say?"

"Three hours and seventeen minutes, assuming that Dr. Fellkirk's observation is correct about when the seizure came upon her. I've arranged for an IV unit if there's no improvement in the next hour or so. Do you object?" Ferenc Nagy favored Giles with a sardonic smile. "We're no further now than we were three weeks ago, are we?"

"No," Giles said slowly, and turned back toward the bed. "If only there was some indication of *why* this happened, we might have a key." He touched Fayre's cool hand as it lay on the spread, and had a moment of vivid recollection: Fayre's hand pressed against his back as they made love. Almost guiltily he drew away.

"One does not wish to intrude," Ferenc said dryly, "however, I cannot help but notice that your concern is more than clinical. Do you think that entirely wise?"

Giles continued to look down at Fayre's face. "Yes. I think it's about the wisest thing I've ever done."

Ferenc Nagy cocked his head but said nothing more. He came and stood on the other side of the bed. "If I were you,

Giles, I think I might keep your involvement a private matter
for the time being."

"Why?" Giles asked, startled. "I hadn't planned to shout it
from the rooftops, but I see no reason to conceal . . ."

"Until Mrs. Schoenfeld is . . . herself again, it might be
best to grant her as much privacy as you can." He cleared his
throat again.

"You mean that because of this, her feelings may change
and it would be wrong to coerce or embarrass her?" Giles
kept his voice low, but as he spoke he felt both anger and
worry building within him. Perhaps Ferenc was right and
Fayre would no longer be interested in him when she had
recovered. Perhaps he had been an escape for her, a means to
forgetting the terrible experiences she had had, and now that
she was once again in the throes of a seizure, their new relationship might be tainted in her mind. . . . He let his fingers
wander lightly over her face. "Very well, Ferenc, I'll keep
quiet about our relationship. I trust you'll do the same."

"Of course." His eyes met Giles', calmly, steadily. "If you
want my opinion, I think it is good for her to have someone
like you. I think it gives her reason to recover. Unless you
are not happy together?"

"I was happy," Giles said softly. "I have never been happier." Now his fingers touched her hair, and he remembered
the texture of it against his face.

"And she?" Ferenc spoke in a low, compassionate voice.

Giles found he could not speak. He nodded once as he
drew a deep, unsteady breath. Reluctantly he pulled his hand
away from her and gave his full attention to Ferenc.

"Do you know if she said anything to Dr. Fellkirk?" Ferenc had sat down in one of the comfortless chairs by the window.

"No, I don't. I didn't say anything. It didn't seem appropriate. Prentiss has so much on his mind."

"And so much invested in Mrs. Schoenfeld." He motioned
Giles to join him. "I will leave you in a few minutes, and
make arrangements for you to remain here as long as you
think necessary. Then I plan to have something to eat and
I'll look in some time after eight. The nurse assigned to Mrs.
Schoenfeld is Elena Mitabas. She's an excellent nurse. If you
need to leave at any time, Nurse Mitabas will relieve you. Is
that satisfactory?"

Giles looked helpless. "As much as anything can be."

"I feel I ought to interject a question here," Ferenc said

thoughtfully. "Mrs. Schoenfeld is not your only patient, and although she is your greatest concern, understandably, do you think she ought to take all your time?" He laughed once, mirthlessly. "The care you give this woman is the sort doctors only give their patients on TV shows."

Giles refused to be distracted. "I have Will Hensell covering for me this evening. Obviously I'll have to go back in the morning, no matter what. And if there's no change by then . . ." He found he could not continue.

"Precisely. We'll have to make such arrangements as to allow for that circumstance, but I pray it won't be necessary." He got to his feet. "Do you have any idea what might be done for her, aside from what we have done already?"

"No. No. I can't *think*." He was accusing himself.

"Perhaps while you're watching her. I'm willing to try anything reasonable. Well, after I return, we can discuss it." Ferenc had stopped once more to look at the still figure in the bed. "A pity. If this were a stroke, or a tumor, or even a chemical imbalance, there would be measures we could take. But this? What is it?" He did not expect an answer and got none as he went to the door and let himself out, leaving Giles to wait in silence.

It was nearing midnight when Giles decided to try talking to Fayre. Earlier, before the IV unit was brought in, he had asked Nurse Mitabas to help him massage Fayre's arms and legs, but there had been no response. Now, knowing he would have to leave shortly, he could think of nothing else to do. He sat on the edge of her bed and took her nearest hand into his own. For several minutes he could think of nothing to say, and felt almost silly. But the sight of Fayre, pale, quiet, so strangely distant, brought a desperate hope to him.

"Fayre? Fayre, it's Giles. I'm with you, Fayre. I want you to come back to me. I don't know what to do, Fayre. You're still. You're like a shell or a husk, abandoned. If I could draw into you and find you." He felt absurd, but refused to stop. "Tell me where you are, where I must come to find you. I won't let you leave me, Fayre. You can't. You can't." Her hand was cool, limp and soft in his. He squeezed the fingers, hoping for an answering pressure, but there was none. "Fayre, please. Don't you realize how much I want you back? Don't you know that I'd do almost anything to have you back again? I'll do anything but harm you, anything but lose you. If you'll come back, I'd let you go, never touch you again, if that's what you wanted, just to have you real again. This . . . this is like talking to a wall. I think it's folly, but, Fayre, I won't stop. Do something, anything, if this is doing one jot of good. Frown, scream, blink, wiggle your toes, anything." He watched her for a sign. "Oh, Fayre." Had he ever felt so saddened? he wondered. "My dearest, dearest Fayre. I'm so greedy for you. I want you in my life, as much as you're willing to be. I bought groceries, Fayre, and I'm having my piano tuned. If you like, I'll play for you. I play very well. Music says things that there are no words for, and I could tell you things in music, and they would not be awkward or constrained. Tell me you'll listen. Promise me you'll listen."

It was no good, he decided, and he put her hand back on the spread. Not a flicker of her eyelid, not the most minute change in breathing, not even a hint of flush to her face. He stood up slowly, defeat turning his limbs to cement. The thought of leaving filled him with wordless, profound despair. He could think of nothing more to do, and he was still an hour from his house. He would have to leave, and the very idea repelled him. His coat lay over the back of a chair and he drew it on slowly, prolonging the time for leaving. He pushed the switch to summon the night nurse, and stood still, waiting for the middle-aged woman who had replaced Nurse Mitabas at ten. "What is the use?" he asked the air. When Nurse Jackson arrived, he gave her a few terse orders and left the room quickly. He found a phone and tried to reach Prentiss, but there was no answer, and after ten rings, he hung up. It was—he consulted his watch—two minutes to twelve. Where the devil was Prentiss? Giles admitted to himself that there was no new development to discuss, and that, given Fayre's condition, he might as well wait until morning to give Prentiss the unpleasant news. He wondered if perhaps Prentiss had stayed on at the lab, and might be reachable there. Giles pulled out his address book and discovered he had only the switchboard number, and not the private line to Prentiss' office. He knew it was useless, but called the lab switchboard, letting the phone ring twenty-five times before giving up.

Giles was still sitting by the phone five minutes later when Nurse Jackson found him.

"Thank God you've not left, Dr. Todd," she said rather breathlessly as she put one pudgy hand to her bosom. "I was afraid you had."

"What's wrong?" It was impossible to say more; dread had stopped his voice.

"It's Mrs. Schoenfeld," Nurse Jackson said unnecessarily. "You'd better come quickly."

"Christ!" Giles stumbled to his feet. "What happened?" Was she dead? Had she started to convulse? Had she gone mad?

"She's awake, Dr. Todd. She says she must see you."

Fayre was wan and there were shadows under her eyes and cheeks, but at least there was no longer that terrible vacancy about her. Her eyes flew to Giles as he rushed through the door, and she lifted her arms toward him.

"Fayre." He embraced her as he sank onto the bed at her side. He ignored Nurse Jackson's stifled shriek of dismay.

"It happened again, didn't it?" Fayre demanded as she clung to Giles. "Didn't it?"

"Yes, love." He wanted to be reassuring but there was no way to keep the worry out of his tone.

"How long? What time is it? God, what *day* is it?" She drew back to look at him but her hands were sunk, clawlike, into the sleeves of his jacket.

"You've been here since this afternoon. Prentiss brought you here after you collapsed." He wished that he knew how to assuage her terror, and to be sure that nothing hurt her again.

"Dr. Fellkirk?" She stared at him, more puzzled than frightened. "What does he have to do with it?"

"You went to the lab to see him. Don't you remember?" The slow negative shake of her head brought him fresh anguish. Very carefully he began to explain. "Prentiss called me earlier today—yesterday, actually—and said that you'd stopped by the lab to see what was going on, and that while you were in his office, you collapsed."

"Like before?" She had let go of his coat and now her hands were held tightly against her chest, the fists pressed to her shoulders.

"I don't know." He reached out to touch her, but she drew away.

"I went to the laboratory? This afternoon?" she said, her voice rising. "Why? I don't remember . . . anything."

Inwardly Giles was as alarmed as Fayre, but he said, "It might be some time before you remember. You've obviously had some sort of shock, and occasionally there's amnesia about the whole event, even the time leading up to it."

"I had amnesia before and it hasn't gone away." She looked around her. "Who brought me here? Dr. Fellkirk?"

"And Dr. Nagy," he said. "They called me and I came down as quickly as I could. Dr. Nagy and I took turns keeping an eye on you most of this evening. I was about to leave when you . . . came out of it." With an effort he kept his words calm and level, and as he spoke, he reached out and touched her tightly clenched hands. "How do you feel?" It was a question he should have asked before, but had been too apprehensive.

"I don't know. Cold. Frightened. Lonely. Oh, Giles, what is it? Where do I go?" Her breathing was unsteady as she held back sobs. "Giles?" There was a subdued agony in her face that he could hardly bear to see. He moved a little closer to her and pulled her into his arms. "Shssh," he murmured as he held her. "There's time for that later. You're back, and that's all that matters now."

"But it isn't," she cried out. "What's happening to me? What causes it? Why?"

"We'll find out," he promised her and his arms tightened.

"But how? I can't remember. I don't know what happens, or where or why or who does it. Maybe I do it myself. I don't know. I don't remember. I don't remember. I don't remember." Her breath shuddered then, and she began to sob.

Prentiss had agreed to meet Giles at the Medical Center two days later when Fayre was due to be discharged, and in fact arrived shortly before Giles did and was able to meet him as he stepped from the elevator. He seemed less ruddy than usual, and some of his overbearing enthusiasm was missing. As he drew absentmindedly on his pipe, he said, "Good to see you, Giles. So good. I very much appreciate your coming down like this. Frankly, I wouldn't blame you if you decided to wash your hands of this entire case, considering the unconscionable way Mrs. Schoenfeld has been endangered. I do realize, of course, that there is probably nothing you can do that Ferenc Nagy hasn't done already, but dammit, I feel I owe it to Mrs. Schoenfeld to have the best possible care, and I've always known that you're the finest surgeon I've ever met."

"That's a little thick, Prentiss," Giles scoffed kindly. "But I am pleased that you asked me to come down today." It was no more than the truth. Even if Prentiss had not requested that he be here, Giles had made up his mind to see Fayre as soon as she was discharged.

"Thank goodness. I'm so terribly, terribly upset. What a dreadful thing to happen! I had no idea when she came to the lab that she'd react this way." It was the same thing that Prentiss had been telling Giles for the last two days, and Giles was no longer interested in hearing it. His concern was for Fayre, and nothing else, including his old friend's conscience. He contained his annoyance and said, "I understand, Prentiss. Believe me. We agreed, didn't we, that there were too many unknowns in this case. We'll simply have to be more careful until we know precisely what we're dealing with."

"But I feel *responsible,*" Prentiss insisted. "I feel it was *my* doing. I can't help but realize that I *wanted* her to come back into the program, and that otherwise I might have refused to have her into the building when she came by."

"She doesn't remember doing that," Giles said, feeling more disturbed by that than he wanted to admit. "Don't talk about it unless she brings it up."

"Of course not, of course not. But if you'd been there . . ."

Giles felt cold at the thought. He had never seen one of Fayre's seizures, and although he knew that her case would be easier to treat if he had seen one, he hated the thought of what such a seizure did to her. "Prentiss, you can't be certain that her visit had anything to do with the seizure. We'll have to regard it as coincidental, and be thankful that if the seizure was going to happen, that it occurred in the lab where she could get the prompt attention. Suppose she had collapsed in a supermarket? What could have happened to her? It might have been hours before you or I learned it had occurred, and she might have been made worse by inadequate treatment." He was privately horrified at the thought of Fayre in irresponsible hands, which, at this moment, meant any hands but his.

"Then you don't think that the lab might have . . ."

"There's no way of telling, Prentiss." As he said the words, Giles wondered, as he had for the past two days, if, perhaps, there was a connection between this second seizure and Fayre's visit to Prentiss' laboratory. It was tempting to think so, for it made the case very easy, and for that reason, Giles doubted it. He decided to mention one consideration. "It might be that being in the lab again triggered the reaction, but, Prentiss, I question whether it would have happened if there weren't other factors operating." And how very much, Giles told himself, he wanted to learn what those factors might be.

"I hope you're right. It's kind of you to say this, in any event. The devil of it is," Prentiss went on, some of his accustomed vigor returning, "that there's no way to find out for certain without risking another seizure, and that's absolutely unthinkable." Prentiss put his pipe back in his jacket pocket after poking it with his thumb to be sure it was out. "I admit that I'm vastly disappointed. I had hoped to have Mrs. Schoenfeld back in the program again, and soon, but it's not reasonable, or wise, to expect she'll be able to participate for some time."

"If ever," Giles said shortly. They were almost to Fayre's room.

Prentiss took Giles' elbow, stopping him. "Giles, be honest with me. Do you think there was anything at the lab to bring about this seizure? I'm not asking just for Mrs. Schoenfeld now, but for all the others we're testing."

Giles met Prentiss' narrowed eyes and had an odd, fleeting impression that behind the bluff, professorial exterior there was deep cunning. This brought him up short. He had known Prentiss for well over twenty years. They had been boys together. It had been Prentiss' suggestion that Giles come to America. Certainly, Giles allowed, Prentiss had always been fairly self-centered, and now, with so great a risk before him, it was hardly surprising that Prentiss would be cautious, observant. There were many years of Prentiss Fellkirk's life tied up in his research, and all of it was in peril, thanks to the mystifying seizures Fayre had had. Giles understood it well, and was much in sympathy with his old friend, but he chose to answer carefully. "I'm not certain of anything yet, Prentiss. It could be—and let me emphasize that *could* is highly conditional—that some aspect of your research or a particular condition of your setup there might have an unexpected effect on those who are already vulnerable to certain varieties of psychic disturbance. Perhaps there's someone in the program who scrambles the signals for Mrs. Schoenfeld. Perhaps it's like an allergy, and it's triggered by very definite environments. Perhaps it has nothing at all to do with your work.

Really, I can't be any more specific than that. I wish to heaven I could."

"You'd do a sociologist credit," Prentiss said wryly. "You see," he went on more earnestly, "it would be one thing to lose Mrs. Schoenfeld, or even one or two of the others . . . but to have the whole project invalidated by this when we're so bloody *close* . . . My Lord, Giles, it would be wholly disastrous. Not just for me, though of course I won't pretend to be pleased, but for a great many others involved in similar research. We'd be back to the old there-are-things-man-was-not-meant-to-know nonsense. It's *exactly* the pious *garbage* that Alan Freeman's been spouting. It's so utterly demoralizing. And think of the *knowledge* we'd lose. Knowledge is power, my friend. Think of all the *force* that would be wasted!" He released Giles' arm. "Sorry. I get wound up sometimes. But thank you, Giles. I am truly grateful for all you're doing for Mrs. Schoenfeld. I'm certain she is, too."

Only Giles' dislike of Prentiss' ridicule stopped him from telling him then that his concern was for Fayre, not for Prentiss or psychic research. He did not trust himself to do more than nod as he went into Fayre's room.

"Oh, hello, Dr. Todd. I wasn't expecting you," Anna Dubranov said as she looked up from packing Fayre's overnight case.

"Good afternoon, Mrs. Dubranov," Giles said quite formally, and hoped that Fayre would be equally distant.

She was. "To you, too, Dr. Todd. Dr. Nagy said you were coming down. I don't think there's any more information now than there was two days ago, but it was a nice gesture." She looked stronger and the polite acidity in her tone encouraged Giles. Her smile was forced, but it was an improvement on her wretchedness following her seizure. "Have you seen the reports yet?"

"All but one," he said, recalling the maddeningly normal analyses of her condition that Ferenc Nagy had sent him that morning. "I hope, however, that you'll be willing to come up to San Francisco tomorrow or the next day and let me run a few more tests."

She shrugged, resigned. "Very well. Monday afternoon, perhaps. What time?"

"Around four?" He would be able to take her to dinner if she came later in the day. He remembered Prentiss and nodded toward him. "Dr. Fellkirk has been quite concerned about you."

A shadow of anxiety clouded her face. "Oh? Why?" She studied Prentiss, an oddly penetrating look in her eyes. "Because of the program? I don't imagine you want me back for testing, not after this."

Prentiss raised his hands. "Hell no. Not if we do anything that is the least risk to you. If it turns out that it's safe for you to resume work in the program, I'd welcome you back with brass bands. . . . Under the circumstances, though, we must be very circum*spect*. Dr. Todd agrees. Mrs. Schoenfeld, you must realize that an ability like yours is so rare, and we know so *little* about it. You can hardly blame me for hoping that I'll have a chance to work with you further."

"Cautious." She looked at Prentiss again, with that same disquieting stare. "Cautious. I suppose . . ." Then she closed her eyes. "I want to know what happened to me. I want to know why it happened. I want to know what I've done. Dr. Fellkirk, what *did* I do?"

Prentiss glanced quickly at Giles before he answered in a guarded tone, "Nothing to be ashamed of, my dear. You were . . . well, it was very *strange*. It was almost as if you had left us and . . . were gone . . ." His laugh was embarrassed. "Not very scientific, I'm afraid. But . . ." He gestured helplessly.

"And was there anything else in my place, or was I just gone?" She had not opened her eyes.

"To be candid, Mrs. Schoenfeld, I was too distracted to notice. There was so much I wanted to do, and very little time, I thought. I kept asking you to speak. Do you remember that? I think at one point I quite literally *commanded* you to speak." Prentiss was very uncomfortable, and although he tried not to show it, he found the whole drift of the conversation intolerable. Giles, watching him, recognized all the signs: the fast, clipped speech, the hands clasped behind his back so that he would not fidget, the tightness around his mouth. Whatever had happened to Fayre, it had exercised a profound effect on Prentiss, too.

"Did I speak?" Fayre was searching for information, and Giles could feel the force of her concentration across the room. He wanted to stop this peculiar fencing between Fayre and Prentiss, but he feared that cutting the questions short would distress Fayre more than any response Prentiss could give her. "Well, Dr. Fellkirk? Did I say anything?"

"There was an answer," Prentiss said after a moment, adding, "It might not be appropriate to discuss it here."

"Ah." Her voice was at once sad and knowing. At last her eyes opened. "Thank you, Dr. Fellkirk." She sat up straight and turned to her aunt. "I think I'm ready to go now, Aunt Anna."

"Very good. I've got the car out in the south lot, near the fence. Kip's waiting there." She smiled as she mentioned Fayre's boy. "He's missed you, but Sally Rider and I have been with him most of the time, cheering him up. But he's such a smart kid, and he understands that you need to be away." She shook her head slowly. "He can be a rascal, sometimes. Yesterday he wanted to give the Gibsons' cat a bath." Her chuckle was as low and infectious as Giles remembered. "That poor cat. Well, it's time we left. Good afternoon, Dr. Fellkirk, Dr. Todd. It was kind of you to be here. I know Fayre appreciates it."

Fayre shrugged. "Yes, of course. Let me take the case. There's nothing wrong with my body." There was the slightest emphasis on the last word, and a defiance in her posture as she stood that dared them to contradict her.

Anna Dubranov was already out the door when Giles stopped Fayre with one last question. "You'll remember the appointment?"

"I will."

"If you have any new or disturbing sensations between now and then, make a note of them, or call me. Also, I'd recommend keeping a pad of paper and a pen by your bed. You might get an impression in your dreams that you'll want to write down."

She considered him a moment. "Do you mean I might remember what happened?"

Giles knew not to promise her anything. "I'm not sure. It might help. I don't think you should neglect anything that could be of use. Do you?" He wanted to put his arms around her, but there was no way to do it with Prentiss at his elbow. He contented himself with a private, wistful smile.

"Okay, Dr. Todd. I'll keep a foolscap pad on the nightstand. And I'll let you know if anything comes of it."

"Foolscap?" Prentiss said softly when Fayre had left the room. "Clutching at straws, Giles."

"It might work. We might learn something," Giles responded, disliking the scorn in Prentiss' eyes.

"Oh, of course it might," Prentiss agreed in patent disbelief.

"I'll get you a cup of coffee, if you like. Or do you still drink tea?" Prentiss had gestured Giles to one of the modern chairs in his office.

"Either will do. I want to discuss what Fayre said during her seizure, but I can't stay long. I have a patient I must check on." He was still feeling some of the discomfort of his few moments with Fayre. She had looked well, he thought, but so distant, as if she wanted to escape entirely. The thought made him wince inwardly and he glanced at Prentiss, hoping the expression had escaped his keen observation.

It hadn't, but Prentiss misinterpreted it. "A patient? On a *weekend*? I thought you had matters better in hand than that. If it's that important . . ."

"The man is succumbing to a spreading paralysis and we don't know why. Every test we've made comes up negative. It's enough to make me believe in curses." Giles' outburst surprised even himself, although what he said was quite true. He was concerned about this case, this frightened, doomed man, but the emotion had come from his concern for Fayre.

"Curses?" Prentiss' eyebrow raised sardonically. "Why, Giles, I thought medicine had progressed rather farther than that."

"Sometimes I wonder." Giles sighed. "What about the coffee?"

"Oh. Of course. Of course." Prentiss hurried out of the room, slamming the door behind him, leaving Giles to stare into space as he tried to sort out the confusion that filled him.

Yet, when Prentiss had not returned some ten minutes later, Giles frowned, rose, and went in search of him.

He found him in the hallway near the computer room, two Styrofoam cups in his hands, his stance belligerent and a wrathful edge in his voice as he glared at a tall man of lupine face and body whose pursed expression was somewhere between piety and superciliousness. He did not need Prentiss to tell him that this was Alan Freeman, for he had seen him on book jackets and television interviews several times over the last three years.

"Now, *wait*, you medieval theorist," Prentiss was saying, his volume and pitch going up. "You forced your way in here with your high-handed theatrics, and you haven't yet given me a reason not to throw you out!"

Several of the staff had come into the hall and were watching, some with enjoyment, some with apprehension.

Giles recognized three of them from his previous visit, but said nothing.

"We run testing on weekends, Freeman. We have work to do!"

"This isn't work, it's evil." Freeman was the lucky possessor of one of those beautiful voices that tolled like a bell, making everything he said sound profound enough to be carved into stone.

"We've had this discussion before. You lost." Prentiss was not enjoying this confrontation. Giles knew that it was a major effort for Prentiss to control his temper, which was not the eruptive sort, but the kind that expressed itself in cold, systematic, destructive rage. There was a tightness to Prentiss' nostrils, a certain whiteness at the corner of his eyes that told Giles it would take very little to push Prentiss too far.

He stepped forward. "I wondered what happened to you. Is the coffee hopelessly cold?"

For a moment there was no response from either man, then Prentiss looked down at the two cups. "Quite likely," he said in his normal tone.

"We'd better get refills, then. I have to leave soon, and we must talk." He touched Prentiss on the elbow and nodded once to Alan Freeman. "Excuse me. If this were not important, I wouldn't have interrupted."

Alan Freeman had stood up as if struck and his long-jawed ruin of a handsome face froze into an offended stare. "I had not finished."

Giles nodded. "I realize that. But then, neither had I, and I have the prior claim to Dr. Fellkirk's time." Occasionally Giles·found in himself a certain odd gratitude for the aristocratic haughtiness of his uncle, and when he wished, could assume the manner himself. He favored Alan Freeman with a slight, contemptuous smile and nudged Prentiss toward the canteen door.

"Who are you?" Freeman demanded, although he had stepped back from Giles.

"I'm Dr. Todd, Giles Todd. Giles Roderick Daveth Todd." He gave Alan Freeman one short nod before he followed Prentiss into the canteen.

Prentiss sat at one of the small, horridly bright plastic tables. The cups were on the table before him, and his big hands were clenched to keep them from shaking. "You know, it's men like that that make me understand murderers." He laughed once, and it was not a pleasant laugh.

"I wondered why you hadn't come back." Giles sat down opposite Prentiss.

"I *promised* myself I would *not* become angry," Prentiss said unsteadily. "Fine job I did of it. Sodding bastard!"

"Yes," Giles said, and moved the cups aside.

"You put him in his place, though. Your uncle to the life." This time his laugh fared better and he loosened his hands.

"It worked." Giles always had mixed feelings when he assumed that particular manner. Part of him always chided the rest of himself for being a fraud.

"Good thing, too. It *is* a bit of a disappointment not to have been allowed to smash his skull, but this is much wiser." He got up abruptly. "Coffee. Coffee. Not that this tastes *anything* like real coffee; it's more like silt. Better than nothing, I suppose."

Giles said nothing while Prentiss pressed the tap on the four-gallon urn. He was trying to think what it was about Freeman that had most disturbed him.

"Shall we go back to my office?" Prentiss offered.

"Not unless we're likely to be interrupted here. You don't want to run into Freeman again, do you?" He took the cup that Prentiss held out to him.

"We won't be disturbed. The next break in the tests won't come for almost forty minutes. Not but what this batch is probably wholly useless, thanks to that ass." He sat down and glanced once at the first two cups. "What waste. As co-director of this project, I should set an example, don't you think, and use my cup at least once?"

"Co-director?" Giles had been unaware that there was any other person in Prentiss' position. "Who is the other director?"

"Sort of a silent co-director. Miriam Fuchs is in on this too." He mentioned the world-famous researcher with elaborate casualness. "She's in Amsterdam for the year, but if all goes well here, she should be joining us here next February."

So that was Prentiss' academic plum. The most respected, most honored psychic researcher in Europe was part of his project. No wonder Prentiss was so determined to have a real success. No wonder he was anxious to have Fayre back again. "Impressive," he said slowly. "I didn't know you'd met her."

"In Seattle. She attended the conference. Everyone else was . . ."—he swallowed suddenly—"shall we say skeptical? She contacted me a few months later, giving her encouragement

and support. Of course, this must be confidential. I haven't
her permission to use her name publicly until she's satisfied
with the sort of thing we're doing here." He took a deep sip
of the hot, tasteless coffee. "So you see."

"I'm beginning to." Giles nodded.

□ 9 □

The woman beside Veronica Beaufort was of medium height,
middle-aged, stout, dressed with quiet, military neatness in a
dark green suit, wore glasses that almost hid the glint in her
greenish eyes. She carried an attaché case on a shoulder strap
that, from time to time, made a sound that suggested it was
filled with something other than paper. She looked like a case
worker or an attorney. She was a witch.

Giles encountered them on the sidewalk as he crossed Parnasus toward the hospital. "This is Alice Hartwell," Veronica
said with a wicked grin. "You remember, you were the one
who suggested that I ask Hugh to find me a shaman. He
came up with Alice. She's been working on Mr. Limmer."

"Any success?" Giles asked as he fumbled in his pockets
for the new house key he had made that morning.

"It's hard to tell," Alice Hartwell said in a pleasant voice
that had a lingering trace of a Virginia accent. "I think that
he's been fooling around with one of those groups that call
themselves covens and are out for a few thrills. Cocks' blood,
mild drugs, indiscriminate sex, that type of thing. There are
quite a few covens of that sort in the Bay Area."

The light changed and they crossed the street together.
"Are you working on him today?" Giles asked.

"No, I'm here to show Dr. Beaufort a few tricks that ought
to keep Limmer in line." From the way she said it, Giles felt
certain Limmer would improve if he knew what was good for
him. He nodded, saying, "I would have thought, given the
number of universities in the area, and the high level of edu-
cation, that there wouldn't be much of that sort of thing."

"Not at all," Alice Hartwell objected politely, and rose to
the bait. "Wherever you gather together inquiring minds,
some of them are bound to go into less accepted areas of

research. That's the source of progress, eventually. It wasn't so long ago, Dr. Todd, that chemistry was considered a Black Art and the practitioner could be burned for his science just as easily as an herb woman could be burned for giving digitalis, as foxglove, to a peasant with heart trouble. Though when you tally up the burnings, more of the herb women died than the chemists." She smiled suddenly and her plain, monkey face was transformed. "Don't let me get onto my hobbyhorse, please. I've been known to go on for hours."

Giles had opened the doors for the women to enter the hospital, following them into the building. "You express yourself very well."

"I hope so," she said in mock dismay. "I do enough lecturing."

"Lecturing?" Giles said with a hint of disbelief.

"Yes. At those universities you just mentioned." The sharpness disappeared from her voice. "I always seem to be on the defensive around you professional-scientist types. You have some very distorted impressions of what I do."

Veronica came to her rescue. "It was quite fascinating to watch her," she said with genuine respect.

Alice Hartwell dismissed this. "Trivial. Your Mr. Limmer was interested in the show, not the purpose."

"You sound like Hugh on religion," Giles said as they reached the elevators. "I'm afraid I have to leave you here."

"Religion and science are not that far apart," Alice Hartwell said, giving no sign that she had heard his polite dismissal. "And quite often the place where they come closest to each other is in my field. Witchcraft isn't the mummery most people think it is. Only the rankest novice would have believed that ceremony I performed on Mr. Limmer."

The elevator arrived and Giles let it go. "Why?"

"Because it was all ritual and no magic. There was no focus of the ceremony, just a lot of chanting and waving of knives and wands. The worst sort of mumbo-jumbo. It was obvious that he had been dealing with the most rank amateurs. All form and no content." She gave Giles a measured look. "I wonder if you believe me."

"I let the elevator leave," he pointed out.

"That's no answer." There was a militant look to her, although she still smiled.

"Then let me say that I don't disbelieve you. Will you accept that?" He hoped she would, because it was the truth.

"Of course." She started to turn away, then added, "They

aren't all novices, you know." Her mobile brows twitched into a frown. "There are a few covens in the area that are really very powerful. One or two of them are dangerous. Left Hand Path is the fancy term for it. We've got as much occult-babble to contend with as Veronica has psycho-babble, and I suppose you have neuro-babble."

Giles paused, taken aback. "Every profession has its jargon, I suppose," he said stiffly.

"And its babble—for when you don't want to answer a question, or when you want to identify yourself as part of the tribe," Alice Hartwell said affably.

As Veronica laughed quietly another elevator came and went. Giles glared at her. "I don't quite agree."

"I wouldn't expect you to," the self-proclaimed witch said without the least embarrassment.

He wanted to leave now, but he also wanted to shake Alice Hartwell's self-possession. "And you think, then, that there are dangerous groups around? Left Hand Path covens, you called them."

Alice Hartwell was serious at once. "Yes. It would be a great error to underestimate them. Men like Mr. Limmer can become victims of such covens. They're often searching for gullible people, or gifted people to use in their ceremonies. Mr. Limmer might be approached with an offer of initiation that could turn out very badly for him."

Giles glanced up as another elevator arrived and five people got out, one of them Nancy Lindstrom. He returned his attention to Alice Hartwell. "Gullible or gifted—what does that mean?"

"The first is perfectly obvious. The second, well, that would mean those with certain talents. Those covens might want to recruit a medium, for instance." She saw Giles' face and reproved him. "Don't scoff, Dr. Todd. There have been mediums for longer than there have been surgeons. A gifted medium can do quite remarkable things."

"Talking to dead uncles?" Giles suggested sardonically.

"Some do. I don't regard them very much. There are a few who talk to other . . . beings."

"And that's what the dangerous covens are recruiting? Mediums who talk to other things?" At last Giles was beginning to enjoy himself. "Where's the danger in that?"

Alice Hartwell took some little time to answer. "There are persistent rumors throughout the local occult community that one of the covens has celebrated an Oracular Mass." Plainly this disturbed her. "I was telling Veronica about it earlier."

"An Oracular Mass?" Giles asked. "It sounds impressive." His slightly raised brows denied his words. He had heard various tales on his uncle's estate from the caretaker's wife and from a few of the women in the village three miles away. Herb women and summer bonfires were familiar to him, but Oracular Masses sounded as pretentious as some of Alan Freeman's more flamboyant writings on macabre literature.

"Don't mock it, Dr. Todd. It's a very serious business. Only very advanced covens can do it, or have even heard of it." She had all but snapped at him, and her expression showed that she herself was quite apprehensive. "The purpose of the ritual is to gain certain sorts of information, prophetic information. It takes a great deal of skill to do it at all, and generally the Vessel, the unfortunate person chosen to transmit the information, ends up idiotic or dead." She had explained this in a curiously flat voice, and her bright eyes were flinty. "You must want the information very badly to do that ceremony. The cost, if it's bungled, can be very high. To say nothing of the response of the law if the Vessel dies."

"Ms. Hartwell," Giles began patiently, "I respect your intelligence and your sincerity. But don't you think that what you're saying is, well, unrealistic?" He wanted her to agree with him, for he had the first awakenings of genuine dread in the depths of his mind.

"Unrealistic?" she asked with asperity. "I suggest you read the reports in Belgium from three years ago. Two people, a man and a woman, were found dead under what were described as bizarre circumstances. One of my closest colleagues was called in to be part of the investigation. The two had died as part of such a ritual. They weren't murdered in the standard sense. No gun or knife or other violence was used on them, but their minds were wholly destroyed."

"Isn't that a bit melodramatic?" Giles asked, folding his arms across his chest. His irritation was coming back and he wanted to be rid of Alice Hartwell. "Just how were their minds destroyed, and how was that determined? You make this sound like one of the worst stories by Lovecraft."

Alice Hartwell gave Giles a tight, mirthless smile. "The two Vessels were psychics, Dr. Todd. So is my friend. He felt them die."

It had taken Giles almost an hour and a half to get home. A late storm had blown in from the ocean, sending rain and high winds battering at the coast, bringing darkness to the sky more than an hour before sunset.

When at last Giles pulled onto his muddy private road, he was exhausted. His arms felt heavy from tension and although the heater in his Land Rover worked well, he was chilly. As he hurried to his door, the wind-lashed rain added wet to the cold.

He took the time to build up a fire before climbing to the second floor to make himself a supper. Once in the kitchen, he discovered that fatigue had robbed him of hunger, and he elected to heat up some soup, wanting the warmth more than the nourishment. While he set the soup to cook, he poured himself a little brandy and let its fire trickle into him.

"Those old monks had the right idea," he said aloud to his empty house. "All that's needed is a St. Bernard."

He drank the soup from a mug and forced himself to have seconds. His head felt achy and his arms were stiff. He went down to the living room and sat by the fire, attempting to interest himself in a particularly unpleasant mystery Hugh had loaned him. He considered going upstairs and playing the piano, which had now been tuned, but the thought of that cold room and the soreness in his arms robbed the idea of all of its pleasure. Not that the book held his interest. He found himself reading the same paragraph two and three times without any real understanding.

Now that he was alone, his mind kept returning to his meeting earlier that day with Alice Hartwell. He wanted to dismiss her as an opportunist, which she certainly was not. He tried to tell himself that she was a credulous zealot with a new kind of religion and a convert's fervor, but this was not evident in her manner or her attitude. He tried to think of her as irrational, but was forced to concede that did not appear to be the case. The last thing she had told him, before he had retreated to the safety of the elevator, echoed in his mind. *The two Vessels were psychics, Dr. Todd. So is my friend. He felt them die. He felt them die. He felt them die. He felt . . .*

Giles got up abruptly and began to pace the room. It was crazy to believe that Alice Hartwell was right. He knew that his concern for Fayre had triggered this new worry, and the mention of a powerful, dangerous coven had played on his fears for her. But who would be so foolish, so arrogant as to try such a thing? The image of Alan Freeman came to his mind. Freeman was just the sort to prefer the illicit ritual to legitimate research. Giles told himself that he was being irresponsible, clutching at straws. He castigated himself. Just because he could not discover what was wrong with Fayre Schoenfeld, he had to find some ridiculous excuse for his failure. How easy it was, he marveled with loathing, for a sensible, educated, reasonable man to succumb to the lure of superstition. A little frustration, a little anxiety, and his own arrogance created vast, sinister forces that would thwart him. Why couldn't he simply admit that he was baffled? Was it because he could not bear to be wrong? Was it because he believed that medicine should be able to treat all human ills? Or was it because Fayre meant so much to him that this sense of futility was enough to drive him mad? Of all the people in the world, why must he fail Fayre?

He stood staring into the dying fire. At least with witches and covens and evil there were things one could do. He could ask Alice Hartwell to make amulets and talismans for Fayre's protection. He could learn the spells and brew up the potions that would keep her safe. He tried to laugh at this, but his voice broke and again he felt that desolation of spirit that had filled him since she had had the second seizure.

The wind had risen, shrieking off the tumultuous ocean in demented rage. The lights in Giles' house flickered as the electric lines whipped in the gale.

This brought Giles out of his unpleasant reverie. He bent to put more logs on the fire, then went in search of candles. It was not unlikely that the power would fail before the storm blew itself out. It had happened five or six times since Giles had moved into Montara. The candles, he remembered, were in the kitchen, and he had about ten candleholders, simple brass, most of them, in the shape of bamboo.

He had not yet found the candles when the lights went out. In the kitchen he stood up too quickly in the sudden dark and hit his head on an open cabinet door. He cursed comprehensively, secretly grateful for the excuse to swear, then lit a kitchen match and resumed the search.

The candles were behind the aluminum foil in the bottom drawer where he had put them before Christmas. He pulled them out and lit one. The light did not carry far, and though Giles could see a few yards around him, the darkness seemed vaster, more threatening now that he had light, but so little light.

There were several branches of candles burning on the first two floors of Giles' house when he heard the sound of a car through the howl of the wind. He thought it might be one of his neighbors, for occasionally the Lynches shared their kerosene lamps with him on such nights. But he did not recognize the sound of the motor, and the Lynches' jeep had a very distinctive growl.

Curious, Giles went back down to the living room, and before he piled more logs on the fire, he glanced out through a slit in the draperies. Leaves slapped at the window and rain spattered against the glass so that aside from the flash of headlights, Giles could see nothing of his visitor.

The engine died, the lights went out and a door slammed. Giles went to the door and opened it, holding a candle sheltered in his hands as he peered into the dark torrent.

There was the sound of running steps, and then Fayre came into the flickering glow of the candle. She sobbed out Giles' name as she reached out for him.

He was so stunned that he nearly dropped the candle he carried. What on earth was she doing here? he asked himself as he put his arm around her shoulder. "What possessed you?" he demanded roughly, his rush of worry turning his voice harsh. "Driving here on this kind of a night . . . !"

She said nothing. Her face was pressed tightly to his shoulder and she was trembling.

He drew away from her long enough to close the door, and cursed as a sudden gust of wind extinguished his candle. He turned back to her in the gloom. "Fayre?"

"I had to. I had to." She pressed shaking hands to her face, and began suddenly, convulsively, to sob.

Giles reached for her again, and held her tenderly. He knew a certain contrition for his first angry outburst. "You're okay, Fayre. You're safe here."

"I know," she said thickly. "That's why I came to you. I had to. Otherwise . . ." The words were lost.

At this Giles pulled back from her and led her into the living room. There was more light here, from the candles and the fire, and it was warm. The sound of the wind buffeting the trees rose over the clatter of the rain, but now it only served to counterpoint the new emotions fired between Giles and Fayre as they sank down on the rug before the fire.

For some time Giles held her in his arms, saying nothing, while she wept and murmured in disconnected spurts. But at last her tears stopped and her thoughts cleared. She moved so that she could look up at Giles. "I'm frightened," she said in a clear, sensible voice.

"Of what? Of me?" The second question was born of his worry, and she seemed to know that, for she answered the first question.

"That's what makes it so frightening. I don't know what's happening to me. Tonight, when Kip came in and said that he'd seen the devil-man again, I thought it was a bid for attention, or perhaps his dislike of the storm. He's always been frightened of bad storms. But then when he didn't calm down, and all the *noise* started—"

"What noise?" Giles interrupted her.

"I can't explain it. It was"—she gestured helplessly as she shook her head—"I don't know. It was all around, like being in the middle of a hive of bees. It wasn't good to listen to it." Involuntarily she put her hands to her ears. "It was as if the sound were inside my skull, eating away at my mind!" Her voice had risen again, and fear came nakedly into her face.

Giles drew her tightly against him, worry vying with confusion for his attention. Absentmindedly he kissed her hair and murmured a few reassurances to her as he tried to think what might have caused this new development. There had been no sign of a tumor in her tests, and as strange as her behavior had been, he did not want to make another mistake.

"It isn't organic," Fayre said in a calmer voice. "I know it isn't, whether you believe me or not." She became stiff in his arms, and tried to draw away from him.

"I don't doubt your sincerity, Fayre. I never have." He held her, unwilling to let go of her. "And if you're right, it might almost make things easier. But don't you see? I have to exhaust everything I know before I tackle anything I don't know."

"Can't you just trust me?" she pleaded. "Please?"

He felt her desolation go through him, cold and forlorn, and he swallowed quickly to keep back tears. "Oh, Fayre."

She spoke steadily now as she leaned close to him. "I know that. But you're just as limited in your vision as anyone else. You want to fit what's wrong with me into your frame of knowledge no matter how much you have to distort it."

Giles started to protest, then nodded slowly. "It's my training."

"And you're very good at what you do. Truly, Giles. I know your reputation from Dr. Nagy and Professor Fellkirk. No one could do your job better. But there are things that aren't part of your job, and God help me, this is one of them." She clenched her hands on his arms so tightly that he winced. "I don't doubt *you*, but you doubt *me*. Giles, when I tell you that I feel I'm being drawn out of my body and drifting away from it, I'm not resorting to metaphor. I mean that's exactly how I feel." Her shudder was brief but intense. "I'm trying to stop it. That's why I came to you."

"And Kip? And your aunt?" There was no criticism in his tone, but he wondered if he should call them and tell them that Fayre was safe.

"They're down the street, at Sally's place. They're fine." She pulled a few stray wisps of hair off her face. "I made sure they got out of the house. With everything that was happening, and Kip getting so wild . . ."

"How wild?" He rose to put another log on the fire.

It took Fayre a moment or two to answer. "He was almost hysterical. He kept running from room to room, saying he had to find the devil-man or it would find him. And there *was* a very strange noise. I told you about the noise."

"Yes," Giles said gently as he sat down beside her again.

"It was terrible. I can't tell you how terrible. I'm . . . I'm better now, but that noise . . ." She looked toward the draperies as if wanting to see the storm. "That's nothing out there, only wind and rain. This was much, much worse."

"But to drive through wind and rain, Fayre, you might have had an accident. Those roads are treacherous in this weather. I had the devil's own time getting from Pacifica to here." He looked into her eyes. "I worry about you, Fayre. I don't want anything to happen to you."

"That's why I came to you," she said, as if it were painfully obvious. Then she faltered. "You won't make me leave?"

"Of course not." He was inwardly shocked that she should think he would turn her, or anyone, out into that storm.

"Will you make love to me?"

The blunt, anxious question startled him, but he had to admit to himself he had wanted to from the moment he had seen her coming toward him through the rain. He held her face in his hands and kissed her lingeringly. The suddenness of this change in Fayre bothered him only an instant, then he rose, pulling her to her feet beside him. "It's cold upstairs," he warned her.

"It doesn't matter." Her arms went around him and she stood close against him, her eyes shut.

"I've got to bank the fire," he said, the sound of his voice strange even to him. "Wait a moment." He worked swiftly with the poker and shovel, finding it hard to concentrate on his task. When he was satisfied, he reached out one hand. "Come on, then."

They went upstairs quickly, blowing out candles as they went until there was only one branch of them still burning. These Giles set on the table by the headboard before he turned to Fayre.

"Listen," she whispered, for the rain was much louder. There was another sound, a groaning, breaking sound.

"Tree branch," Giles said, holding his arms open for her.

She went into his embrace eagerly, welcoming his kisses and the searching of his hands. In the soft, reddish light, they undressed each other, then scrambled into bed in unromantic haste as the cold raised gooseflesh on their skin. She snuggled against him for more than warmth.

"I wanted you here again so much," he murmured to her as his lips brushed the rise of her breasts. "So much."

They made love long and slowly, each caress, each look, each movement savored. The storm had played itself out before they had exhausted themselves and fallen into sweet, disheveled sleep.

Giles whistled as he crossed the street toward the hospital. He had left Fayre curled under the blankets after getting her sleepy promise that she would not leave until he got home that evening. In the wake of the storm the sky was wonderfully clear and the entire city looked new, freshly painted. He stopped to look toward the leafy density of Golden Gate Park before going into the large building. He was a trifle early, and he wanted to have a few moments to himself before turning his thoughts to the grim world of the hospital. What an incredible night it had been! He was deliciously sore.

"Giles!" Hugh Audley called as Giles stepped out of the elevator. "Just the man I want to see." He walked up briskly. "Veronica told me you were the one who set her onto me in this Limmer thing."

"Limmer? Oh, the witch, Alice Hartwell. How did that work?" He was somewhat condescending and he knew it. He tried to change his tone. "Is Limmer any better?"

"I guess so," Hugh said. "It's Alice. She called me last night, talking about a coven in the South Bay. She said that they're gathering strength again. She thinks they're building up to something big." He was genuinely agitated as he followed Giles to his office. "Alice isn't a hysterical type. If she says that there's something going on, then you can be certain there is."

"That's unfortunate," Giles said, wondering what sort of a response Hugh expected from him.

"Yes. She was quite distressed. She's called a meeting of her coven to try to find out what's going on." Apparently he read skepticism in Giles' face, for his tone changed somewhat. "It's not a laughing matter, Giles. Those people can do some very real damage. Whether you believe in it or not, there are links that can be forged between people, willing or unwilling."

"Naturally. And I do believe that," Giles added with sincerity as he had a momentary vivid recollection of Fayre's overwhelming response the third time he entered her as the storm had flailed its last strength at the windows. All of her was open to him, and he had experienced a kind of intimacy that went far beyond the glorious physical passion consuming him. Their closeness had not ended when their bodies were no longer joined, and the intensity of their emotion sustained itself even while they slept.

". . . and a force called Eilif is being invoked . . ." Hugh broke off as Giles turned toward him. "You haven't heard a thing I've been telling you."

"Sorry, Hugh. I'm . . . preoccupied."

"No kidding. You don't seem depressed, though."

Giles smiled. "I'm not depressed. Believe me."

"I believe you. I can see it." He looked at his watch. "I'm in a bit of a hurry, though. We've got a young woman on the third floor we're very worried about. One of Carey's patients. Ordinarily she wouldn't be within my area, but you know what Carey is. The poor kid's terrified. Carey's got her convinced she's going to die or be hideous or ruined or something equally reassuring. Gordon asked me to have a talk with her. There are times when I'd like to give Carey a little of what he likes to give." He gave Giles' shoulder a squeeze. "I'll try to catch up with you before you leave, but if I don't, I'll talk with you tomorrow. Alice really is worried, and it might have some bearing on that case you've got." He turned down the hall with an easy wave as Giles stopped to pick up his messages and mail from Mrs. Houghton.

"You've had three phone calls from Professor Fellkirk this morning. He's very anxious to talk to you. He wants you to call him immediately." There was an unstated criticism in this announcement, a suspicion that underlay much of her conversation.

"Thank you, Mrs. Houghton," Giles said with a pleasant smile. "I'll call him now. Did he happen to mention where he was?"

"At the lab, he said." She favored Giles with a sniff as he went into his office.

Prentiss picked up the phone before the second ring. "Giles?" he demanded.

"Yes, it's me. You wanted to talk to me?" He guessed it was about Fayre, and was not disappointed.

"I don't know how to tell you this. Mrs. Schoenfeld . . . she's disappeared. I've tried everywhere, even that twit Freeman. Her aunt said she just left the house last night. *Left!* In all that rain." He lowered his voice. "I've called the Highway Patrol, and we're checking with the hospitals now—"

"Prentiss, she's okay," Giles interrupted kindly. "She's—"

"You've talked to her?" Prentiss cut in, and there was a quality to the question that startled Giles.

"Yes, I've heard from her," he said, wondering why he was not telling Prentiss the truth. "She's fine. Apparently the weather and all the pressure got to her, and she took off for a couple of days. It could do her a world of good." He wished he didn't feel quite so smug as he said that. "She'll be back tomorrow or the next day. Remember, you suggested that she should get away for a few days." Fayre had told him that, he remembered, in the slow times during the night.

"But do you know where she *is?*" Prentiss almost shouted. "Do you know that?"

This time Giles lied outright. "I don't, not for sure." He was afraid that if Prentiss knew of his relationship with Fayre, it would be endangered, mocked. *Relationship,* he chided himself. What an empty word. What a silly, overused word. What he and Fayre had was love, and he would not limit it with the addition of "affair."

"If you hear from her again, have her phone me immediately." Prentiss sounded almost angry. "You should have *insisted* she call me. She can't be left on her own. She might have another seizure. Didn't you think of that?"

Now Giles frowned. "I thought of that, but—"

"Then it's damned *irresponsible* of you to assume she's *capable* of dealing with, oh, *anything!*" Again he made an effort to control his voice. "If anything happens to her, I *will* hold you *personally* responsible."

"Prentiss, I appreciate your concern . . ." Giles was both irritated and puzzled by Prentiss' hostility.

"*Concern*? Don't you know what that woman *represents*?"

"Yes, I do." He spoke very quietly.

"And you let her go off to the devil knows where?"

"Prentiss, why are you fighting with me?" Giles asked in a reasonable tone. "You yourself suggested that she should get away for a few days. She's taken your advice. I'm certain that if there is any danger she'll have the sense to contact us."

"I didn't *intend* her to go anywhere *alone*. I wanted her to come *here*, where I could, well, *study* her."

"You mean," Giles corrected him, controlling his anger, "that you still want her in your program and you wanted to find out if she'd respond better in private."

"Well, wouldn't *you*, in my position? I've *got* to have more data on her. Without her, my grant's in danger, and think of what we could *lose* in knowledge if we had to stop now." Prentiss was at his most emphatic, using what Giles thought of as his lecturing voice, pouring a forceful sincerity into his words that would give credit to a commercial voice-over. "And *she's* as eager as the rest of us. She's *anxious* to be in the program again. *Ask* her, Giles. If you don't believe me." This last was very nearly contemptuous.

"Of course I believe you," Giles lied. "But it won't hurt her to have time to think about things. It's good for her to get away from the pressure. Even the sort of pressure you represent, Prentiss. Let her work out her feelings. She'll be more effective if you do. And perhaps there won't be another incident like the last one. Or is that unimportant to you?" He almost succeeded in keeping the challenge out of his voice.

"You and your damned *scruples*," Prentiss said with an edgy laugh. "Very well. I'll go along with you, for now. Precious little else I can do, is there? But, Giles, if you talk to her again, have her call me, here or at home. She has the number, and if I'm not there, I'll have Lupe take a message."

"Lupe?" Giles did not remember meeting anyone by that name at Prentiss' lab. "Who's Lupe? Your maid?"

"No, my private secretary. She does all my notes and manuscripts for me. She's really quite a remarkable woman. You must meet her sometime. She helped me out, that first time Mrs. Schoenfeld had a seizure. Lupe was here until just before the ambulance arrived."

Giles had no response to make to this, so said, "If I hear from Mrs. Schoenfeld again, I'll give her your message. But, of course, I can't guarantee she'll call. I'm certain you understand that." Why was he treating his friend so shabbily? he thought again. It made no sense, yet he couldn't stop. After all he had said, he couldn't tell Prentiss the truth now. There would be no acceptable explanation for Prentiss, or for himself.

"Naturally, naturally. I admit that I'm not being quite fair to you." This wry concession made Giles squirm inwardly and he listened as Prentiss went on. "Mrs. Schoenfeld is my most solid accomplishment on the project, and she's a very *personable* woman. Almost the sort that would make me want to mix work with pleasure, except that might invalidate everything we've accomplished."

For the second time, Giles had no comment. Prentiss' casual lechery often baffled him; now it outraged him.

Unaware of Giles' feelings, Prentiss went on, "You might not have noticed, but she can be a very attractive woman, when she isn't in one of those states. A widow, too, which probably means that she'd like a little stuffing now and again. If she can't come back into the testing"—Prentiss paused to chuckle—"there might be a few compensations, after all."

At that moment, Giles wanted to hang up on Prentiss, but he maintained an icy control as he said, "Yes, she is quite attractive. You're probably right about keeping your distance, though. You don't know how much of her talent is associated with sexual frustration. Remember that celibacy is supposed to enhance psychic abilities."

"Oh, *that* old myth!" Prentiss scoffed. "You should read up on the field some more. There's whole *schools* of occultism that include positively frenetic sexuality." His chuckle this time was richly amused. "One of the few advantages of some of the practices, really, because most of the traditional procedures are amazingly dull. Backward masses, hours of peculiar recitations, all for the most *transitory* effects." He was warming to the subject and Giles decided to let him talk. "You can't *imagine* the sorts of tedium those old-school witches and wizards and alchemists put themselves through. Oh, they got results, after a fashion, but it was by blundering into them, not by any genuine understanding."

"You've studied a lot of it, then?" Giles asked, not really surprised.

"Certainly. Parapsychology ain't all that far from witch-craft, when you come right down to it. But as a scientist engaged in the most stringent research, I've had to pare away the nonsense and the rituals and the superstitions to investigate what is *really going on.*" His emphasis on the last three words was quite heavy, like the pounding of a fist. "It's strange, but the less mumbo-jumbo, the better and more consistent the results. Well, take Mrs. Schoenfeld's case—if this were the sixteenth century, she'd probably be burned or hanged as a witch, and she'd very likely believe that she was, because of her exceptional gifts. The *waste* of it!" Prentiss exclaimed, indignant even at the idea. "We've just begun to explore the possibilities of the mind, the soul. It's *important* that we have the chance to learn everything, everything!"

"Prentiss," Giles said calmly, "you don't have to convince me. Save it for your grantors. If it will make you feel any better, I'll concede that there are an enormous number of things we are wholly ignorant about, and that all of them should be explored."

"My damned enthusiasm!" Prentiss said in mock chagrin. "You're very indulgent."

"Well, what are friends for, if not indulgence?" Giles said with a lightness of manner he did not feel.

"You're right," Prentiss agreed. "Well, thank you very much for your time. And I may call you tomorrow if I haven't heard from Mrs. Schoenfeld." He hesitated. "Giles, if there's anything the matter with her, you *will* tell me, won't you?"

There was a slight hesitation as Giles felt again that strange sense of danger. "Of course I will. You've got every right to know." It was true, and yet Giles could not tell him what had truly happened to Fayre.

"I'll look forward to talking to her again. Tell her that, will you?" That slightly arrogant, imperious tone grated on Giles.

"I'll tell her." He looked up at the clock. "I've got to go now, Prentiss."

"Um. I've kept you far too long. Ta." He hung up immediately, without waiting for Giles to say good-bye.

Giles held the phone, puzzled still more by the odd conversation. Then Mrs. Houghton interrupted his thoughts and reminded him that he was expected to meet Dr. diGiorgio in five minutes.

□ 10 □

Fayre gazed out at the sunset, half-smiling at the subtle changes of color above the horizon. The storm had left the air clear, so that the faintly shining stars were like highlights on a brilliant surface. She put her hands into her jeans pockets, letting the light wind lift her pale hair.

Behind her, in the door to the dining room, Giles waited for her to turn. Supper was waiting for them, but he could not bring himself to say her name and pull her from her reverie.

"In a moment, Giles," she said, still looking out over the Pacific.

"Whenever you want," he said easily. It was a joy to stand there, looking at Fayre, letting his senses recall her; the sound of her voice when she said his name, the cascade of her hair on his shoulder as she slept beside him, the curve of her mouth, the tangy scent of her body, the way the curve of her hip fit his hand . . .

Her laughter was low and happy, and at last she turned away from the splendor of the sunset. "About dinner."

"Waiting for you." He stood aside for her to come back into his house.

It was over the dishes that he remembered to deliver Prentiss' message. "He really is anxious to hear from you."

She stopped drying the stoneware plate and frowned. "I don't want to talk to him quite yet.

Giles felt a spurt of pleasure as well as a quiver of worry. "I know it's difficult, and I admit that I'd rather keep you to myself, but he has a certain genuine interest in you." He began to scrub at the Pyrex bowl where some of the pot roast had stuck.

"It's more than that," she said rather vaguely as she put the plate onto the shelf and reached for the two cups.

"Then call that secretary of his—Lupe is her name, I think. He said you have his home number." Sighing, he took the plastic scouring pad and worked harder on the Pyrex bowl.

"Yes . . ." She put the cups aside. "Giles, I don't like that woman. I don't want to talk to her at all. I can't explain why, except that she raises my hackles. It's probably because she was there when I had my first seizure, but . . ." Her voice faltered. "I don't know what it is. I wish I did. If I could remember what happened . . ."

Giles put the glass bowl aside and reached to hug her, his wet, soapy hands spread lightly on her back. "Don't let it bother you, Fayre. We'll learn something in time, and then it will all be over. You'll be fine."

"Will I?" She snuggled against him. "God, I hope so. I've always known what was going on before. I'm not used to this ignorance. It's frightening."

He kissed her forehead where the hairline began. "Don't worry," he said softly.

"But you're worried, Giles," she pointed out.

"That's different. I'm supposed to worry." This time he kissed her mouth, quite thoroughly.

When they returned to the dishes, Giles said, "If you like, I'll call this Lupe for you, or I'll call Prentiss."

"You won't tell them where I am, will you?" she asked as she looked around the kitchen for the right shelf for the Pyrex bowl.

"Second cabinet on your left there, first shelf. No, of course I won't tell them where you are, just that you're safe and you'll be back in Palo Alto tomorrow or the next day."

Fayre nodded slowly. "I called Kip this afternoon. He was doing fine. Sally's kids like him. He didn't mention the devil-man again, and Aunt Anna said that he slept well, no nightmares, and no real disturbances."

"That's good," Giles said, thinking that he had never believed he liked children until he met Kip. Was that because he was Fayre's child, or because Kip was intelligent and responsive? he wondered.

"I'm glad you like him. He likes you, and he doesn't often get along with adults. Kids can be strangely prejudiced against older people. It might just be because they're bigger, but I think there's more to it than that." She dried the serving spoons and the copper pot in which he'd made soup. "You ought to polish this, you know. It's getting pretty tarnished."

"I know. But I don't like it much. Usually my cleaning lady does it, but I've been cooking for myself so rarely . . ." He reached for a towel to wipe his hands. In the sink the sudsy water began to drain. "Maybe I should get the dish-washer fixed. Then we could spend this time over coffee."

"But we can have coffee now. And that gives us more time together." She put the last of the dishes away and glanced at the stove. "Is there water in the kettle?"

"Yes. I filled it before dinner." He reached to turn on the flame, then nodded toward the dining room. "Do you want to sit up here, or go downstairs?"

Fayre started. "I'm sorry. I wasn't listening." Her eyes were troubled. "I don't understand."

Giles stood very still. "You don't understand what?"

"Oh, nothing," she said, taking control of herself. "It seemed as if someone were calling my name. It's odd." She shrugged, but there was apprehension beneath her casual manner.

"I'll make the coffee." He wanted badly to be busy, for the haunted look of Fayre's face troubled him.

"What kind of a name is Eilif?" she asked suddenly. "Is it a name?"

Now, where had he heard that before? Giles asked himself. It was familiar, but he could not place it. "Eilif? Where did you get that?"

"I don't know." Her attempt at laughter was shaky. "When I thought I heard my name, there was another name. It was Eilif. Is that a place or a person?" She reached out to take Giles' hand. "I'm letting my fears get to me. Don't let it bother you, Giles."

"I can't help it." His fingers tightened on hers.

"You don't want to help it," she corrected him.

He agreed promptly, and would have taken her in his arms once again but the sound of water boiling in the kettle distracted him and he went to make coffee.

"Say, Hugh," Giles called as he was about to leave the hospital, "was it you who mentioned the name Eilif to me? I can't for the life of me remember."

Hugh Audley turned away from his assistant. "Eilif? Yes, I told you about it."

"It." Giles nodded. "It's a place then?"

There was an annoyed frown on Hugh's face as he answered. "No, it's not a where, it's a what or a who." He looked back at the young man beside him. "I know how you feel, Dan, and discussing it again doesn't change it; but you haven't failed, truly. Not everyone can work in death coun-

seling, and it's just as well you admit it and find another way
to help. You don't do the dying any good by trying to stick
it out, since they're the ones we're supposed to help."

The young man named Dan flushed uncomfortably. "I
wanted to do this, though," he muttered.

"I know. And perhaps in time, you will. But you've got to
get over your fear of death, and you mustn't expect the dying
to do that for you. Give it a while, and see how you feel in a
couple of years. Dr. Beaufort gave you an excellent recommendation for working with psychiatric outpatients. You may
find that better for your abilities. Come and see me occasionally." Hugh almost filled the hall with his compassion, and
the young man was mollified. "Yes, I will. Thanks, Reverend
Audley."

Hugh winced at this formal title. "It's still Hugh, Dan.
Okay?" He held out his hand and waited for the young man
to take it. "Okay?" he repeated.

"Sure, Hugh." Dan shook his hand, then took up the
briefcase beside him. "Well, I'll be talking to you, I guess."
He gave an awkward smile, then turned and went down the
hall away from them.

"He seems disappointed," Giles observed.

"Of course. He wanted to be a saint before he was thirty,
and he's being deprived of the honor," Hugh said when Dan
was out of range. "He's got ability, but he's still a pious ass,
all full of charity, ideals and unreasonable ambition." He
shook his head. "Wanted to do a trial by ordeal, and comfort
the dying with his wisdom. One of the kidney patients almost
threw him out of the room."

"Is he that bad?" Giles asked, surprised.

"Not bad, just young and egotistical." Hugh looked at his
watch. "Are you on your way out?"

"I think so. Are you?" Giles did not mention that he had
lost another patient that day. It was too raw a hurt for him to
discuss. He was grateful that he could go home to Fayre, but
he knew she would have to go back to Palo Alto this evening,
and that filled him with sadness.

"Yep. Inga's been complaining that I haven't been home
enough of late. She's probably right. What was it you asked
me?" He had started toward the door and Giles walked along
beside him.

"About a name—Filif." He held the door for Hugh.

"I told you about that yesterday. Don't you remember?"
It was chilly on the street, with a wind coming off the

ocean cutting through the spring warmth. Fog hung off the coast, draining the warmth from the setting sun to nothing. Giles hastily pulled on his jacket. "I wasn't paying that much attention, I'm sorry to say. Was it associated with that Hartwell woman? You were saying something, yesterday, wasn't it?"

"When you don't pay attention, you *really* don't," Hugh said, almost laughing. He was pulling on a heavy hand-knit sweater over his multicolored shirt. "Yes, it was about Alice, whom you insist on calling 'that Hartwell woman.' She was concerned about a coven performing an Oracular Mass. She said that the force they were invoking through their rites was Eilif. It comes from a Teutonic root. 'Ei' means forever, as in 'forever and aye.' Same word, an older spelling. 'Lif' is life, and the name means 'ever-living.' In terms of what that particular force can do, the name is not so much an honorific as a threat." They crossed the street together. "Where are you parked?"

"Down the hill," Giles said, indicating a direction vaguely northwest of where they stood.

"I'll walk with you." Hugh fell into step beside him, and as he walked, he went on. "This coven, whoever they are, are quite serious about what they're doing. They're determined to get prophecies from whatever reliable medium they can force to work for them."

"Hugh, really," Giles said with a tolerant, uneasy laugh. "You make this sound like the Middle Ages. Any minute now, someone will invent the Inquisition."

"I devoutly hope not," Hugh said quite seriously.

"Surely you don't believe this, do you? Oh, I'm certain that there are people who indulge in all sorts of foolishness for sexual gratification or power and ego trips." He thought of Alan Freeman, and wondered if the imposing professor dabbled in Black Masses and other occult practices. He seemed the right type. He passed the simplified statue of the University of California bear that stared outward in the general direction of the Golden Gate. "I like that bear," he remarked.

"You don't get me off the subject that easily. I like the bear, too, but it's not what we're discussing." Hugh was strangely autocratic as he regarded Giles. "How do I convince you that there is something going on, something very dangerous? Why did you ask about Eilif?"

"I remembered you mentioned it last night." He shied away from saying that Fayre had asked about the name.

"Did you? Why?" Hugh didn't wait for an answer. "Was it anything Fayre Schoenfeld said?"

Giles tried to conceal his surprise. "What does she—?"

"Because if it was," Hugh went on ruthlessly, "then it might mean she's the target of the coven's use. Which would mean that she's in a great deal of danger." He fell silent and waited for Giles to speak.

Giles was glad for the steepness of the hill, since it gave him an excuse not to talk while he wrestled with the sudden conflicting emotions that rose in him. Could Fayre, his lovely, loving Fayre, be the victim of a crazy cult that sought to use her particular talent for their own ends? "It's ridiculous," he said with little conviction.

"Of course," Hugh agreed, his tone one of flat contradiction.

Another, more pressing consideration rose in Giles' mind. "Why did you ask me about Fayre Schoenfeld?"

"Lord God protect me from brainy simpletons," Hugh said to the air with a gesture of impatience. "You go wandering around behind invisible walls three feet thick, you blame yourself for things over which you have no control, you look like you're heading for one humongous crack-up, and then you come in whistling, you're smiling, you've stopped berating yourself, and when you mention Fayre Schoenfeld, you do it *so* carefully, well, what else should I think? The care you're taking of that woman is far beyond any medical requirements."

"Her case is special," Giles said emphatically. "I've never seen anything like her problem before."

Hugh nodded sagely. "I don't doubt it."

"Stop being smug," Giles snapped. Then he felt another pang of concern. "Hugh, don't mention it to anyone, will you? Please? It's no one's business but ours."

"All right, if that's what you want. But we aren't all blind, you know. Veronica wanted to know what had happened to you to turn you human again. Neither of us thought Prudence was responsible."

Giles pointed out his Land Rover. "Do you want a lift back to the parking lot?"

"No, thanks. Tell me about Fayre Schoenfeld."

His mouth tightened to a thin line. "No, Hugh, I don't think I will."

Hugh shrugged. "If you like. I only hope that you learn to trust your happiness enough to share it." His grin turned impish. "I'm nosy, remember? All those years as a journalist did it. I can't help it."

The grin was infectious. "You mean you don't want to help it," Giles corrected him as they came up to the Land Rover.

"I've never denied that." Hugh waited while Giles unlocked the door. "Think about what I told you, Giles. I'll see you at staff meeting in the morning."

"Okay." He climbed into the driver's seat and started the engine. "Tomorrow morning. Thanks for . . . cooperating."

Although Hugh seemed inwardly troubled, he gave Giles his familiar easy smile. "Whatever you want." Then he stepped back as Giles swung away from the curb and into the street.

"I wish I could stay another night, Giles," Fayre said very slowly. "I want to stay here with you."

"Then do." His throat was strangely tight. "Stay as long as you want."

She put her arms around him, her body excitingly familiar next to his. "You're tempting me."

"Good." He kissed her for what seemed the fiftieth time since he had got home little more than an hour before.

She looked up at him. "Don't make it so hard for me, Giles," she protested gently, then a mischievous light came into her face. "And don't you dare say what you're thinking. You're outrageous."

Giles laughed low in his throat. "Well, if I can't say it's hard, will you let me demonstrate?" He had never exchanged banter like this with Prudence, who would have been shocked if he'd said he had an erection outside of the privacy of their bedroom, let alone joked about it. Had she changed, he wondered fleetingly, since she had gone to Dario? He hoped that she had, that she had learned truly to enjoy her body.

"Hedonist," Fayre murmured.

He held her more tightly to him, the pressure of his stiffening penis against the line of her hip firing his need for her.

Fayre closed her eyes a moment. "Giles, please. I won't be able to keep my mind on driving if you do this to me."

Reluctantly he released her. "I can't argue with that. It's a difficult road, and I don't think I could stand it if anything happened to you." As it was, he knew he would worry until she called, saying she had arrived safely.

"If you feel that way, you can follow me back to Palo Alto," she suggested, a touch of indignation in her words. "I'm not a fragile infant, Giles. Not that I wouldn't be glad of your company."

"In a car behind you?" he asked incredulously.

"Anywhere. I don't need you in the seat next to me to be with you. You can sit in front of the fire and read if you prefer. I can reach you there, if I want to." Suddenly she started to grin. "You aren't comfortable with it yet, are you? You revel in it, and you refuse to believe it exists. Well, I've never known quite what it is, but I do know it's foolish not to trust it."

"You call it 'it.' Don't you have any better idea than that?" He had one hand on her shoulder. "It's my training. Weird powers are outside of my learning." He kissed her lightly again. "Give me a little time, Fayre. I've got thirty-nine years to set aside, and it isn't easy."

"Easier than you think," she said. "Compared to when I met you, you're wide open."

He recalled Hugh's words as he left the hospital. "Apparently I am." He stood back. "Would you like me to follow you?"

"That's not necessary. It probably isn't desirable. You'd distract me even more." She went across the parking area and waved. "I'll be back in a few days."

"Thank God." He was entirely sincere. The thought of being without her for more than a day was almost physically painful to him.

"You'll get over that after a while," she said as she started to open the door. "It's the newness."

"I don't think so," he said. "You might be right, but I doubt it." He was about to turn away so that he wouldn't have to watch her go. "Call when you get home."

"Of course. Otherwise you'll send me the jitters all night, and that won't . . ." She broke off. "Damn!"

Without being aware of his actions, Giles turned and hurried toward her. "What is it? Are you all right?"

"I'm fine. It's this tire!" She kicked at the left-front tire, which was sagging. "It's almost flat."

"I'll change it for you," Giles offered, relieved that it was the car and not Fayre that needed help.

"You can't. The spare's flat, too. I was going to take it in tomorrow, after my mid-month check came in. It's always a few days late, and I couldn't afford to replace the tire until now. Oh, shit!"

Giles glowered at her. "Do you mean that you came driving over that road in a storm *without a spare tire?* Christ, what would have happened if you'd had a flat then?"

"But I didn't," she pointed out reasonably. "It was important to see you." She touched his anger-thinned mouth. "I was safe, Giles. Truly."

He waited a moment before speaking. "How are the other tires?"

"Not bad for retreads. I can get a couple thousand more miles out of them." She was still staring down at the car.

Abashed, Giles realized he had little or no idea about Fayre's financial situation. He had assumed that since St. Matis was an expensive and private university, she was well enough off to meet general expenses, but now he wondered if it were so. A widow with a child, living with an aunt, perhaps it wasn't just for the free baby-sitting or the sharing of scut-work. Perhaps Fayre had no choice, and was getting by on much less than he had assumed. He should have asked. He had been stupidly complacent about her circumstances. He had always deplored doctors who ignored the financial reality of their patients' lives, and now, with the one person he should have learned about, he had joined the most arrogant of his colleagues.

Her voice interrupted his silence. "I'm not broke, Giles, but it's true that I don't have a couple of hundred bucks lying around to pay for extra tires."

His next question embarrassed Giles. "Do you need money?"

"I need tires. I have a little money. Harold left military and some private insurance, enough to take care of Kip without hardship. I've got a small trust from my father's estate—it pays me about three hundred a month. I've had small scholarships and a few study grants that Dr. Fellkirk has arranged for me, but considering the way things are turning out, I might not have any more of them. I've done part-time work off and on. It'll be another year and a half until I get my MS, and I'm careful with money. I'll make it, and then I can get a much better job. I want to have a career in the humaner sorts of experimental psychology, maybe in parapsychology. In a couple of years I will." She touched his arm. "Thanks for caring."

He glanced at her battered old Volkswagen. "Look, I'll drive you home tonight, and pick you up tomorrow evening. In the meantime I'll arrange for the tires. You can take your car home then. And if you don't want the tires as a present, you can pay me back later. You've got to have reliable transportation if you're going to come to see me, and I don't intend to let bad tires get in the way of having you with me."

She gave him a provocative smile. "In fact, you're only helping me out of a deep sense of selfishness."

"Naturally."

"You keep telling fibs like that and your nose will grow," she said quietly. "But I'll go along with the plan. I want to be with you, too."

Anna was delighted to have Fayre home again. "That Professor Fellkirk has called several times. I can't tell you how concerned he is about you."

"You didn't tell him where I was, did you?' Fayre asked, looking uncertainly at Giles.

"Certainly not." She nodded happily. "I didn't think you wanted to be interrupted. Of course Dr. Fellkirk means well, but I imagine he would have insisted on visiting you, and that would not have pleased you."

Giles laughed aloud. "I gather you approve. Why?"

Anna Dubranov opened her bright little eyes very wide. "I trust Fayre. If she trusts you enough to go to you for help, then I trust you, too. It's difficult for Fayre to be happy, and she's happy with you. I'd be a poor excuse for an aunt if I objected. She's a grown woman, and a sensible one." She picked up the embroidery she had set aside when Fayre had come into the house.

Giles stood watching, feeling uncertain. "Anna, I don't know . . ." He stopped again. What did he want to tell this unpretentious middle-aged woman? That he loved her niece? Did he? Or was this his last desperate lunge at youth? Was he trying to escape from fear and disenchantment and stultifying age? The possibility had nagged at his conscience for the last week, and with the growth of his passion, the questions had become louder, more persistent. Was this an oddly delayed rebound from Prudence, a bolstering of his esteem now that his ex-wife was marrying someone else? Was he running from his increasing fear of failure? Knowing that some of this turmoil must show in his face, he compromised and said, "It's very new to me."

Kip had come into the room and was talking quietly and earnestly with his mother, and Fayre had bent to listen to him. Then she straightened and looked at Giles with troubled eyes. "Giles, don't . . ."

Anna's bright currantlike eyes went swiftly from Fayre to Giles and she said, "I've got some laundry to go into the dryer. If you'll excuse me . . ." She started toward the door, then stopped. "Kip, did you turn off your train set?"

"Sure. I think." He smiled winningly at his mother's aunt. "I'd like to turn it back on. If I get it set up right, maybe I could show it to Dr. Todd. You like trains, don't you, Dr. Todd?"

Giles had never seen or operated a model train in his life, and had no idea what he should say. It was obvious that the boy wanted to show off his treasure, and Giles liked Kip. "I know I'll like yours."

"Then come along and get it ready," Anna said, holding the door by the small dining area open. "It's in the garage," she explained to Giles. "It'll take about ten minutes to get everything taken care of. You can come out then. Don't mind if I haven't finished folding the clothes." She patted Kip's shoulder as he slipped by her and closed the door behind them.

"She's very deft, your aunt," Giles said to break the awkwardness.

"What's worrying you, Giles?" Fayre did not come near him. Her hands rested on her hips and there was a determined line to her jaw.

"Nothing. Nothing real. I don't know." He sank into the fake Victorian chair by the front window.

"Do you want some time to yourself?" The words were calm and only the whiteness around her eyes revealed her upset.

"I . . ." He looked up at her. "God forgive me, Fayre, I'm not sure. I want you. Jesus, how I want you. And that worries me. What if it isn't you I want, but something else? The guy that used to be chief of neurosurgery is living on a commune in Mendocino. Terry's happy, but he's running. It's the only way he can live. I don't want to be like that. But what if this is the same thing, only disguised? What if I'm kidding myself about you? Don't you see? I love you so much, I think it would kill me if it weren't real." He put his hands over his face. There was panic inside him that gnawed at his throat from the bottom. His jumbled emotions, now freed by words, crowded in on him like a suffocating force.

"You don't want me to drive without a spare tire," she pointed out. "That's not the usual ploy of an escapist."

Giles was inwardly shocked to hear himself giggle. He rubbed his eyes to avoid looking at her just yet. "Hugh's been lecturing me about a middle-age crisis, and I guess he's right and this is it. What a sodding bore!"

"Does it make it easier to call it that?" Fayre had come closer but she made no attempt to touch him.

"Labels always make things easier. That way a diagnosis is, really, a label. Yes, they make it easier. Not better, not clearer, not more right, just much easier. It's as seductive as cynicism, and there's all sorts of pressure to give in to it."

"Is that what you're doing now? Giving in? Succumbing to a label you don't really believe in?" Fayre put one strong hand on his shoulder. "What do you want, Giles?"

"All the other touching," he blurted out, and turned startled eyes to hers. "I . . . What I mean . . ." What had he meant? he asked himself.

"I know," she said, nodding, and he could read in her expression that she did, indeed, know.

His arms encircled her waist and he pressed his face close to her, the curve of her breasts against his forehead. "Someday, someday, will you explain it to me?" He knew that the touching he meant was more complex than the meeting of flesh, but he had no words to tell her this.

"Explain what? So you can have another label?" She put her hands on his soft brown hair. "You don't need an explanation. There isn't one. There doesn't have to be."

"Why not?" How could something that had taken over his life more completely than an invading army could have done have no name and no explanation?

"Giles, when you're playing the piano, how do you know when it's right?" Clearly she didn't expect an answer, and when he tried to give her one, she put her fingers to his lips. "Come on, you've got to see Kip's train set. It's very impressive, really. He did almost all of it himself. I try to get him another engine or car every couple of months, and sometimes he does odd little jobs to buy something he wants particularly."

"Trains," Giles said, accepting her refusal to talk any more about his confusion. He followed her toward the door on the far side of the dining area. It really was a very small room—

nicely furnished, but nothing fancy except the hutch, and that, he guessed, had been in the family. Again he felt uneasy guilt pricking at him. If he had looked at the house more closely when he had been here before, he might have realized Fayre's circumstances and done something—what?—about them.

"Coming?" Fayre said from the doorway. "And if you buy an armload of train-set accessories, I'll never speak to you again." Laughter took the sting from her threat, but he knew she would not tolerate his intrusion into her life through money.

The concrete area behind the garage had been designated by the builders as a patio, but nothing could have made that dull white square more than what it was—an extension of the foundation of the garage. On the far side, against the fence, there was a makeshift greenhouse, and through the glass panes Giles could see ranks of pots on flimsy shelving. "Your aunt's?" he asked.

"No, mine. I like gardening." She opened the door at the rear of the garage. A light glared in the otherwise dark room, and it made Fayre's face ghostly pale.

Anna Dubranov nodded from a few feet away. Her arms were full of freshly folded towels that she was loading into a basket. There was a crumpled mass of sheets and pillowcases at her elbow. The washing machine was running and so was the dryer, making a strange counterpoint to the running of the model trains.

"We got the table at a flea market. For six dollars. Kip fixed it up himself," Fayre said softly, with amused pride.

Hearing his name, Kip looked up. "It's great, isn't it?" he asked as three separate trains caromed around mountains and across little bridges and through tiny cardboard towns. Kip watched all this with intensity. "I gotta keep track of 'em, or there might be a wreck."

As he looked at the elaborate train set, Giles realized that while he seemed immune to the charm of the little engines, he was captivated by Kip's delight. "Show me how it works, will you, Kip? I've never seen one of these in action before."

"See?" Kip said to his great-aunt. "You said he wouldn't be interested, and he is!" His young face glowed with triumph as he began a careful, painstaking demonstration.

"I should have called Professor Fellkirk hours ago," Fayre said as she refilled Giles' coffeecup for the third time.

"Call him in the morning. It's almost nine and I haven't any idea if he likes to be disturbed at night." Giles was seated on the other side of the little round table in the closet-sized space that was designated a breakfast nook.

"Okay. I don't feel much like talking to him tonight, anyway." She touched Giles' hands again. "What time tomorrow?"

Giles thought for a moment. "I'll be leaving the hospital a little late. We've got a difficult case. Hugh's asked me to spend a little time with the woman. If I leave by seven or seven-thirty, you can expect me here about eight-thirty. If I'm going to be later, I'll give you a call." The coffee was percolated and had a metallic taste that he disliked, but he drank it gratefully, glad for the excuse to remain with her a little longer.

"I'll be ready. Do you want me to stay the night?" She asked it with the same directness that occasionally disarmed Giles.

"Of course. Do you want to stay?"

"Yes." She lifted his hand and kissed it.

"And you can follow me in to San Francisco for your checkup. You're scheduled for Friday, aren't you?" He wished he could sound as casual, as reasonable as Fayre did.

"We could go in the same car. It might make more sense, and it would give you another excuse to keep me out at your place another day." She was teasing him, very near outright laughter.

"Fayre," he said, so oddly that the smile faded from her face at the tone. "Come live with me." *And be my love,* he added to himself, remembering Marlowe.

She started to shake her head.

"There's room for Kip. There's even room for his train. We've got schools out in Montara, well, in Half Moon Bay, and there's a bus. I've got two acres of hillside he can play all over. There's the beach. He likes the beach." He said it all eagerly, wanting to postpone the moment of her refusal.

"Is is Kip or me you want?" Fayre's eyes did not mock him, though her question did.

"You. Both of you. I like your boy. And you won't come without him. I'm trying to think of your position, what you'd be concerned with." Until he pictured her in his house, each day, sharing meals and toothpaste, he had not been aware of how empty his life felt without her.

"What about you?" She had tasted her coffee automatically.

"What about me?" he echoed.

"You're telling me about schools and beaches and real estate as if you're the chamber of commerce. I'm not interested in those things primarily. They're nice, and they're important, some of the time. But what about you?" She started to rise to pour more coffee, then thought better of it. "Do you want me out there, Giles?"

"Christ, don't you know that?" he demanded, almost upsetting his coffee as he reached to touch the smooth, firm line of her lips. "You, of all people?"

She nodded, then said in a small voice, "When I want something very much, I don't trust feelings that confirm it. It might be wishful thinking." She sighed, getting a grip on herself again. "I have to finish up this semester, and I can't just move out on Aunt Anna. She can't afford to have me leave without making other arrangements. I have studying to do. And both of us need a little more time. You said yourself that all this is contrary to thirty-nine years. It's important, I think, that we're a little more comfortable. Otherwise . . ."

"Otherwise what?" Giles said when she had stopped speaking. Now that he knew she was willing, he found he no longer needed to insist on a response. He stood slowly, strangely, wonderfully calm, as if the tempests in him had turned to a lucidly clear confidence. "If we have more time together, then we can worry about otherwise." He had almost told her that she was as necessary to his well-being as amino acids. Not very romantic, but certainly true. The thought that she might not want to stay with him was more terrifying to him than his fear of earthquakes. He cared for her with the same intensity that he cared for life itself. He hoped to God that it was all real.

"What a skeptic you are. What an idealistic skeptic," she said, shaking her head. "I'll think about it. But I'll need time to work things out with Aunt Anna and Professor Fellkirk, and Kip." She laced her fingers through his. "There's a way."

"We can talk about it tomorrow." He felt almost giddy as he said it. She would be with him again tomorrow, and they would talk about living together. Fayre Schoenfeld wanted to live with him. He bent down to kiss her. "Tomorrow."

"I'll walk you to the door," she said, rising into his arms.

□ 11 □

The narrow, rutted road wound between high, well-clipped hedges and massive gates. Occasionally Giles could see lights on the fronts of sprawling, elegant buildings behind screens of trees. Woodside was a rich, horsey community with a kind of self-conscious small-town look. The poor roads were part of the look. They were also part of Woodside's wealthy citizens' civic stinginess, Giles thought, as he at last found the small lane that led to Prentiss Fellkirk's house.

Since his talk with Fayre the night before, he had been uncertain about her position with Prentiss, and now that he himself was so committed to her, he had decided that he owed it to his old friend to be a little more open with him.

Five cars were parked in the wide driveway that led in a graceful curve to Prentiss' home. Giles pulled his Land Rover in behind them, and wondered if it was an appropriate time, after all, to talk with Prentiss. He had almost decided to leave when the door to the house opened and a tall, slender woman with short-clipped dark hair stepped out and came toward Giles' car.

"Are you lost?" the woman called when she was a little nearer. Her voice was low, enticing, and she projected a sensuality that astounded Giles.

He had just got out of his car. "This is Prentiss Fellkirk's house, isn't it?" he asked her as he closed and locked his car door.

"Yes."

"I'd like to see him. I'm Giles Todd. We've been consulting on a case." He did not add that they were old friends.

The woman smiled, then shifted her stance so that her hips thrust forward. She was wearing a long, clinging tunic over a straight dark skirt that was slit on the right side almost to her hip. From the drape of the cloth, Giles knew that she wore no underwear. "Giles Todd. I'm Lupe, Dr. Fellkirk's private secretary. He's told me a great deal about you. Won't you come in? We're having a meeting here tonight. . . ."

"Then perhaps I'd better come another time." Giles was

determined to see Prentiss, but he made the proper protestation. "I'll call him tomorrow."

Lupe moved a little closer and put her arm out to snag his elbow. "I'm sure Dr. Fellkirk wouldn't think of it."

Giles remembered that Prentiss had intimated that this Lupe was more than a secretary to him, and Giles recognized the dramatic allure of the woman as being of the type Prentiss found most desirable. He let her draw him toward the house, and smiled slightly as her thigh pressed against his as they walked. "I won't be long, Lupe, but there are a few things that Prentiss and I should discuss about Fayre Schoenfeld."

"Yes," Lupe said, with a touch of breathlessness in her voice. "Mrs. Schoenfeld. Dr. Fellkirk is very interested in her. She has amazing abilities. Amazing."

Was she jealous? Giles wondered as he glanced at Lupe's profile. The severely cut hair framed her face like a helmet and shone as if it had been waxed and buffed. Her ripe, wide mouth was petulant; then she turned to Giles and smiled. "We've been worried about her. Dr. Fellkirk was so grateful when you took her case. The trouble he had with Dr. Nagy . . ." She stopped, shrugging.

Prentiss had made no mention of trouble with Dr. Nagy, and Ferenc, when Giles had talked to him, had not mentioned any disagreements. Giles told himself that it was probably nothing more than a clash of egos, for both Prentiss and Ferenc were strong-willed and inclined to be overbearing. He held the door open so that Lupe could pass into the house. "I'm glad that Prentiss is satisfied with my work."

Lupe motioned Giles to follow her as she crossed the foyer. "We're in the study, Dr. Todd. It was supposed to be a family recreation room, but it's where Dr. Fellkirk does most of his private work. It's that last door on the right, just beyond the dining room."

The hall was graciously wide and lined with tall bookcases, all filled. Knowing Prentiss, Giles thought that there would be a catalog somewhere in the house, and that each area would have its own designation. He glanced at the titles to his left. *Isis Unveiled, Magic and Mysticism, The History and Practice of Magic, The Encyclopedia of Occultism, Magic and Religion, The Book of Ceremonial Magic, The Seventh, Eighth and Ninth Books of Moses, The Secret Teachings of All Ages, The Secret Lore of Magic, The Arts of the Al-*

chemists, The Phoenix, Oahspe. Giles stopped and stared. "My God," he said.

Lupe turned toward him, and laughed once, low in her throat. "That's the occult section. Archaeology is next, then anthropology. It *is* all very peculiar, isn't it? Still, some of these books are really quite rare. *Oahspe,* for example, is very hard to find, but then . . ."—she pulled a book from one of the other shelves, holding it out to Giles—"so is this. *Sino-Iranica, Chinese Contributions to the History of Civilization in Ancient Iran.* And next to that are *The Travels of Ibn Battuta* in three volumes."

Giles nodded. It was typical of Prentiss to have his most controversial or rare books out on display like this. He fingered the turquoise-blue cover of *Oahspe.* "I don't remember him having so extensive a library. Particularly on occult studies."

"Well," Lupe sighed, as if going into a familiar routine— "it's about the only place where you can find any good material on parapsychology written before 1940, and even then, most of it is useless. Some of the ceremonies are interesting, anthropologically. I took my degree in anthro, in fact, on concepts of magic and religion in contemporary Brazil."

"Really?" Giles said politely. "Master's?"

"Doctorate," she corrected him, then replaced the book in the shelf before motioning Giles to follow her again.

For a moment Giles was struck by the oddity of a woman with a doctorate in anthropology working as a private secretary for Prentiss Fellkirk. Then he dismissed the thought. He knew how ruthlessly competitive the academic world could be. Perhaps Lupe had decided not to play those particular politics, and perhaps she liked working for a parapsychologist. With her background, Prentiss would find her invaluable in his work.

The door at the end of the hall on the right was open, and as he approached, Giles heard a suspension of conversation. Then Prentiss' familiar, resonant voice asking why they were being interrupted.

"The car wasn't someone lost," Lupe said. "It's your friend Giles Todd."

As if on cue, Giles stepped into the study. "Sorry to bother you, Prentiss." He glanced about the room. There were bookcases floor to ceiling on three walls, and a large desk at the far end of the room flanked by filing cabinets. In the center of the room, however, was a long table and three large couches. At the moment these were occupied by ten people, only two of whom were known to Giles. Prentiss was already coming across the room, his hand out, a wide smile on his face.

"What a wonderful *surprise*. I tried to call you today, but I was told you were in surgery. Mrs. Schoenfeld is back, thank goodness. She said that you told her to get ahold of me. Giles, I can't tell you how *relieved* I am that she's back." He gave Giles' hand a hearty shake, then motioned to the others. "This is Giles Todd. You've already met Lupe. I'll have you know I couldn't get along without her." He reached out possessively and put one large hand on Lupe's shoulder. "This is part of my study group. You met one or two of them at the lab. We're reviewing the latest test results, comparing them to a couple experimental methods we're interested in."

"Oh?" Giles said, not letting himself sound too curious.

"We've tried trance states for some of the subjects, but the results are unpredictable. Some of them respond very well, with significantly higher scores, and others simply go to pieces. I would like to establish a pattern there, but so far, no luck." Prentiss pulled Lupe closer to him. "Lupe has some ideas, based on her earlier research, that look promising."

"Prentiss . . ." She pouted, turning a little so that her breast pressed against his upper arm.

The others, watching this performance, were faintly amused, which Giles found oddly alarming. One of them said, "Save it up for later, Prentiss."

His laugh was openly lascivious. "Soon," he corrected, and let go of Lupe as he turned to Giles. "Do you want to join us? Mrs. Schoenfeld was under discussion a little earlier."

Giles had been trying to think of a way to introduce Fayre into the conversation, but now that he was given the opportunity, he did not know how to begin. He knew that the longer he waited to tell Prentiss of his relationship with Fayre, the harder it would be, and the more angry—justifiably angry— Prentiss would be at the deception. Yet Giles could not bring himself to discuss Fayre in this disquieting place, with strangers listening. "I don't think I'd have a great deal to say," he ventured. "I'm not at all conversant with your techniques, and I'd probably be something of a fifth wheel. However, I would like to talk to you about Mrs. Schoenfeld when it's convenient."

There was a new tension in the room, as if all ten pairs of

eyes had grown brighter, more glittery. Even Lupe abandoned her overt carnality as she watched Giles.

"Any trouble?" Prentiss asked, an edge in his voice.

"In the last set of tests," Giles improvised, not knowing why he was lying, "we detected certain anomalies in her scan pattern. It may be that it's nothing important, just a passing phenomenon, and that it has no bearing on your experiments. However, until we can check further, it might be a good idea to give her a leave of absence from the project." He was genuinely uncomfortable now, and the feeling in the air was stronger. "I know how interested you are in her talents," Giles went on, almost desperately, "but this could mean that her well-being is in danger." He directed his remarks to the ten sitting down, purposely not meeting Prentiss' hard gaze. "If there is a late-emerging brain dysfunction, we're going to have to be prepared to act quickly on her behalf."

"What do you think is wrong?" Prentiss snapped.

"I don't know," Giles answered truthfully, but he was not speaking of Fayre. "It might be a chemical imbalance, it might be something as minor as a developing blood clot, which we can be rid of through pharmacological methods. Until we have more to go on, I can't say anything for sure. I wanted to talk to you first," he plunged on, as the idea came to him, "because I don't want to alarm her any more than necessary. If you can reassure her that her contributions are of use to you and that you'd want her to resume the project as soon as she's able, I think it might help her deal with any anxiety that she would feel."

"How bad might it be?" Prentiss asked quietly now.

"It could, of course, be very bad. But perhaps it's to the good. This might be part of her talent, and at last we'll have the means to study it as we study other brain functions. Who knows? she might get her memory back because of this." He had added this last as encouragement, but the reaction was not good. The men and women on the couches shifted uneasily, and one of the women whispered furtively to the man beside her. Giles felt a sudden desire to run out of the house, away from the strange, silent, shiny-eyed gathering.

Prentiss broke the mood with an odd, tight laugh. "I hope she does remember, if that will bring her back to the project any sooner. Well." He put his hands on his hips. "Thank you very much. I realize you probably didn't want to tell all of us about this, and it's not difficult to understand why. I'm certain that we'll all respect your confidence, but, to be candid, it *is* quite a disappointment to have this news. You're proba-bly right, though. We should be cautious until you're sure she's well enough. We're running a few new experimental techniques this summer, and it would be wonderful to have her back with us in June. The next new series will begin in August, and that's quite a time away. Still . . ." He nodded and grinned. "If we have to wait, we'll wait."

Giles knew he was being dismissed, and he felt enough of an intruder that he was genuinely anxious to go, but he hated being turned away like an unwelcome messenger.

"Good. I knew you'd understand." Dissatisfied, he started to turn away.

"Why don't you ask Ferenc Nagy to go over the new tests with you, Giles? He might have a few ideas."

To Giles it seemed that the suggestion was made out of malice and that the smile Prentiss favored him with was one of intense hatred. He wished his conscience had a less acute sense of guilt, or that he was a better liar. Rationally, he knew that Prentiss was being sensible, and that ordinarily he would have welcomed the chance to have Nagy's advice. He forced himself to nod appreciatively. "Yes. I plan to call him in the morning. I figured you'd want to know the latest be-fore we started a new kind of monitoring on Mrs. Schoen-feld." Which, he said to himself, was the strangest euphemism he had ever come up with for living together. He would, of course, have to talk to Ferenc Nagy, but that was for later, when he could find a plausible way to keep the canny Hun-garian neurosurgeon away from Fayre.

Lupe slipped by Prentiss, her hand pressing his crotch as she went. She looked up at Giles. "Shall I see you out?"

"If you would, please. Sorry I interrupted your meeting," he said to the room at large. "Since I was on the Peninsula anyway, I thought I should come by."

"Why *were* you in Woodside?" Prentiss asked, so casually that it hardly seemed a trap.

It was one question Giles had prepared himself to answer. "Oh, one of the electronic firms has come up with an im-proved device for probing the brain. They wanted me to have a look at it, and I thought as long as I was here, it was fool-ish to waste the opportunity." It was true that he had been to see an electronic firm about such a probe, but that had been some time before. If anyone checked—why, Giles asked him-self, did he think that anyone would check on him?—they might discover the deceit.

"Sounds intriguing," Prentiss said with a slight wave. "We'll talk about it soon. I wish I had more time to spare, but with so many people . . ."

Giles nodded. "Of course. It was good of you to give me so much time." He shook Prentiss' hand, then went down the hall with Lupe.

At the door she studied Giles. "I wasn't sure what to expect, Dr. Todd. You've been his friend for so long."

"Yes," Giles agreed. "We weren't quite ten when we met. Now I'm almost forty, and so is he."

"Strange," she said, more to herself than to him.

"How? That we should age?" It was meant as a mild joke, but Lupe took it seriously.

"No. That you should be friends." Without an explanation, she smiled and closed the door.

"Hugh?" Giles said into the phone when he had reached the Audleys' number. "Do you know of a book called *Oahspe?*" He looked across Anna Dubranov's living room to Fayre and Kip bent over a book about the history of railroads. Anna herself was in the kitchen making a dessert.

"*Oahspe?* Yes, I've heard of it. It's very, very rare. Where did you hear about it?" Hugh waited a moment, then pressed for an answer. "Do you have a copy?"

Giles laughed. "No, I don't. I saw it at Prentiss Fellkirk's house, in a bookcase filled with occult stuff, and this was one of them. The name stuck in my mind. I thought either you would know or would know someone who knows what it is."

"It was written about a hundred years ago by a dentist from Ohio, whose name was John Ballou Newbrough. He typed the manuscript in a kind of trance, and the first manuscript was partially destroyed." Hugh sounded somewhat distressed. "Newbrough was a very strange duck all around. He said that he'd had a visitation from a supernatural being he called Jehovih, spelled with an *i* instead of an *a*. The book was supposed to be a brand-new bible, taking all major religions into consideration, as well as emerging scientific theory. The book was quite controversial when it came out—it still is, for that matter. There were two editions of it, the second one prepared after the original manuscript was damaged, and there are some surprising differences."

"Where did you learn about it?" Giles interrupted him to ask. Hugh still had the capacity to amaze him.

"When I was studying for the ministry," Hugh said in a

thoughtful tone, "I had an excellent course in the occult and religion, starting with the *Kabbalah* and coming up to the present. *Oahspe* was part of the course. I read part of it, not all, because it's a big book. I tackled the Book of Thor, the Book of Judgment, and the Book of Cosmogony and Prophesy. Very strange stuff, even for that kind of writing. It has a lot to do with vortices of energy and polarity." He stopped a moment and Giles knew that he was musing. "Alice might have more practical knowledge than I do about it. I'll give her a call, if you like."

Giles considered this, and decided he no longer wanted to deal with Alice Hartwell. "It's not necessary, Hugh. I was just curious about the book. Prentiss said that he'd been reading a lot of occult books to get some ideas for new ways to run his tests. I was a little surprised." He realized that he was trying to reassure Hugh, and he wasn't sure why.

"Well, you'll have to tell me what else he has in his shelves, sometime. It sounds like he's got an enviable collection, if the rest is up to that standard." Hugh paused. "Maybe you'll have a little spare time next week, and we can kick some of the ideas around. If you're interested."

"I don't know," Giles said, his eyes on Fayre, eager for the chance to be alone with her. "Next week might be busy."

"Giles, why don't you bring Mrs. Schoenfeld to dinner next week?" This was suggested with such exaggerated patience that Giles felt embarrassed. "Nothing fancy, just whatever Inga is inclined to cook, since she's got classes. You and us, and that's it. You won't have to face the stares of your colleagues or the threats to her. All you'll have to do is eat with us, and then you can leave, or play Monopoly, or bridge—better not, because I hate bridge—or sit and talk over some tawny port. We'd love to have you over. Ask Mrs. Schoenfeld what she thinks when you see her. Okay?"

If Giles hadn't been so irritated with himself he might have snapped at Hugh, but as it was he was almost sheepish. "I'll talk to her about it."

Fayre had raised her head. "About what?"

Giles motioned her to be quiet. "If you think of anything about that book, give me a call at home in about an hour."

"Aren't you there now?" Hugh asked, then chuckled. "I won't insist on knowing where you are, but if you aren't alone, I hope that she's happier than you are."

"For Chrissake, Hugh!" Giles was exasperated.

"Don't be angry. You're my friend. I wish you could believe that, Giles."

"Of course I believe—" Giles started to protest.

"No, you don't," Hugh cut in, suddenly somber. "You want to believe it, but you don't. You don't trust me, you don't sincerely believe that I value your friendship. It's the truth, Giles, and I wish it weren't." He cleared his throat. "You might remember it, though, in case you ever decide to put the matter to the test."

Giles answered slowly. "I've put the matter to the test, once or twice. Oh, not with you, Hugh, but I learned my lesson. Don't be offended. I've simply stopped expecting certain . . . shall we say courtesies? . . . from people."

"Does that include Fayre Schoenfeld?" Hugh demanded, and quickly corrected himself. "Sorry. That was a cheap shot. I'll accept what you say for the time being, but whether you believe it or not, I am different. See you later. Remember to ask about dinner next week." Before there was a chance for Giles to say another word, Hugh had hung up.

Fayre, who had been watching Giles for a few minutes, now handed the train book to Kip and got to her feet. "Did you get the information you wanted?"

"Yes. Most of it." Giles took her hands. "Hugh wants us to come to dinner next week. What do you think?"

"Hugh's the minister, isn't he?" She had gone to the dining area to take her coat from the back of a chair.

"Yes. You've met him. He and his wife live in Berkeley. He used to be a hotshot journalist, ten years ago. He got the call late, it seems." Giles had risen, and crossed the room to take her overnight bag. It seemed strange to be so casual about their relationship. Fayre's aunt approved, and Kip, in spite of everything that Giles had read about sons and suitors, seemed to like him, and to be pleased that his mother liked Giles, too.

"The brownies are almost ready, if you want to wait a few minutes and take a couple of them with you," Anna said with a rosy smile. "They're very good brownies."

"They are," Fayre agreed. "Do you mind waiting, Giles? What's ten minutes?"

Giles shrugged. As much as he wanted to be alone with Fayre, he liked Anna Dubranov and he was growing very fond of Kip, although he was not certain how to deal with the boy. "Ten minutes? Okay."

It was rather more than half an hour later when they sat at the dining-room table, the few remains of the first batch of brownies cooling in the baking pan in front of Anna.

"We'll give you a call when we get over the hill," Fayre was saying to Anna when the phone rang.

"I'll get it," Anna offered, and got slowly to her feet. "You finish up the stuff here, and then you'd better get under way." She went down the hall, and lifted the receiver before the phone could ring a seventh time. Then she called, "Fayre? It's for you."

"Who is it, do you know?" Fayre called back, making an annoyed face.

"It's Professor Fellkirk. You'd better talk to him. Dr. Todd will understand."

In that instant, Giles felt his body grow cold and contract, squeezing inward. He reached for Fayre's wrist as she rose. "I haven't told him . . . anything. Not about us. Say that I just dropped by. Make up something."

"All right," she said, plainly puzzled. Then she turned away from him and started down the hall.

Anna returned in a moment. "He was very surprised to hear that you're here," she said to Giles. "Old friends like you two are, I thought he knew what's going on."

Giles was sufficiently embarrassed by this question to stammer when he answered. "Well, it . . . it's not that, exactly. Prentiss has a . . . different philosophy about . . . relationships, and . . . uh . . . considering that Fayre is his . . . subject, I didn't want to drag . . . to drag the emotional . . ."

At last Anna took mercy on him. "Dr. Todd, if you want to keep your affair private, that's fine with me. I wish you'd told me, that's all. I can appreciate the difficulties you might have with Dr. Fellkirk—he's a difficult man, and I'm certain he would not take kindly to your involvement with Fayre. Anything," she said firmly, "that spares her further anxiety and pain, I'm all for. But next time, tell me."

Still feeling abashed—and he knew it was with good reason—Giles said, "I should have warned you. I never thought that we'd have to deal with Prentiss this way."

"You'd better think of it, if you're planning to live with Fayre. You can't keep her wrapped in plastic. You've got to open up sometime."

Giles nodded, his face feeling stiff. He studied Anna Dubranov's face, liking the sturdiness of her, the lack of pretense. "It's very new to me, and I'm afraid to trust it yet.

When my wife divorced me, I tried to insulate myself from that kind of hurt. In a way I accomplished it. I don't like the price I paid. And it's wrong to compare my feeling for Prudence with what I feel for Fayre. They're vastly different women. Who knows? Perhaps I'm a different man, now." He was deeply relieved to see kindness in Anna's small, bright eyes.

"Dr. Todd, I don't want you to think that I'm asking your credentials, but you've taken a load off my mind. Fayre hasn't got many friends, and I'm her only relative close by. Her in-laws are much more interested in Kip than they are in Fayre. She doesn't kid herself about that. I'd be pretty upset if you were just conducting an experiment." She reached out and broke off a piece of one of the few remaining brownies. "She's had enough of that."

"I give you my word this isn't an experiment," Giles said slowly.

Anna Dubranov nodded.

They were talking about children's books when Fayre finally came back into the room. "Professor Fellkirk wants to see me tomorrow morning, first thing, before I come up for my appointment."

Giles sighed. "What does that do to tonight?"

"Well, I've got to come get the car. I could get up very early, maybe, or leave late. We'll work it out." She reached for her case again. "We'd better get going, Giles."

"Yes." He rose, and once again held her coat for her.

"Drive carefully," Anna said, not getting up from the table. "And if you expect to come back tonight, call me before you leave." She smiled her rugged smile at them. "If there are any more calls, I'll handle them. Fayre's in the bath. It's simple."

Both Fayre and Giles were courteous enough to laugh before they left the house.

They were almost to the Skyline Boulevard turnoff when Giles broke the silence. "What's the matter?"

Fayre shook her head. "I don't know. Talking to Professor Fellkirk made me . . . uneasy. I don't know why. I can't figure it out."

"Maybe it's just that you haven't been in the program for a while. Maybe you're nervous." The two cars ahead of them made the left-hand, south-bound turn onto Skyline Boulevard, that long two-lane road that wriggled along the crest of the hills between the cities of the peninsula and the splendidly desolate Pacific coast.

"Lupe, Dr. Fellkirk's secretary, lives on Skyline, a few miles this side of Skylonda," Fayre remarked inconsequentially. "She had a party there once, last fall. It's pretty. The house is back from the road, with oaks and redwoods around it. There's a kind of grove down the hill at the back of the house. We had a picnic there, and she mentioned that she has night parties there, sometimes."

They were past the turnoff and heading down the winding road that led to Half Moon Bay.

"Does that disturb you?" Giles asked, knowing that for some reason it did.

"I don't know. I think I almost had a seizure there. It bothers me to think about it." She snuggled into her coat more deeply. "It's crazy, Giles, feeling this way."

"No, it's not," he said quickly, and was glad his response was honest. "We don't know what it is yet, but it's not crazy."

She tried to chuckle and almost succeeded. "What other name would you give it? Demented?"

"No," he snapped. "And I won't have you calling it that, either. Christ, if you don't respect your talent, what do you think will happen? You'll be dismissed as a harmless nut, that's what will happen. It's a waste. You deserve better than that." He held the Land Rover around a steep, descending turn. "Let's not argue while I'm driving."

"We're not arguing," she insisted.

"Well, even if you're not, I am." He put his foot onto the brake as a small animal raced across the road just ahead of him.

"What was that?" Fayre asked, her interest reawakened.

"I didn't get a good look at it. Probably a skunk. Too big for a squirrel, too small for a raccoon." He was driving more cautiously now, his lights on high beam.

"Did you ever hit anything?" she asked, with obvious distaste.

"Once. I think it was a fox. I stopped the car and got out, but I couldn't find it. There was some blood on the road, and some reddish fur. Not a lot of either. I felt somewhat sick for a bit." As he told her about it, the queasiness came back again, like a thickness in his throat. "You'd think a surgeon would get used to blood, but I never have." His self-deprecating laugh was strangely shaky.

Fayre made a noncommittal sound, and turned away to look out into the growing density of the night.

Twice more Giles tried to draw her into conversation, then gave up with a sigh and turned all his attention to the road.

"There you are," he said as he turned on the floodlights of the parking area. "All new tires, a full tank of gas and a tune-up. My mechanic says you're going to need a valve job in a few more thousand miles."

"I know that," Fayre said as she walked to her Volkswagen. "Thanks, Giles. It's a relief . . ." She touched the door of the car. "I really feel lost without wheels."

"They're necessary out here," he agreed and waited while she inspected the tires. He sensed her tension and wished he knew what bothered her. "Fayre? Coming in?"

"Yeah. In a minute." She looked out toward the dark horizon where the ocean and the sky merged their two shades of night. "I keep thinking that something is going on, and I ought to know what it is. It's right under my nose, and I don't see it."

She startled him, because that same, disquieting feeling had been disturbing him most of the evening, though he had no name for it. He had had it before, usually when he first met a particularly difficult patient. It was almost physical, that feeling, as if there was something faintly alive in his stomach. "You're probably looking too hard. Come in and have a drink and a bath. I want to make love with you. I want to do everything that gives you pleasure." His frankness disturbed him, but his concern was erased by the smile Fayre gave him as she turned to him.

"Everything?" she asked with raised brows. "But I don't know all the things."

"Then we'll have to explore," Giles said, smiling, and holding the door open for her to pass into the house.

"I wish you didn't have to leave," Giles said for perhaps the tenth time.

Fayre had pulled on her slacks and was buttoning her shirt. Her face was still flushed and there was fullness to her lips when she grinned at him. "I wish I didn't have to, too. If I don't go now, though, I'll have to leave at six-thirty, and I don't want to drive with the sun in my eyes. Also," she added as she tucked in the shirttails and began to pull her sweater over her head, "if I stay here now, I won't *want* to leave here

in the morning at six-thirty." She leaned over and kissed
Giles. "You don't have to get up, really."

He was already half out of bed and reaching for his robe.
"We British," he reminded her primly, "know manners. If
you insist on going, I'll escort you to the door." He peered
under the bed trying to find his slippers, and gave up. He
could put up with cold feet if it meant he could be with
Fayre a few minutes longer. "Remember to call Anna. She
said she wanted to hear from you."

Fayre nodded. "Thanks for reminding me." She sat on the
side of the bed and reached for the phone, dialing quickly and
then waiting for the answer. "Aunt Anna?" she said at last.
"Fayre. I'm leaving Montara now. I should be home in a
little under an hour. You don't need to stay up."

Giles touched her arm. "It's faster along Two-eighty."

She nodded absently, listening to her aunt. "Okay. I'll tell
him. Good night, Aunt Anna." As she hung up, she said,
"Aunt Anna wants you to know that she let Dr. Fellkirk
think that she doesn't like or approve of you. She's determined
to throw him off the scent, as she put it."

Some of the apprehension that Giles had felt earlier that
evening returned, but he quelled the feeling. "Good for her.
I'm only sorry to have to impose on her."

"Don't be silly," Fayre said as she tied her shoes. "She's
enjoying herself." She stood up. "Okay, Dr. Todd. If you insist on walking me to the front door, get up."

Obediently Giles rose, and reached to embrace her again.
"Next time, stay all night."

"I'll try. I don't like having to leave any more than you
like me to go." She kissed him slowly, some of the languor of
the aftermath of love still with her.

His arms tightened. It was so good to hold her, to touch
her! His hands slipped down to the curve of her buttocks and
he felt her lean into the curve of his body.

"Giles," she said wistfully, "I must go."

He relented, giving her forehead one brush with his mouth
before he stepped back from her. "Okay. Maybe next time
we can spend longer."

"I hope so." She had gathered up her bag and started to
pull on her coat. "I'll see you this afternoon. One-thirty is the
time, isn't it?"

Giles shrugged. "I guess so. I don't remember. Get there
when you want. I have to deal with a handful of residents at

three. Come early, if you can, around eleven-thirty, and I'll take you to lunch."

"Your office?" She bent to pick up something on the floor, then tossed his slippers at him. "You wanted these?"

"Thanks." As he pulled them on, he said, "My office is fine. If I'm not there right on the dot, wait a bit."

"Of course. Come along when you can." She stood in the door now, her coat on, her bag in her hand, and the sight of her this way brought a sudden welling up of loneliness to Giles. He didn't want her to leave. "You don't have to come down, if you would rather not," she said warmly. "I can let myself out, you know."

"All the same," he responded with a formality that was out of place with his bathrobe and the caress of his voice, "I'll be a proper host. It goes against the grain not to be." He went to her side as he spoke and walked downstairs with her, through the darkened house, to stand in the front door while she started her old blue Volkswagen.

After she had gone and he could no longer hear the sound of her car as it went down the hillside, Giles went back to the third floor, not to his bedroom, which now seemed too empty to sleep in, but to the room beside it, to his piano. He sat and played, not really hearing the sounds of the instrument as he went from Fauré to Debussy to Schumann and finally to an elegantly sad piece by Mozart. Each note reminded him of Fayre, of her touch, of the color of her hair, the depths of her eyes, the way she moved, the clarity of her voice.

The sky had begun to lighten by the time fatigue drove him back to bed.

Giles was still in the intensitve-care pavilion at twelve-fif- teen when Nancy Lindstrom reminded him that there was someone waiting in his office. "I think it's that woman with the weird brain. You're scheduled to do tests on her today. Again."

Looking up from the monitor and the grim message of the tracing needles, Giles said, "She knows I may be late. This is important."

Nancy's laugh was unpleasant. "Getting cozy with her, are you?"

"What makes you think that?" Giles knew he should not respond to such goads, but his nerves were already taut and this petty outburst from Nancy stung him. The needles continued to move erratically. "Where the hell is Hensell?" he demanded of Nancy and the resident beside her.

"I don't know," the resident said, looking miserable.

"I see." Giles knew that meant Will had already left for lunch. The lure of scotch-and-water was getting irresistible to Will, and it was beginning to take up a large part of his day. "Well, when he comes back, tell him to see Dr. Gitani immediately. That is, if you can't reach him first. This patient is going to need help soon. If Dr. Hensell isn't available, I'll leave a number where I can be reached. I don't want to authorize surgery without Hensell's okay. The shape this man is in, anesthetic alone might kill him. I don't know his history, but it's my guess that surgery at this point is a very last-ditch gamble, and probably useless." He left the bedside. "You'd better keep someone with him at all times. If there is any change that is consistent for more than twenty seconds, get Hensell or me *immediately*."

The resident nodded nervously. "What about Dr. James?"

"Fine. If he's around." He went to the glass door of the cubicle and motioned the resident to come with him. "Anything we do," he said in a low voice, "won't make a bit of difference, most likely. In addition to the series of strokes, his lungs are shot. The report gives him less than twelve-percent capacity in his lungs. If Hensell wants to operate, that's his business, but I don't think there's any chance of survival."

"What about changes?" the resident asked, steadier now.

"They're important. It depends what's involved. I noticed he can't breath enough to talk. You might try giving him a pad of paper and a pencil when he's a little more lucid." Giles admitted to himself that he would be surprised if the man would recover consciousness to that extent.

"All right. Paper. What about his relatives?"

"Wife?" Giles asked.

"No. Not exactly." The resident paused significantly. "He's homosexual. Apparently he's been living with the same man for almost twenty years. They haven't let him visit, because he's not family. . . ."

"Not family?" Giles repeated, incredulous. "After twenty years, what the hell else do you call him?" He motioned to Nancy Lindstrom. "Nurse, this man has a friend here. I think he ought to be allowed in." He turned back to the resident. "What's the lover's name, do you know?"

"Bill Something. I didn't get the last name. Merchant's

been asking for him occasionally." The resident seemed embarrassed now. "Hensell wouldn't allow the visit."

"Hensell's out to lunch," Giles snapped. "I'll go have a word with him, and then send him up. Are you going to be here still, or is there another resident on duty now?"

"I'll be here until two," the resident said. "I'll get the paper, in case."

Giles smiled a little, liking the resident suddenly. "Good. When there's nothing else to give, a little compassion makes it easier. On both sides." He caught the sarcastic look that Nancy Lindstrom gave him, but decided to ignore it this time. "You're doing good work. Remember to call me if you need me and you can't reach Dr. Hensell."

The resident nodded and stepped back into the small glass-walled room.

"Very moving, Doctor," Nancy said when Giles had got a few feet away from the door. "Worthy of a soap opera. Compassion indeed. What a load of crap!"

"What else can we do?" he asked her, hoping she would be more forgiving.

"Be honest, for once. Christ on a bicycle! You're the most pompous, self-satisfied, arrogant, holier-than-thou prick I've ever known in my life!" She had managed to keep her voice down, but the venom was potent in her soft words. "You getting all sentimental over that new bit of nooky you brought in? Oh, I know you're fucking her. It shows. Noble doctor cures hopeless patient with magic cock. Headlines everywhere. Medical science is astounded. Honors pour in."

Giles winced under this attack. There was enough truth in it, and enough of his fear, to make it impossible for him to deny what she said. He stopped walking and looked at her. "I realize you won't believe this, but I'm sorry for what I did to you. I would undo it if I could."

"That's mighty white of you, Giles. A little *mea culpa* always looks good. It's a great salve to the conscience, too." She looked away from him. "You came on so nice, so concerned and wounded and lonely, and you're a shit. I should have known better, but those big eyes and the posh accent, they really snowed me. I was thinking all kinds of dreck about you and me, just as if I hadn't been around this hospital for eleven years. Oh, you were a smooth, smooth bastard, no doubt about it. And I was ass enough to believe you."

Shocked, Giles stood silent while Nancy turned on her heel

and started to walk away. Had he treated her that way, so selfishly and shoddily?

"You know," Nancy said as she reached the bend in the hall, "Tim Carey is good to me, in his own way. He's even faithful."

There was nothing Giles could say. He watched Nancy as she rounded the corner, and wished in vain that he could explain it all to her.

The man in the intensive-care waiting room was not obviously homosexual. He had none of the outward and flamboyant characteristics that were the mark of much of the gay world. Giles watched him a moment before he approached him. "You're Mr. Merchant's friend?" he began as the man rose.

"I'm Bill Turner, yes." His neat, expensive clothes looked all rumpled now, as if he had not changed them in a couple days. His square face needed a shave and under a sunlamp tan he was almost gray. "Is Dan . . . ?"

"Do you want my honest opinion?" Giles asked as gently as he could. "I'm not actually on the case. I was called in while Dr. Hensell was occupied elsewhere." How easily he lied, he thought. Closing ranks in the face of the public. For a moment Giles wanted to tell this Bill Turner that Will Hensell was out for a four-martini lunch, but even the idea of such an admission shamed him into keeping his silence.

"You've seen him?"

"Just now. His condition is very, very bad. It's unlikely that he'll live . . . much longer. Conditions like this are very hard to deal with, and if there is a history of such conditions in his family . . ."

"Dan's a foundling. We went over this with Dr. Hensell. We tried to find out, but it's been a long time, and there was no way . . ." His voice broke and he sobbed once before he could bring himself back under control. "I'm sorry. We're such old . . . friends."

"I understand, Mr. Turner." Giles hesitated. "Mr. Merchant's been asking for you. Would you like to see him? Before you answer," Giles continued hastily, "you'd better realize that he is under heavy sedation and might not recognize you. Because his condition is so precarious, you'd have to be as calm as possible. We don't actually know how much he hears or understands, but anything that distresses him may have very bad effects on him." As he spoke he studied the middle-aged man facing him. There was a great deal of strength in his eyes, and in spite of his anxiety, now deeply etched in his face, he listened to what Giles told him intelligently. "Perhaps you'd want someone to go in with you. There is a resident with Mr. Merchant right now. He'll need to have someone like that with him all the time. Although you would probably prefer more privacy, it's important that he have that protection."

"Yes," Bill Turner said with a slow, unhappy nod. "I understand that. I want to see him. I won't go to pieces, not in there, anyway. It's so hard, waiting. I imagine terrible things . . ." He forced himself to stop. "Thank you." He held out his hand to Giles, and Giles was pleased that there was so much strength in the grip, and only the slightest tremor.

"It's the fourth compartment on the right. I hope . . ." He stopped, thinking that this was beyond hope. He held the door into the intensive-care pavilion open for Mr. Turner, then started toward the elevator, determined to detour by Will Hensell's office before meeting Fayre. He felt a despairing rage at Hensell and was grateful now that Fayre would be with him that day. Without her, the same forces that had nearly killed Terry Dawes and now had him making pots in Mendocino would overwhelm him as well. Until Fayre had come into his life, he had had no idea how close he had strayed to that terrible brink.

At lunch, he promised himself, we won't talk about any of this. We'll talk about when she can move in with me, when we can be together. It's all that matters now. Soon enough he would be like Dan Merchant, or Bill Turner, waiting for the ebb of life. With a quiet curse, he began to walk faster.

□ 12 □

"Giles, you sly devil!" Prentiss beamed at him, holding out his hand. "Mrs. Schoenfeld mentioned her plans today. My, my, *my*, are you surprising!"

"Do you approve, then?" Giles asked with forced good humor. It was almost three weeks since Fayre had made her plans to spend the summer—at least the summer—with Giles at Montara, and Giles was still feeling odd about it. It would take so little to have her change her mind, he feared, and that disappointment would be more than he wanted to think about.

"I couldn't wish for better hands." Prentiss grinned and stood aside for Giles to enter his office. "She'll get the best care in the world from you."

There was a flicker of irritation in Giles' mind. He resented Prentiss' calm assumption that Giles was interested in Fayre for medical reasons. That may have been the case at first, he admitted, but no longer. Considering his words carefully, he said, "Just as I'll get the best care from her."

"Keep talking like that and they might make you an honorary lesbian." Prentiss chuckled as he sat behind his big desk. "I never thought you'd have it in you to get involved with another woman after your dreadful experiences with Prudence. Really, you know, she was a *dreadful* woman. You were fortunate when she left you. One night in bed with her was all *I* needed to convince me that she was simply *poisonous*." He added cream to his coffee as he spoke, apparently oblivious to the effect his words had had on Giles.

In all their years of marriage Prudence had never once mentioned Prentiss except as a friend of Giles'. There had been no hint that their relationship had been anything more. When had Prentiss slept with her? Giles asked himself. Before he and Prudence were married? After their divorce? While they were husband and wife? Prudence spoke of Prentiss as a colleague, not a former lover.

"Don't poker up that way, Giles. It's ancient history. But I was *certain* she put you off the domestic dreams forever. Well, time heals some surprising wounds, doesn't it?" He smiled his wide, confidence-inspiring smile and leaned forward on his elbow, reminding Giles forcibly of a television ad for insurance or headache remedies. "You're to be given a *great* deal of credit for this. With Mrs. Schoenfeld's history, well, you're being remarkably *optimistic*."

"Why do you say that?" Giles asked, forcing himself to smile in response to Prentiss.

"There are those spells of hers, first off. And I can't imagine it would be easy for you, with your passion for *privacy*, to have a woman with Mrs. Schoenfeld's particular gifts around. She's so apt to *intrude* on your thoughts, one way or another." He made a gesture of self-deprecation. "I know *I* couldn't handle it. And the child too. She's bringing the boy, isn't she?"

"Yes, Kip's coming along. We're turning the two downstairs bedrooms into his area, one room for his trains and one room for him. He'll have a private bathroom, and there is a side entrance at the end of that little hall, remember. We can give him part of the south side of the garden to play in." He had talked it all out with Fayre in great detail, and it was still new enough to Giles that it had an air of unreality.

"Thirty-nine is rather late to take on a family," Prentiss said reflectively as he sipped coffee.

"Are you discouraging me?" Giles wanted to know.

"Hell, no. Why should I? It's marvelous for you to have such a beautiful woman after you. I hope you're not disappointed, and, naturally, I'm apprehensive for you because I *know* that I couldn't handle it."

"Well," Giles said gently, "I'm willing to give it a try."

"All for love, then, is that it?" Prentiss smiled indulgently. "You've become a romantic in the last couple years. I hope, for your sake, that you're not disappointed."

Giles managed to keep his attitude light. "Why would I be disappointed?" What was wrong with Prentiss, anyway? Was he behaving this way because Giles had fallen in love with his prize test subject? Was he jealous? Why should Prentiss treat a friend so . . . shabbily? He had no answers, and it disturbed him very much. He had never thought that Prentiss would deal with him in so hostile a manner.

Prentiss stirred his coffee, as if buying time. "Well, you realize, Giles, that Mrs. Schoenfeld isn't precisely *stable*. Oh, she's been doing quite well, but anyone with as highly developed a talent as hers, it's never easy. To be candid, she *could* have another seizure, or seizures. It's likely that she will. And what the long-term effects of those seizures are, well, we can't even *guess* at it yet. Of course, she's quite attractive, and I imagine sex with her will be *very* intense. Her ability, again, coupled—if you'll pardon the pun—with the physical experience. In a way, I envy you that. Still, I don't think I could accommodate that sort of relationship day after day after day." He sipped at the coffee, watching Giles over the rim of the cup.

"You may be right. There's nothing long-term planned yet. At the end of summer, we'll make some decisions." Giles looked toward the window. "Provided that all goes well, Fayre might be back in your program in the fall. No matter what her final decision is, it won't affect the work she does with you." He hoped that this would calm Prentiss.

In fact his next comment was somewhat mollified. "We *are* looking forward to having her with us again. Perhaps the vacation with you will help her."

Giles did not like living with Fayre being called a vacation, but he held his peace. "I'm glad you agree with me. Now, I want to know if there is anything Fayre can work on in the meantime while she's with me."

Prentiss seemed startled. "Work? With you?" He put his coffee down so sharply that some of the liquid in the bottom of the cup splashed out onto the papers on his desk.

"Certainly. Fayre wants to keep up her research and she is interested in resuming her work with you. That means that she will be ready to do anything to help keep her in practice. Would you like her to work with Zenner cards?" Giles was not entirely convinced that Fayre should be returning to psychic research so soon, but he did not want to oppose her when the studies meant so much to her.

There was an odd flicker to Prentiss' eyes, then he cleared his throat. "That *is* encouraging," he said warmly as he finished blotting up the spilled coffee. "By all means, if she is willing to do a few tests . . . Zenner cards, naturally, are of value. There are other tests she can run. I think it might be a good idea if she found time to come by the lab in a month or so, and we'll show her a few of the new techniques we're using."

"Is that a good idea?" Giles asked, suddenly cautious. "Remember what happened the last time she came by the lab."

"Yes," Prentiss agreed. "I see your point. Well. Yes. That *does* make it difficult." He considered the problem. "If you don't object, perhaps I might come to see her at your home. That should be familiar enough to her. The tests themselves aren't *threatening*, just new and somewhat, um, *demanding*. How about two or three weeks?" He flipped through his desk calendar.

"Don't you think that's pushing it, Prentiss? How about a month at least? By then we'll have a better idea what's going on, and if she's done the regular experiments without . . . mishap, then she might be able to work quite successfully on your new methods." The smile that Giles was keeping firmly spread over his mouth was beginning to ache.

"I suppose it could be put off . . . But look here, Giles, I'll be visiting some friends near La Honda in a few weeks. I could take a short drive up the coast road and see you then. We can work something out then, when you've settled in a little more." His confident manner indicated that he was already certain that Giles would go along with the plan.

"Well, come for lunch, in any case. We'll see what Fayre feels about it then." Giles prepared to rise, but Prentiss stopped him.

"Very sound attitude. Mrs. Schoenfeld is fortunate to have you. No, I mean that. I've never been one for love, myself—it seems damned unproductive, but that's not to say you shouldn't try it out."

Until that moment Giles had not felt any real sympathy for Prentiss, but the casual admission that he was not interested in love because it was unproductive filled Giles with a sense of sadness for Prentiss. "Don't you think it might be worth trying out for yourself?"

Prentiss laughed. "I'm probably not the type. Don't get into a lather over me, Giles. I have what I want, or almost. I'm not giving up *any*thing, believe me." He rose along with Giles. "I confess I was *concerned* about this affair of yours, but it may all turn out for the best. I'll have someone I trust taking care of her, you won't try to get her out of the program, and if anything more *should* happen to her, you'll be right there, and you'll be able to take the responsibility necessary." He opened the door now, almost bowing Giles out of his office. "I'm glad you stopped by in person. We'd have had trouble doing this on the phone."

"Possibly," Giles said, thinking of the many times he had wanted to see his patients when they called him, knowing that he was apt to learn more from one quick look than from ten minutes of description. "I know my way out."

"Fine, fine. I'll give you a call before going out to La Honda. Take care of Mrs. Schoenfeld, will you?"

"I'd be delighted to," Giles said with a wave as he turned down the hall, leaving Prentiss standing in the office door, watching him go.

"I don't want to go to the beach," Kip complained the following Sunday afternoon when the last of his train equipment had been brought into the house. "It's cold and foggy and there's devil-men down there."

Fayre exchanged a quick glance with Giles, then said to

Kip, "You said you wanted to build a sand castle. The sand's at the beach."

"That's sound reasoning," Giles said softly. "You'll like it, Kip. We'll have it all to ourselves, and we can watch the ocean." Immediately after he said that, Giles realized he had made a mistake, for the boy stiffened. "It won't be like before," he went on quickly, hoping to recover his lost ground. "There's nothing to be afraid of. It's not like last time. You're smart enough not to go so far out on the rocks."

"I guess so," Kip said sullenly. "But it's cold. I don't like the beach in the cold. It should be hot in summer."

"There's always some fog in the summer," Giles said, wanting to be fair with Kip. "That's what makes the land around here so pleasant and green most of the year, not all brown the way it gets inland. The fog does that, and it cools off the air so that we don't get as hot here as people on the other side of the ridge."

"I like it hot," Kip announced, crossing his arms.

"Tell you what," Fayre said before the situation got any worse, "you can come down to the beach with us, and if, after half an hour, you want to come back here, then we'll do it. Is that okay? All we ask is that you give it a chance. If it doesn't work out, we won't force you to stay there any longer."

"Well . . ." He turned to look out the window again at the thin white fog that drifted against the coastal hills. "Half an hour only, you promise?"

"We won't stay any longer than that if you don't want to." Fayre stood back and looked at Giles. "Do you agree, Giles?"

"Of course," he said quickly. "And if you decide you want to come back, we'll make some sandwiches as a snack before dinner."

Fayre raised her brows. "Sandwiches?"

Giles shrugged. "The roast won't be ready until seven-thirty. Sandwiches at four shouldn't ruin his appetite." He held out his hand to Kip. "Come on. Half an hour."

Reluctantly Kip took the hand. "You're not wearing a watch. How'll you know when the time is up?"

Just as Fayre was about to show Kip her watch, Giles reached into the little pocket in his jeans and pulled out an old watch case. "This will tell me when. It belonged to my grandfather and he gave it to my father, who left it to me."

He held it out to Kip and showed him how the catch opened. "It's very old and it keeps excellent time."

"Hey, wow!" Kip said, fascinated by the pocket watch. "That's *neat!*"

Fayre laughed. "If we stop to show off watches now, we won't get to the beach until sunset." She put her arm through Giles' elbow and grinned at Kip. "Come on."

Kip held out for one condition. "I get to look at the watch when we get out of the car. Okay?"

"What a skeptic you are!" Giles laughed. "Very well, you can look at the watch, and you can tell us how much time we have."

The breakers were frothing over the rocks and there was a brisk wind driving them. It was a typical foggy summer day, just as Giles had said. There were two other parties on the beach: a group of scuba divers with a pile of equipment laid out along with several wet suits, one or two in bright colors, but most of them in black; and between them and Giles, five teenagers sat around a small driftwood fire toasting hot dogs.

"Okay, it's seventeen minutes until four!" Kip declared as he consulted Giles' watch. "That means that it's . . . uh . . . that we leave at . . . thirteen minutes after four. Right?"

"Very good," Fayre said as she tousled his hair. "We'll ask you then what you want to do."

Kip nodded critically, then got out of the Land Rover and walked toward the sand, his old sweater and faded jeans giving him the look of an urchin. He stopped to study the other two parties farther up the beach, then started toward the rocks at the south end.

"Careful of the rocks," Fayre warned, remembering what had happened on the rocks at the other end of the cove.

"Oh, yeah!" Kip called back as he began to search along the high-tide line for something interesting.

Giles dragged the old army blanket out of the back of the car. "You feeling okay?" He was worried at the paleness of her face and the fine lines that were settling in around her eyes.

"Tired. Moving is always such a chore. I hate it." She leaned back against the Land Rover and shaded her eyes as she peered into the fog. "Do you think it will get any thicker?"

"Probably. Then along toward midnight it will all blow away and tomorrow will be bright." He put an arm around her shoulders and felt her shiver from the cold. "We English are supposed to like fog, but if you'd rather go back to the house and warm up . . . ?"

She shook her head. "No. I like it here. I need to get out. Walking by the ocean is . . . quieting. It's like clearing away all the noise and the cobwebs and the gunk people carry around with them."

Giles was mildly startled to hear her say this, because he had always thought that his soothing affection for the sea was, if not unique, at least rare. He zipped his jacket. "Madam, will you walk?"

"Oh, God!" She came precariously close to giggling, but she put her arm lightly over his and let him lead the way to the beach.

The sand was cold, and where the tide had left it, clammy. Occasionally a stranded jellyfish lay in their path like a bit of gelatin. There were pieces of crab shells and an occasional strand of seaweed curving like question marks where the ocean had left them. Over the shouting and hiss of the waves there came the lowing cry of foghorns.

Fayre stopped and bent to take off her shoes. "I might as well. Otherwise we'll bring half the beach into your house."

"I have a vacuum cleaner," Giles reminded her, but took her shoes as she handed them to him.

They walked together, saying little, the sound of the waves enough of a reason for their silence. It was a companionable walk, as if they had always walked here on Sunday. Giles liked the way the wind blew Fayre's pale hair into fine moving tendrils, like the fog itself. He was unwilling to speak, to intrude on their quiet, but he said at last, "Do you think about the project, ever?"

She was not surprised by the question, he was certain, because there was no quick change of expression. "I think about it. Not often. I've wondered if I should. Dr. Fellkirk is determined to have me back this fall. He said so when I spoke to him. I suppose he said the same thing to you."

"Yes, he did."

"You can't blame him for being so single-minded. If he proves his techniques, he'll be the most influential man in the field. He'll have a tremendous amount of . . . power." On the last word she faltered, then stopped walking. Her head was turned away from Giles, toward the line of breakers.

"What is it?" Giles asked quickly.

"I wonder why I said 'power'?" she remarked in a distant voice.

"Prentiss has always wanted to be the best, the first, the authority. Even when he was young, he had to be the one to do the best and the first. Very American of him, really. He got teased about it then." He tried to chuckle, but the thought of Prentiss came back to him.

Fayre was frowning when she turned to him. "He's not a boy now. He's a grown man, turned forty." Her eyes grew strangely hard. "He still has to be first and best. He wants to control people. I've seen him do it." She shoved her hands deep into her jeans pockets. "I think that's what's bothered me about the project, from the beginning. I wasn't really aware of it until just now. I thought it was me, you know. I thought that it was too much sensitivity coming out of my abilities. But now, I don't know. I've been away from it for a while, and I've had you. It's given me a different perspective." She looked out to sea as they walked and Giles respected her privacy. A little later she began to speak again.

"Maybe that's why I have seizures. I don't want anyone but me to control this. Maybe the seizures were survival for me."

"It's possible," Giles allowed, hoping that she would continue to talk.

"God, I wish you were doing psychic research instead of neurosurgery. You're not like Prentiss Fellkirk, you're more compassionate. You don't need to control." She stared down at her feet, at the little sprinkles of sand that preceded her footprints. "I can't quite grasp it. There's something I'm missing. It's very nearly in reach, but I can't seem to focus on it."

Giles put his arm around her shoulder and pulled her nearer. "Don't force it. It will come in time."

"It's so frustrating, wanting to know." Her voice was very small. "You'd think it would be easy for me, but it's not."

"Why should it be easy?" Giles asked after a moment.

"You know. It's this ability. I ought to be able to sense or see what's going on around me. I ought to be able to figure out what it is about Fellkirk that makes me uneasy."

"Maybe it's because you've had your seizures when he was around and you associate him with them." Giles was not entirely sure he believed that, but it was a reasonable explanation, and he badly wanted a simple and reasonable answer to Fayre's worry.

"It could be. That would be enough to put up some peculiar blocks in my head." She slipped her left arm around Giles' waist. "It feels like that. As if there's a barrier in here . . ."—she touched her head with her free hand—"that I can't open or break down or get over."

"But what could it block, and why?" Giles thought aloud. "It could be the amnesia surrounding the seizures—"

Kip's scream stopped both Giles and Fayre suddenly. The sound was loud, as angry as it was frightened, and in the wake of the scream, Kip ran up the beach toward them. "Mommy! Mommy! Devil-men! Whole bunches of them!"

Fayre hugged her boy tightly as he ran into her arms. "Devil-men? What . . . where did you see them, Kip?" She tried to pry his arms loose, but he clung to her as he started to cry.

"Devil-men!" Giles stared down the fog-bound beach and tried to imagine what the boy had seen, or thought he had seen.

He hadn't long to wait. Three of the scuba divers came toward them as quickly as their clumsy flippers would let them, the first of them already pulling off his face mask so that he could call. "You've got to excuse us!" he shouted to them in a voice that would have been pleasant but for the high, edgy sound his upset had given it.

Fayre looked up. "Skin divers," she said, half in revelation, half in digust.

"Not skin divers, scuba divers. And the Pacific around here is too cold to go into in bare skin, most of the time." He had come up to them and held out his hand to Giles. "I'm Arnold Grosstein. I'm studying oceanography at Stanford. I'm really sorry we scared the kid. These outfits can look pretty outlandish if you aren't used to them, I guess." As he spoke, the other two caught up with him.

Giles had taken his hand. "Of course. Unfortunately the boy was scared on those rocks once before, and you reminded him of it."

Arnold Grosstein nodded. "I know how that is. My ten-year-old daughter has a thing about toads. We tried giving her a small toad of her own, but it only made it worse." He looked at the others. "These two reprobates are my students. Kathy Jamison and Ralph Fitzsimmons. There are a few others still back on the rocks. Honest, I didn't know the boy was there." He tried to touch Kip's shoulder, but he shrieked and cringed away.

"Kip!" Fayre admonished him sharply. "These are ordinary

people in special clothes. You're old enough to know that. Turn around and accept Mr. Grosstein's apology for frightening you."

Reluctantly, very reluctantly, Kip released his hold on Fayre. His eyes were troubled. "You're a devil-man," he announced petulantly before he turned back to his mother.

Giles decided to intervene. "He doesn't mean to be rude, Mr. Grosstein. I hope you'll understand." He glanced quickly at Fayre, curious that she had not repeated her insistence that Kip face the scuba divers.

"Well, I know how it can be. But let me warn you that Linda Tsiao has her class here from San Francisco State and there's going to be divers all around the place. I also saw a couple nonacademics out for a lark. Perhaps he'd better be taken home, if he's so easily frightened." Grosstein looked down at Kip. "I didn't mean to be so disturbing, young man. I know we all look strange. I hope you'll get used to us. Then, maybe someday, you'll want to dive, too." He motioned to his students. "I want to take one last look at that slippage before the tide turns. Let's change tanks and get back to work." Just before he walked away, he said to Giles, "You might want to remember that there's a lot of us out on foggy days like this one. That way we don't have to worry about swimmers and about occasional surfboards, though most of that's down on Half Moon Bay. Much more of this and we'll have to have shifts to keep the coast from being so crowded that no one can enjoy it." Then he waved and walked away.

Puzzled, Giles waited until Grosstein and the two students were out of sight around the outcropping of rocks before he looked at Fayre. He realized that she was more upset than he had realized at first, and so he was anxious to hear what she would say.

He had prepared himself for a great many comments, but her question, when it came, still startled him. "Giles, why would anyone put on scuba gear to scare a child?"

"You don't think that . . ." He stopped in mid-sentence.

"I do think it. Kip isn't lying when he says that's what his devil-man looked like. I know he isn't lying, Giles. Do you trust me?" One hand was on Kip's shoulder, and she reached with the other to hold Giles' fingers.

"Yes," he said, nodding slowly. "If you say that was what he saw, then it must have been. But it doesn't make any sense. Why would anyone . . . ? Do you think it might have been an accident? There are scuba divers around here who sometimes bring in a few illegal fish. Perhaps . . ."

This time Kip himself protested. "No. It was a devil-man. He was mean because he wanted to be. He could've hurt me. He wasn't that man"—he gestured toward the rocks where Grosstein and the students had gone—"he was a lot bigger, and he talked like he didn't like anyone." His fear was strong enough to make him hold onto his mother even though this plainly embarrassed him.

"Well," Giles said after a moment, "I'm not certain I understand what really happened, but I know you were a long way out on the rocks, and I don't think you went there simply out of curiosity. Tell you what, Kip: if you want to go home, I'll take you now, but if you think you can stay here awhile longer, it might be a good idea. Otherwise you might get frightened again, later on, and that wouldn't be good for you or anyone. What do you want to do?" As he spoke, Giles wondered what Kip's reaction would be. Giles was not sure his ploy would work, and he watched Kip closely as the boy thought it over.

"There was a devil-man at my grandparents' house, too. I might as well stay here a bit." He raised his head and tried to look quite calm.

Giles saw at once that Kip was not nearly as confident as he wanted to appear, but he thought that the boy deserved credit, so he reached over and touched his light hair. "There's nothing to be ashamed of, Kip. People get frightened. I get frightened. The time to be ashamed is when you let your fear rule you, so that you can do nothing but feel afraid."

Fayre smiled at him, then looked down at her son. "Giles is right. If you're afraid, tell us. Then we can find a way to deal with it. Fear is a good thing, Kip. It's only bad when is more important than you."

Slowly Kip nodded. "Okay." He swallowed. "I'm going to look around again. And if I see any divers, I'll just watch them." With visible effort he moved away from his mother and started down the beach, casting an occasional apprehensive look at the rocks at the south end of the hollow.

"Scuba gear?" Giles said softly. "In Manteca? In the San Joaquin Valley, for God's sake?"

Fayre shook her head. "I don't know. It's what he thinks he saw, Giles."

"But that doesn't make sense. Unless someone wanted to scare him. Why would anyone want to scare Kip? This isn't a

schoolyard prank we're talking about, this is much bigger."
He had made an attempt to keep his voice low, but the words
came out like soft explosions.

"I realize that." Fayre was frowning. "I hate to see him
like this, particularly now. I wanted it to be easy for him to
move out here." She still held Giles' hand and her grip
tightened.

"But it doesn't make any sense," Giles protested as they
resumed their walk down the beach.

For several moments Fayre was silent. "No, I can't figure
it out. Certainly it isn't that Kip's a rich kid, because he isn't.
There's no point in frightening him. About the only thing it
accomplishes," she added with a shaky laugh, "is that it
drives me almost half-crazy with worry."

Prentiss sounded very hearty on the phone when a few
days later he called ". . . just to see how things are going. I
hope I didn't interrupt your dinner?"

"No," Giles said with an odd smile. "We haven't eaten yet.
I was held up at the hospital for a few hours, so Fayre gave
Kip a few sandwiches and we're going to have a meal in half
an hour."

"You mean she can *cook*, too?" Prentiss asked, chuckling
at his own humor. "I thought only plain women learned to
cook these days. Remarkable woman, Mrs. Schoenfeld."

"Yes," Giles agreed.

"You're no doubt cursing my intrusion, too," Prentiss said
at his most knowing. "But I warned you I might call you.
Lupe and I are spending a couple of days at her place up on
Skyline, and I thought perhaps we could get together tomorrow night. You know, a meal and a hand of cards, or whatever it is you do for excitement in Montara."

"I'll have to talk to Fayre . . ." Giles began, feeling ill at
ease, and realizing that it was because he was not yet ready
to share Fayre's society with his overwhelming friend.

"Oh, come, Giles," Prentiss chided him. "Be a little kind.
You can't keep that *treasure* to yourself forever. I don't intend to *ravish* her, man, I only want to talk, see how she's
coming along. In case you have forgotten, she *is* my discovery."

It was all true, Giles told himself. Perhaps he was being
unfair. He wondered how he could explain to Prentiss without offending his old friend, and so was grateful when Pren-

tiss himself said, "If it's a problem, you figure it out and I'll give you a call tomorrow evening. How's that?"

"Fine. I'll talk to Fayre tonight." He wished he could understand his reluctance to have Prentiss over. Perhaps it was that Lupe would certainly be with him, and part of Giles was both attracted to and repelled by the woman.

"Or perhaps the two of you could come out here. Lupe's having a little party come Wednesday week. There'll be a few people Fayre knows."

"Oh?" Giles asked, realizing with a start that he had not heard Prentiss use Fayre's first name before.

"Yes, we're having a few people from the lab. She might like to see them again, in relaxed surroundings. Lupe's place is very nice. Ever-so-slightly decadent, if you get my meaning. Sauna, redwood tubs, water beds in *very* discreet places. Ferenc Nagy will be here. You won't be the only one."

Against his better judgment, Giles said, "That sounds like it might be fun. I'll see what Fayre thinks." He looked up as she came down the stairs from the dining room, and motioned her to silence. As always, he marveled at the surge of emotion she brought to him by her very presence.

"*Won*derful. I'll call you tomorrow evening. It will be a real pleasure to have you with us."

"I'm not certain we'll be able to come, yet," Giles warned him, then mouthed over the receiver, *it's Prentiss,* and put a finger to his lips quickly to keep her silent.

"She's not a hothouse flower, Giles," Prentiss reminded him in a manner that was both indulgent and condescending. "You'll have to turn her loose in public *eventually.* There will be people she knows there, and it isn't the lab. Who knows? it might be therapeutic."

"I'll tell you tomorrow," Giles promised. "You may be right about the party. It's no reflection on you, but I can't help remembering that it was with those particular people that she had her last seizure. It might be too soon—"

"Nonsense!" Prentiss interrupted. "You talk to her, and you'll find that she shares my opinion. I'll call you tomorrow at eight-thirty. Give my best to the woman. She's a remarkable lady." He chuckled once, almost nastily, then hung up before Giles could speak again.

"Fellkirk?" Fayre asked as Giles hung up the phone.

"Yes. He wants us to come to a party at Lupe's place a week from Wednesday." It was not reassuring to be so perplexed by a single phone call, he thought, and one from his oldest friend.

"What's the matter, then? Prentiss isn't going to spirit me back to the lab, Giles. Think of how careful he's been with me, and how protective . . ." She broke off. "I wish I could remember what caused those . . . episodes. I've tried, but I can't. You'd think I could." She sank onto one of the huge cushions that had been added to the living-room furnishings.

"Well?" Giles said, dropping to one knee beside her. "If you want to go, we will. If you'd prefer not to, that's fine." He touched her hair and then, suddenly, caught her in his arms and pulled her tightly against him. He had had a moment of fear, and from it had come an instant's vision of his life without her. It would be much worse than vacant, it would be a terrible desolation of his soul.

"I won't leave you, Giles," she whispered fiercely. "Nothing could take me away."

He was still not used to her tendency to answer his thoughts, but now he was grateful for it. "Is that a promise?"

"Of course." Her arms were strong and her need for him matched his own desire. "Kip's watching TV," she said, a little breathless, as she pushed back from him. "We can go upstairs."

Had it been later, he would have been tempted to make love to her on the pile of cushions in front of the cold fireplace, but Kip was still awake, their dinner was not yet ready, and he did not want to be rushed.

"All right. But for the time being, I'll play for you. Later, we can be private. What do you like better? Mozart or Scarlatti?"

She laughed easily, her eyes large and sparkling. "A romantic pragmatist—you don't want to be interrupted."

"Particularly by a rumbling stomach. I think we'd better have a meal and a bath first." Lightly he touched the curve of her breasts, then the rise of her hips. "Do you mind?"

"Play me some Scarlatti until dinnertime. If you do one of those wistful, poignant Mozart things, you won't get dinner until after midnight." She took his hand in hers. "Giles. Giles. It's good being here with you."

He tried to chuckle in order not to reveal the painful relief that took hold of him. "I do my poor best." His throat was tight as he spoke and he blinked once to keep tears from his eyes.

"Why does caring bother you?" she asked, touching his jaw first, then the place on his temples where his hair was white.

Giles answered with difficulty. "If I didn't feel so much for you, then it probably wouldn't bother me. But, you see, this is not to be treated as trivial. I'm like a blind man who is given sight, and that sight is of things beautiful. . . . I feared to open my eyes because I didn't want to see desolation and ruin . . . God, I wish I could say it better." This time his laugh was less strained as he tugged her after him up the stairs to his music room and the scintillating elegance of Domenico Scarlatti.

□ 13 □

"Did you have any trouble finding the place?" Prentiss asked Giles as they strode out onto the deck of Lupe's house. "The turn for the drive is easy to miss if you aren't looking for it."

"No trouble."

The late-afternoon light dappled through oak and redwood, bright summer gold in the green gloom. The deck, a large expanse of unfinished redwood, ran the length of the south side of the house, overlooking a graveled drive well-parked with cars. There were sounds of conversation from the tables in the small grove farther down the hill, and a scrap of song drifting from the outdoor hot tub where four of the guests were soaking together in the deep, warm bath. The air smelled of trees and resin and dry summer grass as well as chickens basted on a spit over an open fire.

"You're lucky. The Yamadas overshot us by almost twelve miles. It's easy to do," he repeated.

"There isn't much margin for error," Giles agreed and thought that this conversation was more inane than any he had had since he had arrived with Fayre almost an hour before. "We turned onto Skyline and drove until we came to the entrance. Fayre did the navigating." He took another sip of the gin-and-tonic Prentiss had made for him, and said, to be polite, "Quite a gathering."

"Yes." Prentiss nodded with the start of a smug grin. "Once a year Lupe and I get together and do something a little special for all the hard workers in the lab. Socializing helps, particularly now in the slow season. Summer can be deadly dull on a university campus, even one as large as St. Matis. This lets us get together, trade gossip and ideas. And, of course, men like you and Ferenc Nagy are welcome. As outsiders, you're apt to see things we miss, being so close. What better setting than this?"

"It is beautiful," Giles said, thinking that his home above Montara was not one whit less beautiful.

"Did you meet everyone yet? We've got some of our subjects here, those that are leaving the project."

"Leaving?" Giles repeated, baffled. "Why did you ask Fayre, then? I thought you wanted her back in the project."

"Oh, we do." Prentiss paused to wave to a middle-aged couple coming up the path from the grove. "Her case is rather different. She already knows most of the people involved in the experiment, so there's no reason to exclude her. And, of course, she won't be working with anyone here. We're *extremely* careful about that."

"For any specific reason? I can understand why you might want them not to discuss their work, but I confess that this passion for anonymity is beyond me." The gin-and-tonic was getting warm now that the ice had melted and Giles debated whether to drink it quickly or to set it aside and ignore it.

"But it would throw all the results into question, if it could be proved that the various subjects knew each other. Do you remember the woman we were testing the first time you came to the lab?"

Giles nodded. "Indian, wasn't she? Very Western, I think." He was surprised how well he could recall the woman he had seen only on a monitor screen.

"Yes, that's right. She and her partner were getting quite remarkable results, and then, one afternoon, she was having coffee in the student union and she saw a young man come into the room. She claims she knew who he was the moment she saw him, but I'm inclined to doubt it. It was the same young man you saw working with her that day, George Brenner. After that it was *useless* to test them together, since they were in regular contact. Chadri is planning to continue in the program, but George has left it. It's a shame in some ways, but I suppose I ought to expect it, dealing with the gifted psychics we've had in the program."

"I can't see that their socializing is a problem," Giles persisted as he set the warm glass aside.

"It's that they're getting too . . . well, *involved*. Oh, it's nothing so simple as *sexuality*; they're setting up a certain link, rather like a private phone line. We can't get unimpeachable results with conditions like those." He had turned and leaned his elbows against the top of the railing. His shirt was open at the collar and the lightweight sweater-vest that matched his slacks was his most obvious concession to his carefully cultivated professorial image. In this setting he seemed slightly out of place.

"I see your point."

"It would be helpful to have someone like you in the program, too. Oh"—he held up his hand casually to defer any of Giles' protestations—"I'm not asking you to leave Cal and throw in your lot with me. I know how you feel about surgery, and you must stay where you feel most *comfortable*. However, it would be quite *beneficial* to have someone who understands the *brain* as well as you to provide some additional *insight*."

"But I don't know much about the brain," Giles objected as reasonably as he could. "No one does. I'm hoping that your research will be of use to me. Now you tell me that you're planning it to be the other way around."

Prentiss laughed, this time with a kind of mockery. "I'm damned if I'll admit that we're all in the dark. Do think it over. With you and Fayre both in the program, we might make some major strides forward. *Think* what it would mean if we could *use* this sort of talent constructively and predictably." He beamed at the idea. "We would be able to *change* so much. . . ."

A third man had come out onto the deck—a tall, thin man with a lupine face and dark hair faintly silvered, which was wet just now. His clothes were more formal than Prentiss' or Giles' and he carried himself with gloomy dignity.

"Why, *Alan*," Prentiss said, sounding not too sarcastic, "you decided to come, after all."

Alan Freeman gave Prentiss a long, disapproving stare, and then turned his famous, penetrating gaze on Giles. "We were down at the beach and decided to stop by on the way back. There are too many people at Half Moon Bay, too many surfers."

"Alan likes to dive," Prentiss explained to Giles, then turned back eagerly to Alan Freeman. "Surely you can't object to surfers seriously. They're entitled to enjoy themselves. Or do you think that they're an evil influence, too?"

Giles wished that Prentiss would not bait Freeman so, but was reluctant to object since Prentiss might then turn his attention to him, an occasion that Giles was anxious to avoid.

"You delight in misinterpreting what I say," Freeman announced. "I've only warned you that you are dealing with powers and influences beyond your understanding, and that our whole literary and cultural history is filled with cautionary tales about those who would not heed the warning and were destroyed. Consider Mary Shelley's *Frankenstein*, which is much different than the interpretation given her work in films, and think of the real danger she dealt with, including a comment on those who deal with questions of the powers beyond ourselves; powers of life and death, of the soul."

"Excellent, Professor Freeman," Prentiss said as he began to applaud.

Alan Freeman answered this with a stony stare. "You don't want to admit that you are delving into areas that might be quite dangerous. You think that you're doing all this for science and that there is no harm in knowledge, but you forget those poor men and women who believed that and found themselves lost to Christ and promised to Satan, eternally a part of evil." He crossed his arms over his chest and waited for an answer.

Prentiss was delighted. "If you mean those Mass-backwards Christians," he said, grinning at this witticism, "they were the most devout of the lot. All that rigamarole, the liturgy said backwards, the candles, the ceremony, why, all that *proves* the strength of their Christianity. If they didn't believe in the power of Christ, then all they would have to do is reject it, go somewhere else. But no, they develop a long, elaborate parody of Christian worship, with holidays and a particular canon and ritual just as complex as the regular Christian forms. Now, *that's devotion!* Who do you know today who has enough real faith to go to such lengths to refute it?" He winked at Giles and raised his brows as he turned back to Alan Freeman.

"Nothing you say changes the contempt and danger that are part of those rituals. . . ."

"Contempt? What do you mean?" Prentiss shook his head, the sardonic light shining in his eyes. "You've been reading too much Huysmans, Alan. You're starting to believe all that perverted, purple prose of his. If you want to have an orgy, it isn't necessary to celebrate the Mass of Saint Secaire to do it. That's like using a sledgehammer to kill a fly—the fly will

certainly die, but what a waste of energy." Before Alan
Freeman could object, he went on. "I'm not saying that such
rituals don't focus energy, because they obviously do. But
most of it is drained off into theatrics. That's why my kind of
research is important, Alan. Because I'm trying my poor best
to find out how to release that energy without all the trappings, and turn that force from display to power and useful
knowledge."

Giles thought that if the setting had been slightly different,
Prentiss would have taken a bow for the last statement. He
decided that it was time to end the game. "Freeman, let's
change the subject. Neither of you will persuade the other.
Tell me about Half Moon Bay. Where do you go there?"

Alam Freeman favored Prentiss with a smoldering look,
then managed to answer Giles. "We have a group of friends
who like scuba diving. I've done it for many years. It was
more enjoyable ten years ago. There was a fad for it then,
but there were also fewer divers and it wasn't so difficult to
find unusual sights near the shore. Pollution and popularity
have made much of this coast pretty boring." He sounded
fairly enthusiastic now, with a kind of genuine pleasure that
was as charming as it was surprising.

Almost against his own private wishes, Giles asked, "Do
you ever dive around Montara Beach?"

"I? Not recently. I think the last time we went there was
two or three years ago. Now we go to Princeton-by-the-Sea
and dive off the point. Last year my wife and I went to Baja
California, and that was quite fascinating." Freeman paused
as he looked for a deck chair, and went to drag one nearer so
that he could continue the conversation.

"Scuba diving?" Prentiss said softly. "I didn't know you
were interested in such things."

"I'm not, particularly." Giles looked around as laughter
erupted from the direction of the hot tub once more. "Have
you ever tried it?"

"Once or twice." Prentiss nodded. "But it takes something
more important than fish and seaweed to get me into one of
those damned wet suits. The only time I feel claustrophobic is
in one of those contraptions."

Alan had dragged the deck chair near them, and now he
settled his long limbs in it. "You'd get over that if you did
more diving," he assured Prentiss. "They are a little disquieting the first few times you wear one, but it passes. My wife's
been trying to organize some sort of club for divers, so that

they can compare experiences and learn about the latest advances in the technology."

Prentiss snorted. "For a man who normally reacts to technology the way deer react to lion shit, I'm *amazed* to hear you say that."

Freeman stiffened. "I'm not objecting to the technology. I'm objecting to its uses."

The terrible suspicion that had been building, unbidden, in Giles' mind prompted him to ask, "How do you mean that?"

"Use never bothers me, Todd, it's misuse that causes all the trouble. I don't see that air tanks and wet suits and masks are a misuse of technology." He leaned back, and added, "Ginny's been happier since the equipment has got prettier. She worries about aesthetics, and black wet suits and dark tanks depressed her."

"Oh?" Giles was not certain how this new revelation affected him.

For the first time since Giles had met him, Alan Freeman smiled. "You should see Ginny in that yellow wet suit of hers. She's great! Watching her in the water, she's like a bit of sunlight." This confession was apparently too much for Alan, because he made his face somber and added, "Of course, I feel like a perfect ass in orange, but it is a great deal more visible than black or blue."

Giles' suspicion faded as quickly as it had risen. Unless Alan Freeman were a good deal more subtle than Giles thought he was, it could not have been Freeman who had threatened Kip. According to the boy, his devil-man was black, not orange or yellow. He moved to one side of the deck chair. "Well, I think I'll pour myself another drink. Do you want another, Prentiss?"

Plainly, Prentiss was very pleased at the prospect of having Alan Freeman all to himself for a while, so he waved. "No. I'm fine. There's extra tonic in the frig, if you need it." Then he turned to give his full attention to the man in the deck chair.

Giles was strangely glad to escape Prentiss. This discomfort he felt around Prentiss Fellkirk was new to him, and he wanted to understand it better. Was it because of Fayre? The question had nagged him before and it returned now. Was there really that much competition between them, that so little could disrupt it? Or was that being kind to Fayre? She was much more important to Giles than anyone else he had known, and if it came to a choice between her and Prentiss,

Giles knew, though the knowledge saddened him, that he would always choose Fayre.

In the kitchen he opened the refrigerator and found, aside from mixers and beer, a large container of iced tea. His relatives in England had been horrified when they discovered that Giles had developed a taste for iced tea. He was glad now to have it available, since it made it possible for him to have an acceptable amber-colored liquid in his glass and not have to drink alcohol. As he poured out the tea, he thought of Will Hensell, and as always when Hensell's image crossed his mind, he worried. Giles was no prude. He liked wine and spirits, but not daily, not in ever-increasing amounts. He had known other surgeons with minor drinking problems, but not like Will Hensell's. Was Will, like Terry Dawes, beginning to slip, to lose that arrogance that was required of surgeons?

"Well, Dr. Todd," his hostess said from the doorway. Today Lupe was wearing raw silk dyed and cut to look like ranch-hand denim. Her checked shirt was silk, as well, and only the lowest button was fastened. Her polished hair glistened in the light.

Giles turned, feeling strangely guilty. "Hello, Lupe. I was just making myself another drink." He was absurdly glad that she had not seen him pour the tea, and that there was scotch and brandy conveniently near.

"Oh, good. I always want my guests to have a good time." She came nearer and Giles smelled her perfume, which was a woody musk scent, like a dark place in the forest. "Is there anything you want?"

"No," Giles said, anxious to leave the room. "I'm fine. You give an . . . im . . . impressive party." He motioned vaguely to a buffet laid out in the dining room. "I like that smoked turkey. I was going to make myself a sandwich."

"It is tasty," she said, staying beside him, her hip now pressed against his. "Are you sure that will be enough for you?" She had slipped her hand through the crook of his elbow, and her smile was one of blatant invitation. "There are three water beds downstairs. I'm pretty sure that one of them is free. It's early yet."

Giles sensed an inner warning that he must not respond with the deep indignation he felt. "You know, Lupe, Prentiss and I are very old friends . . ."

"He won't mind," she said lightly. "He knows how I am about men. It doesn't bother him."

"But you see," Giles said gently as he began to assemble

himself a sandwich. "*I* mind. It may be foolish, but I could never forget that I have an obligation to him."

Lupe laughed. "An obligation? To Prentiss?"

"It probably sounds quaint to you, but we did go to school together for many years, and all through the time, we were each other's strongest ally. I know that sounds like Good Old Boy crap, but in this case, the feeling is genuine." He had piled turkey and ham onto dark pumpernickel bread and reached for mustard.

"You sound like something sentimental out of Dickens. No one feels that way anymore, Giles Todd. Prentiss warned me about you, but I thought he was kidding." She put her hands on her hips, not in anger, but to make herself more provocative.

Giles wanted very much to ask what Prentiss had told her, but he could not bring himself to do that. He took a bite of the sandwich, buying himself time, and realized the whole thing tasted like sawdust.

She moved closer to him again. "You're an attractive man. I imagine women like you. You act as if you were a virgin in the company of a rake. I'm not asking you to give up Fayre Schoenfeld, I only want you to fuck me."

Her nonchalance amazed Giles. Over the years he had had a few invitations, and his occasional affair with Nancy Lindstrom was, for a time, an uncomplicated outlet. He had avoided other women, those of the innuendos. He had never experienced a woman like Lupe. "I'm . . . committed elsewhere." In his own ears the words sounded dreadful, but he had no way to change them.

"What are you? A Victorian? Let me tell you, those were the worst lechers that ever existed. There were half a million whores in London when Victoria reigned. And they had a lot of customers. There's nothing wrong in wanting me. I like that. Don't you like dark hair? Are you afraid you'll catch something? I'm careful. I get blood tests regularly." There was a contemptuous edge to her smile as she reached for Giles' free hand. "Here. Try that. Doesn't it turn you on?" She put his hand under her shirt, over her breast.

Giles quickly pulled away. He was deeply upset now, though no longer embarrassed. He wished he had an easy way to leave this party, which had become so disturbing. "I'm sorry."

"No, you're chicken," Lupe corrected him. "You're not willing to take what you want. You're afraid that Fayre might find out about it, since she's psychic. She probably can. Have you stopped to think about the tyranny she's imposing on you? You'll never be able to admit to being bored, or interested in someone else. She'll always know, and whether you admit it or not, she'll be aware of everything you do. You say you don't want me now. What about six months from now, when you're over the novelty of her? What happens then?" She had gone to the head of the stairs that led to the lower floors. "Sure you don't want to change your mind? Maybe you'd like to watch some of the others, for inspiration?"

"No, thank you." It was an effort of will not to throw something at that lovely, smiling face. Giles had rarely felt such overwhelming revulsion as he did at that moment. He not only wanted to protect Fayre from this strange attack, but was deeply offended by the distorted picture Lupe conjured.

"Always so proper. Prentiss warned me about that. I still can't get over your being friends." She slid her shirt aside and let Giles get one good look at her naked breasts, then turned and went down the stairs, whistling to herself.

Giles stood in the dining room holding his sandwich and staring rather blankly at the far wall. He found it hard to believe that the conversation had taken place. It made no sense. He tried to account for Lupe's odd behavior, to explain it to himself, and found he could not. Unless, he thought after a moment, unless Lupe had been on something. There had been marijuana joints making the rounds earlier, but Giles doubted very much that so mild a drug, even when mixed with alcohol, would make so great a change in Lupe's manner. He had not been told of anything stronger available, but it was not impossible. He had almost made up his mind that some unknown drug would account for it when Alan Freeman came into the dining room.

"Not a bad party," he allowed with a somber nod to Giles.

"It's quite interesting," Giles said, somewhat at a loss for words. He picked up a paper plate and put the rest of his sandwich on it, and carefully took a knife and cut it in half.

"Fellkirk always intrigues me." Freeman was inspecting the buffet with a critical eye. "Do you happen to know if there are any deviled eggs left? I confess that my one demonic delight is deviled eggs." He did not smile at his ponderous humor but there were more creases around his eyes.

"Try the kitchen. There aren't any left out here." He held

the plate in one hand and his glass of iced tea in the other, and was eager to leave.

"Of course. I wish there were a way to prove to Fellkirk that his work is dangerous. Nothing I say does any good. All he does is talk about knowledge and power." From the kitchen, Freeman added, "I'm afraid I can't help remembering the adage about power and corruption, particularly in relation to this sort of power. Ah! Deviled eggs! Thank you, Todd."

Whatever else Alan Freeman might have said, Giles did not stay to hear. He went out the open front door and began to look for Fayre.

"Do you think it would be okay to leave soon?" Fayre asked as they finished the sandwich. "I can't help it, Giles. I'm having a terrible time." Her face looked more drawn than Giles liked and there was a tremor in her hands.

"Anytime you like. Is something the matter?" He spoke softly, as she had done, with the odd feeling that otherwise they would be overheard—deliberately overheard.

"It's hard to define. I feel drained. I don't have any energy. It's as if they're all gobbling it up." She gave him a wan look. "It's one of the things that happen to people with my sort of talent. We're prey to these sorts of things. It might be that someone is using my energy, but it's more likely that I'm oversensitive to the weird ambience here. It *is* weird, isn't it, Giles?" This last was almost a plea.

He nodded. "I think so. Well, don't let it worry you. I'm ready to go when you are. We can always say that Kip's sitter has to be home in an hour and it'll take us forty minutes to get back."

Fayre was plainly relieved. "Anna would stay with Kip until doomsday if we asked her," she said as they began to walk back toward the house. "I don't know why it is, but I feel this house is oppressive. I shouldn't. Look at it. It's pretty, and open, and there are all sorts of people here, and they're having a good time, and I feel as if the breath were being sucked out of me."

As she spoke, Giles looked toward the house and saw Prentiss on the deck. It was a trick of the light, but suddenly he seemed massive, and threatening. Then the wind touched the trees and there was light on the deck as Prentiss waved to them.

"Giles! Fayre! I was starting to get bored up here. Come and talk with me!" He motioned with open arms.

Giles paused a moment and looked quickly at Fayre, then called back, "I wish we could, but Kip's sitter won't stay past seven-thirty and it's six-forty now." He stopped almost underneath the deck and grinned upward. "We were just coming to thank Lupe for having us. It's quite a group you've got here."

"Fascinating, aren't they? Are you sure you can't stay? Lupe's got some great things planned for tonight. You can call your sitter and tell her you'll be a while longer." Prentiss had leaned forward, his folded arms on the railing. "Stay a little longer. Chadri's going to do some Indian dances for us in an hour or so. She's *very* good. Alan's going to do us a reading, probably from James or Stoker. Good, blood-curdling horror. He does it very well, with real *conviction!*"

"It's tempting," Giles lied. "It would be exciting, but it isn't fair to the sitter. She has other responsibilities, and I know it would be difficult for her to stay later." He shrugged. "If you'd told us that this would be an evening thing as well . . ."

"You mean you didn't know?" Prentiss scowled a moment and his big hands knotted into fists. "*Damn!* I was looking forward to having you here tonight!" The scowl vanished. "Well, next time you'll know. We do this sort of thing off and on throughout the summer, on a smaller scale. We'll have other chances." He straightened up. "I'll walk you to your car."

"It's not necessary," Giles said quickly. "I wanted to thank Lupe for the afternoon, though. Can you tell me where she is?"

Prentiss gestured expansively. "She and Alan went downstairs about half an hour ago. I'll convey your message. I don't think," he said, smiling lasciviously, "that an interruption just now would be tactful."

So it was true, Giles thought. Apparently Prentiss didn't mind Lupe's involvement with other men. "Well. Thank her for us, then."

"I'll be glad to. After I've had a little time with Mimi Bradeston." He read the disapproval in Giles' face. "Poor Giles, you certainly have a limited view of life." He looked away, then turned back to Giles and Fayre. "If you ever change your mind, let me know. Lupe's taught me a lot and there are so many women who crave a little variety, just like men. There are things they want to do, but not regularly, and *not* with their *husbands.* Parties like this are *great* places to experiment." He leaned down toward them, saying quietly, "Mimi's the kind who likes to be tied up a little, ravished." He rolled his *r*'s lavishly. "Nothing really rough, but a touch of the old rape fantasy. She'd go completely to pieces if anyone were *really* rough with her. So. Another time, then. Take care. Drive safely." He straightened up and started across the deck, pausing only once to look back.

"I don't want to go to another party there," Fayre said when Lupe called later the next week. "Tell her we're doing something else. Say we're going into the city to the theater or something. I don't want to go through that again."

Giles lifted his hand from the mouthpiece of the receiver and said, "Lupe? I'd forgotten that I'd got tickets for the Pops concert that evening. I don't think we can make it." He tried to infuse an element of regret into his words, but was not at all sure he'd succeeded.

"Well, if you change your mind, come ahead. We're having quite a gathering. I'll call you that morning and find out what's happening, okay?" She paused, then said in a lower voice, "There's going to be a lot of people here. You'll have time to yourself, if you want it."

"Yes." Giles felt a spurt of anger. "Perhaps your library would interest me, but not a week from Sunday. It's also difficult for us to get sitters during the summer. I'm sure you understand." He was about to hang up when Lupe added one last word.

"Prentiss would like it. It bothers him that you're withdrawing this way. You might think about it. Talk to you later, Giles." She had hung up before Giles could say another word.

"I don't like her," Fayre announced. "It's not only because of her sexual thing with you." She avoided Giles' eyes. "I know about it. It was kind of you not to mention it to me, but I'm not so naive that I don't know she's after you. I don't blame her, because I like you, too." There was mischief in her eyes. "But don't let her get to you, Giles, okay? Not for the reason you think. I'm not jealous, really. I know you're going to look at other women and perhaps, someday, do more than look. I know you still have a certain affection for Prudence, and that's good. I remember Harold lovingly, though I admit that if he had lived, our marriage wouldn't have lasted."

Giles was not yet used to Fayre's openness, and for that reason he faltered. "It's . . . different. I'm not used . . . to what you can do. I haven't wanted to mention your husband, or my ex-wife, for that matter. You're so special, and I haven't wanted to intrude on . . . anything." He still held onto the phone and considered a moment whether or not he should make a call to someone, anyone, as an excuse to avoid what could easily become a painful conversation.

"I'm not going to force confidences on you, Giles," Fayre said as she started toward the kitchen. "But you've been saying that we ought to call the Audleys and make up for that dinner we missed. Why don't you do that?"

As she passed him, Giles reached out and took her arm. "Fayre, wait." He set the phone aside and pulled her close to him. "You're more than I ever thought I could have, and sometimes it frightens me. I want to protect you from all the hurt there is, because you're so vulnerable to it, and you have been . . . wounded already. I don't want to wrap you in cotton wool. If I try, you must stop me. But please let me care for you. It's one of the few things I know how to do."

Fayre turned her head to kiss him, and when they were ready to part again, stood back from him. "You do more than that. Remember what I was like when we met? I couldn't have managed without you. I'd probably be in a hospital somewhere, right now, filled with drugs and the darling of all the experimental types." There was ill-concealed detestation in her face at the thought. "You were willing to help me when no one else was."

"Oh, come on," Giles protested, flattered but too honest to accept her praise. "There was Prentiss. He brought me into the case. I wouldn't have known about you if he hadn't asked me." There was also Frank Crocker, dead now, who had forced Giles to change his mind about medicine.

"Prentiss brought you into the case so that he could save his own ass if anything went wrong." Fayre spoke with asperity. "He knew you're too ethical to refuse assistance, and he was scared silly that I might go completely to pieces on him and he'd have to take full responsibility, and that would ruin his pet project."

"Well, you can't blame him for wanting to protect his work," Giles said reasonably, then stopped. "He was more worried than that."

"Was he? He wanted to keep me on because of my ability, not because of my trouble. If I hadn't had the test results I did, he would have been glad to be rid of me after that first seizure." She looked both sad and angry now. "You were the one who really cared, Giles. That's what made the difference. If you hadn't been there, I would have been lost."

A loud blast from the lower floor brought them both out of their private worlds. "Kip's got his trains running," Fayre said as Giles blinked. "Let's go down and have a look at them."

Two nights later Fayre woke with a shriek late in the night. She was almost straight upright in bed and her body was slick with sweat.

In a moment Giles was beside her, his arms around her as he tried to calm her. He waited for the onset of another seizure, but though she trembled uncontrollably and her eyes were oddly glazed, she did not slip away into that other state. For over an hour they sat together, Giles with his arms around Fayre, in the chill after midnight, as she waged an invisible battle.

Giles was desperately worried, but dared not reveal it by so much as a quiver in his voice. He kept his words low, his hands as steady as when he performed surgery, his whole being as strictly mastered as that of a religious adept. He hardly knew what he said, but the words came steadily, and his arms were firm as he held her.

Finally there was a lessening of her tension and her eyes focused on the draperies by the window, which stood open to show the dark sky framed by a few trees. She lifted her hand to her face, brushing back her pale hair. For a little time she tried to speak, and then she began convulsively to sob. This was as distressing as her silence had been and Giles forced himself to stay calm. He knew that if he failed her now, he might lose her, and that fear gave him the courage to hold her in her suffering and not to succumb to it himself.

When the sobs had ceased and she leaned against him, limp from her ordeal, Giles allowed himself the luxury of admitting how terrified he was. "Fayre?" he said in a voice husky with contained emotion. The time it took her to respond seemed endless to him.

"They were calling me out of myself," she said quietly as she looked at him at last.

"They?" It was a stupid question, and he felt wholly inadequate as he asked it. "Who?"

"I don't know! The ones who want me!" Her voice was very loud and she started to cry again.

"Fayre . . ." He was frightened now, a new fright that quickly began to change to rage. "I won't let them." He had no idea whom he was fighting, but he was no longer willing to be passive. He had many doubts clamoring in his mind for attention, all the questions that Prentiss had posed earlier. Was Fayre indeed too unstable now, could he deal with episodes like this, was he martyring himself to his new intimacy? None of that mattered when Fayre was in such pain.

With one arm still around her, he reached for the phone.

"What are you doing?" she demanded as he began to dial.

"What I should have done weeks ago."

"But it's three in the morning. You can't," she protested and tried to stop him. "I don't want anyone to see me like this. It's hard enough when *you* do."

Grimly Giles hung on to the phone and was shortly rewarded with the sound of a sleepy voice on the other end of the line. "Hugh, this is Giles. Can you come over right away?"

The sleepy voice mumbled, and then cleared. "Trouble?"

"Yes."

"I'll be there in an hour."

The line went dead and Giles turned to Fayre. "Hugh's on his way."

It was almost four-thirty when the white Datsun station wagon pulled into the carport. By that time Giles had fixed coffee and both he and Fayre had bathed.

"I'm not certain he can do anything," Fayre said as Giles started down the stairs to open the door.

"I'm not certain he can't," Giles answered, and hurried to let Hugh in.

Only the greater unruliness of his hair and a slight darkness around the eyes revealed that Hugh Audley was not used to being up at this hour. He was dressed neatly, as always, in slacks, patterned shirt and sweater, with a wool jacket over the rest. "Sorry it took so long. My car had electrical trouble, so I took Inga's." He waited while Giles closed the door. "Okay: what's wrong?"

Giles shook his head. "I don't know. Fayre woke up a couple of hours ago, in a terrible state. Something is very wrong, and I thought you could help."

This announcement did not seem to surprise Hugh, but he

asked, "Why did you call me? Why not another surgeon? Or that parapsychologist you've been working with?" The questions were sharp but the manner in which they were asked was not. Hugh went to the foot of the stairs. "How is she now?"

From the second floor Fayre answered, "I'm better. For the moment."

Immediately Hugh looked up. "What's the trouble? Can you tell me about it?" He had started up the stairs, Giles behind him.

"I don't know. It's all fragmented in my mind, and it terrifies me when I try to understand it. . . ." She put her hands into Hugh's as he reached the top of the stairs. "Giles said you can help. I hope that's true. Someone has to help me."

"I'll do everything I can, but it might not be much," he said.

"I've got coffee ready if you want some," Giles remarked as he came up the last step. "Do you think it's okay to have coffee?"

Hugh nodded. "Sure. Why not? I need something hot to wake me up. It won't hurt you, either." He looked from Giles to Fayre. "Well? Which of you will tell me what happened? And then tell me what you want me to do."

There was an awkward silence, then Giles said, "When Fayre woke up, she was so badly frightened that she seemed to be in some sort of shock. I tried to get a response from her for some time, and after a while, she started to cry."

"Why didn't you take her to the hospital?" Hugh asked in a reasonable tone. "Couldn't you have done more for her in a hospital?"

Giles stared down at his slippered feet. "It didn't seem to be that kind of problem. I didn't think it would do any good. I called you because . . ."

"You wanted my sort of perspective?" Hugh suggested, and did not wait for a reply as he turned to Fayre. "Were you frightened?"

She nodded. "It was almost like what happened . . . before, except I felt I was being called . . . out of myself. I thought that someone else wanted me to go away so . . . so I could be used. It was . . . I felt lost inside myself . . . I knew Giles was there, but I . . . couldn't touch him. I was too far away inside. And I thought that if I ever let go, I could not get back again, that I'd always be gone." She put her hands to her mouth. "It sounds so crazy. It happened that way."

"It doesn't sound crazy," Hugh said sympathetically. "It sounds very real and you had every right to be scared." He walked over to the dining table and took one of the seats. "No need to stand around this way. Join me. This might take time."

While Fayre seated herself across from Hugh, Giles went into the kitchen and poured three cups of coffee. When he came back to the dining room, Hugh was in the middle of a complex explanation.

"So whether or not you believe in psychic attack, you can still be the victim of it. One of the best ways to make such an attack is to undermine the victim's trust, not in others, but in him or herself. If you get people to distrust their own thoughts and hunches, you've gone a long way to getting them under your control. It sounds to me as if you've both had a lot of that to contend with." He reached out for the cup. "Thanks, Giles. Sit down. I want to check a few things out with you."

Giles sat next to Fayre, his hands around the cup before him. "What do you want to know."

"I'm trying to make sense out of what's going on. Oh, I know what seems to be going on, but that's another matter entirely. I'm not interested in appearances. Let me get this straight. You're no longer prepared to consider Fayre a patient . . ."

"Not now, but . . ."

"I don't mean because you're living together, I mean because you don't think she has a medical or neurological condition. Is that right?" Hugh had produced a small lined notebook from one of his pockets, and he scribbled as he talked.

"Yes. Whatever she's got, we're not dealing with disease pathology. I'm not certain what else is happening, but she isn't ill."

Hugh nodded. "And you don't think she needs a psychiatrist or you would have called Veronica, not me. Since you've called a minister, part of you thinks this is, somehow, theological." He sipped his coffee. "I hope you have more of this."

"There's a good amount in the pot," Giles said.

"Well? Is it theological? Or were you hoping that I had

some insight from all the things I did while I was a journalist?" He waited, watching Giles.

"I think," Giles said slowly, "that I called you because I trust you, and because I have no idea what we're dealing with. I thought you'd know something."

Hugh nodded again, rather slowly. "It's humbling to be trusted. It's the trust that matters, isn't it?" Plainly he didn't want an answer. "Fayre, are you prepared to trust me, too?"

She met Hugh's eyes. "Yes. Only it isn't really trust; I can read you too well."

"Well, that's something." Hugh drained his cup of coffee. "Why don't you bring the pot in?" he asked Giles, then wanted to know, "Where's the boy?"

"Asleep. His room is on the ground floor. Is that okay?" Giles said as he went for the pot.

"We won't disturb him too much, then, unless things get really bad. Thanks." The last was for the second cup of coffee. "Now tell me, as simply as you can, what seems to happen to you when you have moments like this last one. What do you feel? What do you think is going on?"

Fayre opened her hands and stared at them. "I'm not sure. It's as if I'm being displaced. I get very cold, and then I feel all stretched out. Tonight was different, though. Instead of being drawn away, I thought I was being called, or lured. I felt that there was something waiting to take my place, that wanted to use me, and that if I left . . ." She stopped, trembling.

"Did you feel this way when you had seizures before?" Again Hugh was writing in his notebook.

"I don't think so, not quite like this. But I've always had amnesia associated with it." She had locked her hands together and now she twisted them as her knuckles whitened. "If I didn't have that . . ."

Hugh put his hand over hers. "You've got to stay calm, Fayre. We don't want to start the cycle all over again." He looked at Giles. "Do you have any medication that is a relaxant? Valium or the like? I want to see if we can stop the tension now and then go over what happened." As he looked back at Fayre, he asked, "Are you willing to try that?"

"Anything," she said quietly. "But can I have some time to prepare?"

"How? What? It makes no sense to delay. It only means that your impressions will become more confused, and the less of a chance we have of breaking this thing." He shook his head. "I work with the dying, and I've learned to do things quickly; the dying don't have much time."

Fayre took her lower lip between her teeth and forced herself to agree. "I'll do what you think best. I don't know what else to do."

With the Valium, the fatigue, and the gentle, persistent suggestion of Hugh Audley, Fayre was able to achieve a light trance state. She leaned back on the cushions in the living room, her eyes fixed unsteadily at the only light that glimmered from a candle on the other side of the room.

"Are you certain this won't hurt her? Prentiss warned me that she might respond badly . . ." Giles said, worried now that he saw how vulnerable Fayre was to further manipulation.

"No, I'm not certain, but can you think of anything better?" Hugh demanded softly. "You asked me to come, and I said I'd do whatever I can. You've got to help me, Giles, not be crippled by doubts. Now, are you ready? You'll have to do exactly as I say, no matter what happens."

Giles murmured his assent. He forced himself to shut out his doubts and came across the room with Hugh, who knelt beside Fayre in the darkness. "Fayre, this is Hugh. We're going to do some hunting, you and I. Do you want to do that?"

"I suppose so," she said dreamily.

"I want you to seek out the people who are trying to hurt you. I want you to follow the trail back to them. Will you do that?"

"I'll try." She swallowed. "Yes. I will."

Hugh looked relieved. "Good. I want you to keep your eyes on the light. Look only at the light, and obey only my voice. The light is Giles, and he will not lead you to the wrong place."

Giles was startled to hear that, but remained quiet, watching Hugh as he worked.

"What is it you're supposed to do for the people who call you?" Hugh asked, still sounding as if he were having a conversation about the weather. The deepening of the strong lines around his eyes accented his tension, but his voice stayed casual and steady.

"It's Eilif they want." Fayre gave a minute shrug. "I can channel him for them. They have to have me to get him." There were tears in her eyes. "They don't want me to say this. They want me to keep silent."

"But you won't do that," Hugh said quickly. "You're going to obey only my voice."

Giles unclenched his fists and whispered, "Eilif. You said that before."

Hugh nodded. "Alice Hartwell told me."

"Alice Hartwell. What's this Eilif, then, some sort of demonic presence?" He had wanted to sound sarcastic, but his voice cracked.

"The only real demons are the ones we build inside ourselves, but they can be very dangerous, just the same." Hugh shifted his weight so that he moved more freely. "This Eilif is a nasty name for some of the less lovely parts of human beings. It's a name for having knowledge and power over everything. Kind of infantile in concept, and just as unreasoning and demanding as a frightened baby can be." He motioned Giles to silence and focused his attention on Fayre once again. "Why do they want to call Eilif? What do they want to know?"

"They want power. They want to know about future events, so that they can use the knowledge to get power." There was an unheard scream in her voice. "They'll do anything for that power."

Hugh leaned forward a little. "What do they need you for?"

"For Eilif. They want me to go away, and then Eilif will speak. They were calling me so that they could bring Eilif." She sounded remote, almost mechanical.

"Fayre!" Hugh said her name sharply. "Fayre, there is no Eilif, there is only their desires. You cannot be displaced by this Eilif. You can shut it out because it is only their will that is being used. You have a will, too. You can resist them, because your gift makes you stronger than they are. That's why they call you, but you can refuse." He reached for her hands and held them tightly. "Think about Giles, and watch him in the light. You must resist or you will lose Giles."

"No. No. I won't lose him!" Her voice had risen, but it became soft again quickly. "They will try again. They have been trying for a long time."

"Then you must force them away. Giles is here. You cannot leave him." Hugh leaned closer to her. Giles could see that he had begun to sweat. "Who wants to talk with Eilif?"

"I can't tell you!" She turned ghastly pale. "No."

"Why?" Hugh asked as he put one hand on her shoulder and motioned to Giles to do the same.

"Because they've forbidden it. It will mean that Eilif will replace me forever!" She was weeping now.

"But there is no Eilif," Hugh said firmly. "There is only their desire. And they are not strong enough to replace you. They are weak, or they would be able to talk to the Eilif part of themselves without your help." He was insistent and his hands were on her shoulder and back. He glanced at Giles. "Keep touching her. You've got to, Giles. I wish there were a way you could make love to her now, but do everything you can. Keep her aware of her physical body. Do things that give her physical pleasure, including masturbation, if she seems to respond."

Giles was bewildered, but he accepted the instructions, starting to caress her shoulders. He felt awkward and foolish, but it was important to continue, because Hugh nodded his approval. How strange it was to touch Fayre this way, feeling his love for her almost as a physical presence in his mind, but being completely unaroused by the sensation of her skin, the languor of her body. As Hugh talked, he moved closer to Fayre, so that she lay against him.

"Fayre, you don't have to obey them. They cannot hurt you. If they tried, you could stop them."

"But there are so many," she whimpered.

"So many? How many?" Hugh rapped the questions out and waited to write the answer in his notebook.

"I'm not sure. Fifteen, twenty. They're all eager. They want to control . . ."

"They cannot control you!" Hugh insisted. "Who is in charge of them? Resist that person first. The others will follow."

"They're not calling me now. That was earlier." She moved closer to Giles, snuggling into the curve of his body.

"You can resist them anytime," Hugh said patiently. "You can turn their feelings back on them. What do they want you to tell them?"

"The future. The things that will happen."

"And can you do that?" Hugh asked, somewhat startled.

"Not very often. That's why they want Eilif. Eilif tells them . . . things."

Hugh glared. "What they want to know, of course. That's one of the reasons for creating him."

"Eilif . . ." Fayre muttered, and turned her face to Giles' shoulder. "No more Eilif."

"That's right," Hugh agreed. "No more Eilif. We can make

him go away, from you and from the others. Then we'll know who they are."

"It's the power," she said slowly, slurring the words. "They want the power. It's Eilif."

Giles held Fayre close against him, disturbed by her remote expression and the lack of response she gave him. He could feel she was cold, but he had no way to warm her. As he listened to Hugh, he was more upset than he thought he would be. Who had been so cynical, so mindlessly ambitious that they had almost sacrificed Fayre's amazing talents and her sanity to a single-minded drive for power? At that moment, Giles felt an intense hatred he had never known before, and had thought himself incapable of feeling.

"Fayre," Hugh said as he sat beside her on the carpet, "Tell Eilif to return to those who made him. Tell him that now."

"Go away, Eilif," she said like an obedient child repeating a lesson.

"Say it again," Hugh ordered. "And then follow him to where he goes."

"Go home, Eilif," Fayre said, and closed her eyes.

"Keep your eyes open. Watch the light!" Hugh told her, staring at her intently until her eyes opened again and sought out the brightness. "Where did Eilif go?" he asked as soon as she had settled snugly against Giles.

"Home."

"Where was home? Who was it?" Hugh reached to take her hands. "You've agreed to obey me."

"No. No. I don't want to tell you. It's bad. I don't want to." She was weeping again, her face pitifully sad. "I can't ... It's hard ... Betrayed."

"Hugh, do you have to do this?" Giles whispered as he tightened his arms around Fayre.

"If you don't know who's doing this, how are you going to be able to stop them?" He waited while Giles made up his mind.

"Okay. Sodding bastards!"

"At least." Hugh gently turned Fayre to face him. "Fayre, where did Eilif go? Who made him?"

Her mouth quivered before she said the name, and in that instant, Giles knew who it was, and wanted to stop the words from being spoken as the recognition went through him like a knife.

"Eilif went to Prentiss. Prentiss Fellkirk."

□ 14 □

The sun had been up for almost an hour and the ocean out the dining-room window was touched with ruddy gold. Hugh sat across from Giles and Fayre, all three of them exhausted and listless, the platter of scrambled eggs turning cold as they spoke.

"But I've known Prentiss since we were boys. It doesn't make sense that he'd do a thing . . . like this," Giles protested for the third time. "He's not a monster; he's ambitious. No question about that. He always was. You're making him out to be . . . I don't know what. Prentiss is deeply involved in his work, I grant you that, but it isn't . . ." He stared at Hugh, feeling very helpless. Was it possible that all those years he had been mistaken, that his closest friend had never been a friend at all?

"He's always been helpful and concerned about me," Fayre said as she took Giles' hand. "Dr. Fellkirk was the one who had faith in my talent, and who worked with me to develop it. Couldn't it be that I've conjured him up in my mind because of that? Or there may be associates of his who are using him as a kind of psychic front . . ."

"Do you really believe that?" Hugh asked her soberly.

Fayre could not meet his eyes. "No. I don't. But I don't want to believe the other, either."

"Consider what's happened," Hugh said, making his voice dispassionate. "It was Fellkirk who found out about your abilities, and it was he who urged you to more comprehensive tests. You've had seizures when in his company, and you suffer from amnesia afterward. You said that Fellkirk was solicitous of you then, and that makes sense—he could afford to be, at least until you remembered what had happened. He convinced you that without his assistance, you'd be abandoned, turned into a guinea pig for unscrupulous psychic investigators. He brought Giles into the case as demonstration of his sincerity, knowing that Giles would not question his motives. It's a beautiful setup, and you took it on trust." He looked at his watch. "Six-fifty. When does your boy get up?"

"Around seven-thirty." Fayre looked at the eggs and sighed. "Do you want any of these?"

Neither Giles nor Hugh answered her. "Kip won't eat them cold. I'll put them in the frig until I can think of something to do with them." She took the platter as she rose, and carried it into the kitchen.

"You're going to have to be very careful now," Hugh pointed out, raising his voice so that it would carry. "Once Prentiss knows that you've traced him, he'll take steps to change that."

Giles was shocked. "Oh, come on, Hugh. It's one thing to play around with psychics, and another to take after them. He wouldn't do it. It might ruin his project."

"He'd rather do that than give up Fayre. You mustn't underestimate him." Hugh leaned forward onto his elbows. "He had a great thing going for him—Fayre brought him academic praises at the lab, and acted as medium for his own personal demon the rest of the time. He isn't apt to bow gracefully and exit simply because you've found him out. For one thing, he's still quite safe. Who can you complain to, and what could they do about it? What would a cop say if you showed up claiming that Fayre had been forced to be a precognitive medium for a recognized, well-reputed academic, particularly when all he would have to do is show that she had been part of his experiments, but had developed a history of seizures. All the cops would do, if they got that far, would be to apologize for disturbing him and figure you and Fayre for nuts."

Giles studied his hands. "I wouldn't want to involve Prentiss in anything like that."

"Why? Because you've been friends so long? Because you don't want to admit that he's dangerous enough to try to control you, to stop you?" Hugh glared across the table at Giles. "Why do you want to protect him? You saw what he did to Fayre. He'll do it again if he can. In fact, you're letting yourself in for a lot of trouble if he finds out that you've figured out what's going on. He won't wait for you to make a move—he'll act as quickly as possible."

"You can't be sure of that, Hugh," Giles objected, but it was with little conviction. If Prentiss had done this much already, he would be prepared to do more. Giles felt sick at heart. When Fayre had been in travail, he had wanted to kill the person who was the cause of it, but he could not bring himself to want Prentiss Fellkirk, whom he had known most of his life and whom he had always regarded as his oldest and best friend, to die. There had to be an explanation. "Maybe," Giles ventured, "maybe it was his association with Lupe that made him want to do . . . this."

"Probably the other way around," Hugh said. "He knew what he wanted and he sought her out, because she had the knowledge he lacked. You can't make me believe that she's under his influence. And that means she was already involved in this sort of thing before they met." They were silent as Fayre came back to the table.

After several minutes, Giles looked up. "Very well, Hugh. What do we do now?" Inwardly he ached as he asked the question. Against his will he had admitted at last that Prentiss could do the deliberately destructive things that had been done to Fayre. If there were mitigating circumstances, he wanted to know what they were, otherwise he had to believe that all the good fellowship had been deliberate sham.

"Don't blame yourself, Giles," Fayre said. "You're not disloyal. He's forfeited the right to your friendship. If he hadn't, I wouldn't agree to . . . stop him." She sighed. "How do we stop him? What's he doing that we *can* stop?"

"I'm not certain. But if he can use you, he can use others, and that demon he's built himself is pretty damn powerful." Hugh got to his feet and began to pace. "First off, we've got to give you more protection. Is there anyplace you can take your boy? Is there anyone who can stay with him, or he can stay with, whom you trust?"

"My aunt," Fayre said promptly. "She'll take him, or come here, whichever seems wisest."

"Do you think she'd mind taking the boy for a couple of days, until we know where we stand?" He stared up at the ceiling. "Giles, do you think you could call Prentiss today, just a social call, and find out what he's going to be doing for the next few days? We have to know what his movements are going to be."

"Do you think he'd tell me?" Giles asked, and knew that he dreaded making the call. "I'm not sure I can talk to him, not the way I'd have to. I want to demand an explanation from him, and I know I can't do that."

"Tell him you want to see him, or that there's some question about Fayre's talents. You can, if you like . . ."— Hugh's hazel eyes got very bright—"you can tell him that you might be close to discovering what's causing the seizures.

That will force his hand, but he might do something desperate. We'll have to think that out a little more."

"I want this over. I don't want to have to worry any longer about what's going to happen to me, or when, or how, or . . . to what purpose." Fayre looked at Giles, her face determined but calm. "I want this behind me. So I can work on my abilities without fearing what they might do. And I don't want to have fears about us. Let's get it over with, Giles, finish it."

Giles looked at Fayre, then Hugh. The room was growing light, and he rose to turn off the large brass lamp that hung over the dining table. Did he, he wondered, want to end it now? Perhaps it was wise to settle the matter quickly, for prolonging it could only cause pain. He closed his eyes, a furrow between his brows. "I want it finished, too."

Hugh studied Giles' face, then came back to the table. "Let's get ourselves a plan. We don't want to take any unnecessary risks."

"We've got enough risk as it is," Giles said quietly. "Christ, I wish it were over."

Kip was delighted at the chance to have a trip with his aunt. "I'll take some of my accumulated sick leave," Anna Dubranov said as she smiled down at Kip. "I have an old friend who lives outside of Santa Rosa on the Russian River. She usually has her grandchildren up for the summer, and I'm sure she'll be glad for another kid. I'll write her name and address down for you, and a phone number. We should be up there this afternoon."

Fayre nodded absently, a frown dragging her face down. "If anyone, anyone at all, should call or come by and ask about Kip or me or Giles . . ."

"Why, I haven't heard from you in a few days. I have no idea where you are. In fact, I'm surprised they can't reach you." She beamed at them. "Most people expect dumpling-shaped middle-aged women to be honest, eager to please and rather stupid. Sometimes it comes in handy. Most times it's irritating." She gave Fayre an affectionate pat on the arm. "You don't have to worry about me. I'll do it right. I don't like the idea of people using others against their will. I'll have them truly baffled."

"Aunt Anna," Kip said as he tugged at her sleeve, "will there be horses?"

"Why, yes, Fiona has two horses she keeps for her grandchildren. I'm sure she'll let you ride one." Apparently she sensed Fayre's reservations. "The horses are used to children, very gentle and steady-tempered. Fiona wouldn't have them if they weren't." She thought of another treat and told Kip, "She had a couple of boats, too, and you can go on the river. I know that Matt would be glad to take you out with him. He likes to go fishing in the early morning."

Kip's eyes widened. "Fishing! Hey, I caught a couple fish once, when Granddad took me with him. I'm good at it."

The anxiety lifted from Fayre's eyes. "Good. You'll have fun, won't you, Kip? I'll call you every evening, and you can tell me what you've done."

"Speaking of calls," Giles put in, "be sure that Kip does not answer the phone. If they learn he's here, then there might be an attempt to harm him. Be very careful."

"Keep him in, if you can, Aunt Anna," Fayre said, and looked to where Kip sat with a magazine on his lap. "Kip, listen a moment, will you? I know it's hard, but I want you to stay in the house until Aunt Anna is ready to leave. It'll only be an hour or so, and maybe you can watch TV. There are some mean people who are looking for me, and they will want to find you, too."

Kip grinned, excited by the newness of the danger. "Will they do terrible things if they catch us?"

"Yes, Kip, they will," Fayre said. "Please, honey, don't turn this into a game. It isn't. It's very serious and you could be badly hurt if you got caught. . . ." She turned to Giles, her eyes pleading with him.

"Okay." Giles went and squatted down next to Kip's chair. "You remember the devil-man, the one that forced you out onto the rocks?"

His eyes grew wide. "I remember."

"These are the same men, and they will do worse than that if they catch us this time. So it's very important that you help us, and not go outside or answer the phone or let anybody know you're here. Once you're at Fiona's place, then you'll be okay, and you'll have a grand time, but until then, you've got to be very careful. Will you do that for your mother?" he asked. "It's a big thing, I know, but you're old enough and smart enough to handle it, aren't you?"

Kip stared at his magazine and nodded slowly. "I won't make it a game, Giles. I promise."

"Good. We're depending on that." He rose and turned back to Anna. "We've got to go. We don't want to stay here any longer than necessary. Do you have my number at the hospital?"

"Yes, I do. I'll call you from Fiona's. Don't worry, he'll be fine. You take care of yourselves now, and leave Kip to me." She smiled efficiently and pointed them toward the front door. "I'll plan to be back in a week unless you tell me otherwise."

Fayre hugged her aunt, then tried to speak. The words choked her and for a moment she clung to the older woman.

"Never mind that," Anna said with a sniff. "You'd best be going. Be sensible, Dr. Todd."

"I'll try," Giles said as he held the door for Fayre. He knew that he meant it, but could not decide what a sensible course might be in a situation as difficult this one.

Prentiss was not at the lab. When Giles called from the hospital a cool young woman told him that Dr. Fellkirk would not be in that week.

"All right. Thank you. Tell him that Dr. Todd called, if you will." He hung up without waiting for a response.

"Any luck?" Hugh asked. He was sitting in one of the two chairs in Giles' office. Fayre was in the other.

"He wasn't at his house and he isn't at the lab. They said he'll be out for the rest of the week. Where should I try next?"

"Lupe's place?" Fayre suggested. She looked tired now, with dark smudges under her eyes and a whiteness to her upper lip.

Giles shrugged. "I can try. I don't know where else he might be." He picked up the phone and got an outside line as he fumbled for his address book. The number was a fairly melodic one but the pure electronic notes had little effect on Giles.

"This is Lupe's phone robot," said the device at the other end, "and I am answering for her because she is not available just now. If you will leave your name, the number or numbers where you can be reached, and the time of your call, I will see that she contacts you at her earliest opportunity. There is time for a sixty-second message following the tone."

As he listened, Giles said, "She's not there. I've got her answering machine. What should I do?"

"Tell it something," Hugh said.

There was a low beep and Giles stumbled over the words. "Uh . . . Lupe, this is Giles Todd. I'm . . . I'm trying to get

ahold of Prentiss. Have him call me at the hospital today, or
at home tonight. . . . Uh . . . It's important that I talk to
him." He decided that was enough, and hung up. "Fayre, will
you stay here for a while? No one will bother you in here.
I've got rounds and a lecture and a few other things to do.
I'll take you to lunch, and then we'll go downtown and I'll
get us a room at one of the hotels."

"Okay. Do you have anything to read in here?"

Giles flushed. "I've got a few paperbacks in the top desk
drawer. You're welcome to them." He glanced at Hugh.
"What're your plans?"

"I've got rounds to make, too, and a meeting to go to
later on. I'll try to stop by here on my way to dinner. We'll
work out the rest of the plan then."

"If you get any ideas, jot them down," Giles told him, then
touched Fayre's shoulder. "If you get bored, you can always
go over to Golden Gate Park. Just tell Mrs. Houghton where
you're going and when you'll be back. I'll panic thirty minutes
later." He bent to kiss her.

"I'll keep that in mind," she said, attempting a smile. "It is
nice out, and I don't think that anyone is going to try to take
me out of Golden Gate Park in the middle of tourist season.
I might go to the Japanese Tea Garden if it isn't too
crowded. Thanks for thinking of it." She leaned back in the
chair and crossed one leg over the other. "And then again, I
might nap."

Outside his office, Giles turned to Hugh. "Do you think it's
okay for her to go to the Park?"

"I'd imagine so. She's probably as safe there as she is in
your office." He patted Giles' arm. "Don't get worn out yet.
There's still a lot to do. I'll see you later."

"Okay. Thanks."

"It's my job," Hugh said with a self-deprecating grin as he
turned and went down the hall.

Shortly before six that evening Giles was on the last of his
rounds. It would be another half hour and then he and Fayre
could go to dinner and enjoy the evening. In a burst of ex-
travagance, he had taken a room at the Fairmont at the top
of Nob Hill. It would be a lovely evening, he promised himself, with a good meal and luxurious surroundings. There
would be time to talk with Hugh before they left. Giles was
starting to recover from the shock of that morning. He had
already decided that Prentiss must be reasoned with, not

fought, for an open confrontation would benefit no one. Now that he had had some time to think about it, he was certain that Prentiss could not be as desperate as he seemed, that this Eilif manifestation was only an experiment that had got out of hand. With her talent, Fayre would be able to help deal with Prentiss so that she would not have to give up the work she loved, but would not be at the mercy of Prentiss' overambitious projects.

The emergency code on the PA system brought him out of his reflection. "Brady," he said sharply to the nurse in the room, "I've got to go. See that Dr. Sheng or Crawford finishes up these evaluations." He did not stay to hear the answer, knowing that a nurse as competent as Linda Brady would not neglect patients for any reason.

By the time he reached the emergency/neurological area, he found only one other doctor there: Will Hensell, still feeling his cocktail-hour martinis, stood with the emergency-room staff looking over an elderly man racked by convulsions.

"Hey, Giles, we got a winner!" Will called out, waving Giles nearer.

The others chuckled, but Giles was shocked. "What's the matter?" he asked as he came up to the gurney. "What's happening? What's the history?"

"Can't get it from him in this condition," Will protested sagely. "Look at him—no way to communicate."

"Who brought him in? Are they here? Can they help?" He rapped out the questions and the paramedics and two interns stopped their amused exchanges.

"There's another man with him, I think. He said he was a nephew or something." The intern was starting to be disturbed by what he had seen. "I'll go, if you like."

"Someone had better go. Right now. What about blood series? Get someone in here to draw him. Urine, stool, saliva, the whole works. I want an EEG and an EKG as fast as you can get them. Now!" When only he and Will Hensell were left with the stricken man, Giles turned to his colleague. "What's the matter with you, Will? Being drunk is no excuse. This man could be dying, and you're cracking jokes about it. I've heard that surgeons have to be callous, but I never thought it meant this. Who's on call tonight? Other than you?"

"No one," Will answered, his face growing red. "You've

got no right to talk to me like this, Todd. You aren't the chief of surgery, or—"

"Do you want to hear this from the chief of surgery?" Giles shot back. "Who else is on? You're in no condition to deal with this man. If you have to operate, you'll kill him."

"I don't have to—" Will began, swaying slightly with anger.

"Yes you do. If you can sober up in half an hour, I won't stop you—I'll protest formally, but I won't stop you. Now, who is supposed to be on call tonight?" He wanted to turn his whole attention to the man on the gurney, but it was plain that Will Hensell was determined to challenge him.

"Jeninne Nessien. She went home earlier with some kind of rash. She was exposed to measles a couple weeks ago." Will was turning sulky. "I'm a better surgeon than she is, anyway."

"I doubt it. Jeninne doesn't drink when she works." He bent over the patient, and with an effort lifted an eyelid. Only a small crescent of iris showed. Giles shook his head.

"Get him ready for X rays, and CT scans if that doesn't do any good. Let me know as soon as we've got a lab report so we can give him something to lessen the convulsions." This was said to the paramedic who had returned from the lab.

"Okay, Dr. Todd." He began to secure the patient to the gurney.

Giles stuck his head out of the cubicle. "Nurse!" he called to the woman standing nearby. "Call my office and tell them that I'm going to be delayed down here. And let Reverend Audley know where I am. Then get an emergency team together."

The woman turned to do his bidding.

As she turned, Giles saw that there was another nurse who had been talking with her. Nancy Lindstrom stood watching Giles for a long moment. She moved a little closer, and looked Giles up and down with cool, incurious contempt. Then, without a word, she turned on her heel and followed where the other nurse had gone.

It was after ten o'clock when Giles left the operating room. He was exhausted, emotionally and physically, and his nerves were wire-taut. The fight for the elderly man had been long and grueling, and the outcome was still uncertain. He had survived the surgery, but Giles doubted very much that he

would last more than a few days. The damage had been too
massive and the repair too drastic.

"You did your best, Giles," Carl Minton, who had assisted
him, said.

"Great." Now that they were out of the operating room,
Giles felt the places where sweat plastered his loose green
tunic to his arms and back. He tugged the tight cap off his
head. "God, I look like a butcher shop. I want the shower
first."

Carl inclined his head. "It's yours. You earned it."

Now that he could let up on the fierce concentration of his
work, Giles thought, rather guiltily, of Fayre waiting in his
office. Ruefully, he remembered the evening he had planned
out for them, and promised himself he would make it up to
her. As he stripped and stepped into the hot shower, he wondered if he had better call Hugh. The needle-sharp spray and
billowing steam sought out the fatigue in his body, as his
wandering attention found it in his mind.

By the time he stepped out of the shower and began to
towel himself off, Giles wanted nothing more than the luxury
of a good bed and Fayre to sleep beside him. He dressed
slowly, rubbing the stubble on his chin. For a man planning a
seductive two days, he was off to a lamentable start. He debated with himself about shaving, and decided that he would
do it later. Fayre would be waiting and she had seen him un-
shaven before.

Some of his good humor was restored as he walked toward
his office. In half an hour they would be at the Fairmont, and
they could wake to a long, lazy morning.

He knocked on the door. "Fayre?" She might have dozed
off, or was busy reading.

There was no response.

"Fayre?" This time the knock was louder. "It's Giles." He
opened the door onto a dark room. Puzzled, he turned on the
light.

The room was empty, and only a used coffeecup suggested
the place had been occupied.

Cold panic gripped him, hard as a physical blow. Then he
got hold of himself. She might well have gone down to the
lobby, since it was so lonely and oppressively quiet at night.
He went to Mrs. Houghton's desk and picked up her phone.
"Front desk?" he said when he was answered. "Will you
please page Mrs. Schoenfeld for me? This is Dr. Todd."

He waited, listening to the impersonal voice repeat "Mrs. Schoenfeld, Mrs. Schoenfeld," as if the name were a chemical formula, and when the page had been repeated without success, Giles thanked the front desk and hung up. He slumped against the wall, telling himself that his fears were foolish, and that nothing had happened. On impulse he picked up the phone again and this time called the Fairmont, and asked the operator to ring their room. The ring went unanswered.

Giles was staring at the wall, refusing to admit his fear, when a friendly voice spoke at his shoulder. "Can't locate her?" Hugh stood beside him. "You're worried?"

"Yes. And I can't think. I've been trying to think." He put his hand to his eyes. "It's absurd, but I keep thinking that somehow, somehow, Prentiss has got her. I can't bear to think that. But it keeps coming back, again and again."

"Why couldn't Prentiss have her?" Hugh asked.

"How could he get her away from here? This is a big hospital. My receptionist was out in front until five-thirty. People can't just wander in and drag someone out . . ." His hands slapped to his sides. "I don't think it could happen, but I'm frightened that it did." He looked at Hugh. "What are you doing here?"

"I was waiting to see you. I didn't get out of my meeting until almost nine, and I found out you were still in surgery. After everything you've been through today, I thought it might be easier to talk."

"Did you see Fayre?" Giles asked, hoping that Hugh would give him the answer he wanted.

"No, I'm sorry. I was having coffee with Veronica until a few minutes ago. I wanted her opinion on this case, but in confidence. She's kind of upset about it." Hugh shook his head. "Where have you looked for her?"

"I've had her paged, I called the hotel . . ."

"Did you call home?" Hugh suggested.

"No. Why should I? Why should she go there? How would she get there?" His sense of helplessness washed over him like a tide.

"Have you asked the staff if anyone saw her or spoke to her?" Hugh sounded so reasonable that Giles made himself think clearly.

"I haven't asked. I suppose I ought to." He picked up the phone and tried the front desk again. No one on duty there could remember seeing her. "No luck," he said to Hugh with a twisted smile.

"Try emergency. She might have gone down there."

"Why?" Giles demanded, but obediently pushed the button for emergency. "This is Dr. Todd. Is Mrs. Schoenfeld there, or has she been there?"

"I haven't seen her, Dr. Todd, but I'll ask." The nurse pushed the hold button, and in a few minutes there was a voice on the line. "Dr. Todd? Dr. Ensenbach says that he saw her earlier talking with Nancy Lindstrom and a woman she didn't know. Would you like to talk to Dr. Ensenbach? She's still here."

"Is Nancy Lindstrom still there?" Giles demanded.

"No, she went off shift at eight. I should imagine she's home by now." There was enough primness in her tone to imply that Nancy had left with Tim Carey.

"Just a moment," Giles said, then relayed the information to Hugh.

"Ask what the other woman looked like. Dr. Ensenbach might be able to tell you." Hugh was starting to pace again in his impatience.

"Nurse? Will you put Dr. Ensenbach on, please? Unless she's busy." Giles waited, his anxiety growing.

"Giles? This is Penny Ensenbach. I hear you've mislaid a patient."

"Yes, you might say that," Giles said, realizing that under other circumstances he would be tempted to turn her comment to a pun. "You mentioned you saw her down there?"

"That's the woman with the lovely blond hair, isn't it? She was here with Nancy Lindstrom about two hours ago. They were talking with a woman I didn't recognize."

"Can you describe her?" Giles asked quickly, motioning to Hugh to hand him a pencil.

"I think so. She was very striking. Let's see, she was quite slender and fairly tall, I'd say early to mid-thirties, olive skin and black hair cut short, you know, like a Norman helmet."

"Lupe!" Giles stopped writing.

"She said something about an emergency in Palo Alto. I caught a name, Kirk Something. I wish I'd seen more."

"It was enough. Thanks very much, Penny." Giles was about to put down the receiver, feeling a new torment in his heart.

"You might be interested that Nancy seemed very pleased with herself. She mentioned to me that at last she'd met someone who wasn't afraid to get back at you. Whatever it is you did to that woman, she definitely holds a grudge. She also said that you could beg for it from now on. I gather she's been wanting to harm you for some time."

"Then she can congratulate herself, because she's succeeded," Giles said through clenched teeth. "I'm glad you told me."

"Sorry it's bad news." Penny Ensenbach hung up after one short bit of cheer. "You'll manage, Giles."

"Lupe's got her? Who helped her?" Hugh said as soon as Giles had hung up.

"Nancy Lindstrom helped her. I don't know how she got Fayre to leave my office . . ." He stopped, overwhelmed by fear and fighting the tears that welled in his eyes. "Hugh?"

"Hold on, Giles. We'll find her." He took the phone from Giles. "What's Nancy Lindstrom's number?"

Giles forced his attention away from himself. "It's here, in my address book." He handed it to Hugh. "If she's not there, have the desk call Tim Carey's place. They're seeing each other these days." It was difficult to say that, to admit that Nancy had allied herself with Tim Carey.

Hugh pressed the number and waited. "No answer."

"Tim's, then."

There was a wait, but at last Hugh nodded to Giles. "Tim? This is Hugh Audley. . . . No, I'm still at the hospital. I was wondering, is Nancy Lindstrom there? . . . Yes, it is fairly important. I wouldn't call if it weren't."

"Let me talk to her," Giles said.

Hugh shook his head, and went on to Carey. "Something happened a little earlier, and I was told she might have some information that could be helpful. I'm sorry to interrupt like this. I know you don't want to be disturbed, but it . . . Thanks." He looked toward Giles. "Let me talk to her. She won't tell you anything, but she might say something to me." Then he turned his attention back to the phone. "Nancy? Hugh Audley. Look, I was wondering if you'll be willing to help me. There was a young woman with Dr. Todd today, and she's disappeared from the hospital, and apparently you were the last person to see her. Do you know why she left and where she went?" He listened, a slight look of pain in his weathered face. "I see. Do you have any idea where they might have gone?"

"Let me talk to her!" Giles whispered fiercely.

This time Hugh's gesture was almost forbidding. "Nancy?"

he said to the receiver as he motioned Giles away. "Why did you do that? You could have guessed the coffee was drugged. . . . I'm not trying to pry, but if you knew that Mrs. Schoenfeld was in danger . . . All right. . . . No, I won't." He held out the receiver. "She hung up."

"Well, what the bloody hell did she say?" Giles demanded.

"She said that Lupe wanted to talk to Fayre in private, so she took her to your office. She said Lupe brought her a cup of coffee. She did it to get back at you, Giles."

"Tim Carey must be teaching her some new tricks," Giles interrupted. "Why couldn't she have taken her anger out on me? Why Fayre?"

"Because how else could she hurt you?" Hugh asked gently.

"She's done that, all right." Giles crossed his arms, hating the doubt, the worry, the fear that was eating away at him. "What else did she say?"

"Not a great deal. She did mention that the woman said something about Fellkirk, and that's all."

"Fellkirk! That's to be expected. But where have they gone?"

"Possibly to the lab, or to Prentiss' house. Didn't she have one of her seizures at Prentiss' house?" Hugh tried to look hopeful, and though he failed, his compassion touched Giles.

"We'll try there. If not there, then the lab." He had started to pull on his coat. "Hugh, I'm sorry. It may be stupid, but I don't want the police involved if I can help it. If you don't want to come along, I understand. It isn't your fight."

Hugh stared at him, but his eyes were seeing something at a great distance. "You know, when I was a reporter in Vietnam, I tried to tell myself that, that it wasn't my fight, and that I had no obligations except to file honest stories. Then I spent a week with an interrogation unit. That's the new word for torture. I saw an American sergeant use a cattle prod on the genitals of a thirteen-year-old boy. It wasn't necessary because the sergeant already had the information he wanted. He was making sure that we weren't double-crossed. There were other things, too, that I don't want to remember. I couldn't write that story, or any story after that. When I sat down at my typewriter, I would literally shake so badly that my fingers could not type. I was given a six-week vacation by my paper, and told to fuck around for a while. But I couldn't. And after a few days, I ended up drunk in Saigon, and a young MP dragged me out of a fight and almost opened my skull with his truncheon." He stopped, clearing his throat. "The concussion wasn't too bad, but I was in rotten shape. Anyway, sometime while I was lying in my hotel room, I began to realize that there were things that are humane and sane and there are things that are not, and that I had to make a choice between humanity and inhumanity. I've never figured out if that's being called by God, or what. Maybe that's why I became a Unitarian instead of some other, more formalized religion. I know I became a minister because it was my only weapon. So it is my fight, Giles. I signed up for it long before now."

Giles looked away, astonished at what Hugh had told him. He had guessed that Hugh's late vocation for the ministry had come out of his war experiences, but he had always imagined that it was a heroic encounter on the battlefield or a moment of revelation when hope was exhausted. He was not prepared for this, for the sordidness of it. He cleared his throat. "Perhaps you'd better call Inga. We're going to be late."

□ 15 □

They made the run to Woodside in less than an hour. The freeway was almost empty at that time of night and Giles drove his Land Rover at as high a speed as he dared. Hugh sat beside him, saying little, remarking once that Giles needed more rest than he'd had in the last twenty-four hours.

"I can't stop for a rest just now," Giles said grimly.

"No, of course you can't. Just keep it in mind."

Prentiss' house was dark and there were no cars parked in front of it. "What do you think?" Giles said as they pulled up in the wide driveway.

"I don't know. Should we go around to the back? He could be wanting us to think he's not here." Hugh had already opened the door and was stepping out of the car.

Giles joined him. "Let's try the door first."

"And warn him?" Hugh asked.

"If there's any reaction at all, we'll know someone is in there." He felt foolish as he rang the bell. It would be too easy for Prentiss to bring Fayre here. There was the lab, there was the privacy of Lupe's house on Skyline. He tapped his hand against his thigh, whistling slightly through his teeth.

"No answer," Hugh said. "Do you want to look around the back? There could be a light on we can't see."

They had just started around the side of the house when another car pulled into the driveway. Giles plucked at Hugh's sleeve and started back toward the newly arrived car.

"Hold it right there!" came the command, and a bright light lanced out of the darkness at them.

"What?" Giles said, lifting his hand to shield his face.

"Police." The voice announced the word like the sound of closing doors. "Hands up. Over here by the car. Fast."

"Look, officer," Giles said as he moved to obey. "I don't know why you stopped us, but let me identify myself and explain."

The policeman shoved Giles and Hugh against the car. "Hands against the roof. Quick!"

It seemed impossible to Giles. He was being frisked by a policeman in front of Prentiss Fellkirk's house. He might be detained for hours. "There's identification in my wallet, inside my coat. I'm Dr. Giles Todd. I'm associated on a case with Professor Fellkirk."

"Sure," the policeman said, and began to frisk Hugh.

"I've got identification, too," Hugh remarked with asperity. "Right-rear pocket, in my wallet."

From inside the car a second policeman said, "I called in the license number. No warrants against it. The car is owned by a Dr. Giles Todd, all right."

"This is absurd!" Giles burst out. "We're trying to find Professor Fellkirk. It's an emergency. He was supposed to meet us here." He turned around slowly. "Officer, this isn't a joke. We have to find Professor Fellkirk, and soon."

The policeman stood with Giles' wallet in his hand. He opened it and studied the contents. "You're Giles Todd, all right. But you haven't said what you're looking for."

Hugh interrupted before Giles could answer. "Does Fellkirk have a silent alarm? You got here very fast."

"Yep," the policeman said. "Let me have your wallet, mister."

"Reverend," Hugh corrected, smiling sweetly.

The policeman sniffed, but took the wallet gingerly. "Shit! Reverend Audley." He gave the wallet back.

"I believe I have a parking ticket about five days old that I haven't paid yet," Hugh said at his most good-natured. "Check it out on the computer, if you like."

"It isn't outstanding yet," the policeman snapped.

Giles wondered if perhaps he could capitalize on the policemen's mistake. "We do have to find Professor Fellkirk. Is there any way you could suggest? Can you help us?"

"Is it Woodside?" the policeman in the car asked.

"Probably not, if Professor Fellkirk isn't here," Giles admitted, feeling new helplessness.

"Then we can't do very much. We can give the other officers in the area a call, though, and tell them not to pick you up again. We'll describe the car, and that way, if you go poking around you won't get hauled in, or have to go through this again." The policeman looked hopeful. "If it's a life-and-death matter, we might be able to stretch the rules. Is someone dying?"

"I don't know," Giles answered honestly. "That's why we have to reach Professor Fellkirk."

"Then I don't think we can do much, but we'll pass the word about you guys. Hey, be glad you aren't real thieves. You'd be real bad at it." He motioned them away from the side of the car.

"Thanks, officer," Hugh said. "We appreciate your help."

His irony was lost on the policeman. "No trouble. Just remember when you do this again, some of these people have guns in the house and you might get shot. They get jumpy when folks come skulking around in the night. Keep it in mind." He slammed the door, and gestured to his partner. The car's engine roared and then the pale green car was gone.

"It might help," Giles said, not convinced. "We'd better try the lab next. It's closest." As they went to the Land Rover, he began to be frightened at the enormity of their task. Prentiss need only move Fayre from place to place and it would be days before he could find her.

"Well, it keeps interference to a minimum," Hugh said dubiously. He got into the passenger's side of the car. "The lab."

The building was well-lit but the doors were locked and there were no lights in the offices that Giles could see. He went around the building twice, then returned to the parking lot. "I didn't find anything," he said miserably.

"Neither did I. There's no one in the basement, and I can't

find a way in. The thermostat is turned down to sixty, so they can't have anyone there, I don't think. What time is it?" Hugh looked around uneasily. "I don't like it."

"It's almost midnight." He laughed awkwardly. "Traditional witching hour. I wish I could get that thought out of my mind. It's childish, but that's the hour when . . . things happen."

"Coaches turn into pumpkins, for example," Hugh growled. "I'm going to give Alice Hartwell a call. She might be able to tell us something."

"Good idea," Giles agreed, and no longer thought it remarkable that they should seek the advice of a self-avowed witch.

The Seven-Eleven store was still open, and Hugh called from there. Giles waited in the car, impatient, thinking of what might have happened to Fayre by now. No, he told himself firmly, you can't believe that. You must believe that she's still all right, that they haven't harmed her. Too much. He thought of her lying still in a hospital bed, cool and wholly unresponsive. I can't let it happen, he said inwardly. I won't let it happen. It mustn't happen. He wished Hugh would finish the call, for he grew more anxious each moment. He wanted to be off to Lupe's. That house, with its quiet, secluded rooms and the deep grove behind it in the splendor of the redwood trees. It would be a good place to meet, very private, not likely to disturb anyone. Where, for the love of God, was Hugh? Giles had not smoked in almost ten years, but now he found himself longing for a cigarette, so that he could do something, and his hands, at least, would be busy. What would they do to Fayre? he asked himself. What did they want now, and how could they get it? He dreaded the answers his mind suggested.

"I got Alice," Hugh said as he opened the door. "She said the only group she has contact with meets down near Big Basin, but that this is not a pagan holiday, and that whoever is having a celebration on a night like this doesn't know the calendar." He slammed the door closed. "She mentioned that powerful coven again, and said she'd call around to find out if anyone in her group has more information. Apparently most of the witch community is pretty worried about this Eilif thing. I don't blame them."

"But you don't believe in demons," Giles reminded him,

hoping to make light of the new information. "You said yourself they don't exist."

"I believe in the power of malice," Hugh said, his mouth closing to a thin line. "Get going."

In the dark, the La Honda Road up to Skyline was even more treacherous than it was in daylight. It wriggled and twisted up the steep hillside, making hairpin turns and long switchbacks. The tires screamed as Giles held the Land Rover on the road by force.

"This thing isn't a sports car," Hugh said quietly as they raced up one of the few straight bits of road.

"It doesn't have to be," Giles replied. He was concentrating on the road with intensity born of despair and fatigue. He dragged on the steering wheel and pulled the car around a tight curve.

"There are deer on this road, and raccoons."

"They can hear us coming and get out of the way," Giles promised him.

"Fine. What happens when we go into a ditch? I know these things have a winch, but that won't get you out. It won't help Fayre if you wreck us, either." He hung on to the brace above the passenger door. "You're an excellent driver, Giles, but—"

"Hugh, shut up." His voice was soft, but the set of his jaw made up for that.

"Okay. But you'd better stop at Skylonda for gas. The tank's almost empty, and it won't do us any good to run out of gas up here."

Giles looked at the gas gauge. It showed that they had less than a gallon in the tank now. It would be impossible to get back down the road to a service station before running out. There was only the little station at Skylonda. "Isn't it closed?"

"The guy who runs it has a house next to the station. Summertime like this, there's usually someone up, looking for people like you and me." Hugh sounded resigned now. "I can call Alice, too, and find out if she's got any more information for us."

An old station wagon filled with teenagers sped past them, racing down the hill. The sound of their shouts drifted back to the Land Rover.

"Gas at Skylonda, then," Giles said, going cold again as he thought bleakly of the lost time.

After persistent knocking, a middle-aged man came out of the little house near the two-pump service station and glared at them. "It's after midnight," he snapped.

"We're out of gas," Giles said quickly. "I'm a doctor," he rushed on, holding out his wallet. "Check my ID, if you like. This is an emergency."

The man looked at the wallet, sniffed once or twice. "What's your car take?"

"The best you've got," Giles said, almost weak with relief. "And check the oil. It should be okay, but the way I've been driving tonight . . ."

"Sure, sure, I know the drill, Doc," the man said, rubbing his thinning gray hair. "I'll get you on your way again in a little."

"Thank you. Thank you very much," Giles said fervently.

"And is there a pay phone?" Hugh interjected.

"Across the road there, by the café. There's a light in it. You'll see it." He pushed past Giles and wandered over to the two pumps. Reluctantly he turned on a light and one very bright bulb flooded the little service station with light. "I don't see many of these," he observed, patting the angular hood.

Hugh touched Giles' shoulder. "I'm going to call Alice. I won't be any longer than I have to." Then he sprinted away into the dark.

Giles was tapping his steering wheel with impatience as the attendant finished adding oil. Hugh had been gone for almost ten minutes, there had been one other car down the road, and Giles was ready to scream.

There was a sound in the night, a sound that Giles had known well in the years he had lived with his uncle, the sound of a walking—no, a limping horse. He turned toward the sound, and in a moment a rangy woman in twill riding slacks, high boots and a leather hacking jacket walked into the light. She was leading a big handsome bay gelding.

"Hi, Camille. Something wrong with Shiloh there?" The service-station attendant paused in his examination of the dipstick. "He don't look hurt."

"He's not," said Camille. "We were coming up the road two, maybe three hours back, and five cars came by us fast. Shiloh freaked, almost threw me, which isn't like him, and stumbled. Now he's got his off-hind shoe hanging on by a

"Pardon me," Giles called, "but we are in a hurry."

"Your friend ain't back yet," the attendant pointed out and grinned at Camille. "What were you doing out so late, anyway?"

"I was over at the Jacksons' place and stayed too long. You know how they are. D'you mind if I make myself a cup of coffee? I'm beat." She plainly didn't expect any opposition as she started toward the little house.

"What were all the cars doing on the road? I thought Shiloh was used to cars." He had slammed the hood now and was walking back to the pump to check the price of the gas.

"It's that crazy bunch that go down to the big new place between La Honda and San Gregorio. I can't remember their name. You know the ones, they go in for meditation and chanting and all kinds of outlandish things. They lock the kids up in the house and go off for who-knows-what. Damned fools, if you ask me."

The words caught Giles' attention. He looked up and glanced at the woman as she looped an end of her horse's bridle around a fence rail. "Ma'am!" he shouted. "Ma'am, just a minute!"

She looked back as Giles got out of the car and came toward her. "Yes?" Her manner was frosty and she stayed next to her horse.

"I didn't mean to upset you," Giles began, trying to be more collected. "I'm Dr. Giles Todd. I've been trying to find an . . . associate of mine most of the night. Can you tell me a little more about the people you saw?"

She smiled sarcastically. "If you're a doctor, you aren't likely to know that bunch. They're weird ones. They aren't the right bunch for anybody to associate with, least of all doctors."

"I realize that. That's why I want to find him. Can . . . can you tell me anything at all?" He wasn't sure that she believed him, or if she did, if she would be willing to help him.

"What kind of doctor are you?" she asked suspiciously.

"I'm a neurosurgeon. Nerves, brains, that kind of surgeon. I work at the University of California, at their hospital in San Francisco, where the medical school is." He wished he could grab her by the shoulders and shake her until the information fell out.

"The big hospitals on Parnasus, right?" She nodded once. "I'll tell you everything I know, but that's not much. There's a group that goes out to that new ranch—not that they do much ranching out there. They were out there last night, and again tonight, which is pretty unusual. Most of the people around here stay clear of them."

"Where's this ranch?" Giles asked impatiently.

"That'll be nine-fifty," the attendant said laconically at Giles' shoulder.

"You go down this road, through La Honda, and out toward the ocean. It's on the south—the left side of the road, a big white-and-green house with a fancy stone patio, a couple hundred yards back from the road. There's barns off to the west of the house. There'll be half a dozen cars there now, I guess. You can't miss it." She patted Shiloh's nose and went to check the loosened saddle girths. "If you're planning on going down there, I'd be pretty careful. They're an unfriendly lot."

"Thank you," Giles said sincerely as he handed a twenty-dollar bill to the attendant.

"I don't have change," he said with what might have been a wink.

Giles sighed. "Keep it. Keep it." He held out his hand to Camille. "Thank you again. It might make a big difference." And he added to himself: it might not. If these were not the people he was searching for, he had to face the possibility of losing Fayre, for a short time or forever. His hands shook as he turned back to the Land Rover, and started the motor.

Almost five minutes later Hugh came jogging across the road and ran toward the car. He was slightly out of breath as he tugged open the door. "I've got . . . what might be a lead. . . . Just a rumor, Alice said. . . . There's a group meets out near San Gregorio . . ."

"Beach," Giles finished for him. "I just heard. Get in. I'll tell you about it."

"Good." Hugh pulled himself onto the seat and tugged the door to. "Drive on. I'll tell you what Alice said as we go."

La Honda lay spread against the foot of the hills, a sleepy town, almost entirely dark. Giles hardly slowed down as he went through it. "Keep an eye out. I think the place is coming up in the next two or three miles," he told Hugh. He hung onto the steering wheel with arms sodden with fatigue.

"Slow down a little. I don't want to miss the turn." Hugh leaned forward in his seat to watch the road on the left.

Reluctantly Giles eased up on the accelerator. "Just give me fair warning so I can be ready for it."

Hugh made no answer, his concentration already on the curve of road.

They were out of the hills now, entering a long, gentle slope that led to the ocean.

"Lights up ahead," Hugh said a little later. "On the left. There's a white fence and a gate. It looks like it might be the place. There are cars out in front of it."

"Right." Giles braked cautiously, and shifted down. The Land Rover shuddered as it slowed, and Giles lugged on the wheel to bring the car in line with the driveway. "Hang on. It's going to be tricky."

"Ready." Hugh had grabbed the brace and tightened his seat belt an extra bit. "Do your worst."

Gravel sprayed wildly as the Land Rover swung onto the drive. The car bounced and teetered, then righted itself as the engine whined.

"Steady on!" Giles shouted as he fought for control of the wheel. A deep pothole nearly wrenched the wheel from his hands before he had control of the vehicle again.

"Amazing," Hugh said in a low voice. "We'd better stop before we reach the house. We don't want them blocking off the route of escape."

"The house is dark," Giles pointed out as he braked and turned off the engine. "Except those two upstairs windows."

"That doesn't mean anything. They've got to be somewhere. Maybe out behind the house—there might be a garden back there. Or it could be they're in the barns."

Now that they had reached what Giles hoped was their destination, he began to be afraid. There were going to be several people at this gathering. What could he do to take Fayre away? He could not go up to Prentiss and simply ask for her back. He could not try to distract them—Hugh alone could not provide a diversion. With kids in the house, they couldn't break in to call the police. "Oh, Christ!" His hands were high on the steering wheel still, and he leaned his forehead against them.

"What's the trouble?" Hugh asked. He had already opened the door and he was puzzled as he looked at Giles.

"The trouble? I don't know what to do next." The anguish in his voice disturbed him. "Not without cops."

"I think I do. Get out of the car. Don't lock it, but take the keys. If we have to get in, it might be in a hurry, but we don't want anyone driving off with it." He looked across the darkened ranch. "No smell of livestock. They probably have a different use for those barns. Let's try there first."

"Okay. The barns first." As Giles got out of the car, he realized he was not sensibly dressed for this venture, but it was too late now. He wished in vain for a heavy wool shirt and his hiking boots. It didn't matter, he insisted mentally. What mattered was getting Fayre out. He watched Hugh strike off across the small enclosed pasture. Fighting his own sense of impending disaster, he closed the Land Rover's door and followed his friend.

In the second barn Giles and Hugh found what they were looking for. The building had been converted into a small recreation hall. The far wall was dominated by two huge bookshelves, while on either side the stalls had been replaced with little booths with couches and low tables. It was a well-lit room for its size, and would have been pleasant but for its occupants.

There were fifteen of them, most of them on chairs in an irregular circle around a high, simple bed. Fayre lay on the bed, her face waxen. She was very still. Prentiss stood near her head, watching the hanging IV unit beside him. Lupe was on the other side of the bed, leaning over Fayre.

"Say that again, Eilif," Lupe ordered as Giles peered around the edge of the door.

A voice wholly unlike Fayre's sounded in the room. It was a strange, deep tone, commanding yet oddly impersonal, a voice filled with power and contempt. "It should not be necessary. I have told you what you want to hear." The words were slurred.

"She's drugged," Giles muttered. How could he help her when she was in that state? He did not know what Prentiss was putting into her veins. He felt rage again, and forced himself from breaking into the room.

"Hold on. We've got to do something. Let me think." Hugh looked over toward the other barn. "They may have horses in there. We can use them."

"How?" Giles implored him. "We can't ride in like Lochinvar to the rescue."

"No," Hugh said very softly. "But we can panic them. Do you have any matches?"

"Matches?" Giles asked, horrified. "It isn't safe—"

"Isn't safe?" Hugh hissed. "What's going on in there isn't safe. How are you planning to get her out? Walk in, excuse yourself, and walk her out? She's largely incapable of that right now. Whatever Fellkirk is using, it's done a good job on her. She won't be of much use to anyone but him, at least for a while. If you want to change that, we've got to take some risks." He looked squarely at Giles and said even more softly, "I'm not planning to hurt the animals. But if we don't frighten them, we've got no way to break up that little prayer meeting."

Just as he finished speaking, there was a terrible, distant cry from inside the barn. Giles turned in spite of himself and would have called out but Hugh's hand was suddenly clamped over his mouth.

"Giles, get ahold of yourself!" he muttered.

He knew that Hugh was right. His fear would not help, and his exhaustion was even more dangerous. He was always jittery after surgery, and the long emergency he had handled earlier that evening had taken more of a toll than he realized. He could not afford to be weak, or tired, or frightened. Slowly, carefully, he reached up and took Hugh's hand away. "I'll be okay," he said softly, his stress revealed in the prominence of his English accent.

"Matches?" Hugh whispered.

The cry came again, and as Giles took a long, uneven breath to keep from rushing into the barn, there rose a murmur of voices, and Giles heard Prentiss say, "We will provide you this vessel as your home, Eilif, if you will continue to speak to us."

"Matches!" Hugh ordered softly, and Giles, strangely numbed, said, "In the car, the glove compartment, right-hand side."

Since they could not find enough paper, Hugh suggested that they cut up the canvas jacket Giles kept in the back. "It'll stink, but it'll burn more slowly than paper. If we put these in the barn and open the door so that the horses can escape . . ."

"We'd better drive them toward the second barn," Giles warned. "Otherwise they're apt to let them go until they've moved Fayre into the house, or away . . ." He forced the thought from his mind. He had to use every small advantage he could find. If Prentiss knew what he planned, he would have Fayre hidden more securely, and drugged.

"Have you got anything to cut with?" Hugh asked.

"No . . . Wait a minute, there's a couple scalpels in my

emergency kit. Under the rear seat. Better use just one." He helped Hugh remove the case and pointed out which of the scalpels would serve best for cutting cloth. "There're scissors, too, but they won't be of much use. They're not designed for this kind of cutting."

Hugh took the scalpel and began silently to cut up the canvas jacket.

It had taken more than forty minutes to cut the jacket, soak it in gasoline, and find places in the stable where they could start a fire without damaging the horses. There were seven animals in the large box stalls, and they were nervous as Giles and Hugh moved among them.

"Before we light these damned things," Giles said to Hugh, feeling his pocket for the matches one last time, "check the stalls to be sure the doors are open and that none of the horses are tied in any way. That stall near the door—there's a mare in foal in it. Lead her out as you leave, otherwise she might be hurt. When you get outside, stand between the path to the barn and the house, and make noise if the horses start to run toward you or the house. A loud shout should do."

"You? An expert on horses?" Hugh asked.

"My uncle belonged to the local hunt. I haven't ridden much in the last few years, but the old habits stick." He held up the gasoline-soaked rag in his hand. "I'll light this in"—he looked at his watch—"five minutes. You'll be ready?"

"I'll be ready," Hugh promised him. "Five minutes."

It seemed to Giles that hours had passed by the time the first horse bolted from the smoking barn. His watch told him it was less than twenty minutes, but the wait had felt interminable. He was glad to see the sorrel quarter horse race toward the barn, for it meant that the others might follow him.

"They've stopped listening," Hugh said. He was standing a few yards nearer the barn than Giles was. "I think they might . . ."

The barn door opened and half a dozen people stumbled out into the night, cries of shock and anger mixing with the neighing of the panicked horses.

"But we *can't* stop now!" Prentiss' voice rose above the feld . . ."

rest. "We're just getting ready to house Eilif in Mrs. Schoen-

One of the horses, a big Percheron-hunter cross, thundered toward the barn, as if seeking a safe building. People fled before him as he galloped to the threshold of the brightly lit meeting place. More of the group inside were up and moving, some toward the horses, with shouts, others away from the frightened rush.

"We can't stop!" Prentiss shouted.

"The stable's on fire!" cried another voice that sounded familiar to Giles, almost like the organ tones of Alan Freeman.

A woman screamed. "There's someone out there! Someone is driving the horses!"

Hugh turned to Giles. "Get down! If they find both of us, we've got trouble."

Smoke was billowing out of the barn, but there were no flames. The air was tainted with the stink of the burning rags and hay, and Giles felt his eyes water.

The horses were beginning to mill in front of the barn and a few of the group had gone to investigate the smoke in the stable. "Probably kids!" Giles heard one of them say. "Childish kind of stunt. The horses might have been hurt."

"You know kids," was the answer.

"We've got to go now!" Giles whispered to Hugh. "If we don't, they'll get away."

"I'll take the front, then, and you take the back. Christ, I wish we had some kind of weapons." He began to move, waving to Giles as he ran toward the far end of the barn.

As Giles burst though the rear door of the barn he heard Prentiss' smugly confident voice. "*There* you are. For a moment I was afraid that one of my company had got *zealous.* Luckily not."

On the far side of the room, Hugh stood very still. "Giles!" he called sharply. "Do exactly as he says."

Prentiss smiled. "Yes. Do that, Giles, O friend of my youth. Otherwise I will be forced to deal *harshly* with Mrs. Schoenfeld. Do you see this?" He held up the long steel needle and Giles made out a narrow runnel of blood leading from where Prentiss had taken it from Fayre's arm. "It's three inches long. If I drove it into her, just under the *ear,* with an upward *thrust* . . . Three inches is a long way." He looked at Giles, a certain irritated perplexity marking his features. "Why the devil did you have to *interfere?* It was going so *well.*"

Fayre stirred slightly, a moan fluttering on her lips.

"If you wanted to get laid, why didn't you *tell* me? Hell, Giles, I know *fifty* women who'd be *delighted* to land a neurosurgeon, short- or long-term. Why did you have to pick *her*? And what prompted you to this *foolhardy* kind of heroics? You're not the *type*, Giles. You're too old. You're too moral. Right now, you couldn't walk up here, take this needle out of my hand and shove it in my eye, *could* you?" Prentiss waved the needle at him. "No, of *course* you couldn't. But I warn you right now, Giles, *I could*."

"Yes," Giles said softly. "I realize that."

"Good." Prentiss looked down at Fayre. "She'll be out from under this in about half an hour. Groggy, as you'd expect. If you *had* to break in, I *wish* you'd waited awhile."

"Where are the others?" Giles asked, fearing the answer. It would be like Prentiss to devise a show for them.

"In the house," Hugh said. "He sent them there, with that woman, Lupe."

"Otherwise it might be *untidy*." Prentiss smiled his English-country-squire smile. "It isn't necessary to *involve* them in what you're going to do for me." He paused. "And Eilif."

Prentiss was in the back of the Land Rover, Fayre propped up beside him, her head lolling against his shoulder. It was hateful to Giles to see that as he drove. That Fayre should be so dreadfully passive, and dependent on Prentiss . . .

"When we get to the coast road," Prentiss informed Giles enthusiastically, "I want you to turn south and stop in the first beach parking area that we find without a telephone. You . . ."—he tapped Hugh on the shoulder—"are going to leave us there, Reverend Audley. It should be several hours before you get any traffic along here. You might use the time for prayer. Or do Unitarians pray?"

"Just like the joke says, Prentiss, 'To whom it may concern.' " Hugh was half-turned in the passenger seat so he could watch Fayre. "She might get carsick. Had you thought of that?"

"I'm not worried, Audley." Prentiss touched Fayre's flaccid hand where it dangled beside him. "And you should have other things on your mind now. If I had time to do it right, I'd kill you."

"Where do we go after that?" Giles asked, keeping his voice steady. If Prentiss were prepared to abandon or kill Hugh at the roadside of California Highway 1, he would expect to be rid of Giles himself. He would have plenty of time, Giles realized grimly, to do it right.

"We go toward Santa Cruz," Prentiss said lightly.

That would not be the real destination, for Prentiss would not reveal his destination to Hugh, who might have them followed, however belatedly. "And then?" How long, he wondered, would he live?

"Well, it's *unfortunate,* but somewhere along the road, and I'm not quite certain where, you will meet with an accident. Your Land Rover here will go ever-so-slightly out of control, which, on the coast road, can be very dangerous. You might live through the crash, but probably not high tide." He met Giles' eyes in the rearview mirror. "*Why* did you have to do this, Giles? I don't want to kill you. Why are you *forcing* me to do it?"

"Killing me is your choice, Prentiss. You haven't understood about Fayre and me. I don't think you'll ever understand. What are you going to do with her?" Though he tried, he could not quite keep his voice steady for the last question.

"What I began back there. Give Eilif a home. You've never grasped the *significance* of Mrs. Schoenfeld's abilities. She's a perfect *channel,* a tuner, a receiver for Eilif's power." Prentiss was becoming enthused again. "Once Eilif is housed—"

Hugh cut into his comments. "There is no Eilif," he spat. "That's in your mind, Fellkirk. You're right about Fayre's talent being a tuner, but she's only bringing out part of you that you can't handle. And that's dangerous, Fellkirk. You're acting in ignorance." He turned to look ahead. "The beach's coming up," he said at his most laconic. "I think I get out here."

Not far away the road on which they were driving ended where it met Highway 1. Beyond was a grassy, then sandy slope down to the gentle curl of waves. Giles pulled up at the junction and asked, "Left?"

"Left. Keep looking for a likely place to leave your . . . friend." Prentiss settled back. "Don't try anything crazy, Giles. I still have this needle. It would be a *shame* to have to use it."

Three, four, five miles down the road and there was one of those small, unexpected coves tucked between towering rocks and rising bluffs. A small gravel turnout gave access to the beach, which was narrow and steep. The headlights of the

Land Rover flashed across large warning signs: swimming and surfing were strictly prohibited.

"*Okay*, Audley," Prentiss said, "this is where you get out. Ready?" He leaned forward, half-standing in the back, his fingers on the door handle. "Be careful how you go. No missteps. Got that?"

"I've got it." Hugh's face was set, and behind the fatigue and defeat there was rage.

Prentiss opened the door for him. "Go gently, Audley."

Hugh moved slowly, deliberately as he climbed out of the Land Rover.

"Now, turn around. Face me!" Prentiss ordered, and as Hugh obeyed, Prentiss slammed the door outward, the bottom edge of it crashing against Hugh's legs with a sound that came in part from breaking bone.

Hugh roared in agony and reached out to keep from falling, and grabbed Prentiss' arm. His sudden weight caught Prentiss off-guard, and with a startled sound he fell against the front seat.

It was a desperate chance to take, Giles knew. He threw the Land Rover into reverse, then gunned the engine. The car leaped backward several feet, and Prentiss, with Hugh still clinging to his arm, fell half out of the door. Giles braked the car.

"Hugh!" he shouted. "Hold on!"

"Yeah!" came the answer in a tone distorted by pain.

Giles flung open the door and raced around to the other side of the car. He could use Prentiss' own plan for himself; abandon Prentiss here on the beach, put Hugh in the car, and drive for help. "Get him out! Get him out!" he shouted as he ran up to Hugh.

"I'm trying!" He had transferred his grip to Prentiss' shoulder, tugging at him.

"Move over!" Giles reached to haul Prentiss out of the car. Apparently the impact with the front seat had winded him slightly, because his struggles were ineffectual as Giles and Hugh pulled harder.

At last Prentiss fell out of the door, landing in a heap on the gravel. His face was flushed and he took a shallow breath before lashing out at them with his arms. One blow struck Hugh on his broken leg. The scream it brought was terrible.

"Hugh! Get back in the car! Check Fayre! Quick!" Giles had grabbed the back collar of Prentiss' coat, and was trying to drag him away from the Land Rover.

"You don't! *You can't!*" he raged. Prentiss was a bigger, heavier man than Giles, and he was quickly recovering from his rough handling. He began to fight back.

Giles stopped trying to drag Prentiss away from the Land Rover long enough to deliver a few well-placed kicks. He knew from the force of impact and grunts that Prentiss answered with that he had inflicted very little damage on his antagonist. Where, he worried, was that long steel needle? Had Prentiss dropped it?

Suddenly Prentiss surged off the ground, slamming into Giles with all his weight. Giles staggered under the shock, but by luck stayed on his feet. Once down, he knew that Prentiss would not hesitate to smash his skull with his foot. Backing away from Prentiss, he almost lost his footing where the gravel of the turnout gave way to the rough sand of the beach.

"Giles!" Prentiss howled. "I'm going to *kill* you!"

Beyond any doubt, Giles knew that if Prentiss fought him, he would win. As he pursued Giles toward the water's edge, Prentiss was utterly changed from the erudite college professor that had long been familiar to Giles. Now Prentiss wore the face of his own demon. He lunged at Giles once more, and Giles evaded him. The beach was small and the water was rough. At the mouth of the cove breakers clawed at the cliffs. All Prentiss would have to do was drive Giles into the water far enough and the Pacific Ocean would break and smash him with an impersonal fury beyond anything Prentiss could do.

"Hugh!" Giles cried out. "Hugh! Take the car and go!"

The reply was almost lost in the crashing of the waves. "I can't. My leg won't work!"

"Try!" The word was his will. Fayre had to get away. Hugh must take her. Otherwise it would have all been useless, a waste. The cold waves pulled at his shoes, spilling around them. Giles took another step backward.

"You're a stupid, sentimental fool, Giles!" Prentiss bellowed as he rushed again, trying to force him off his feet, back into the beckoning water. "You could have *used* her. You could have had *anything* you wanted!"

"I got what I wanted," Giles said quietly, knowing that Prentiss could not hear him.

"You had *no right!*" Again he pushed out sharply, trying to hit Giles in the chest or shoulder.

The water was up to his knees, incredibly cold, roiling

about his legs. Giles wished it were light, for in the dark he could not find a weapon. He dared not get too close to Prentiss, to be caught in his powerful grasp and forced under the waves. If he could pick up a rock, a branch washed in, anything.

"Come on, Giles. Stop this. End it." Prentiss was mocking now, confident of his victory. "The longer you wait, the harder it'll be. I'll be angrier, for one thing. I'll take my time."

"No." In daylight, Giles would have taken his chance with the ocean, diving into the deepening water and getting far away from the threat. At night, in an unfamiliar cove, the risks were too great. He shouted again, "Hugh! *Go!*" If there was an answer, or if Hugh could hear him at this distance, Giles did not know.

"You're getting deeper, Giles. The breakers are right behind you. Can you hear them? Do you know what they can *do* to you?"

It might be worth it, Giles told himself, if only Fayre gets away. Gets away and can still be Fayre. "They might get you as well," Giles said. The water was higher than his waist and it was getting difficult to walk. Twice he had almost been knocked over, and he could feel the drive of the surf behind him.

"Fellkirk!" The shout came from the water's edge. Hugh's tone was ragged, almost a sob, but he stood—incredibly, stood—at the edge of the ocean. He lifted one arm and threw with all the strength he had left.

The rock was not large and it missed by more than a foot, but it distracted Prentiss a moment. He turned, infuriated, and yelled incoherently at Hugh.

Giles wanted to rush Prentiss while his attention was on Hugh, but the water slowed him down. Then the matter was taken out of his hands. A wave, one of the large ones that are supposed to come every ninth time, topped the rocks at the mouth of the cove like a huge, descending hand. Giles was caught in its rush and carried forward. He was off his feet, rolling in the cold turmoil, arms and legs flailing. He careened into Prentiss, sending him sprawling into the water.

"Giles!" Hugh cried out.

He broke the surface and gulped for air. His lungs hurt and he could feel his heart closing like angry fists in his chest. He looked for Prentiss and could see him getting to his feet.

They were both in shallower water now, and the next wave was minor. Prentiss waded toward Giles.

The second rock that Hugh hurled hit Prentiss on the shoulder, but he ignored it in his determination to reach Giles.

Hugh started into the surf, limping slowly and in dreadful torment. "I'm coming!"

The cold was becoming painful. Giles could no longer move as fast, as carefully as he had to. He wanted to believe that the frigid waters were taking the same toll of Prentiss, but he could not.

Then Giles tripped over a submerged rock, and an instant later, Prentiss was on top of him.

Water rushed into his eyes, his nostrils, his ears, closed over his head with a hungry gurgle. Prentiss had fixed his hands in Giles' shoulder and was trying to grab his throat.

With all his remaining strength, Giles pushed upward, coming out of the water coughing and pushing against the hands that held him.

"You earned this, Giles!" Prentiss yelled, and lurched toward him, trying to drive him under the water again.

Hugh was almost upon them, the air rough in his throat, his movements jerkier with each terrible step he took.

There was a sound then, or perhaps it wasn't a sound at all. Giles seemed to hear Fayre speak, as if she stood beside him, but her words were not for him.

"Eilif! Eilif! Go home! Go home! *Prentiss Fellkirk!*"

Prentiss stumbled, moving back. He made a strange sound in his throat, and looked over his shoulder. Where there had been murderous intent there was now hunted fear. He started to move away through the water, holding his hands as if to fend off a presence.

"It's yourself, Prentiss Fellkirk," Fayre's voice said sadly.

Prentiss turned again, stumbling into the path of a wave. With deceptive gentleness, the water lifted him, and even as he turned with its compellingly easy grace, he was brought down with huge might onto a small outcropping of rocks that lay just beneath the surface of the water. He didn't have time to scream.

Giles stood, stunned, as he watched the water gently rock Prentiss' shattered body like a child playing with a doll.

"Help me back," Hugh said, and not even his great strain could hide his horror or his compassion.

They were halfway back to the Land Rover when Hugh

collapsed. Giles knelt beside him in the sand, his eyes filled with unheeded tears. He held Hugh gently, helplessly, feeling more desolate than he had ever felt in his life.

When he looked up, Fayre was coming toward him.

□ Epilogue □

The Highway Patrolman finished scribbling in his notebook and nodded to Giles. "Thanks, Dr. Todd. We'll get a full report from you later. The sheriff will want to talk to you."

"You know where to reach me." How tired he felt. His body was stiff and soreness reached fingers into every part of him.

"The ambulances should be here in another twenty minutes. I still think you ought to go along for a check. You've got a bunch of bad bruises, and that cut over your eye is a mess."

"Don't worry," Giles said slowly.

"Good thing you had those morphine ampuls with you. I think Reverend Audley will be tolerably comfortable until they get a cast on him."

"Yes," Giles agreed.

"And the lady?" The Highway Patrolman waited.

A customized van and an old station wagon, both filled with teenagers looking for an early start at the surfing beaches farther down the coast, came around the curve and stopped to stare at the Highway Patrol car, the Land Rover and a shape that lay under an old tarpaulin. Irritated, the Highway Patrolman waved them on.

"She's with me," Giles said. "I'll take her in myself this afternoon."

On the beach the long red smear that marked the place where Giles had dragged Prentiss from the water was already being erased by the incoming tide. Dawn cast long, bright, wraithlike rays down the hill toward the cove. The ocean beyond was already glittering in the new light.

"Pity about the professor," the Highway Patrolman said, looking for more information.

"A great pity," Giles said softly.

"Did you know him well?" The dark eyes were probing.

"No, not really. We went to school together when we were kids." He looked toward the Land Rover on the other side of

243

the turnout. Fayre sat in the front passenger seat while Hugh lay in the rear.

"Lucky thing about that fire. We might not have checked it out if we hadn't got that complaint from the woman up at Skylonda. Things like that are usually pranks, and that bunch isn't popular with the neighbors. From what the cops said, they were messing with things people should stay away from." He lifted two fingers in a casual salute and walked away.

Giles stared out at the ocean beyond the breakers at the entrance to the cove. The patrolman's words stayed with him. Messing with things that people should stay away from. Was that really true? he asked himself. He walked slowly down to the tide line, hating the feel of his wet clothes and the sand that chafed his skin. Maybe the patrolman was right, he thought. Look what had happened to Prentiss. His shudder wasn't entirely from clammy garments and morning chill.

"No," he said at last. He refused to make the mistake that Prentiss had. There was nothing wrong in knowledge, in study. What had been wrong was the ignorance, the superstition that had done the damage. Prentiss had been possessed of a devil of his own making because he could not bear to learn about himself.

"Giles?" Fayre put her hand on his arm.

He looked down at her, then back out to sea. "How are you?"

"Rocky," she said serenely. "I'm coming out of it. You?"

"Getting better." The sun was brighter, climbing higher up the morning, and Giles felt its warmth through his sodden clothes.

"Do you want to leave?" she asked. "You don't have to stay here."

"Just a little while longer, love." He looked at the rising waves, and the line of his shadow across them. Early-summertime traffic was increasing on the narrow highway. The whine of engines with an occasional radio blare cut through the battering of the waves and high screeches of gulls.

"How's Hugh?"

"Floating," she said. "We're waiting for the ambulance, but after that?" She leaned against his arm.

"We can leave," he finished. "We'll be contacted later."

A second Highway Patrol car pulled up at the turnout.

"Fayre, do you still want to do testing?" Giles asked without looking at her.

Her answer was prompt, confident. "Yes."

He thought of Prentiss lying dead under a tarpaulin. He recalled Hugh's declaration that there were no demons, only the dark places of the mind. He remembered the strange, misguided sincerity of Alice Hartwell. He thought of how Fayre answered his thoughts, not his words. "So do I."

Silently then she took his hand, and turned toward the Highway Patrol cars, the Land Rover where Hugh lay, away from the ocean. Toward all that was left of Prentiss Fellkirk.

"The ambulance just turned at San Gregorio," the patrolman called out. "You ready to go when it gets here?"

Giles squeezed Fayre's hand. "Yes. I'm ready," he said for both of them; he had felt her answer with his mind.

ABOUT THE AUTHOR

CHELSEA QUINN YARBRO, a young woman of many interests, has written science-fiction, detective, and occult novels. She lives with her husband in California.